THE JEFFERSON PROPHECY

THE SECOND NOVEL IN THE PAUL MARCUS TRILOGY

BY

TOM LOWE

K

KINGSBRIDGE ENTERTAINMENT

Library of Congress Cataloging in—Publication Data, Lowe, Tom, 1952
ISBN-13: 9781723357893
ISBN-10: 1723357898

The Jefferson Prophecy by Tom Lowe - First Edition, 2018

1. Thomas Jefferson—fiction 2. Cipher wheel—Fiction. 3. Barbary Pirates—Fiction. 4. Battle of Derna—Fiction 5. Liberty Bell, Mt. Rushmore—Fiction - Title: *The Jefferson Prophecy*

The Jefferson Prophecy is distributed in ebook, print and audiobook editions. Audible Studios is the publisher of the audiobook.

Cover design by Damonza.

Book layout by www.ebooklaunch.com

Also By Tom Lowe

A False Dawn

The 24th Letter

The Black Bullet

The Butterfly Forest

Blood of Cain

Black River

Cemetery Road

A Murder of Crows

Destiny

Wrath

ACKNOWLEDGMENTS

My thanks and deep appreciation for the people that helped put this novel together. To my wife, Keri, who is always my first reader and editor. To Richard Brockman, Ph.D., for his expert advice on cryptography and American history. To Adrian, John and Dane and the talented team at Ebook Launch. To Alicia, Damon, and the graphic designers with Damonza. To Helen Ristuccia-Christensen and Darcy Yarosh for their extraordinary beta reading skills. And finally to you, the reader. If a book isn't read, it's like a song that's never heard. Thank you for reading and being part of the journey. I hope you enjoy *The Jefferson Prophecy*.

To the memory of Thomas Jefferson—a true visionary who, more than once, knew when to draw a line in the sands of time.

"The secret to happiness is freedom, and the secret to freedom is courage."

- Thucydides

For Jim Kelel and Rachel Pruitt

PROLOGUE

London, England - 1786

Thomas Jefferson didn't know it at the time, but as he stood in a cold, light rain, waiting for the door to open, his life was about to change forever. His close friend, John Adams, took a closer step and knocked on the solid wooden door again, more forceful. Jefferson, at a height of six-two, chiseled face, towered over Adams as they waited for someone to answer.

"Maybe the ambassador from Tripoli has forgotten our appointment," Adams said, his round, fleshy cheeks pink. "He was late for the meeting I had with him last month." Adams pulled his collar up around his neck. "Welcome to England, Thomas. It's almost May and cold in London."

"Not unlike Boston," Jefferson said with a smile. He listened for movement inside the home that served as an embassy as well. "I think I hear someone coming."

It was a chilly and gray afternoon in the heart of London. The draft through the misty rain brought the odor of horse droppings, burning coal and the scent of blooming hyacinth in front of the building, which resembled a two-story brownstone townhouse in the Knightsbridge section of the city.

A horse-drawn carriage rattled down the street, coming closer. The carriage was enclosed, and the only passenger was a woman. The driver's narrow face had a gaunt look, his cadaverous skin the color of old bones. He wore a rain-soaked, black top hat and a long leather jacket. The driver stopped the horse as an elderly man crossed the street, the man's overcoat soaked at the shoulders.

The woman inside the carriage glanced out the window, looking at the tall man from Virginia standing under the eave. He turned toward the carriage, locking eyes with the woman for a moment. She smiled as the driver jostled the reins, the horse responding. When the carriage pulled away, she looked out the back window, never to know that both men who stood at the doorstep would be elected as presidents of the United States.

The door of the home opened, yellow light flooding the faces of Jefferson and Adams. A dark-skinned man in his late twenties, red housecoat, a brown taqiyah on his head, looked at the visitors and smiled. Eyes black as his beard. "Good evening, gentlemen. Please, come inside and out of the rain. Ambassador Abdrahaman is expecting you."

Jefferson nodded and let Adams enter before him. They were ushered into a foyer where the attendant took their overcoats, hanging them on brass hooks in an alcove. "This way, gentlemen."

He led them down a hallway and into a large room with books lining two of the walls. An orange fire crackled in the large fireplace, the slight smell of coal and oak burning. A framed painting on one wall depicted tall-mast schooners and sailing warships, their sails stretched by the wind, the white froth of a dark sea at the bows. Another painting was of an older Muslim man wearing a turban, dark red robe, lighting a brass lamp, the light from the lamp caught in his dark eyes.

The attendant said, "Ambassador Abdrahaman will join you in a moment. Please, make yourselves comfortable." He bowed slightly and exited.

Jefferson studied some of the books lined on the walls. Most were books about philosophy and history. One was about religion. Jefferson reached for a copy of the Koran, removed it, and turned to the first chapter. He glanced up at Adams and said, "It's in Arabic, of course. I purchased one of the first copies to be translated into English."

"Why the interest?"

"I had read much of the Bible. I was interested in learning more about Islam."

"All right, Thomas, tell me … what did you learn?"

The door opened and in walked Ambassador Sidi Haji Abdrahaman with two servants, both male. The younger men carried three pipes with smoke curling from the bowls. Abdrahaman wore a black housecoat over a long, beige robe, white turban, and sandals. His beard was black with streaks of gray; the stringy whiskers came to the center of his chest. His face and hands were the color of coffee, the yellow flames from the fireplace reflected off his dark eyes.

"Good afternoon, gentlemen," Abdrahaman said, his voice guttural with an Arabic accent. "I have had the pleasure of meeting Mr. Adams last month. "You must be Thomas Jefferson, the American minister to France." He made a slight bow at the waist.

Jefferson smiled. "I am very pleased to meet you, Ambassador Abdrahaman. John has told me a lot about you. I have been looking forward to this meeting for some time now."

The ambassador nodded. "Let us sit. We will smoke some fine Moroccan tobacco and have Turkish coffee." He led the men across the room to an area where red, blue and white pillows were arranged in a semi-circle next to Victorian furniture. He gestured toward the pillows. "I prefer sitting on the floor."

He sat on a large pillow, Jefferson and Adam taking seats across from him. The servants handed each man a pipe and then stepped back. Silent. Ambassador Abdrahaman took a long drag from his pipe, the smoke exiting his brown nostrils. He turned to his servants and in Arabic said, "Bring us coffee and water."

The younger men bowed and quietly left the room.

John Adams inhaled the burning tobacco through his pipe, face shiny in the firelight. Jefferson puffed from his pipe, allowing the smoke only into his mouth and blowing it back out.

Ambassador said, "Mr. Jefferson, I understand this is your first visit to England."

"Yes, it is. I am looking forward to seeing London and some of the countryside. I have an appointment with King George in two days, and I meet with Queen Victoria before I depart at the end of the month."

"Please give King George my best regards."

Jefferson nodded, keenly aware that the ambassador didn't include Queen Victoria in his salutation. The men spoke about the subtle differences in tobacco grown from Morocco compared to tobacco harvested from Virginia soil. The servants returned with Turkish coffee and left the men to their discussions.

Jefferson said, "Ambassador Abdrahaman, my country is young. We have done nothing to Tripoli, Morocco, Algiers or Tunisia, yet the Barbary States have been aggressive toward American merchant ships. As you know, your country has seized one of our ships. You are holding Americans hostage and demanding ransom money. Congress has authorized Mr. Adams and I to negotiate a peace treaty with you and the other North African nations."

The ambassador leaned closer. "I am listening, Mr. Jefferson. What are you willing to bring to the table?

John Adams interjected. "What are you offering, sir?"

"English is not my primary language, so I will try my best to be understood. We offer a safe trade route passage into the Mediterranean Sea through the Strait of Gibraltar. For an annual fee of thirty-thousand English guineas, plus the ten percent I receive as broker, your American ships can come and go as they please."

Adams sipped his coffee and asked, "Are you speaking only for Tripoli? What about the other three nations, would the thirty-thousand be spread amongst them?"

The ambassador touched his beard, a slight smile working in the corner of his mouth. "No, you will have to pay each country. I should think the price would be the same, thirty-thousand each, plus a commission." He raised his shoulders. "It is a small price to pay for entrance into the Mediterranean market, the largest on earth. It is simply the cost of conducting business."

Jefferson shook his head. "No, it is not. The Barbary States do not own the Mediterranean Sea anymore than someone could own the universe. You do not have any rights from any source to charge fees. Our nation is young. We are not in a position to generate that kind of money, and even if we did, America will not be a victim to extortion and ransom."

"Then we have nothing further to discuss, Mr. Jefferson. In the meantime, I'll let my envoy know to hold American sailors as slaves. We shall take ownership of your vessels as well."

Jefferson said, "That would be a big mistake."

"Do not threaten us. You have no idea what we are capable of doing."

"What has America done to you? Nothing. You have no right to—"

"No! We do have a right." The Ambassador leaned closer, the firelight twisting like white lighting in his black eyes. "It is written in our Koran that all nations, which do not acknowledge the Prophet Muhammad, are sinners. It is the right, and it is the duty of the faithful to plunder and enslave the sinners. It is written that for Mussulmen who are slain in this warfare will go to paradise."

Jefferson didn't blink as he stared into the man's hard eyes. Adams cleared his throat and said, "If I understand you correctly, you are saying that Christian sailors are fair game, or sinners?"

The Ambassador raised his hands and shrugged his shoulders.

Jefferson said, "Any man can use doctrine to justify beliefs that are not universally shared. May I suggest to you, Ambassador Abdrahaman, on this matter, the Koran has something written on the subject that I recall reading. It says ... 'fight in the cause of Allah to those who fight you, however, do not transgress limits ... for Allah loveth not transgressors.' Have you read it, sir?"

John Adams glanced at the bookshelf and then at Jefferson, stunned.

Ambassador Abdrahaman's jaw muscles popped. His eyes narrowed, his voice was just above a raspy whisper. "Mr. Jefferson, with respect to you because you do not know the Muslim history and that of Islam, and by virtue of that, you cannot interpret our Koran. Please, take my message back to your Congress. Your country may be young, but you are about to face an adversary with centuries of fighting experience. If you want a future for America ... I suggest you study our history and do not make the same mistakes our enemies have made."

ONE

Isle of Panarea, Sicily - Present Day

As Paul Marcus approached the Isle of Panarea harbor in a forty-foot sailboat, he removed his sunglasses, glanced up at the surrounding hillsides, never able to shake the feeling he was being watched. Paul, mid-forties, brown hair and eyes as blue as the surrounding Mediterranean Sea, smiled at his wife, Alicia, and four-year-old son David. They sat in the cockpit as Paul adjusted the throttle and steered for the boat slip.

Alicia's hair was pulled back in a ponytail, high cheekbones, tanned skin. She stood, watched the distance narrow between the boat and the long dock. "The tide is up at least a foot since we left two hours ago," she said, looking back at her husband. The air was briny and smelled of oyster beds and blooming bougainvillea.

"Look!" said little David, curly, dark hair tousling in the wind. He pointed to a ragged fishing boat coming into the harbor, a flock of squawking gulls dipping and diving above it. The old boat resembled vessels from a thousand year lineage, high bow, short wheelhouse, and a large cockpit. Blue smoke puttered from the single diesel. Two brown fishermen readied spring lines as the seasoned captain eased the boat up to the dock. A few tourists watched, eager to see the catch.

Alicia turned to her son. "David, stay here with Daddy. I'm going to help tie up the boat."

"Can I come?" he said with a toothy smile. "Please?"

"Okay, but hold my hand."

He grinned as he stepped with his mother along the side of the boat and up to the bow. Paul watched them, slipped his sunglasses back on, and looked toward tourists debarking from a hydrofoil ferryboat one hundred feet away. He watched closely, looking for anyone that seemed to be observing his family beyond the inquisitive gaze of a tourist.

One of the dockhands, a teenage boy wearing khaki shorts and a blue T-shirt with the words *Marina de Panarea*, came running down the long dock. He signaled for Alicia to toss the rope to him. She made sure David stood behind her and then threw the end of the rope to the teen. He grabbed it and pulled hand-over-hand to help secure the boat. He quickly tied the rope to a dock cleat. Alicia placed a rubber bumper fender to one side, keeping the sailboat from touching the dock.

Paul cut the engine and tossed one of the stern ropes to the teen. As he tied the rope, he asked in a heavy Italian accent, "Did you have a good sail?"

"We did," Paul said, reaching in his wallet for a Euro note. He handed the teen the money and said, "Grazie."

"No problema." The teen pocketed the money, nodded and hustled to another dock where a sixty-foot Azimut cruiser was approaching.

Alicia turned to David and said, "Let's help Daddy close up."

"Okay." He followed his mother as she began securing the sailboat.

Paul set his sunglasses on the console, adjusted two more rubber fenders, glancing at the ferryboat. Alicia approached him and touched his arm. "You're so relaxed at sea … but as soon as we come into the harbor, I can see the tension build in your face. Paul, it's been five years. We'll be fine." She smiled.

"I know. But I also know these people have a long memory. You and David mean too much to me to ever let my guard down."

She kissed him and went below, David following her.

The Isle of Panarea, one of seven Aeolian Islands, is two hundred miles north of Sicily. For the first few years, Paul and Alicia Marcus never left the island. They couldn't take the risks. But as David turned three, the family began short excursions to the other Islands in the Mediterranean, taking a ferryboat to Salina, Lipari or Stromboli.

They could have been tourists, like the rest. Island hopping. Experiencing the history of the ancient archipelago—islands in the stream of time.

But they weren't tourists.

Paul Marcus was the most hunted man on earth.

Paul locked the boat and walked with his family up a winding gravel path bordered by old walls of stone, lush with red and white bougainvillea. The trail led past sleepy resort hotels dotting the hillsides. Paul noticed a slight movement on a wooden terrace filled with bougainvillea. He picked David up and stepped closer to a lizard almost invisible against the brown wood. "Look at that, David. The lizard is rare here on the islands. I've only seen one or two in the last few years."

"Does he bite?" David asked, staring at the lizard, its tongue flickering.

"Let's don't find out," said Alicia. "Come on, guys. Ice cream and Italian ice are definitely on the agenda. Let's walk to the Café Sicilia. We left our cart near there."

Paul set David down, held his hand and continued walking. White houses dotted the rolling hillsides of the volcanic island. They leisurely strolled the two blocks on the narrow roadway, laughing and talking as a family. There were no cars on Panarea, only golf carts and Vespa motor scooters.

Café Sicilia was an open-air coffee shop with seven tables under a wooden lattice covered with blooming bougainvillea. Alicia and David sat at one of the outdoor tables. Paul glanced at the sidewalk café fifty feet across the plaza. A few tourists sat at the tables under umbrellas and ate fresh fish, most of the glasses filled with white wine.

One man sat alone.

He read a newspaper, *La Sicilia,* and sipped an espresso. He wore a tropical print shirt. White Panama hat. Early fifties. Stubble of whiskers on his lean face. Marcus locked eyes with the man for a millisecond, the man casually looked down, turning a page in the paper.

For the first time in five years, Paul Marcus knew that someone recognized him.

TWO

Near Benghazi, Libya

Delta Force commando Eli Dexter smiled and shook his head as he watched the old farmer use a camel to plow rows in the Libyan soil. The farmer, his brown skin dry as the earth, walked slowly behind a camel strapped to a hand-held plow, the animal snorting and pulling the single blade through the sandy soil. Dust puffed like smoke behind the camel's hooves. The farmer wore a sweat-stained, red-checkered keffiyeh on his head, the cloth touching his stooped shoulders. His long sleeve shirt was tattered, soiled—the color of used cooking oil. Baggy pants, no shoes.

Dexter, like all Delta Force members on assignment, wore civilian clothes. He was in his late twenties, wide shoulders—a week's growth of stubble on his face. Dexter watched the old man plow and thought of his own grandfather who'd worked his Virginia farm for sixty years. He remembered the Ford tractor and riding in Grandpa's lap in the fields. Dexter had been in Libya for a month when he learned of his grandfather's death.

There was no way to attend the funeral. Not with the mission at hand. He and eleven other commandos, six Navy Seals and two FBI agents, were on a hunt. Their task was to find and capture at least seven known leaders of the attack on the US embassy in Benghazi. Their orders were to bring them back alive, if possible. *Back* meant to the United States where they would be tried in a federal court for killing the U.S ambassador to Libya and three other Americans.

The harsh sunlight broke across wind-torn rock formations and rolling hills of fractured land and sandstone. Dexter stood under the shade of two date palms near an adobe-like compound that served as a temporary headquarters for his team. The ancient structure, built from mud six hundred years ago, would be where they stayed for the next three days. Then, they would relocate. Constantly moving. To remain in one place too long was to create suspicion, and that invited trouble. The compound was three kilometers from the desert town of Suluq.

Dexter unscrewed the cap off a water bottle and took a small sip. The water was warm. The air smelled of camel dung and dust. He looked at the dry, cracked earth, a panorama that resembled a Martian landscape. A goat cried out from where it stood, tied to an olive tree near more earthen brick homes scattered in the agrarian desert. Excluding the old farmer, Dexter could see no one else. He looked at his watch and mumbled, "Where the hell are you guys?"

There was the sound of boots against the hard-packed earth that led from a back door of the compound. One of Dexter's team members, Captain Mike Nolan, tall, rawboned, stepped from the shade of the walkway and approached Dexter. Nolan said, "They should have been here fifteen minutes ago."

"Yeah … it's not like Preston to be late."

"Maybe we should cut 'em some slack. Federal agents just don't get the training in punctuality that we do. I'll go back inside and try to reach them on the sat phone. Why don't you get out of the sun?"

A teenager on a recycled Vespa sped by, the motorbike belching white smoke out of the exhaust pipe. Dexter watched the teen for a few seconds and said, "I'm gonna give this bottle of water to the old guy across the street plowing that field. In a way, he reminds me of my grandfather. He worked the fields in Virginia and ran cattle 'till he dropped dead under a windmill used to pump water for livestock." He smiled, looking toward the farmer in the distance "If my granddaddy could have seen a man using a camel to plow a field, he'd split a gut laughing."

"It's too bad you couldn't go to his funeral. I know you were tight with him."

"Yeah, I was. Grandpa taught me how to ride a horse, how to hunt. He taught my dad how to shoot, and years later my father set records with a sniper's rifle." He blew out a breath, moved the water bottle to his left hand.

Nolan nodded. "Your dad had a helluva eye in his day." He glanced at the farmer in the dusty field. "Maybe you shouldn't give the old guy water. These people are like that damn camel … they seem to go forever with little water. And we don't want to breed familiarity with the locals. It's your call."

"That's why we relocate every three days. We'll be outta here tomorrow. Giving an old man some water can't be too risky, Cap." He started across the dirt street to the field about eighty yards away. Nolan looked up and down the road before turning to walk back inside the compound.

Within less than a minute, Dexter was near the farmer. He watched a moment as the elderly man spoke to the camel in Arabic, like he was talking to an old friend. As the farmer turned to plow another row, he spotted Dexter and stopped, his craggy face filled with suspicion.

Dexter lifted up the water bottle and approached. When he was closer to the old man, he said, "Water."

The farmer nodded, tied the reins to one of the wooden plow handles and reached out his leathery hand, taking the bottle. He slowly unscrewed the cap and took a small sip. In Arabic he said *thank you*. He placed the cap back on the bottle and started to give it back.

Dexter smiled. "No, it's yours. Keep it."

The old man smiled and wiped his lips with the back of his sandpaper hand. His dark eyes scanned the area. The camel opened his mouth in a wide yawn, its eyes sleepy. A dog barked in the distance. Dexter turned to leave. He heard the farmer give the camel orders and then the scrape of the plow chewing through rocks and sandy soil.

As Dexter started to cross the road, he paused. There was the sound of a vehicle coming. "About time," he muttered. Within seconds a blue van approached. Dexter didn't know what vehicles the federal agents were using. The driver was dark skinned. Full black beard. The van slowed.

Something wasn't right.

Dexter watched a second. When the van came to a stop, he reached for his sidearm beneath his untucked shirt. The side panel door flew open and three armed men, all bearded, opened fire. Dexter got off one shot, hitting a man in the stomach. The gunfire was too much. A round traveled through Dexter's throat, exiting from the back of his neck. The men ran to him, one shooting Dexter in the head. They lifted his body and carried it to the van, throwing it inside.

Three Delta Force commandos came running from the compound. They used handguns to fire a barrage of rounds at the van as it sped off. One commando stood in the street and emptied his clip, two rounds smashing through the van's back window. But the driver kept going, almost veering of the road. The van was soon gone, and with it, the body of Lieutenant Eli Dexter.

The old farmer looked across the field at the scene, smoke drifting in the air from the barrage of gunfire, the men in jeans and T-shirts distraught, running to a Range Rover they kept behind the building. The old man stared at the mud-brick and adobe homes, across the plateau of sandstone and cracked hills, his dark eyes troubled and more desolate than the barren landscape.

THREE

Paul Marcus didn't want to frighten his wife—especially in front of David. He was sure he'd been spotted. But what he didn't know was whether or not the man reading the newspaper was friend or foe. His thoughts raced. *In this business, enemies weren't usually seen unless they have a gun, knife or poison intended for you.* Paul didn't recognize the guy. But that meant nothing.

He looked at Alicia and David. "Okay, who wants ice cream and who wants Italian ice?" he asked.

"Chocolate," David said.

"Please," Alicia said to David.

"Chocolate, please, Daddy."

"Chocolate it is. How about you, honey?"

"Italian ice, mango." She glanced at David and smiled. "Please. This place makes the best."

"Coming up," Paul walked to the counter and ordered from a woman with her blonde hair in a ponytail. He glanced in a smoky mirror behind the long counter, watching the man at the table. The man looked at Paul's family for a moment, set the paper down, and made a call on his phone. As Paul waited for his order to be filled, he thought about his former life and how much better it was now.

He'd worked as a cryptographer for NSA and the CIA— recognized as the best in the world at code breaking. When he broke an ancient code left behind by Isaac Newton, the results helped destroy one of the most powerful and secretive groups ever to exist—the Circle of 13. They were thirteen multibillionaires who'd conspired, plotted and systematically engineered the take down of governments. They installed dictators, manipulated banks, currencies, helped create chaos and wars, all to build power, position, and money.

Part of the fall of this house of cards was connected to the Middle East, and it came when Paul planted a cyber worm that he programmed to immobilize the Iranian nuclear program in its tracks. Not only did Paul have a bounty on his head issued by three of the known surviving members of the Circle of 13, the Iranian government maintained a standing kill order with has name attached to it.

Paul and Alicia had both worked for NSA before they were forced into what amounted to a relocation program like none other in the history of American covert intelligence. Never before was there a combined bounty of a billion dollars for information that would lead to the capture or assassination of Paul and his wife.

Although they occasionally visited the other islands, they never went back to Sicily. Not since the helicopter they were in crashed six miles off the Sicilian coast five years ago. The pilot died, but they managed to make it to the remote beach of Panarea, and they stayed.

The former director of NSA, Bill Gray, made a clandestine trip to visit them, bringing everything needed to assume new identities and new lives. The conditions were that they would exist completely off the grid. And they could never return home if they hoped to live. Panarea was now home. It probably always would be.

Paul watched Alicia wipe chocolate off David's face. "I'm just thrilled you didn't get any on your clothes," Alicia said, dabbing a bit of ice cream from his chin.

Paul nodded. "We need to leave."

Alicia turned to him. "Buddy will be okay. He has food and water in his bowls. We haven't been gone that long. I wanted to do some shopping."

"Let's go. There's something I need to tell you."

"What, Paul?"

"Not here."

She could sense the tension in her husband's face. "Okay."

They got up to leave, Paul placing his sunglasses on and glancing toward the man who ended his phone call. Paul had parked their golf cart near the café, under the shade of a vine-covered coquina archway. He escorted his family to the cart, placing David in the middle of the front seat, between him and Alicia.

Paul backed out onto the pathway lined on one side by an ancient stonewall, the view of the Mediterranean on the other side. As he started to pull forward, the man from the café approached. "Excuse me," he said in perfect English.

Paul's heart slammed in his chest. He glanced at Alicia. She stared at the man, her lips tight. She reached for David, hands on his shoulders.

"I'm wondering if you can give me directions?" asked the man, newspaper folded under one arm, Panama hat casting shade over one eye.

Paul studied him for a second. "Where do you want to go?"

"Hotel Girasole."

"It's about a kilometer west. There are golf cart taxis at the pier."

"Thanks." He reached inside the folded newspaper.

Paul jumped out, his fist balled and ready.

"Whoa!" the man said, stepping back. "I come in peace."

"What do you mean come in peace? Come from where?"

The man looked around, lowered his voice. "I know who you are. I'm on your side."

"We don't have sides. Who the hell are you?"

"It's not important. What's important is inside this envelope." He pulled a sealed envelope from the fold in the newspaper, handed it to Paul.

"What's this?"

"It's for you. Actually, it's for your wife."

Alicia looked at the envelope. There was no name or address on it. She asked, "What's in there? Who sent it?"

"I don't know. That's the truth. I do know that the former director had it dispatched to you. I've been told that I am one of three people who know you're alive and here on the island. My job is to get this to you and vanish. Something I've made a living doing. What you do with the information in there is up to you. It's been more than five years, so I guess whatever the letter says must be damned important to somebody." He glanced around, his hazel eyes like a wolf's radar, looking in the shadows, tracking movement, on high alert.

"How'd you know where to find us?" Paul asked.

"The former director. He recruited me twenty-five years ago. I still do favors for him, occasionally, when I can."

"How do we know he sent you?"

The man glanced at the Mediterranean, the Isle of Stromboli on the edge of the horizon. He leveled his eyes at Paul. "The director told me to ask about Buddy. He said he bonded with your dog when he traveled with him to this island."

"Others in the agency might have known that."

The man smiled. "Perhaps. The director told me Buddy's missing his left dewclaw.

Alicia took a deep breath. Paul said nothing.

The man nodded. "My time here is up. I have a ferry to catch." He turned and stopped, looking back. "Mr. Marcus, what you did … it made a helluva positive difference in the world. I just thought you might want to know that." He touched the brim of his hat in a slight bow, turned and walked back toward the harbor.

Alicia looked at the blank envelope and then glanced up at her husband. She said, "Why now … what's in here?"

FOUR

Alicia stared at the sealed envelope. Her hands trembled. She looked over at Paul. "I'm almost afraid to open it."

"Don't rip it open. We don't know what's in there. I'll use my penknife to slice through the top."

"Okay." She handed him the envelope.

David watched a blue butterfly dart from the terrace of pink and white flowers. "Mommy, do lizards catch butterflies?"

She glanced down at her son, sitting in the golf cart next to her. "I don't know. We'll have to research that when we get home."

Paul got out of the cart and stepped a few feet away. He looked at the leaves on a bent olive tree. "The wind's blowing from the southwest," he said. He sliced open the envelope, tuned it over and tapped it with two fingers. He reached inside and slowly removed a folded sheet of paper. He stepped back to his wife. "The courier said it was for you." He handed it to her.

Alicia opened the paper and read silently. Within seconds, her eyes welled. She blinked, looking away as a tear spilled down her cheek.

David tilted his head. "Mommy, why are you crying?"

Alicia regained her composure, wiped the tear away. "I'm okay, David."

She lifted her eyes up to Paul. "It's handwritten, and it definitely looks like the director's handwriting."

"What'd he say?"

She handed the letter to Paul and said, "My mother's very ill. Cancer. He said she doesn't have much longer." Alicia moistened her lips. "Bill said Mom's been asking about me, especially after having chemo. Remember when Bill brought Buddy to us, I'd given him the necklace Mom had given me. Before I left the states, I'd told her if the necklace ever gets to her, it meant I was okay … or at least I wasn't dead. Mom's the only one in the family who knows I'm alive. They probably think that when she asks to see me that she's under the effect of the cancer drugs."

Paul said nothing for a moment. He read the letter, folded it, placing the paper back in the envelope. "I'm so sorry to hear this."

"Paul, I've got to go to her." Alicia looked at her son. "Mom doesn't know that she has a grandson. She needs to see David … and he needs to see her."

"We don't know if the letter is a hoax—"

"Who would know that Buddy is missing his left dewclaw? Bill spent a few days with Buddy transporting him from Virginia to this island. We have to make plans to get back to Virginia." She stared at her husband, her eyes hot and desperate.

Paul stepped over and touched his wife on her shoulder. "It'll be very dangerous. You two may have to go alone. It's me they want."

"No, I want you with us as a family. We can figure out a way to get there. You're my husband, and I won't leave without you."

In the distance, Paul watched passengers board one of the three ferryboats in the harbor. The man in the white Panama hat stood next to a railing, portside. "Alicia, somehow, someway, we have to reach Bill Gray. If he confirms he wrote the letter, we'll come up with a plan to get you back to your mother's house."

"Thank you. But how can you possibly reach Bill Gray without going on the grid? With all of the cyber sniffers looking for you—for us, how can you get around that kind of sophisticated trap?"

"By not leaving tracks, at least tracks that will lead directly to us."

"Can you do that, Paul?"

"I can try. If I fail, they'll find us before we can get a flight out of Sicily." He looked down at his young son and then stared up at the

expanse of vast ocean, a large white gull dipping into the breakers. "If I am flagged, and we can beat them from out of this area … we will have to travel at breakneck speeds. And we'd have to do that with a child."

"Where do you begin?"

"By buying a computer. I'm going to sneak through the dark valleys of the Internet and do it without leaving footprints. At least that's what I hope I can do."

FIVE

Central Virginia - Present Day

There was something about the old farmhouse that called to Janice Hawkins like a whisper in the wind. For more than five years, she and her husband, Carter, had driven by the property when they went for Sunday drives from their home south of Charlottesville. Janice was a professor of history at the University of Virginia. Carter was an analyst for the National Security Agency.

Today, they owned a new home that was two hundred years old.

Carter was behind the wheel of their BMW. Janice sat on the passenger side as they drove through the Virginia countryside. After another mile, they turned off the two-lane road and onto the gravel driveway that led more than a hundred yards up to the old home. They maneuvered around poplar trees and stooped oaks with gnarled trunks, heavy limbs, hearts and initials carved into the bark a century ago.

Carter, early fifties, brown hair streaked with gray, looked over to his wife and touched her hand. He said, "It's ours now."

"Yes ... yes it is," Janice said, green eyes beaming. She was a few years younger than her husband, auburn hair back in a scarf, oval face with delicate features.

The old home sat atop a slight hill and overlooked the Blue Ridge Mountains, the foothills the shade of mauve and purple in the distance. The home was made of exposed beams—pines that had been felled two centuries ago. It sat in the center of 125 acres of fields and hardwood forests. A rustic, wooden split-rail fence ran adjacent to the driveway. The out buildings behind the home included an aged barn with slate gray timbers, and a small, rough-hewn cabin with a front porch.

They parked the car in front of the home and got out, the breeze smelled of lilacs and lavender planted at the base of maple trees near the front of the home. Janice said, "I'm amazed that it's only been on the market two times since it was built. I can't believe our new home is almost as old as the nation."

"I like the majority of the updating that's happened, especially the kitchen. And I like the fact that they left a lot of the interior and exterior in its original state. I'm looking forward to making a few remodeling changes and moving our furniture in here."

"I hope we sell our home soon, and then we can move out here and live the rest of our lives away from the city." Janice walked around the side of the home and looked at the fenced pastures. "I wonder how long it's been since this land had a horse or two on it." She turned to her husband. "Let's start out with two horses, a few goats, and maybe a pair of lamas." She laughed.

"That sounds like a lot of work."

"But it's the kind of work that's good for the soul. Let's go inside."

They unlocked the front door and began moving through the house, talking about the little changes in paint and decor they were going to do. As they walked down a hall, the hardwood floors groaning under their feet, Carter pointed to a small closed doorway on the ceiling at the end of the hall. "Never noticed that," he said, gesturing to the attic door that was almost hidden under a coat of white paint.

Janice smiled. "I could tell it had an attic, maybe a small one, but I never saw the entrance either, and I didn't think to ask the realtor about it."

"It looks to me like the attic door was installed later. Maybe there's nothing but a short crawlspace up there. But we can use any extra storage space. The last time I came out here I brought a small toolbox and put it in the laundry room cabinet, a flashlight, too. I'll get them."

"I wonder what's up there, if anything." Janice hugged her arms, suddenly a little cold.

"We'll soon find out." Carter strode off, whistling.

Janice opened the door to one of the adjacent bedrooms. There was an antique dresser in a corner, one of the few pieces of furniture that remained in the home. The edges of the mirror were black, age spots through the looking glass. Janice stepped up to the dresser and slid out one of the drawers. There was something inside. She lifted out a pink bow for hair. Next to it was an antique hair comb, beige with a red rose inlaid into the top portion.

Janice looked out the bedroom window at the pasture, barn and the foothills. She thought about her own daughter, married and living in Los Angeles. She smiled and placed the items back in the drawer, quietly closing it.

Carter returned with a wooden chair in one hand, toolbox in the other. "Let's take a look," he said, removing a knife and a screwdriver. He stepped up on the chair and used the knife to slice through the dry paint, exposing most of the doorframe. And then he used the screwdriver to pry open the door. He managed to expose it enough to get his fingers inside and pull the entrance open. "Ahhh … there's the tip of an old ladder. I think I can reach it."

"Be careful." Janice stepped aside as her husband maneuvered the ladder out and down, dust falling like confetti from the attic.

He slid out the ladder and propped it up on one wall, stepped from the chair and climbed the ladder. When he entered the attic, he said, "Janice, you have come up here. There's some old furniture that looks like it was built in the mid 1700's and a few wooden crates. What a bonus. Maybe we'll find some hidden treasure, long since forgotten."

SIX

Paul Marcus took a deep breath as he pressed the power button on his new laptop computer. He sat alone in a remote corner of the hotel lobby, his slim laptop on the table next to a cup of espresso. He watched as a honeymoon couple, mid-twenties, laughed and registered across the lobby at the reception desk. Two paddle fans turned slowly from the ceiling, tropical plants in the corners. A woman in a maid's uniform approached the ferns and dwarf palms with a brass watering can.

Paul decided to go online in the hotel because it was busy and the Internet traffic coming and going from the hotel would be much greater and more diverse than from a coffee shop on the island's main plaza. Initial anonymity meant blending in with the crowd. From there it was avoiding the cyber snares.

Paul logged on the Internet, mindful of each keystroke and what the implications can mean. *Like stepping through fields with landmines underneath*, he thought. He knew how surveillance worked online, but he hadn't opened a computer in more than four years. New technologies were undoubtedly in place, however, the basic premise was still there. More than ninety-five percent of the Internet traffic under surveillance was computer monitored. The sniffers searched for key words or grouping of words.

Human monitoring usually began when the computers singled out what government or police agencies labeled *"interesting."* From there they'd track and scrutinize the source and the recipients. Packet sniffers in computers search for chunks of data routed between networks. The packets are small pieces of data that can be intercepted and later assembled back into a more complete package. Paul's goal was not to get intercepted due to anything caught or trapped in hundreds of filters.

If he could get to Bill Gray's computer, that meant that others could as well, and from anywhere in the world. Paul could hack his phone, computer and any software he used online. The problem was all of that is designed to be covert. Invisible. To communicate, to connect, with the former director of NSA, Paul would have to take more risks than he wanted.

The challenge was what message could he leave? How long could he afford to leave it there? And how could he frame it so the director's answer would be as innocuous as the question? No red flags. Nothing out of the ordinary. No IP links back to Panarea. Rather than hacking Bill Gray's computer, he decided his port of entry would be Gray's daughter, Rachel. Not her email, but rather her phone and text information.

He drained the espresso, rolled up his sleeves and began. His fingers moved over the keyboard deftly, each tap of a key calculated before he did it. Within less than ten minutes, he'd found the number and IP address of Rachel Silverstein. She was Bill Gray's only daughter. Married to a Department of Justice lawyer. Lived in Georgetown. Paul remembered her as a stay-at-home mom with three children. At least one was a teenager now.

He hacked into her phone, looked at the last text messages she'd sent to her father. It didn't take long. The last was sent at 3:02, Sunday, two days ago. She'd texted a picture of her youngest child, Lisa. The girl, age ten, red hair in a ponytail, was holding a beagle puppy. Lisa flashed a wide smile, braces on her teeth, and a spattering of freckles across her nose and cheeks.

The text read: *Dad, meet Bojangles. Three months old. Lisa is begging us to let him sleep with her. Not until he's solidly house-trained.*

Bill Gray responded by writing: *We got you your first dog, Tippy, when you were about Lisa's age. You were inseparable until you discovered boys a few years later. Maybe your mother and I can meet Bojangles next weekend.*

Rachel Silverstein hadn't responded yet. Paul seized the moment, his fingers moved quickly across the keyboard. He wrote: *That'd be great. Bojangles is missing his left dewclaw. Have you ever seen something like that?* Paul sent the text and waited. The paddle fan above him had a slight squeak as it slowly turned.

The message came back quickly. Gray wrote. *Yes. An old buddy of mine had a border collie that was born missing a left dewclaw.*

A smiled moved across Paul's lips. The former director knew it was a covert sign, and he'd made contact. Paul wrote: *No biggie. Did you write and send the invitations to Mom's surprise party?* He hit send and waited.

In less than thirty seconds the response arrived: *Yes. Should have been delivered today.*

Paul typed: *Great. See you soon, all three of us.* He logged off and sat there for a moment. Another couple entered the lobby, the woman's blonde hair uncombed, as if she'd just come off one of the ferryboats. Her boyfriend wore an untucked white shirt over Bermuda shorts, sandals. Paul watched them register, thinking of how his family would soon be traveling and staying in hotels. International travel and keeping off the grid would be challenging. But it could be done. He had thought about it for the last few years.

And now he was about to do it.

He was about to take his family across continents and time zones, exposing them to unspeakable dangers. Paul knew that the bounty on his head would motivate the world's best assassins. If they were caught and captured, he knew that his family wouldn't be killed immediately. His enemies would make his death, and that of his family, a spectacle. They would use it to set an example. Posting their executions live on the Internet.

Paul left the hotel lobby, slipped on his dark glasses and headed toward the house that he and Alicia had made into a home. If they were seen and identified, if the fact that they were alive was somehow made known in the clandestine world, they could never return here either.

He walked quickly down the old stone paths, the blast of a ferry-boat whistle coming across the harbor, his thoughts racing. It was decision time. He needed a solid plan. There would be no margin for error.

Meaning there could be no plan B.

SEVEN

Janice Hawkins wasn't sure she wanted to go up there. Not that she had any aversion to an attic, even a small attic that wouldn't allow an adult to fully stand. Her apprehension was the unknown. She'd fallen in love with the old house and its pastoral grounds. She'd walked the property with Carter. They'd made plans for updates to the barn, rustic cabin and home.

"Let me give you a hand," Carter said at the top of the ladder. "I wonder how they got this stuff in here."

She could see him slowly moving the flashlight around the dark attic. At this point in time, a few years from a planned early retirement, her goals were simple—to live in harmony with the land and the old home while she was still young enough to easily get around. The attic, and the quick observation that Carter made, opened the door to the unfamiliar. She enjoyed an adventure, but she didn't care for surprises. She stared up the ladder as her husband turned and extended his hand. Janice's thoughts ran. *What if an old crate was a Pandora's box of last wills and testaments, property deeds, land easements, disaffected relatives … two hundred years of the past trapped in an attic?*

"Why the hesitation?" asked Carter.

She smiled, blew a strand of hair from her left eye, stepped up on the first rung of the ladder and said, "I teach history but sometimes I don't like turning over historical stones because you never know what might be lying in wait."

"Let's be optimistic. Maybe there are maps of land trails or clues to hidden spaces that'll give us places to explore on that biggest mountain out our backdoor. Or maybe we'll find the lost gold of the Confederacy. What if General Robert E. Lee slept here." He grinned and helped his wife up the ladder.

When she entered the attic, Janice touched two fingers to her neck. The warm air seemed as if it had been caged for decades—the smell of dry rot, old parchment papers, a trace of perfume—a fragrance entombed between the pages of a worn Bible.

In the light from the flashlight, through the cobwebs and dust, she looked at Victorian furniture handmade two hundred years ago—all appeared in very good condition. A desk. Rocking chair. Baby's cradle. Dresser with marble and an oval mirror in burled wood. A roll-top writing desk.

They had to stoop over as they shuffled around the attic, opening drawers to old dressers and cabinets. Carter used his flashlight to read some papers he found in one drawer. "These are records of sale for horses and cattle," he said. Then he shook his head. "And there are bills-of-sale for humans—slaves. Looks like, at one time, there were at least a dozen slaves on this property."

"Maybe that's why there are two small cemeteries—separated, on the land. One for the landowners and one for the slaves."

Carter stepped over to an old writing desk. He slid out a drawer on the left. Nothing. He did the same for one on the right. It, too, was empty. And then he knelt down and opened the bottom drawer. There was nothing in the front portion. He aimed his light toward the rear, through cobwebs. A worn leather rucksack was at the back of the drawer. He knocked the spider webs down and removed the rucksack, setting it on the desk. "Take a look a this."

"It appears really old."

"Hold the light while I see what's inside."

Janice held the flashlight as Carter carefully unbuckled the two straps securing the satchel. The leather was like aged skin, cracked and dry with tiny veins splintered across the surface. Carter opened the satchel and looked inside. He reached in, removing two sheets of paper. One appeared to be a handwritten letter. The other was filled with random letters and numbers. He saw something else, reached back inside, and lifted out a tubed-shaped wooden cylinder about eight inches long.

Carter took a pair of glasses from his shirt pocket and placed them on, studying the cylinder. "There are twenty-six small wooden wheels," he said, turning one of the wheels. "And it appears that the alphabet, in random order, is engraved on each wheel. If this is what I think it is …"

Janice stared at the device for a moment, raised her eyes up to Carter and said, "It's called a cipher wheel. Thomas Jefferson invented it, and that device, or something very similar, ushered America into the world of espionage with the capability to send and receive covert messages."

Carter rotated the wheel to the far left, studying the letters. "I remember seeing a device like this on display at Monticello. Simple and brilliant."

"When Jefferson became president, he was concerned that letters he wrote and sent to his envoys overseas were being opened and read by postal clerks working as spies. So he sat down and came up with an ingenious way to encrypt. If the recipient had a cipher wheel and the encrypted message, all he or she had to do is use the letters in the encryption to turn the wheels and then look for the plain text below the line of encrypted text, which would literally spell out the secret message. What's on the papers? One looks like a letter. The other is apparently a code."

"Hold the light closer." Carter read silently for a few seconds. He looked up at his wife, his eyes vibrant. "It appears to be a letter written by Thomas Jefferson. It's dated in 1804. The signature below reads *Th Jefferson*. He writes: *Dear Robert, may this letter find you in good spirits despite the challenges that you have endured these last few months. As newly elected president, I assure you that the United States will not tolerate the barbaric and unjustified corsair attacks from the Barbary pirates. It is always our first initiative to negotiate peace and not to purchase it. Should that fail, we as a nation, will not be held hostage to another country's greed nor creed."* Carter looked up from the letter, his eyes distant for a moment.

Janice said, "This letter is a better find than a pot of gold. What Jefferson wrote two hundred years ago could have been written today."

"You're the historian ... why would this letter, this cipher wheel and this apparent code be hidden in this house?"

"The home, as we know, was built by Isaac Kincaid. He had helped Jefferson one day when Jefferson's horse threw a shoe. This house was on the route that Jefferson followed by horseback when he left Monticello for his country house, Poplar Forest. We're near the halfway point. I'd read in a diary and the history of Amherst County that Kincaid, who was a farmer, and Jefferson, developed a close friendship that they maintained for years until Jefferson's death."

"Maybe Kincaid was more than a farmer. He could have been a guy that Jefferson trusted to get messages out ... or to store classified information."

"What does the rest of the letter say?"

Carter looked down and read. '*As you are aware, the pasha of Tripoli has declared war on the United States because of my refusal to pay $220,000 to ensure safe passage of American ships. This piracy shall and will end. As president, I have made plans to eradicate the continued plundering of American ships in the Mediterranean. We will coerce the enemy to a peace treaty on terms compatible with American honor and interests. I have instructed Lieutenants Stephen Decatur, William Eaton and Presley O'Bannon to utilize maneuvers that, we believe, will unleash such force upon the enemy as to leave them rendered helpless. This information is on a separate encrypted letter. This should be sufficient to give our nation access to trade with Spain, Portugal and other Mediterranean nations. However, the goal of safe passage for decades will require something beyond this approach. I have thought about this day since my first meeting with Tripoli's ambassador in London years ago. In that meeting, he told John Adams and I that, according to the Koran, all nations, which do not acknowledge the Prophet Muhammad, are sinners. He said it is the right and duty of the faithful to plunder and enslave the sinners. Accordingly, also on the encrypted paper, I have included information that will reveal what I believe can be a solution to people of nations who think they have a holy or religious right of violence for those who* *do not follow the aggressor's doctrine, but yet wish to live in a peaceful coexistence. Perhaps it is nothing more than conjecture on my part. However, after examining twelve hundred years of Islamic history, I am offering a prediction in regards to that and the global harmony of all nations and people. I look forward to your thoughts and subsequent correspondence.*

Sincerely, Th Jefferson.

Carter looked up, his wife awestruck listening to him read from an unknown letter written by Thomas Jefferson. She said, "I'm not saying this because I teach history at the university Jefferson founded, but this is an incredible find."

Carter nodded. He held up the second two sheets. They were filled with random letters in English and French. And it included a series of numbers from one to twenty. He said, "What in the world did Jefferson predict? It's here on these two sheets of paper. But I can tell you that this encryption is much more difficult than random sequencing of letters. He mixes French with English and numbers with letters. Thomas Jefferson was, no doubt, brilliant, but was he astute enough to offer a forecast into the fate of nations? He and our small American navy won the first war of terrorism ever declared on the nation. So what is Jefferson's prophecy?"

"Surely it can't be that difficult for NSA to break the code?"

"In 1804 Robert Patterson used Jefferson's cipher wheel to write an extremely difficult code. It was broken two hundred years later by a Robert Butler, professor of mathematics at Rutgers. This cypher encryption seems more difficult. I'll take it into the department to see if some of our cryptographers can break it. It'll be damn tough, I can tell you that just by looking at it. If my people can't crack this, I know the one man in the world who might be able to do it."

"Who's that?"

"I wish I could tell you. He's been hiding the last few years. Maybe it's the ultimate witness protection program, the most covert our nation has ever done. Getting to him would be exceedingly difficult, if not impossible."

EIGHT

Alicia Marcus stood on the terrace of her white stucco home and stared at the horizon. There was a fine line where the sky and sea become one, the sapphire of the atmosphere dissolving the cobalt blue of the Mediterranean. The island of Stromboli was to the right. Near it, a volcanic cone rose from the sea, a wisp of smoke like a brushstroke of white paint on the blue face of the sky. Alicia watched little David play chase with their border collie, Buddy, in the yard, the dog barking and David laughing.

Paul stepped out of the house onto the terrace, two cups of tea in his hands. He handed one to his wife and said, "We'll leave soon."

She turned to him, her light brown eyes troubled. "We need to take Buddy. It would break David's heart if he never saw him again."

"Mario can take care of him until we get back."

"Mario's a kind man. He's an excellent gardener, but he's getting up in age. And what if we never come back? This could be the last day in our home."

"Maybe not. I'll do everything I can to get you safely to your mother's house. There are risks, as you know. Bill knows we're coming. I need to contact him to get us a different set of passports. I'll go back to the hotel to reach him. Maybe he can get us into a safe house in the states."

"Are you certain that Bill knew it was you?"

"Yes."

"It would be so nice to go back to your old farmhouse. Buddy would get reacquainted with the farm, and David would have a chance to grow up around horses—"

"Alicia, that's not possible. As much as I'd love to raise our son in the Virginia countryside, it's too risky. You know that."

She looked away, took a deep breath, the air filled with the fragrance of chamomile and flowers. Paul touched his wife's shoulders, squeezed gently and kissed her on the cheek. He said, "We'll be fine. We can take Buddy. It'll make us look more like a family traveling leisurely on holiday and help us blend in as locals when we get there. Okay?"

"Okay. I do love our home here—the fact that flowers grow from every crack in the volcanic soil. We're living in paradise, but paradise has its limitations when it's a small island and the rest of your family is seven thousand miles away. I'm so looking forward to seeing Mom. I was with her often when Dad was fighting his cancer, and now it's her. I'm sure Dianne is doing what she can, but I'm the oldest daughter, and I feel I need to be there. If nothing else, just to hold Mom's hand, to make her feel comfortable and loved." She watched David and Buddy play, and then turned back to Paul. "It seems so little but it is really so much."

"I'll get you home safely. Promise."

Alicia set her cup on an outdoor table and reached for her husband. She hugged him tightly. Over her shoulder, Paul watched David toss a Frisbee in the air, Buddy jumping up to catch it, the distant volcano suddenly reminded him of the pyramid on the back of a dollar bill. The sun reflected off a tuft of smoke like a light in the distance, staring at him, unblinking, somehow ominous. And then the wind changed and the smoke descended, covering the summit as if a pastel veil just descended over the eye of the volcano.

• • •

Captain Mike Nolan and the other members of the Delta Force team got the message at little before 11:00 a.m. They left their compound in four different vans, fully armed. Their job wasn't going to be a rescue. It would be a body recovery. And they had no plans to leave Eli Dexter's body in Libya. Units from Seal Team Six were waiting on a desolate beachhead near Derna to transport the body to a U.S. Navy ship eighteen miles off the Libyan coast.

Special Forces' members used GPS telemetry and photographs sent from NSA of the site where the body was left. It was in a less populated section of town, no more than three blocks from the Mediterranean coast. Mike Nolan opened his radio microphone and said, "We're a kilometer away. Units three and four, head to the eleven and two o'clock positions in the rear of the place. Unit two, stay with us as we come up to the old archway."

Each squad sent a one word affirmative confirmation of the orders and proceeded to their destinations. Nolan looked at a screen depicting a live satellite feed of the site and said, "No indication of organized hostiles, but that means nothing."

"Roger," came a single word over the radio.

Nolan turned to a team member in the front seat. Ron Childers was one of the younger recruits. Early twenties. Full beard. Eyes dark, unreadable. He looked at the Mediterranean Sea to their right, off the coastal highway that snaked through the ancient city of Derna. He glanced at Nolan and said, "We have ISIS here. And we have two more fractured Libyan splinter groups vying for power. Who do you think got to Eli?"

"Could be any of them, or some wild ass who wants to start his own coup in this part of the country. But, in about three minutes, we'll have a better idea."

NINE

The scene reminded Captain Mike Nolan of a lynch mob. But the victim was already dead. Slaughtered. And still more than two-dozen Islamic jihadists, morbid onlookers, and children—holding their parents hands, looked at the body of the American. Some took pictures and video using their phones. Some screamed insults at the dead man's body, some spit on Eli Dexter's corpse. Others took sticks, hitting it like striking a piñata. A few just stared for a short period and walked away.

Nolan and his Delta Force team, in innocuous cargo vans, parked about one hundred yards away from the scene in four separate locations—north, east, west and south. Nolan turned to the men in the back area and said, "We'll assess the situation and move closer. Let's circle the wagons around this mob. The eye in the sky shows us that people are movin' about. We just don't know who the hell they are." He nodded to Ron Childers on the passenger side of the front seat and said, "Hand me the glass." Childers pulled the binoculars from a duffle bag and gave them to Nolan.

He looked through high-powered binoculars and suppressed his rising anger. *It's not personal,* he thought. *Get the job done.* Eli Dexter's body hung under an old stone archway, one of the ancient gates to the city of Derna. His arms were outstretched, tied with ropes looped over the archway, keeping his body vertical. His throat was slit;

dark blood stains covered his shirt. Flies crawled over his pasty face and into the wound.

"Bastards … we're comin' for your sorry ass," mumbled Nolan as he studied the scene. A cardboard sign was tied with twine and hung from Dexter's neck, the sign propped against the stomach area. A few words in Arabic were scrawled across the cardboard. "They wrote something and left it on the body," Nolan said, handing the binoculars to Childers. "You read Arabic better than me. Can you make out what it says?"

Childers looked through the lens, his jawline tightening. "You sick shits …" he whispered. After a moment, he added, "Somebody wrote … 'remember the battle of Derna.' "

"What battle? This whole country is a battlefield, just like most of the Mideast."

One of the men in the back cargo area of the van, a seasoned veteran with a white scar about his left eye, spoke in a Texas brogue, "It's like the saying we have in Texas … remember the Alamo."

"I know what that means," Nolan said. "What the hell does remember the battle of Derna mean, and why did those assholes strap it to Eli's body?"

The team member leaned forward. "Hand me the bi-nocs." He held the binoculars to his eyes and was silent for ten seconds and then blew out a breath. "Eli never signed up for that shit. Death is one thing … mutilation of the body is something else." He handed the binoculars back to Childers. "Let's get Eli outta this shit hole."

Nolan nodded. He opened his mic. "Long-range … move into positions."

One of the men inside Nolan's van said, "Yes sir." He lifted a M-2010 sniper rifle and slipped out the rear door of the van. Three other snipers did the same thing, leaving the other three vans, positioning under cover of trees or buildings. The team had precious few seconds before the snipers were spotted.

Nolan looked through the binoculars again. He watched as an elder man, turban, long gray beard, approached the body. The man had a long knife, the blade serrated. He stepped up to the body of Eli Dexter, spat in the dead soldier's face, mumbled hate in Arabic and pulled pack Dexter's head. The crowd of less than thirty people cheered.

Mike Nolan whispered into the microphone. "Johnston … you take out the guy with the meat cleaver. McNairy … Larson … Reynolds … pick the strongest men in the circle and fire on the count of three. One … two … three …"

Nolan looked through the binoculars. The man with the serrated knife stood in front of Dexter's body and turned to the crowd. He shouted something, his left fist clenched. The moment he turned back to the body, his head exploded. Blood and brain matter splattered across the onlooker's faces. In a split second, three men, all vocal protesters were shot in the head. Their bodies dropped on the spot.

"Let's roll!" Nolan said into the radio mic. The convoy pulled up to the crowd in seconds. The side panel doors flew open and four armed Delta Force team members in each van approached, weapons aimed. People screamed. Hands shot up in the air. Some ran away, screaming and crying. Other stooped and wailed at the bodies of the four dead men. In Arabic Ron Childers shouted, "Hands in the air. Everyone! Stand back! Move away from the American! Now!" The crowd complied.

Nolan and Childers moved through the people. The other team members circled and guarded the perimeter. Nolan looked at two of his men. "Cut Eli down. Put him in unit two." The men moved to the hanging corpse, one man using a Special Forces tactical knife to cut the ropes. The other man supported the body. Within seconds, the body of Eli Dexter was cut down and loaded into a waiting van.

Nolan watched a tall, bearded man in the midst of the crowd reach for his phone. Nolan gestured to Childers and they approached the man, Childers standing a few feet behind, Nolan facing him. The man tried to slip his phone in his pocket. Nolan took a step. He pointed his sidearm directly at the man's forehead. "Pal, who are you calling?"

The man said nothing. His dark eyes cold and hard, staring at the American.

Nolan glanced at Childers. "Tell these people the fuckin' show's over and to leave."

Childers shouted the orders in Arabic. People ran, most toward the city center. The man standing in front of Nolan started to leave. "Not you!" Nolan shouted. "Hands in the air!" He gestured to

Childers. "Tell him he's got five seconds or he'll be the fifth person to die here today."

Childers shouted the orders. The man slowly raised his hands. Nolan said, "Weapons check. And get his phone."

Childers patted down the man, and then removed the phone from his pocket. He looked at the last number called and received. "Local numbers," Childers said.

Nolan nodded. He cut his eyes back to the man standing in front of him. "I believe you know who killed my friend. And I further believe you're gonna tell me."

The man shook his head. In a thick accent he said, "I do not know this, but even if I did … I would never tell you."

Nolan made a cold smile. "I thought you spoke English. Who were you trying to call?"

"My wife."

"To tell her what?"

"That we executed another America pig." He grinned.

Nolan's fist hit the man so fast and hard it knocked him flat on his back. A second later, Nolan had his pistol barrel under the man's chin, the gun buried in his shaggy, black beard. "One more time! Who killed my friend?"

The man tried to speak, blood pouring from his loose teeth and smashed lips. "I don't know. Some call him Fajar. It means the great warrior. It is mentioned nine times in the Koran. He is a descendent from Yusuf Karamanli, the greatest pasha to lead Tripoli. Fajar calls his war against America the closing of the circle."

"Where is Fajar?"

"I do not know. Allah knows I am telling the truth."

"What do you mean … the closing of the circle?"

"It was here in Derna when Muslims fought the first war with America. More than two hundred years ago under your president, Thomas Jefferson. You won that war. The American soldier they hung from the ancient city arch, is the first death in the new war. The sign placed around his neck spelled it out for you. Remember the Battle of Derna. Because now it has began again, and Fajar, with his vast connections and resources, will not lose this time."

TEN

P aul Marcus took the same seat in the corner of the hotel lobby, but this time he was about to take a much greater risk. He'd planned for the six hour time difference between the Aeolian Islands and Washington DC. It was 9:00 a.m. Wednesday in DC. He watched a family from England stand at the reception desk and check into the hotel. After the family left for their rooms, Paul approached the desk clerk—early twenties, fresh haircut, black-rimmed glasses. "Yes sir," the man said.

"Can I get an espresso? I'll be sitting at the corner table, near that palm tree." Paul motioned to the opposite side of the lobby. He handed the clerk twenty Euro.

"Absolutely, sir. I'll have it delivered to you." He started to count the money.

"Keep the change."

"Thank you very much, sir."

Paul smiled. "May I have a postcard of the hotel? It looks like you have a few behind you."

"Of course." The clerk handed Paul a picture postcard featuring the hotel with a view of the Mediterranean in the background.

"Thanks … I should be getting a phone call soon. I see you have a house phone near where I'm sitting. Would you mind transferring the call?"

"My pleasure. What is your name, sir?"

"Gavin Parker."

"I will be happy to transfer the call, and we'll get your espresso to you in a few minutes. Is there anything else you may need, Mr. Parker?"

"No thanks."

Paul returned to his seat. He glanced at the phone number on the postcard, sat and opened a small notepad. He wrote down the hotel's phone number across the top of the page. He stared at it a few seconds, looking at ways to encode the number. Then he wrote a letter beneath each digit in the phone number and spelled: I-S-L-A-N-D-S—the exact number of digits matching the hotel's main phone number.

He opened his laptop and used the hotel's connection to access the Internet. Within three minutes, he had hacked back into the phone of the former NSA director's daughter, Rachel Silverstein. Paul wrote: *Happy upcoming anniversary, Dad! You should take Mom to the ISLANDS. Gavin Parker took his wife. Loved it! Call Gavin ASAP.*

Paul knew that Bill Gray would use the word in all caps, ISLANDS, to find the numeric code in the alphabet, substituting letters for numbers, each letter given a numerical value. The letter A would equal the number 1. The letter I, as in ISLANDS, would represent the number 9. It was simple, efficient, and not overtly suspect.

A waiter, dark-skinned, slender fingers, approached Paul with a cup of espresso on a small tray. The waiter smiled and said, "Sir, did you order the espresso?"

"Yes, thank you." Paul handed the man two euros.

"You're very welcome. Is there anything else I may bring you?"

"No thanks."

The waiter nodded. As he returned to the kitchen, his right shoulder skimmed the fronds of a sago palm in a large cast-iron pot. Paul looked at a clock on the wall near the plant. He could hear the sound of a ferryboat whistle from the docks. He glanced out an open bay window to the sea. Two hydrofoil shuttle boats approached from two different directions, one east and one south.

And then there was the soft buzz of an incoming call. Paul watched the front desk clerk answer the phone. He nodded and looked in Paul's direction. Less than ten seconds later, a white phone rang on an adjacent wicker table. Paul picked it up and said, "You're quick."

"And you make it easy, even for someone like me who has no encryption skills. How are you? How's Alicia?"

"We're all fine. She's anxious, very worried about her mother. Thank you for letting us know about her condition."

"You're welcome. I hate like hell being the bearer of bad news. But I thought she should know." Bill Gray walked by a three-acre pond on the property of his home on the outskirts of Great Falls, Virginia. He was pushing seventy. White hair neatly parted. His face tanned from a recent golf trip to Florida. He wore a cardigan sweater over a flannel shirt and pressed jeans. Gray held a burner cell phone in one hand, a pad of paper in the other.

Paul said, "It's important that she knows. Now, of course, she wants to see her mom."

"When I gave Alicia's mother the necklace—the one Alicia had given me five years ago, I could tell that her mother knew Alicia was alive. All I said at the time was this … they're okay. So I suspect she knew you, too, were alive and with her daughter."

"She doesn't know that she has a four-year-old grandson."

"What's his name?"

"David."

"I bet he's a fine boy."

"He is." Paul looked at the window as a three-hundred-foot private yacht cruised into Panarea's harbor, the yacht gleaming white, a helicopter perched on one end. "Bill, I'll need passports for each of us under a different name to get my family back to that part of the states to protect the other identities you gave us in case we have to up and leave quickly. Can you get them here soon?"

"Of course. Text a photo of David. Go through my daughter's phone. I've given her a heads up that it's business. She's uncomfortable, of course. She feels that her privacy has been compromised. It was most ingenious on your part, though."

"My apologies to Rachel."

"Too bad I can't extend them. Three people know you're alive … me, the agency's director of cryptanalysis, Carter Hawkins, and the president. We can assume that Alicia's mother knows. But because I was vague, she can't confirm it. Maybe in her heart she knows it. That means she can never acknowledge what she doesn't really know for sure. She stays safer that way."

"How quickly can you get the passports here?"

"They'll come from our embassy in Rome. Give me twenty-four hours. I'll have them delivered to your house."

"Thanks. I'll try to stay in touch the best I can en route."

"Paul, there's something else."

"What?"

"I said earlier that I hate being the bearing of bad news. I've done it way too often in my career. Usually I couldn't even tell the surviving spouse how their husband or wife died."

"What is it, Bill?"

"I know how close you are to Liam Dexter and his family. You went to the University of Virginia with Liam, and his son Eli, was your godson."

"What do you mean … was?"

"Eli's been killed. Happened not far from Benghazi in the port town of Derna. I'm so damn sorry."

Paul used one hand to brace himself against the wall. His face was flush, heart hammering, nausea and bile rising in his gut. His mind felt vapid.

"Paul … are you there. There is something else you need to know."

ELEVEN

Paul stepped back from the open window, the phone still held to his ear. He looked across the hotel lobby, the slow turning paddle fans, wicker furniture, ferns and large saltwater aquarium against one wall, the desk clerk staring at a computer screen, light reflecting off his glasses.

"Are you there?" Bill Gray asked.

Paul inhaled deeply, his eyes wet, remembering Eli at family events such as sports and holidays. "What happened to Eli?"

"He was captured outside a compound he shared with other members of Delta Force. He'd gone across the road to give water to an old farmer plowing his fields. On his return, a van loaded with hostiles pulled up and ambushed him." Bill told Paul all he knew and added, "We took out four before recovering the body. One hostile, under severe interrogation, admitted that the leader is someone called Fajar. He allegedly has family ties back to the Pasha of Tripoli, whose name was Yusuf Karamanli."

"Why is that relevant?"

"Because Fajar, or his followers left a message on Eli's body. They had a sign hanging from his neck that read … *Remember the battle of Derna.*"

Paul said nothing. He glanced out the open window, the sea breeze cooling his face. "Derna … you're talking more than two hundred years ago. That battle was the first war the U.S. fought after becoming a nation."

"The pasha of Tripoli was the first to declare war on America. And now it looks like one of his descendants is doing it again."

"Why Eli? He was one of the best of the best."

"That's the question we'd like to answer. The Delta Force team is there along with federal agents and Navy Seals to hunt down and capture those responsible for firebombing our compound in Benghazi and the deaths of four Americans, including our ambassador. We're hunting them down and taking them to be tried in federal court back in the states. This guy, Fajar, his last name is Hamad, spent a lot of time training in Iran. We believe Iranian operatives were actually behind the disaster that went down in Benghazi. And that's where you enter the picture, Paul."

"What do you mean?"

"Maybe it's the answer to your question … why Eli. Let's go back almost five years ago when you set in motion the destructive cyber worm into the Iranian nuclear operation. The destruction put the Iranians back years in their nuclear progress. We know of the outstanding kill order on you and your family. What if Eli Dexter was handpicked to die because of his connection to your family … and most importantly … his connection to you? What if they somehow knew that and used the opportunity as leverage to get to you."

"But the world thinks Alicia and I died in the helicopter crash off the coast of Sicily."

"Because the only body recovered was that of the pilot, your enemies like the Iranians, what's left of the Circle of 13—throw the former Russian president in for good measure … they are and always will be suspicious. So I'd surmise that any opportunity they have to eat away at your Achilles heel is something they'd pursue with a vengeance."

"You really think Eli was killed to get to me?"

"His death was horrible enough … but they wanted to send a message to the world. They strung him up by his wrists under the archway at the old gateway to the city of Derna. The same place where the U.S. flag was raised after we beat them two centuries ago. The sign on his body … it all points to ulterior agendas. For Fajar, for his group, it's not enough to kill an American commando, they want to draw a line in the sand that goes back to 1804."

"Why 1804?"

"Because that's when Thomas Jefferson sent our troops in to stop them. They'd been pirating our merchant ships, holding the crews hostage, putting them into slavery. We, as a nation, had been paying what amounted to ransom and an annual fee to the four North African nations—Algiers, Tunisia, Morocco and Libya, referred to as Tripoli in those days. The fee was to allow our ships safe passage into the Mediterranean Sea. When Jefferson was elected president, he said enough was enough."

Paul stared out the window at the Mediterranean, the sea breeze briny. "That's a long time to hold a grudge."

Bill chuckled. "Actually two hundred plus years is a short time for some vengeance prone Muslims to hold a grudge. Usually this type of old vendetta has to do with hatred for other Muslim tribes over land or interpretation of religion. Most folks in the world don't know what their great grandfathers did or did not do. But for some jihadists Muslims, these people go back to the time of Abraham and blame each other in long ancestral clashes where the original cause of the animosity is vague, but the vendetta is palpable in their minds … forever."

"I need to see Eli's family."

"You can't. It's too risky."

"Alicia will be there for her mother. I'll go see Eli's dad, Liam, and his mother Jenny. I won't go to the funeral, but I'll do what I can to ease their emotional pain."

"The more people that know you are alive, the greater the odds are that you won't be for very long."

"I have to do something. I was at the hospital when Eli was born. Saw him play sports, graduate from high school and enter West Point. Please get the passports to us as soon as you can."

"I'll have them delivered quickly."

"By the same courier?"

"Yes."

"Bill you said only three people know Alicia and I are alive … the president, Carter Hawkins and you. The guy you sent with the letter makes the fourth person."

"Guy?"

"Early fifties. He said you recruited him twenty-five years ago. He told me that he does favors for you … and then he vanishes."

"How'd this man approach you?"

"He'd been sitting at an outdoor café. He came up to my family as we were about to take our golf cart back to our home from the harbor."

"What name did he use?"

"He didn't tell us his name."

"No, what name did he call you? Was it your cover name, Alex Perry?"

"No, he asked me if I was Paul Marcus?"

"I didn't send a man. I sent a woman. She's a federal agent out of Rome. She didn't know your real name. Paul, you've been compromised. Maybe that's why Eli Dexter was picked out of more than fifty of our best covert agents in Libya."

"If my family and I have been compromised, why didn't the guy approach our home at night and try to eliminate us?"

"I can't answer that. My suspicion is they have something more spectacular planned for you. Most likely it's something dramatic, maybe something involving other innocent people. Or they could be waiting for you to travel so they can more easily kidnap you and your family. "

"How fast can you get the passports here?"

"Give me twenty-four hours. I'll have them delivered to your house."

"This time, tell me who the courier will be. If not, I'll kill whoever approaches my family."

Bill pinched the bridge of his nose. "Will do." He disconnected and threw his burner phone into the center of the pond, watched the ripples for a moment, turned and walked slowly back to his home.

TWELVE

Paul wore a baseball cap pulled just above his eyebrows as he bought airline tickets at the Alitalia counter. He'd waited until the last minute to make the purchases. He counted the money to the clerk behind the flight desk, a dark haired woman staring at her computer screen, tapping the keyboard. She asked, "Do you need to make connections out of Rome."

"No, we're fine, thanks."

"I need your ID and that of your family, Mr. Miller."

"Of course." Paul handed her British passports. Alicia and David stood behind him. Alicia held Buddy on a leash, the dog silent, observing people. Paul smiled, "I don't suppose our dog needs his passport. Since he's a border collie, he thinks he can cross borders just about anywhere."

The woman looked up from her screen and smiled. "It's a quick flight to Rome. He should be comfortable in the cargo area. There are no other dogs on the flight. He'll have the space all to himself."

"I'll let him know. Thanks."

"We'll bring out a crate for him in a moment. It the meantime, we can process your luggage."

"There's not a lot to process. It's all carry-on bags."

"As long as they fit in the overheads, you're good to go. The flight departs from gate B-17."

A stocky airline baggage handler approached with a metal crate. Alicia smiled and said, "Thank you. We'll get Buddy inside. He's always cooperative, but he hasn't flown in a while." She took the leash off, and led Buddy by the collar into the crate. He sat, tail wagging.

David reached in and petted his dog. "Mom, can I ride with Buddy?"

"Not on this trip. Dogs, Buddy's size and larger, have to ride in the cargo space. He'll be fine. Buddy will probably sleep most of the trip."

"What if he has to go to the bathroom?" David's eyes widened.

"The trip isn't that long. Buddy will have an adventure." She nodded to the baggage handler, who smiled and walked with the crate through the recesses of the luggage processing area.

Paul checked the tickets and said, "Let's go find B-17."

As they walked though the airport, Paul scanned faces—tourists, airline workers, anyone coming toward them. It was a typical busy international airport, people concerned with travel logistics, departing, arriving, making connections—the frenetic pace of travel deadlines and delays. The walk was less than five minutes, and they were soon approaching B-17. Paul touched the boarding passes inside his coat pocket, looked at the departure monitor screen on one wall. All flights appeared to be leaving on time.

And then he saw it.

Out of the corner of his eye.

A man watched them.

Paul chatted with Alicia and David, not looking directly at the man standing on the opposite side from his gate. "Let's sit," Paul said to his family. They sat in chairs that overlooked the airport runways, planes landing and taking off.

"Can we watch the jets?" David asked, jumping up and running toward the large window.

"David, slow down," Alicia said, following closely behind her son.

Paul looked at one of the monitors secured to the support beams. The screen was turned off, black. He could see the reflections as easy as looking into still, dark water. He saw the man in jeans and a sports coat watching his family. The man lifted a phone from his inside pocket.

"Now boarding priority seating on Alitalia flight 1972 to Rome, gate B-17," came the announcement from the overhead speakers.

Paul watched as Alicia lifted David up and pointed toward a jet coming in to touch down on the runway. He had seconds to make a decision. Paul turned and looked toward the man in the sports coat. He casually glanced away, and pressed the keyboard on his phone.

Paul stepped over to the large observation window. He watched as five baggage handlers loaded the luggage onto a moving conveyer belt that led through an open door into the belly of the plane. One of the handlers, in dark jeans with red shoes, took a call, lifting a phone from his back pocket. He answered and glanced around the perimeter as he spoke, his face pinched, nervous. Paul watched him for a moment, the man nodding and reaching into a separate luggage cart. He removed a small, black plastic box. The man then vanished inside the plane.

"Look!" said David, pointing. "I see Buddy." Buddy sat in the metal crate on luggage cart, the last to be loaded on the plane.

"Let's go," Paul said, gently touching his wife and son. "We need to board."

Alicia smiled and looked at her husband. "There's not a rush. Priority seating will be there now or in ten minutes. We want to watch Buddy get on the plane."

"Alicia, trust me on this. We need to move right now."

She looked startled, lowered David to the floor and said, "Okay, Paul."

He led them to an airline employee taking boarding passes. They handed her their boarding passes and walked down the corridor. No one in front of them. An older couple behind them. At the door to the plane, Paul stopped. He motioned for a flight attendant. The woman was middle-aged, brunette, hair pinned back in a barrette, wide smile. "Yes sir, may I help you?"

"Yes, please. There's a dog on the tarmac. He's ours. Don't board him. The dog has become sick and could die between here and Rome. Please just bring him back to the gate. We'll get him."

Alicia looked devastated. Not sure what to say. David stared up at his father, his eyes frightened, unsure. The flight attendant said, "Yes sir. We can do that." She stepped to one side and picked up a red phone, telling the ramp supervisor not to board the dog.

Alicia pulled her husband to one side, lowered her voice, and asked, "What are you doing? David is going to burst out in tears. He thinks Buddy's about to die. Paul, what's going on?"

He whispered. "I think a bomb's been planted on the plane."

"What! Dear God ..."

The flight attendant approached. "Sir, your dog is being returned to the gate. You can get him in a couple of minutes. What will this mean for your family and your flight?"

"We'll have to cancel."

Alicia looked down at her feet. David stared at his dad. The flight attendant nodded and said, "I completely understand. I'm a dog lover, too. My golden retriever is like one of my of my kids."

Paul took a deep breath, looked over the woman's shoulder at the pilot and co-pilot sitting in the cockpit, the silver-haired pilot sipping hot coffee from a Styrofoam cup. Paul said, "Listen carefully to me."

The flight attendant looked slightly taken back, titled her head. "Sir, what do—"

"There are five baggage handlers loading this plane. One is wearing dark jeans and red tennis shoes. From the observation window, I saw him load a small package—a black plastic box. The box came from a food vender's truck. But it wasn't food, and it didn't look like anything food related."

"Sir ... what is your name?"

"That's not important. What's important is to find the baggage handler or the box he put on the plane. You need to share that information with the captain now."

She nodded. "We appreciate you speaking out. It could be nothing, but better safe than sorry." As she turned to go back inside the plane, Paul touched Alicia on her back, picked up David, and walked quickly up the passenger ramp and into the terminal. Paul knew the man in the tan sports coat would be gone. The man would tell his superiors he saw Paul Marcus and his family board the plane.

The deadly consequences were in place and in motion. Paul would have to find another way out, and he had very little time to do it.

THIRTEEN

Buddy greeted his family as if he'd just returned from a long trip. Paul unfastened the door to the crate, handed the porter five Euros and said, "Thanks."

"Yes sir. Thank you." The man tipped the bill of his cap.

Alicia said, "Please, leave the crate here. We hope to board in a few minutes when they're done."

"Yes ma'am. They'll radio me, and I'll get your dog on board quickly." He smiled, turned and left.

Alicia looked through one of the large airport windows at the plane still on the tarmac, airline employees standing about as investigators searched the plane. Two men in dark suits and darker glasses questioned the baggage handler in red tennis shoes.

Alicia snapped the leash onto Buddy's collar, stood and said, "Paul, they've delayed the flight a half-hour, searching the plane. It looks like they haven't found anything."

David wrapped his arms around his dog's neck. "Hi, Buddy."

Paul looked out the window, watching the people milling about near the plane. He turned to Alicia and said, "There are a lot of places to hide something that small on a large aircraft."

She glanced at the gate to the plane. "It looks like they're allowing the passengers back on board. Can we go now? I don't know how much time Mom has, and the more time we're here, the less we'll have to spend with her. Let's just get on the plane and leave, okay?"

"I understand. But I saw something. I saw a field agent make contact with that baggage handler."

"But you can't be sure of that. It was two men on the phone at the same time. Maybe they both look suspicious … but to you, everyone is suspect. You need to move on." She bit her lower lip. "I'm sorry. I didn't mean—"

"It's okay. Considering what we went through five years ago, it's a by-product of our survival."

Alicia watched passengers board the plane. An announcement came across the overhead speakers, "General boarding call for flight 1972 to Rome. This includes all rows and all seats, please board."

Alicia glanced up at her husband. "We need to get Buddy back on the plane, and we have to board."

Paul looked around the terminal, searching for the slightest indication they were being watched. His throat was dry, pulse rising. "Alicia, we can't get on that plane."

"We have to."

"No, we don't."

"Then I'm taking David! We're getting on the plane." She reached for David's hand.

Paul said, "Listen! Somehow, they intercepted my communications with Bill Gray. Somebody knows we're alive, and they'll do whatever it takes to change that. I'll get you to your mother's bedside, but it will not be on that damn plane."

The announcement continued. "Final boarding call for flight 1972 for Rome."

Alicia shook her head. "You have to get a grip on yourself. Maybe it's some kind of PTSD, I don't know, but that plane's been cleared for takeoff. David, you're coming with me."

David looked up at her, his blue eyes fearful. "Mom, the man hasn't come back for Buddy."

Alicia managed a smile. "He will. He knows he has to put Buddy on the plane."

Paul looked at his wife. "I told you I will get you to your mother's house. In all the time we've been together, have I ever promised you something and not seen it to the finish? Tell me, have I?"

She inhaled deeply, her face flush. Eyes fiery. "No, you haven't."

"Then trust me when I tell you I will get us out of here today en route to Rome and then the states." He placed both hands on her shoulders. "Trust me, okay."

David said, "I don't want to go without Daddy."

Alicia nodded. "Okay." She eyed her husband. "How are you going to get us out of here?"

"We'll take a car from Palermo to Messina, then take a ferry across. And we'll catch a train to Rome and fly out from there."

"Okay."

Paul took Buddy's leash, glanced around him, and said, "Let's go."

They hustled through the airport, flagged a taxi outside. Paul opened the front door to the odor of stale cigarette smoke and said to the driver, "We need to go to Messina. Can you drive us there?"

The driver, a husky man, swarthy, round face, with small ears, wore a white short sleeve shirt, top three buttons open. Chest hair spun like steel wool. A silver cross on a necklace rested in the center of his chest like a cross on a steeple in the black of night. He raised his wiry eyebrows, looked at Alicia, David and Buddy. "I can do that. It will cost you four hundred Euros."

"That's fine."

The taxi driver shrugged his wide shoulders. "Very good. I put your stuff in the trunk."

He quickly placed their bags in his trunk, got back behind the wheel, glanced in the rearview mirror at Paul, Alicia, David and Buddy in the backseat. "My name is Carlos. You mind if I play some music on the way. Messina is more than two hours."

Alicia forced a nervous smile. "That's fine."

The man nodded, tuned the radio to a station that played a mix of Italian songs and fifties, American rock music. They pulled out of the airport to the voice of Ricky Nelson singing *Lonesome Town*.

In less than ten minutes, the taxi headed east via the Messina Marine Highway. The road hugged the Mediterranean Sea, small cars and Vespas whipping by as the driver maneuvered in traffic.

Buddy sat next to David, the dog's chin resting on the boy's lap. Alicia sat in the center with Paul to the far left, closest to the view of the sea. Something to the right, in the direction of the airport, caught his eye. A jet was gaining altitude leaving the airport. Paul studied it a moment.

Alicia watched him and asked, "Is that the plane we were supposed to be on?"

He said nothing for a few seconds. "Yes. It'll be heading right above us, banking over the sea and gaining altitude en route to Rome, toward the northeast."

She cut her eyes to the taxi driver, his cologne mixing with a slight body odor, the smell of cigarettes in the fabric of the car seats. She said, "I know you did what you felt was right. I will never fault you for that, Paul. But right now, I wish we were on that plane."

Paul said nothing, watching the jet soar above the highway in front of them and begin an ascent once it was over the sea.

The pilot never had time to begin his climb.

He never had time to do anything.

At that moment, flight 1972 exploded in a massive ball of white and orange flames. The noise was as if two high-speed trains collided head-on.

Alicia gripped Paul's hand, her nails almost cutting into his flesh. "Oh dear God!" she blurted.

The taxi driver slammed on brakes. He made the sign of the cross and said, "Mary, mother of Jesus…"

David stared out the window, watching flaming parts of the plane, its cargo and passengers drop like fiery confetti from the sky. The hot pieces of metal pelting the surface of the Mediterranean, steam rising from the blue sea now covered in oil, jet fuel and blood.

Alicia looked over at her husband, her eyes welled. She could say nothing. Her thoughts scattered and buried deep as parts of the plane dropped to the floor of the ocean.

Fourteen

Tripoli, Libya

Rafa Gamal was a hired gun. But he carried no sidearm or rifle. His weapon of assault was deception—the innocuous look of authenticity, finding the hidden key to open locked doors on the Internet. Gamal was an impostor. If he were a magician, he would be a master illusionist—able to trick his audience into suspending disbelief by creating the pretense of benign reality.

Rafa Gamal was a hacker, a predator—and one of the best in the world.

He sat at his desk in his small apartment and looked at the time on his computer screen. *Less than five minutes*," he thought. Gamal had curly dark hair, a narrow face, pitted from acne scars. His black eyes were partially hidden under eyebrows that appeared cross-stitched into his face, long eyelashes. He celebrated his twenty-eighth birthday three days earlier with two belly dancers he'd bought for the night in Cairo.

Now he was back in his small apartment in Tripoli overlooking the harbor. He watched a container ship unload, a stiff wind off the Mediterranean jostling roadside palm trees. He returned to his desk and sipped Turkish coffee from a paper cup, his computer on, and heavy metal music turned down low. He removed a slim, non-filtered cigarette from behind his right ear, lit it and took a deep drag, exhaling through his nostrils, the left nostril had a tiny hoop ring clipped through the flesh.

He thought about his journey this far. He'd been a computer programmer for five years and traded that to work as a consultant for companies, finding the weak spots in their IT systems and offering suggestions as to how to reinforce them to keep hackers out. He could write code in his sleep, knew every programming language—Java, HTML, Perl, PHP, Python and more.

The first offers came from the dark web.

One job a month. Then two. More flowed in, as did the money— from people with deep pockets who paid well for information and privacy. From governments, groups, individuals, and corporations, most coming in through third-party vendors, assumingly to cover their tracks. Gamal was in such demand, he became very selective. Since he spoke five languages fluently, Arabic, German, English, Persian, and Russian, he could take his programming linguistics to a much higher level.

Gamal didn't care about the client's motives as long as they were willing to pay his fees. How his clients used the information, the personal tracking of people, the images from their phones or computers, their flow of money—none of that concerned him. He wasn't blackmailing or leveraging data to fleece any company or person. But he could open the door to people who had those motives.

One of the skills that made him so sought after was his speed at hacking and his ability to not leave trails. Law enforcement, on the highest levels, was no match for his talents. His encryption skills were as good as his IT covert penetration abilities. Thus far, he'd covered his tracks well and felt sure no one had the skillset to surpass him.

His phone vibrated on his desk, the unfinished wood marked by half circle coffee rings, tobacco ash, and burns left from smoldering cigarette butts. When Gamal was deeply concentrating, following prey on the Web, he often forgot about all else around him. Lighted cigarettes missed the overflowing ashtray. He answered his phone and spoke Persian.

The voice on the phone was deep and raspy. In Persian, the man said, "We want to target an American senator. His name is Harvey Fairchild."

Gamal took a hit off his cigarette and said, "No problem. What are you looking to discover about this man?"

"His routine, if possible. People he associates with after hours. Anything you can get."

"Are you looking to find opportunities for ransom or blackmail?"

"Always. But this mission will go deeper, much deeper. Find the things he likes. Places he goes—his general routine."

"Does he play sports?"

"We know he played American football in college. He is said to maintain a fitness regimen."

"Do you know if he wears a fitness tracker?"

"No, we don't know that. Is it something you can find out?"

"Yes. It will take me longer, you will pay a little more, but it can be done."

"Then do it." The voice on the phone disconnected.

Gamal cracked his knuckles, let his fingers hover the keyboard a moment, and then began a hunt from the shores of Tripoli to Washington, D.C.

FIFTEEN

P aul was about to use one of his three burner phones to do something he was hesitant to do. He needed to make a call to Bill Gray. He didn't know if his pursuers were aware that he and has family were not on the plane as it exploded over the Mediterranean. But it would be just a matter of time before they did. No recovery of bodies. The devastation was too great. There would be a manifest list of passengers on board. The airline would release that within a few hours.

He had a few hours to put great distance between the killers and his family.

Paul needed to get Alicia, David, and himself on a flight bound for the states before the assassins knew he and his family had not been on the plane they took down. He held Alicia and David's hands as they walked up the embark ramp to a massive ferryboat that carried train cars. Alicia led Buddy on a short leash. The wind blew across the Straits of Messina in the port, the water reflecting the blue sky. A large cruise ship entered the harbor, passengers standing next to the deck rails, seagulls laughing.

Paul turned to Alicia and said, "We need to keep inside the boat the best we can, at least until we pull away from the dock and get in the middle of the straits."

"Okay."

"We'll take the train to Rome and hopefully get a flight out to Washington."

"How do we get airline tickets?"

"I'll see what arrangements Bill can make. CIA has operatives in Rome. Maybe someone can help."

"The man who originally handed us the letter from Bill … who the hell was he, and what if he's waiting for us to arrive in Rome?"

"Right now they think we were killed on that plane. We have a little time."

"How much time, Paul?"

"I don't know. A few hours at best."

"It'll take us a few hours on the train trip into Rome. We did the reverse five years ago in coming here."

Paul said nothing. He watched a large cargo freighter ship leave the port, black diesel smoke coming from its stacks, the ship heading east across the Straits of Messina.

David looked up at his father and asked, "Can we take Buddy to the front of the boat to watch?"

"In a little while we can. Let's go inside, we'll see if they have some hot chocolate. Maybe get some water for Buddy, okay?"

"Okay."

They entered the large salon inside the ferryboat, a vessel massive enough to carry four train cars to be slid onto tracks on the opposite shore. Dozens of tourists sat at tables and chairs in front of a small café. Paul and his family walked up to a deli that served sandwiches. The air smelled of fresh ground coffee and baked pastries. "Just get me a coffee," he said to Alicia. "I need to find a quiet corner to make a call." He glanced at his watch. "Let's hope Bill is awake."

Alicia nodded and took David to the counter to order, Buddy following calmly next to her. Paul turned and walked to a far section of the ship's salon, a corner with glass windows. He wanted to get a cell signal while still on land. He made the call and waited, his eyes watching the faces of passersby.

Bill Gray answered on the fifth ring. He sat up in bed, looked at his sleeping wife and stepped quietly out of the bedroom. He walked to his kitchen and looked out the bay window into the night. Moths were orbiting an outdoor floodlight on his back patio. Bill glanced at the kitchen clock in the dim light and cleared his throat, "Good afternoon."

"I wish it were a good afternoon. I assume you haven't received word of the tragedy over the Mediterranean that happened a couple of hours ago?"

"Since I'm semi-retired, I don't receive alerts on an immediate basis. Now it's more of a need to know, and that topic is only one … you and your family. What happened?"

"Someone blew up the plane that my family was supposed to be aboard."

"Good God …"

"They knew we were flying out. Maybe it was the mysterious envoy who delivered the letter from you." Paul told Bill all he knew and added, "After the operative made the call to the baggage guy on the ramp, and after we faked getting on the plane, the man inside the airport disappeared, of course."

"Where are you now?"

"Crossing the Straits of Messina. We're en route to Rome. Can you get us on another plane there? I don't care what area of the states it's headed for … doesn't have to be DC. We just have to get the next plane out as soon as we arrive at the Rome airport."

"I'll make the best arrangements we can. You'll be traveling, of course, using the same names that are on your passports. I hope that won't be the fly in the ointment. Maybe that was the situation that triggered the downing of the plane."

"I don't think so. We paid cash and didn't present the passports until then. The killers knew ahead of schedule. That means once our location and other identities were breached, they were just waiting for us to leave. The closest international airport is Covina. So they waited for us and then set their plan in motion."

"I'll call you back on one of your other phones as soon as I can confirm arrangements."

"If we get unlucky, and they're waiting for us in Rome, can you have agents there to help get us safely on a plane?"

"Yes, of course. Unfortunately, we're one agent short. The woman who was supposed to have been the one delivering my letter to you … she's dead."

"What happened?"

"We found her body in her apartment in northeast Paris. She'd been shot between the eyes. Paul, she was one of our best. Very savvy. Very good. Whoever they sent for you has to be better than that, and that makes them frightening. So damn frightening, they took an entire plane full of people down to get you. That's making an international statement to send shivers around the world. Let me get to work. This won't be easy, it'll be damned dangerous."

Bill Gray disconnected. Paul looked across the ship's salon at Alicia and David, sitting at a table with their hot chocolates. Alicia hand-fed Buddy a snack. She used a napkin to wipe David's face. She kept up the airs of confidence even though Paul knew his wife was more vulnerable now that she was a mother. She was hurting, longing for family connections because of her own mother's impending death. Alicia was always the resolute partner, always strong in the face of adversity. But he could see the cracks just under the surface. When the plane exploded, he felt the absolute terror in her grip, the deep distress in her eyes.

He'd made a promise to get his wife and son safely to her mother's home. But at the moment, that journey felt like traveling to the dark side of the moon.

Unreachable and deadly.

SIXTEEN

It was 6:04 a.m. when Bill Gray received his second phone call of the morning. This one was expected. He was sipping his third cup of black coffee, reading online news accounts of the plane explosion. He looked at the caller ID and recognized the number—Carter Hawkins, Director of Cryptography, at NSA. Bill answered. "Good morning. Did you get arrangements made for the family?"

Hawkins spoke from his third floor corner office, the NSA building in Fort Meade, Maryland. He stood at his window at dawn and watched the morning sun cast a golden outline against the tall trees beyond the vast parking lot. The lot was half-filled. Many of the cars belonged to employees working the overnight shift, monitoring covert information coming from all of the industrialized nations on earth. "Yes, they're booked. We'll have two CIA operatives meet them at the train station, escort them out of the public areas to private security stations and load them on the plane before the other passengers."

"Who are the agents?"

"Richard Barker and Chase Owens."

"I'll let Paul know."

"I wanted to give you an update on the explosion. Our sources indicate that it's definitely tied to the Iranians."

"Let me guess … Fajar Hamad's group, right?"

"Somehow they knew—or someone in his network knew. We believe it may have been Carl Busch. After he breached more than four years ago, he's only been sighted twice. The first time was when you were still with the agency—remember, he was spotted in Moscow? And now the second time was when he approached Paul Marcus. At least that's who we believe it was—he fits the description Paul gave, and we know he was spotted in the Paris airport around the time our agent was killed."

"Who the hell is Busch working for … the Russians or the Iranians? And how did he know."

"We're not sure, and we don't know why he's working more as a scout or birddog rather than the hunter. It's probably for the Russians. You know he speaks the language, and he's fluent in Arabic, Persian and Farsi. He could be the liaison between the Russians, specifically former President Petrov." Hawkins stepped back to his desk. "Petrov hasn't stopped looking for Paul since he exposed Petrov as part of the Circle of 13."

"You think Carl Busch killed Anna Taylor in her Paris apartment?"

"Most likely. All surveillance cameras around the apartment complex were down for more than an hour at the estimated time of her death. He could easily have done that. Your letter to Paul Marcus wasn't found in her apartment."

Bill set his coffee cup down, stared at the Washington Post headline on his computer screen: *Mid-air Explosion Kills 193 Over Mediterranean.* He said, "What a damn shame. All those innocent people."

"Bill, let me call you back in a few minutes. I have something to share with you that's going to sound rather bizarre, but under the existing circumstances, maybe not so much."

• • •

Senator Harvey Fairchild stood in front of a full-length mirror in the bedroom of his elegant Bethesda home and tied a maroon tie into a perfect knot. He would turn sixty in two days, hair more black than gray, broad shoulders, angular face. He looked once again in the mirror and picked off a piece of lint from his lapel. His phone, set on his dresser, vibrated for the second time since he got out of the shower. It was next to his Rolex watch and his fitness tracker.

He stepped to the dresser, strapped his watch on his left wrist and his fitness tracker on his right. Then he checked his phone—four new emails since 6:00 a.m. One was from the company that manufactured the tracker. He read the brief message. He could download the upgrade on the app and use it to further calibrate his walking and fitness routines throughout the day.

"Turn on the news," came the voice of his wife from downstairs, the smell of fresh brewed coffee and bacon filling the home.

"Okay," Fairchild said, hitting the download button from the fitness tracker company. He checked the time on his watch, picked up a remote control, pointed it toward the widescreen TV in the corner of the large bedroom. A network newscast scrolled a banner below the video of rescue ships off the coast of Sicily. Fairchild turned up the sound and the picture cut to live images of a reporter in an open sports coat standing at the Palermo International Airport. He held a microphone and said, "Witnesses say the explosion appeared to originate from somewhere in the center of the plane with an enormous force that literally blew the jet apart in sections, scattering hundreds of pieces into the sea. Dozens of watercraft have been crisscrossing the area, looking for survivors. So far, it appears no one lived through the horrible explosion. Authorities say none of the jet's engines appeared to have exploded. Again, the fireball coming from the center section, and they say this points to the high probability of a bomb somehow loaded either in the overhead compartments or in the cargo section below passengers. The debris fell into an area of the Mediterranean that's nearly two hundred feet deep. So finding the cockpit voice recorder, or the black box, will prove quite a challenge. Police investigators say that no terrorist group has come forth to claim responsibility for the deadly explosion that took the lives of 193 people, including five members of the crew. Jacob Williams, BBC in Sicily."

Fairchild flipped through the channels, pausing to catch as many details as possible. His anger rose each time he changed the channel and caught another story about the downing of the jetliner. "Bastards," Fairchild said as he read emails from his chief of staff, the subject was the explosion of the jet.

His wife, dark hair pinned up, in a beige robe, entered the bedroom with a cup of steaming coffee. Allison Fairchild handed the cup to her husband and said, "How in this day and time can someone sneak a bomb onto a plane, a bomb large enough to do that much damage?"

Fairchild sipped his coffee and said, "It most likely was loaded in the cargo hull. How it got there, God only knows."

"No, the sick people who put it there know."

"I feel so bad for the people on that downed jet and for their families. We know there were at least two Americans aboard. A honeymoon couple from Atlanta. FBI is going through the manifest."

"Which terrorist group is claiming responsibility?"

"None yet. It's going to be a long day in the office. My staff says two of the cable news channels want to do live interviews with me. Right now, I know nothing more than what I've seen on television, and that's not saying much."

Allison used both hands to gently square the knot in his tie. She beamed a loving smile, her eyes playful with her husband of more than thirty years. "You'll do fine."

"No telling how many steps I'll log today around the Senate and Capitol buildings." He glanced at his watch. "Oh, before all of this bad news, I downloaded an app update on my fitness tracker. I'll be able to tell exactly what my mileage is today."

• • •

Rafa Gamal stared at his computer screen, his pupils absorbing the white light as if it was a source of energy. A sinister smile moved across his red mouth. He lit a slim Turkish cigarette, inhaled once, moved the cigarette to the corner of his mouth, closing his left eye from smoke rising like a white snake. He punched in numbers on his phone.

The man with the deep voice answered in two rings. "What do you have?"

"The mouse took the cheese. I will follow him and give you details on where he goes."

"That's all we need."

SEVENTEEN

Washington, DC

It is the most secretive court in America. There are no witnesses. No public hearings. No attorneys arguing legal briefs. The court's sole purpose is to issue surveillance warrants—giving the government legal permission to spy on anyone, citizen or non-citizen, suspected of espionage within the U.S. Due to the nature of its business, the court doesn't keep regular hours. One of a dozen federal judges is on call at all times.

It is the Foreign Intelligence Surveillance Court—FISA, and it's housed on the top floor behind heavy security and locked doors in the E. Barrett Prettyman Federal Courthouse. The proceedings are usually quick, and they're done with one judge and a lawyer from the Attorney General's office, the FBI, or NSA requesting a warrant to permit electronic surveillance of a suspect—a person of interest.

Today, it was a government attorney requesting the warrant. The lawyer, Justin Silverstein, a long-limbed, balding, Princeton graduate in his tenth year of practice, carried the applications in a new briefcase his wife, Rachel, had given him. He set the briefcase on the table in front of the judge who wore dark slacks and a button-down white dress shirt. The attorney unlocked the briefcase and opened it. The interior had the scent of new leather and fine paper stock. "Judge Astor, thank you for coming over here on such a short notice."

Judge Robert Astor, early sixties, sagging face, the start of cataracts in one of his brown eyes, said, "Notice how it's always short notice. I suppose that's the nature of surveillance."

"Yes sir, it is, unfortunately. These are signed requests for two FISA warrants."

"Two? Who are they, and what does the government suspect they're are doing?"

"It's all here in the application affidavit from the Attorney General. The first is a request to electronically scrutinize Senator Harvey Fairchild. The bureau has spotted him having lunch with Avros Sokolov, a Russian diplomat in New York suspected of influence peddling. Also, he met with Egyptian, Jabari Mansour, known to have a dotted line to the Bashier al-Assad in Syria and one of the top Iranian Quds Force leaders. Fajar Hamad."

"Senators meet with diplomats and foreign emissaries often. This had better be something you can sink your legal teeth into, because, when you start requesting to spy on United States senators, you'd better have your damn ducks in a row. We don't need this court to be suspect for no judicial oversight or any kind of political bias. I don't rubberstamp a damn thing."

"Understood. Nor would we want you to do that, sir."

"Who's the second person?"

"Sami Botros."

Judge Astor looked above the frames of his glasses, his face un-readable. "He's one of the president's closest advisors. He went to school with the president, and if memory serves me well, so did Senator Fairchild. Is there some sort of trio going on here … does this lead to the Oval Office?"

"We don't know, sir? We hope to learn more through surveillance."

The judge removed his glasses and pushed back in his chair. He looked out the window to traffic down below on Constitution Avenue, the American flag languidly moving in the breeze, seagulls flying toward the Potomac River and the Tidal Basin. He said, "This is my seventh and last year on the FISA court. I'd like to leave here believing that more than ninety-nine percent of the warrants we authorize were needed and did the nation good."

The lawyer nodded, feigning sincerity. "Yes sir, that's what we strive for."

"In the last year or so, it's come to the point that anyone assumed of being involved in covert intelligence is considered legitimate targets for surveillance … some with FISA warrants … others, I'd surmise, without any warrant whatsoever. The special needs exemption certainly has broadened the definition and muddied the rules of domestic spying." He put his glasses on and read through the briefs.

The attorney started to pull out a chair to sit. The judge raised a finger on one hand and said, "You won't be here that much longer, Mr. Silverstein." He scanned the warrant applications, pausing at the signatures on both papers. The Deputy Director of the FBI, Ward Rosenberg, signed them. Judge Astor snorted, the edge of the cataract somewhat milky in the light coming from the window. He said, "This is the fourth warrant I've seen signed recently submitted by the Deputy Director of the FBI. Is Ward Rosenberg bucking for the director's job? He seems to be on a mission."

"I don't think so, Judge Astor. But I'm just the messenger."

"And a well paid one at that, Mr. Silverstein."

The judge signed the warrants and said, "When the bureau sets up its wiretaps and other cyber sniffing, can you keep it out of the damn media for God sakes? All we need, in light of everything else going on right now, is for this to get into the public and be debated from CNN to Fox and every media type stacked somewhere between the two. Isn't that why this court exists, to authorize surveillance that's supposed to be secret?"

EIGHTEEN

Italy, near Naples

P aul watched the faces. As he and his family walked through the moving train cars, he looked at the passengers. Most were Italian families on holiday going to Rome. Many were international tourists. He overheard languages—German, French and English as he walked behind Alicia and David heading for the last seats in the final car of the train.

He scanned the faces. No one seemed to make eye contact. No one seemed to recognize him or his family. He carried Buddy in a newly acquired wire kennel; a few passengers smiled when they saw the dog. An elder Japanese couple grinned and pointed at Buddy. Paul and his family continued walking, taking their seats in the back of the train car.

At the half-way mark in the trip, south of Naples, Paul took a long, deep breath and slowly released it, trying to ease the tension in his body. David sat next to the window, Alicia alongside him and Paul next to her. Buddy slept in his kennel near Paul. David leaned against his mother's side and was soon asleep.

Paul glanced around the half-filled train car. A dozen families were in the car. Some people looked out the windows at the rolling Italian countryside. Others read, played cards, or engaged with electronic games on their tablets and phones. Four teenagers, two boys and two girls, snapped Instagram pictures.

Alicia watched her sleeping son, her eyes red and fatigued. She looked over to Paul and said, "He's so innocent. I keep thinking about a little girl around David's age that was boarding the plane with her mother. The young mother was probably in her mid-twenties. I see the faces of a honeymoon couple we met waiting to board. The elderly couple flying to visit grandchildren in London." She stopped, her eyes wet. She kissed David on top of his head. "How old do you think he will have to be before we tell him that he's lucky to be alive because a plane that exploded was meant for his family?"

"I don't know."

Alicia said nothing, looked at David's small hand resting on her arm. "I know we're lucky to be alive, and I know how hard you tried to warn the airline. When they cleared it for takeoff, I thought everything was going to be fine, and we'd just have to catch another plane or figure a way to get to Rome for a flight to the states. I never thought we'd take a train because our plane blew up, and we were escaping Sicily literally with the clothes on our backs and in our carry-on suitcases."

Paul reached out and held Alicia's hand. "I'm deeply saddened by what happened back there, especially since it may have been prevented. I want you to know that from the day I fell in love with you, from the hell we traveled through together before being forced to fake our own deaths and take refuge on Panarea, I will always do my best to protect you and David. I will not let anything happen to my family. You come first, and always will."

Alicia's eyes welled. She blinked back tears and squeezed her husband's hand as the Eurostar train approached Naples at 120 miles per hour. After a moment she said, "I hope that we can board safely in Rome, get back home to Virginia, see my family and try to come up with a plan to keep us safe. What frightens me is the fact that our identities were exposed on Panarea but they waited for us to board a plane before trying to do us harm. It's as if they wanted to make a greater impact by killing everyone on board a jetliner when the target was our family. It's not unlike flying planes into the World Trade Centers. They want to cause as many deaths as possible. If they're going to that extreme to destroy us in a grander public arena … where can we go, where can we hide so no one else dies, too?"

• • •

Deputy Director of the FBI, Ward Rosenberg, stood next to a large glass window in his seventh floor office inside the J. Edgar Hoover Building and gazed across E Street. He could see the roof of the International Spy Museum from his vantage point. He was a tall man with a wide forehead, thick wrists, and receding hairline. His wire-framed glasses almost hid a small scar across the bridge of his nose. The mark was the result of an accidental hit from a polo mallet in college.

He sipped a cup of tea and stepped back to his spotless desk. An American flag rested in a stand behind the desk. On one wall were framed pictures of Rosenberg with the last two presidents. Two unopened files were on his desk, near a picture of his wife and teenage son, and a coaster with a Cornell University logo in the center.

There was a quick knock at his glass door. Rosenberg motioned for two agents to enter. The senior agent was Carolyn Latcham, average height and build, shoulder length black hair. The second agent, Oliver Bentley, was wide in the chest, short haircut, eyes the color of a butane flame. Special Agent Latcham said, "We've been listening to conversations from both Senator Fairchild and Sami Botros. Fairchild is always brief, almost quipped in his style unless he's on the phone with a potential donor. Then he's quite chatty. He's meeting Russian Ambassador Andrie Kozlov for lunch today at the Old Ebbitt Grill. Here's something else, Fairchild and Botros have spoken about a dozen times in the last month. Now that we're monitoring conversations from both, we hope to see if there's any collusion between them and the Russians in Senator Alfred Dawson's election. And maybe we'll have a better handle on the leak to Carl Busch."

Deputy Director said nothing, his eyes unreadable behind his glasses.

Special Agent Bentley said, "Sami Botros has close ties back to Dearborn, Michigan, a place he spent a lot of time when finishing his undergraduate work at the University of Michigan. One person he's in contact with is Batil Farrah. Although he tries to be covert about it, Farrah is a known consultant to radical imam, Abdul Massoud, who started the so called Islamic Villages across the nation."

Rosenberg nodded. "Their first compound was a converted chicken farm fifty miles northwest of Dearborn."

"And now there are at least seven others in as many states. We've seen evidence of paramilitary training at some of these camps. We know that Massoud and his followers—a group called the Muharib, are recruiting in person and online here in the states and across the world. The Muharib means *the warriors* in Arabic. They've been targeting what they call the common Muslim, trying to reach an emotional connection with the common disenfranchised man, if you will, to turn him into the uncommon warrior. The Maharib targets disaffected youth—young men, as well as some with criminal records and others that are often societal outcasts. They're good at converting people like this to carry out the lone-wolf terrorist attacks, whether it be driving a truck into a crowd or setting off a suicide bomb."

Rosenberg set his cup on top of a coaster with the Cornell University logo. He asked, "Have we found any link from Massoud to this radical nut with the Thomas Jefferson vendetta, Fajar Hamad?"

"We don't know who Massoud directly associated with while in Libya. But he spent two months there. We have reason to believe he was in Hamad's inner circle because Massoud spouts much of the same propaganda messaging, and he's become a mastermind in the art of al-Qaeda misinformation. His brother was killed in one of our drone attacks in Pakistan. And since that time, Massoud has ramped up his recruitment efforts."

Rosenberg leaned back in his black leather chair. "So what does a member of the president's staff, one of the top advisors in the White House, have in common with people known to be linked with this group, the Muharib?"

Special Agent Latcham said, "That's a good question. Maybe nothing. Sami Botros grew up in Dearborn. His family has deep connections in the Muslim community. One of his uncles owns a popular Lebanese restaurant in Livonia. After hours, it becomes a hangout for marginalized Muslim men who seem to have a lot of free time on their hands."

Rosenberg nodded. "But that doesn't constitute criminal activity. Let's follow Botros closely. Tap all of his electronic devices. Get some of our best language experts on the job. They can look for the subtleties that someone with Botros' intellect and possible cunning might use. Also, let's see what he and Senator Fairchild have in common. This could get very interesting, very quickly."

NINETEEN

C arter Hawkins looked at a manila file folder on his desk marked *T Jefferson,* called Bill Gray and said, "I hate to keep bringing you in the loop on this. You spent thirty-two years chasing the ghosts of bad guys, but you insisted to be brought in if you thought any intel had a remote connection to Paul and Alicia. The explosion of flight 1972 has everything to do with them, especially Paul."

Bill stood at his wooden table in the kitchen and watched two squirrels play tag along a deck railing in his backyard. "Is the safe house ready for them?"

"Yes, how long it'll stay safe is anyone's guess. We know that Fajar has soldiers in the states. Petrov has his top assassins here, too, or when he wants them here. There's a good chance that Petrov has teamed with Fajar. The Russians have spent time and money with the Quds Force. We've spotted a Russian agent meeting with Fajar in Baghdad. The Russians and Iranians keep inflaming the strife in Syria. They're team players, for now. Crimes of mutual convenience."

"I've been thinking a lot about what you told me concerning Eli Dexter's slaughter. You know that Eli was the son of Paul best friend, Liam Dexter. I don't believe for one damn minute that the abduction and murder was coincidental. It was planned. They targeted Eli."

Hawkins nodded. "It was probably engineered to bring Paul out … to expose him to a hit or, God forbid, a capture. Dexter's body will be arriving at Dulles today."

"If this goes back to America's first war with Islamic jihad terrorists—Barbary pirates, when our nation was young, we have one serious problem in terms of this guy wanting to settle a score. I keep thinking about the words they scrawled on the sign around his neck … *remember the battle of Derna*. Carter, it's not unlike the battle cry Sam Houston shouted leading our troops against Mexico in 1846. The rally call was *'remember the Alamo.'* A decade earlier, Davy Crockett, Jim Bowie and a couple hundred Americans died after the third siege of the Alamo."

Hawkins sat at his desk. "We believe the same words, *remember the battle of Derna*, were scrawled on one wall of our embassy in Benghazi. The fire did too much damage to be sure, but the word Derna was definitely seen through the destruction. And it had been written in blood."

"Fajar has probably been thinking about this since he was a kid, listening to the elders tell him about the atrocities of America, never knowing that it was the Muslim nations of North Africa that started that whole mess by capturing our merchant ships and enslaving our crews."

Hawkins nodded. "History is often filtered and then fanned to ignite the smoldering embers of handed-down hate. It doesn't take much to see new flames burning from old ideology, legacy, and leftover grudges. And it stems from what they believe is a sacred edict giving them a right, or even a duty, to defy and obliterate anyone who refuses to embrace their religion."

"I've studied this all my career, and I'm no closer to an answer. How do we ever have real and meaningful negotiations or relations with any group that harbors that kind of mindset? They detest the West and some of their leaders, especially in Iran, have sworn to take Israel off the map."

Hawkins stared at the folder on his desk. "Speaking of Iran, we've learned they have finally restored the damage Paul Marcus inflicted to their reactors. We, and the Mossad, believe it's just a matter of time before they have a nuclear weapon aimed at Tel Aviv. Paul stopped them the last time, but now they've installed state-of-the-art sniffers to detect and destroy cyber worms. That bridge can't be crossed again."

"At least Paul slowed them down. It made the world a safer place for the last few years. Do you have a team escorting Paul and his family off the plane?"

"Of course. They'll be transported to the safe house under heavy guard."

"Alicia will want to see her mother as soon as possible."

"We'll make the arrangements."

Bill ran his right hand through his white hair, his eyes puffy, filled with fatigue. "My gut tells me something horrible is brewing, Carter. We believe Fajar was one of the Iranians in Egypt behind the deaths and destruction in Benghazi. He appears to be responsible for Eli Dexter's death. If the common link between Benghazi and Eli's death has to do with our first war with Islamic jihad pirates—as in remember the battle of Derna, could Fajar and his followers be planning a major showdown two centuries later?"

"I think Benghazi and Eli's death are just the tip of the iceberg. Two months ago, Special Ops raided an adobe shanty sixty miles west of Misrata and picked up one man we know participated in the Benghazi attack. We took him out of Libya in the dead of night, shuttled him out to a Navy aircraft carrier and flew him back to the states to stand trial. His name is Ulan Hamad ... and he's Fajar Hamad's younger brother. You see where this is going?"

"Yeah ... not good. So, let's assume they'd love to capture Paul next. Make an example out of him for the world to witness. And, the Russians, perhaps, want to annihilate him. This could get pretty complicated. Who would have thought the code he broke left behind by Isaac Newton would have led to the dismantling of the Circle of 13 and the Iranian nuclear program?"

Hawkins picked up the folder marked *T Jefferson*, and pulled out the pages—the letter Jefferson had written and the page he'd encrypted. He studied them for a moment and said, "Bill, you remember me telling you about that old house Janice and I bought and began restoring and remodeling?"

"The one in Amherst County?"

"Yes. We were going through old furniture stored in the attic and stumbled across a letter written by Thomas Jefferson."

"That's a hell of a find. What did he write?"

"One copy was written to Robert Livingston who was the Minister to France at the time. As you're aware, Jefferson had invented a cipher wheel he often used to encrypt letters he wrote. The recipient would have an identical cipher wheel to decrypt the correspondence."

"I remember reading about that. Fascinating."

"In a letter to Livingston, and others—Lieutenant Stephen Decatur, Jefferson discussed his rationale for fighting America's first war after the pasha of Tripoli declared war on the states. And in the letter, Jefferson briefly mentions an encrypted dispatch he'd included. The thrust of the encryption had to do with Jefferson's prediction in terms of dealing with extremist nations, those waging religious or holy jihad wars on other countries. I brought the code to work. Thus far, we haven't cracked it, and my people are pretty damn good. If we could crack it, knowing Jefferson, it might reveal something substantial … maybe a key or a way to deal with these people. What if there's a method we can use to diffuse this guy, Fajar Hamad, and whatever he has planned. And just maybe Jefferson gained an early insight that no one else had at the time … or even today."

"If anyone can decipher the code, it'd be Paul Marcus. Make me copies of the letter and the coded letter. I'll speak with Paul."

TWENTY

Senator Harvey Fairchild had a routine. It made him one of the most physically fit members in the United States Senate. It also made him one of the most vulnerable. At age sixty, he was in excellent shape. A successful businessman who entered politics on his forty-sixth birthday, he was now facing a re-election campaign. He was a natural competitor, a man who enjoyed the strategy and challenge of a political race.

He'd built a company, and now he was eager to help build a better country. Deeply patriotic, he wasn't timid about speaking up against anyone or any nation that represented a threat to America. He had the stamina and the drive for the re-election run, and he had the fire in his belly. Fairchild used his home gym to workout three days a week. He jogged two miles at the crack of dawn every Monday, Thursday and Saturday mornings. He was a picture of good health. He watched his diet.

But he didn't watch his surroundings.

His two-mile run laced through the opulent and picturesque old neighborhood of million dollar homes near the Potomac River in Bethesda. The neighborhood was gated, security cameras at the gates. Motion detectors. Large oak trees near the entrance and a decorative wall made from river stone and vaulted wrought iron points that encircled the neighborhood. The wall did not border the river. But the jogging trail did.

Senator Fairchild jogged down the asphalt path, the soft slap of his tennis shoes the only sound at 6:07 in the morning. He glanced at the sunrise over the Potomac, the slivers of mauve and pink reflecting off the dark water. He inhaled through his nose, a fine nose with an ancestral trace to ancient Rome. He took deep breaths, his pulse steady—the rhythm of a runner. He could smell the fetid scent of damp earth and decaying leaves in the air. He thought about the day's agenda.

As Chair of the Senate Select Committee on Intelligence, he would lead a closed-door hearing into the pending charges against the first two Islamic militants captured in Libya, men believed part of the group that left the U.S. Consulate in Benghazi scorched, the CIA compound shattered, and four Americans dead. That was back in 2012. And now, years later, they were finally going to be tried separately in federal courts. *You two bastards first,* he thought. *Just a matter of time before we find the rest of the rat pack.* He thought about the murder of Delta Force member Eli Dexter. Thought about the funeral he planned to attend,

And he ran harder.

Angry.

Down the dark path.

The soles of his shoes popped against fallen acorns on the trail. His left shoe came untied. He dropped to one knee to tie it. There was a noise behind him. *Odd for this time of the morning. Maybe a squirrel.* He looked over his right shoulder just as the man's heavy boot caught him in the face. The hard combat boot heel slamming into Fairchild's nose. The blow shattered the bone and cartilage in his nose, blood squirted across his chest.

Fairchild fell to his back. He pushed to get up.

And then the second man appeared out of the murky light. Both were dressed in black. Both wore the half face mask that are symbolic and identified with ISIS fighters riding in open air vehicles, the ISIS flag fluttering in the wind, rifles clenched in their hands. The second man raised a tire iron and brought it down hard against Fairchild's right knee, the blow destroyed the patella—the kneecap. The second blow shattered Fairchild's tibia bone just below the knee.

He groaned in pain. The man with the tire iron stood with his arms folded, his dark eyes fiery in the shards of sunrise breaking over the Potomac. The second man said, "Senator, your days of running are now history. Speaking of history, you and members of your intelligence committee want to control the fate of the Middle East without real and thorough knowledge of the history of its people."

Fairchild clutched his knee, staring in disbelief, blood pumping from his ruined nose and soaking into his pale blue sweatshirt. He felt cold, bile choking in his esophagus, nausea filling his stomach. He coughed. "Who are you? What do you want?"

The man with the tire iron said, "Old ghosts who will never leave as long as you infidels continue your aggression. Just when you think we are no more ... we come back to haunt you."

"What ... what do you want?"

The shorter man smiled behind his mask. He stepped closer. "We want only a few things ... things that you really owe us. You owe us an apology for your first aggressive move against our people. We want your president to publically apologize for the aggression from America when it attacked Tripoli, killing many of our people in 1804."

Fairchild stared at the men in doubt. "Are you serious ... a war more than two centuries ago? How about the death and destruction your leaders have caused in the last decade, maybe that's where we should start."

"We want your president to release Ulan Hamad. He participated in the fight at Benghazi only to defend our land ... as we did two hundred years earlier when President Thomas Jefferson, sent troops onto our soil. And your land had no bedrock when it comes to such a divisive history. Your Civil War is a good example. Today some Confederate statues are torn down. Jefferson had dozens of slaves, and yet monuments to him still stand. Such hypocrisy."

Fairchild shook his head. "You mention history ... you need to recheck history. Your people have been slave traders for centuries. Off the Barbary Coast, you attacked our merchant ships even before Jefferson was president. You captured and enslaved our sailing crews and demanded payoffs to enter the Mediterranean. We fought only because we had no choice."

"You always have a path to choose, Senator. Our wants are simple, and justified. The nuclear agreement we had with your country gave us time to rebuild. But it was costly. We want one billion dollars routed into the Central Bank of Iran. This is money that it took Iran to reconstruct its nuclear program after an American, Paul Marcus, a man who worked for your NSA, destroyed our program. And we want Marcus. If not, we will unleash jihad against Americans across the world and right here in your country. If we can get to you, Senator Fairchild, in the backyard of the FBI, CIA and all your watchdogs ... we can get to anyone anywhere."

"The president won't negotiate with terrorists." Fairchild sat straighter, nausea building.

"Oh, I think he will. You will deliver the message ... dead or alive." The man leaned closer. "What is your choice, Senator?"

Fairchild was close enough to smell the man's sweat in his clothes, the acrid body odor. "It's not going to happen and you know that."

"Another thing, we want to take a picture with you. Imagine your last photograph in your life with two members of the people you hate most on earth. Perhaps it is only fitting."

"I hate no one. I believe in honorable and fair negotiations among people." Still fast at his age, Fairchild grabbed the man's shirt, pulling him closer, he used his right fist to smash into the man's mouth, lips and teeth shattering.

The man screamed in Arabic, calling for help. The second man brought the tire iron across Fairchild's temple, cracking his skull. Another hard blow to the skull.

Fairchild tried to speak, his mouth unable to form words, his thoughts scrambled like pieces of a jigsaw puzzle scattered across a table. The orange of sunrise. The green of the tree leaves. The blur of a squirrel scampering. The bleary reflection of hate in the men's dark eyes. The numb feeling that his body was being pulled. Somehow he was now propped up against a pine tree. There was the flash of lightning. Or maybe it was from a camera. More blows to his face. In shock now. His eyes swelled, fluid pouring from eyes and ears. He looked at the sunrise over the Potomac. An osprey sailed low over the surface, as if it were flying in slow motion. Fairchild wanted to reach out to the bird. And then it was gone. He tried to visualize his wife and daughter's faces.

Something was shoved in his mouth—between his teeth. Paper. He was too weak to spit it out. Another camera flash. He thought about what he wanted to say last at the funeral of Delta Force member Eli Dexter. *A fine young American.* Fairchild's trembling fingers touched the damp pine needles on the ground. *The day was so short,* he thought as darkness fell across the river and his hands became still.

TWENTY-ONE

As the Eurostar train pulled into the Rome terminal, Paul repeated Bill Gray's words in his mind—replaying the code sentence the operatives would use when or if they met. He thought of the descriptions of the two men, could almost visualize their appearances even from a distance. Bill had been descriptive. He always was. Attention to detail.

Paul and his family sat alone in the last car on the train, Buddy softly whined once in his crate. Paul said, "It's okay, boy. We'll find you a patch of grass soon." The train stopped, passengers standing and waiting to exit into the terminal. Within thirty seconds, the doors opened and the crowd spilled out.

Paul watched them for a moment. He looked over at Alicia and said, "Bill Gray gave me a visual description of the people picking us up. Shouldn't be too hard to spot in the crowd. Although I'm sure they'll see us before I see them." He glanced down at Buddy and smiled.

Alicia looked out the window at the hubbub of people crisscrossing the terminal, searching for travel connections. Some ride-share and taxi drivers stood in the crowd, holding up signs with the names of those they were meeting. Alicia said, "Maybe they simply should have our fake names on a sign." She half-smiled, looked at her sleeping son. "David, time to wake up sweetie." She gently rubbed his forehead.

David opened his eyes and glanced around, not sure where he was at the moment. "I'm thirsty."

Paul nodded. "We'll get some water for you. Are you excited to go on your first plane trip ever?"

"Can I sit next to the window on the plane?"

"Of course." Paul watched the last passengers exit, the final two. An elderly man and his wife slowly made their way down the aisle between the seats, the silver-haired man gently holding his wife's arm. "Let's go," Paul said, lifting Buddy's crate and a small suitcase. He led his family through the center passage and to one of the exit doors.

They left the train and entered the flurry of the Rome terminal, tourists reading overhead signs for connections to the airport, Metro, and dozens of highway routes. They walked through the terminal and exited where taxis, vans and buses packed the arrival area, the smell of diesel fumes on the air. Buddy wagged his tail and barked once at a woman walking a black and white Shih Tzu on a leash.

"Buddy," Alicia said, "no barking. We know you aren't used to seeing dogs on leashes. Not something most people did on our little island." She smiled, holding David by the hand, her eyes darting at faces in the crowd.

In the barrage of taxis and buses, a black Alfa Romeo Stelvio SUV pulled up to the curb. The windows were tinted. The driver parked and got out. The man on the front passenger side exited. They wore jeans and sports coats over golf shirts. Dark glasses. Paul watched them a moment, both men matching the physical traits Bill Gray had listed. They were in their late thirties. The driver was the taller of the two. Both muscular. The passenger had a week's worth of whiskers on his face. The other man was clean-shaven, strong jaw-line, large hands.

The passenger approached Paul and his family while the driver watched the crowd. The man smiled at Paul and said, "We're not Uber service, but we don't mind transporting dogs. My buddy and I have a thing for border collies, especially those with a single dew claw."

Paul nodded. "Good to see you."

"You, too. It's an honor. What you did is legendary in the agency. Let's get you and your family in the car and out of here."

They loaded into the back seat, Paul on one side, Alicia on the other, and David in the center. Buddy, in his crate, was placed in the back. The driver pulled away from the curb. He looked into his side view and rearview mirrors. The man on the passenger side watched the people along the sidewalk and waiting area. Within a minute, they left the train terminal behind, heading for the airport.

David looked around the interior of the backseat, his eyes wide as the cityscape flew by the car. Paul smiled. "Cars are a new experience for you. You'll see a lot of them in the coming days. We might get one after we get to the United States."

"I like riding in cars."

"They can go a lot faster than the golf carts. That's why we must always wear a seatbelt. Seatbelts can help keep us safe if we have an accident."

"Okay. How fast can this car go?"

"I'm not sure."

"Where are we going, Daddy?"

The driver glanced in the rearview mirror and smiled.

Alicia said, "We'll visit some friends."

"Can Buddy come, too?"

"Of course."

"I'm thirsty."

The driver glanced up in the mirror. "We have bottled water up here if you'd like some."

"That'd be great," Alicia said. "Thanks." She took the water from the man on the passenger side. As she started to open it, Paul touched her wrist. She tilted her head at him, eyes questioning. He lifted the water bottle out of her hand and examined it, turning it upside down and gently squeezing the sides. Then he looked at the seal and twisted the plastic top off. He handed the bottle back to his wife.

"Here you go, David," she said, giving the open bottle to her son.

David sipped and asked, "Maybe Buddy's thirsty, too."

Alicia smiled. "We'll give Buddy some water on the plane."

Paul looked at the men. "Which airline are you taking us to?"

"None of the commercial."

"What then?"

"Military."

"We were supposed to Fly British Air."

"There's been a change, sir. Director Parker wants you to leave on an alternative jet."

"Does Bill Gray know this?"

"You are going to meet Mr. Gray upon arrival."

"Why the change in plane?"

"There's been another incident. The president wants to see you."

"What kind of incident?"

"Senator Fairchild was found dead. The killer or killers left something." He glanced in the rearview mirror and looked at David. "The president and Mr. Gray can tell you more."

• • •

Bill Gray had a feeling that his son-in-law had something to say but wasn't sure how or when to say it. Bill, his wife Claire, daughter Rachel, and son-in-law, Justin Silverstein, were finishing a meal at an Italian restaurant. Toward the end of the meal, when Claire and Rachel went to the restroom together, Silverstein, his tie loosened, cheeks blossoming after two vodka martinis, said, "Dad, that murder of Senator Fairchild ..."

"Yes, it was tragic. Harvey was a patriot."

"That's what I thought."

"Did something change your mind?"

"It hasn't changed. After his murder, I'm more convinced now than ever." Silverstein, licked is lips, looked around the restaurant, lowered his voice and said, "I know I shouldn't tell you this, but since you were with NSA for so long ... the DOJ sought and got a FISA warrant for Senator Fairchild."

"What? Why?"

"FBI had intel that indicated Fairchild was in conversations with one of the presidents top aides, Sami Botros." Silverstein paused, choosing his words carefully. That wouldn't raise an eyebrow, however a second FISA warrant was taken out on Botros.

"Why and by whom?"

"Federal agents, tracking Islamic radicals, jihadists in the U.S., spotted Botros meeting with one."

"What if Botros was trying to get information from someone he knew? Was the conversation overheard electronically?"

"No, not yet. FBI is now monitoring his calls, emails and texts."

"Who requested the warrant for surveillance on a U.S. senator and a member of the president's inner circle?"

"The Deputy Director of the FBI, Ward Rosenberg."

Bill looked through the restaurant window at the Jefferson Memorial in the distance. It was bathed in soft light. He thought about the murder of Senator Fairchild and the note the killers left on his beaten body.

TWENTY-TWO

The nondescript Boeing 737 touched down on a private runway at Dulles International Airport. A dozen federal agents waited in black SUVs. The vehicles were parked near a restrictive and highly secure area of the tarmac where commercial planes were not permitted. The jet would taxi over and stop at a section of the airport property only used when the president's plane, Air Force One, and other government flights were sanctioned to take off and land.

Bill Gray sat in the passenger side front seat of a black Ford Explorer, the motor running, two FBI agents in the back seat, the Director of NSA Cryptanalysis, Carter Hawkins, behind the wheel. Next to Bill, on the seat, was the manila folder marked *T Jefferson*. He watched the plane come to a stop, the pilot on the radio in the cockpit.

Four SUV's pulled up to the front of the jet, armed men getting out, their eyes scanning the perimeter, the distant roofs, the aircraft on nearby runways, anything that moved on the ground or in the sky. Three agents pushed the movable air-stairs to the front door of the plane. It opened slowly; a male flight attendant stood in the entrance and helped to position the stairs in place. He secured it, turned and nodded to someone inside the plane.

Bill Gray and Carter Hawkins watched as Paul appeared in the doorway. He waited a few seconds, scanning the tarmac, turned and said something to one of the pilots. After a moment, he gestured for his family to join him. Alicia held David's hand as they walked down the steps. Paul followed with Buddy in his crate. Bill watched the family step onto American soil and said, "They're home. Now let's do everything in our power to keep them safe."

Carter nodded. "It won't be easy. Not after what happened to Senator Fairchild. It's getting more difficult. Maybe Paul can help take them down a notch."

"He did it once. The question is … can he do it again?"

They got out of the SUV and approached the family. Alicia spotted Bill and smiled. He lifted his arms and they hugged a long moment. He said, "It's so good to see you again."

She looked at him through moist eyes. "Thank you for letting me know about my mother."

"I hope it was the right thing to do."

"It was."

Bill looked at David, leaned down, and smiled. "And who is this fine young man?"

"My name's David. And my dog's name is Buddy."

"I know Buddy."

"You do? How?"

"I flew on a plane with him. So this is the second time Buddy has been on a plane."

"He likes it."

Bill stood straighter. "Paul, it's good to see you." They shook hands.

"You, too, Bill. Thanks for the private jet. It certainly made our travels much smoother than the first leg of the trip."

"Such a damn tragedy. I want you to meet Carter Hawkins. Carter runs encryption at NSA. He came on board right after you went off the radar."

They shook hands all around and Carter said, "It's good to have you and your family back home. You're still legendary in the agency. You raised the bar so high, I'm not sure we'll reach that again."

"Sure you will. You have faster and better computers, and AI is now much more in the mix. I'm sure that's creating some pretty interesting work for your analysts."

"The world definitely has changed in the five years since you've been gone, and not so much for the better."

"Let's dare to hope for fair winds."

"Indeed."

Buddy made a slight whine. Alicia said, "Buddy is in dire need of a potty break. Is there a patch of grass somewhere?"

"Matter of fact, there is," Bill said, motioning to a federal agent. The man wore dark glasses, a flesh-colored earpiece in his right ear. He walked up to them, and Bill said, "John, would you escort Mrs. Marcus and Buddy to that large swath of grass adjacent to the hanger. The president's dog occasionally uses it. I'd bet Buddy would love to go to the bathroom there, too. What do you think, David?"

"Yep. He probably has to go pee."

Bill smiled and said, "Let's help him out."

"No problem," said the agent. He gestured to David, "Come on, we can take Buddy for a walk." David grinned, and they took Buddy out of the crate, the dog's tail a blur. Alicia snapped the leash on Buddy's collar and walked with David and the agent to a grassy area near the hangar.

Bill looked at Paul and said, "There's been another tragedy. Carter will update you."

Carter nodded. "Senator Fairchild, the Chair of the Senate Intelligence Committee, was beaten to death less than a mile from his home. He was jogging next to the river, which borders his neighborhood in Bethesda. A woman walking her dog found his body. Preliminary autopsy indicates he had his head cracked open in three places, severe brain hemorrhage. The killer or killers left two nickels on top of Fairchild's eyes, and they left a note on the body. They stuck it in his mouth. It's addressed to the president. They're demanding a billion be paid to the Iranian government. They say it's for the cost to restore their nuclear reactors."

Bill folded his arms and said, "So much for the deal we had with them. That just bought them time to bring it back up. It's not online, at least as far as we can tell, but it's probably close to where it was before you took it down."

Paul said nothing. He looked away, watching the agents observing the perimeter, the pilot and co-pilot coming down the stairs.

Carter continued. "They want the president to apologize for Thomas Jefferson going to war with the Muslim nations off the Barbary Coast of North Africa. That's crazy even for them. We know this is coming from Libya-born Fajar Hamad. He's believed to be the older brother of a man we captured in Libya and shipped here for trial, Ulan Hamad. He's one of a dozen we're tracking down for the Benghazi attack. They want Ulan Hamad released back to them. His brother, Fajar, was extensively trained in Iran. He speaks Arabic and Persian, and he was definitely one of the forces behind the Benghazi attack. From what we understand, for this guy—a radical who's always been the go-to person between Iranian and Libyan factions, especially after the take down of Gadhafi, he's got an ax to grind against the U.S. that goes back more than two centuries. And now he's drawing lines in the sand."

Paul exhaled and said, "A horrific line would be a nuclear-ready Iran with warheads aimed at Israel."

Bill cleared his throat. "One of their demands, Paul, was for us to hand you over to them. Otherwise, their threat is to continue killing American citizens on U.S. soil. The downing of flight 1972 was just, as they put it, a drop of blood in what would result in a sea of blood. They've posted images of Senator Fairchild's body online."

Bill's lips were tight, his face pinched, as Alicia, David, and Buddy approached with the agent at their side. Bill turned to Alicia and Paul. "My car is in the hangar. I'll give you a lift to your new home. We'll have company. Some of the agents will follow us. After you're settled in, Paul, the president would like to speak with you."

Alicia said, "I need to see my mother as soon as possible."

"And you will. Let us get you in the safe house. There are some things you need to know before you venture out anywhere."

TWENTY-THREE

Tourists standing on the observation deck near the base of Mount Rushmore never saw it coming. Never heard it approach. Maybe it was because of the wind blowing through the Black Hills of South Dakota. Maybe it was because the drone pilot had practiced the mission two days earlier over the Badlands. And now it was time.

Visitors to the national park took pictures of the four U.S. presidents carved into stone and history books. Dozens of people walked the Presidential Trail, meandering through the tall pines to get to the closest point to the face of Mount Rushmore. The towering ponderosa pines gave off the slight scent of vanilla. A bald eagle rode the warm air currents above the hills.

"Would you mind taking our picture?" asked a twenty-something mother of two, her blonde hair in a ponytail. She and her husband picked up their young daughters and stood next to the wooden railing, the stone faces of George Washington, Thomas Jefferson, Theodore Roosevelt, and Abraham Lincoln, perched high in the background.

"No problem," said the recently hired young park ranger, wide smile. The mother handed him her phone, and he framed the shot. He snapped it, and the family gathered around to see their picture with the presidents.

Behind the tourists, on the far side of the famed carved mountain, were two men who came to take pictures of the celebrated monument, too. But they were using a video camera attached to a drone. They'd planned it for weeks. And after the death of U.S. Senator Fairchild, now was the time to show how easy an American iconic monument could be targeted—could be destroyed. Not all four of the carved faces on Mount. Rushmore.

Just one.

The face of Thomas Jefferson.

The men could have been international tourists. They could have been geological surveyors in the four-wheel-drive Jeep they'd rented and driven though the hills and countryside surrounding Mount Rushmore. But they weren't. They were killers. Both wore jeans and flannel shirts, untucked. Dark skin and hair. Close cropped beards. And their black eyes shared the same merciless shine of a lynch mob.

They'd staked out the vast property during the course of two days. Tested the direction of the air currents, watched the flow of tourists, stayed away from the National Park Service buildings and the security cameras. They'd looked at the best trajectory for launching and flying a drone from a high altitude directly into Mount Rushmore.

The taller of the two men, E'temad, a small, serrated, ashen scar beneath his left eye, drove the Jeep along Highway 244. "Up ahead," he said. "There's a break in the guard rail. We'll enter there." He glanced in his rearview mirror.

The man on the passenger side, Vafara, young, prominent cheek-bones, long, slender fingers, said, "It should not take long. We will have the altitude. The wind is from the southwest. We will fly in from behind the tourists and strike our target. With the camera on the drone, there is no need for us to see the target in a real time trajectory."

They pulled off the road, drove about one hundred feet behind an outcropping of rock shrouded by pine trees. They shut off the motor, opened the Jeep's hatch and quickly assembled the drone. It was one of the most powerful on the market, able to lift up to thirty pounds, a visual range between camera and operator of almost a mile. It gave the men the advantage of a strike from the opposite side of the mountain, allowing them to be on the highway and almost to Rapid City before police and the FBI could coordinate a manhunt.

• • •

Mike Welch loved the Black Hills and the Badlands. As a boy, he camped and hiked the hills with his parents and sister. He loved catching fat brown trout from the rivers and streams that twisted through hills and canyons. His favorite place was Spearfish Creek. Fast, clear water and the pockets of slower water behind rocks with the promise of rainbows and brookies lurking in the shadows. He thought about that as he drove down Highway 244 in his National Park Service pickup truck. Welch, who had been a park ranger for only three years, came to work early and left late each day. He was lanky, dark hair neatly parted on the left. He wore wire-framed glasses, and his youthful face made him look like a boy scout in an adult's uniform.

His phone buzzed. He lifted it from the truck's console and looked at the ID. His wife was texting. Welch pulled over, off the road, to read and respond to her text. Her message was next to her picture. *Still the most beautiful girl in South Dakota,* he thought. *Maybe the entire nation.* She wrote: Please pick up three jars of spaghetti sauce for tonight's dinner. Love you!

Welch smiled and started to respond. He heard something off the road. It sounded like a den of agitated rattlesnakes had been discovered, hundreds of rattlers buzzing at the same time. He stared in the direction of the noise. Saw movement in the brush, the sun's wink off the bumper of a car, the small tree branches jostling. He opened the truck door. There was no wind. He stood to one side, craned his neck trying to get a better look. The buzzing noise increased and then died down. For a moment, there was silence. He could hear the subdued voices of men speaking. Their talk was quick. In short, staccato bursts. And it wasn't English. Welch had a good ear for dialect.

"Arabic," he mumbled. "Maybe Farsi or Persian."

Welch gently closed the door without making a sound. He stepped through loose gravel and twigs, heading in the direction of the sounds. As he walked around a strand of trees, he froze for a moment. It was the first time in Mike Welch's career that he wished he had a gun. Two men were adjusting something on the underside of the large drone. Welch could tell it was more than a camera.

It was a bomb.

TWENTY-FOUR

Mike Welch didn't move. The men hadn't seen him yet. Any movement in their periphery could get their attention. But right now they were focused on the drone. They'd turned off the motors as they adjusted the payload. Welch heard the hum of a semi-truck in the distance, the caw of a crow above the tall pines. And less than fifty feet away, was a danger far beyond a den of disturbed rattlesnakes.

He could run back to his truck in twenty seconds and radio in to headquarters. The park service might have the road blocked within minutes, and the two men would be trapped. No way out. He stepped backward. A small fallen branch snapped under his boot. The sound was small but, at the moment, it might as well have been a blast from a car horn.

One of the men looked up. Even from the distance, Welch could see and feel the hate in the man's eyes as he said something to his partner and both of them turned. The taller one reached behind his back and pulled out a 9mm pistol.

Welch held up one hand, palm out. He said, "Whoa ... take it easy. Right now it's just a simple misunderstanding. No harm done. You probably have a permit to carry. You fellas are welcome to fly drones in parts of the Black Hills, but just not here. There are too many tourists in the area. I have a map in my truck. I can get it and show you guys places where you can fly that drone all day long if you want to." He started to turn.

"Don't move!" shouted E'temad.

Welch held both his hands up. "C'mon, guys. No harm done. I'm a federal wildlife officer. If anything happens to me, you'll have every law enforcement agent in the United States looking for you."

"Do you think that frightens us?"

"We can talk this out. I haven't seen a crime committed yet. The firearm can go back in your holster and you boys can fly that drone all over the Badlands."

The men approached Welch. The younger of the two, Vafara, said, "But you have committed crimes. Your entire nation has committed deep offenses, and it continues to do so, in spite of our warnings."

"Look fellas … I have a two year old son. I just got a text from my wife to pick up some spaghetti sauce for dinner. I'm not some kinda FBI agent. I'm just a park ranger. And as you can see, I'm not even carrying a gun."

"That is your mistake," E'temad said. He got to within ten feet of Welch. "On your knees!"

"Please, man … in God's name … you don't have to do this."

"God's name?" smirked E'temad. "Your Christian God is like a cartoon. Not real and silly. On you knees! Hands behind your back! Quickly!"

Welch slowly dropped to his knees.

E'temad grinned, pointed the pistol at Welch and said, "Renounce your nation's imperialist agenda and your God."

"Why?" You're gonna shoot me anyway."

"Renounce!"

"No. I can't."

"Then maybe you will meet your God. Renounce!"

"I don't speak Arabic, but I think you'll understand this … go to hell."

"You're wrong about me shooting you."

With lightning speed, Vafara kicked Welch in the lower jaw. The blow knocked Welch on his back, stunned. Vafara pulled out a long knife. He pounced on Welch like a wolf, cutting his throat from ear to ear. Then Vafara stood, blood dripping off the serrated blade. Welch tried to sit up, the blood staining his park service shirt as if he had on an adult bib. Bright red. He held both hands to his throat, trying to stop the bleeding. His heart pounded, blood seeping from between his fingers. He managed to sit up, looked at the men. They were grinning, pacing like two hyenas. They spoke in Arabic, their voices dimming.

Welch fell on his back, still holding his throat. His phone buzzed in his pocket. After three rings it went to voicemail. Even in his pocket, he could hear his wife, Heather, leaving a message, *"Hope you got my text. We need an onion, too. Don't work too late, okay? Love you."* He heard the sound of rattlesnakes again, the loud buzzing. Within seconds, the drone was airborne. It flew directly over him, a bomb attached. From Mike Welch's perspective, the single lens of the camera looked like a one-eyed predator taking flight.

TWENTY-FIVE

Attached to the drone, behind the camera, was a bomb about the size of a large submarine sandwich. It was housed in a black metal box. The bomb wasn't large enough to destroy the entire monument, but it had enough shock wave force to inflict damage to at least one of the carved faces—the face of Thomas Jefferson.

Within two minutes, the drone was flying southeast high over the target. Vafara operated the camera, scanning the landscape below like the eye of a hawk looking for prey. Both men watched the computer monitor as E'temad flew the drone in a half-circle pattern, to the southwest, and then made a route slightly northeast toward Mt. Rushmore. They took the drone to an altitude of more than three thousand feet.

E'temad held it there for a few seconds, waiting for a low-hanging cloud to pass. When it did, the men looked at the renowned monument far below the deadly cargo. E'temad smiled and said, "I will aim for right between the eyes."

He moved the toggles and the drone responded, flying fast and almost straight down. The men watched the image of Mount Rushmore become more defined as the drone flew closer. They could see the four faces. E'temad aimed for the one next to the sculpture of George Washington. Within seconds, Thomas Jefferson's likeness filled the monitor.

And then the screen went black.

E'temad and Vafara could hear the explosion form their vantage point. They looked in the direction as a cloud of white smoke rose from Mount Rushmore. "Praise to Allah," said Vafara. "Let us go."

They sprinted to the Jeep, got inside and drove back to Highway 244, squealing tires on the asphalt.

In front of Mount Rushmore, there were no squeals. Only screams. The bomb and explosion shattered the face of Jefferson, destroying the left eye, nose and left portion of the mouth. Rock shot in multiple directions, debris tumbling down the mountain—a small avalanche of stone and billowing dust.

Rocks pelted the observation stand. People tried to take cover and watched dumbfounded as the smoke obliterated the faces of the presidents. A rock, no larger than a baseball, came out of the smoke and struck one of the twin girls on the temple as her mother and father tried to run from the disaster. The blow ruptured the girl's skull, blood gushed on the Presidential Trail.

"Help us!" cried the mother dropping to her knees cradling her daughter in her arms. "Dead God! My baby! No! God no! Please!"

The onlookers rallied around the family, forming a circle, looking over shoulders at the destruction to the mountain, one man calling 9-1-1. Another called the park rangers. A woman prayed aloud.

The young father knelt down beside his wife and daughter. He wanted to shield his other daughter from the horror inflicted on her sister. "Jenna! Stay there." He held his slain daughter's head in his trembling hands. The blood stopped flowing as the girl's heart quit beating. The mother sobbed. Through her tears, lower lip trembling, she looked up at Mount Rushmore. The smoke rose above the mountain leaving the face of Thomas Jefferson shattered. And at the foot of the mountain, a three-year-old girl lay dead.

TWENTY-SIX

The home was built in 1925, Old World Tudor design. Lots of stone. Vaulted, pitched roof and a full circle driveway. The house was more than two hundred feet from the road, almost hidden behind old oaks, flowering dogwood and redbud trees. A black wrought iron gate crossed the entrance to the driveway. Bill pressed a remote control, and the gate swung open. He signaled for the two agents in the SUV to enter. When both cars were inside the property, Bill closed the gate. "They'll wait outside until they're cleared to go," he said to Paul and Alicia.

He drove down the long brick driveway, the SUV following. Bill looked in the rearview mirror and then used a remote control to open the wide garage door on the right side of the home. He pulled in and closed the door. It was large enough for three full-sized cars. The agents parked in the circle and stayed in their vehicle. "Here's your new home," Bill said, pursing his lips. "At least for a while. Let's have a look."

They got out, and he pointed to a black Audi on the left side of the garage and a Ford Escape in the center. "Those are yours. Your alias names are listed on the registration. All paperwork is in order. You'll receive no utility bills and no mail."

"Thanks," said Paul. "We appreciate all the effort."

"Comes with the territory. A double-edge sword perhaps, but it's the compromise we take entering in this line of work." Paul, Alicia,

David and Buddy followed Bill into the home. He led them through the spacious great room, brick fireplace, comfortable sofa and chairs, fully decorated. Buddy sniffed most of the corners, nooks and crevices. They entered the modern kitchen with state-of-the art stainless steel appliances, vaulted ceilings, and a large cooking island with six barstools on one side.

Alicia smiled and said, "Since we'll be eating at home a lot, this will make it easier."

"Indeed," Bill said. "This place has been a safe house for more than two decades. No one has been here in a year. There are hidden surveillance cameras monitoring the front and back of the property."

He stepped to the wall. Next to the light switch was a cream-colored plastic plate with vents for audio. "It looks like an intercom. And it is, of sorts. Press the button and an agent will answer within fifteen seconds. Someone will be here faster than the fire department. There's one in the master bedroom and in the garage. There are no mics or cameras inside the home. The backyard is fenced and very private. You can't see your neighbor's homes in any direction, and they can't see yours. Motion detectors, cameras and automatic floodlights are all around the perimeter of the home and sections of the property. All windows are bulletproofed. Doors are like a vault, reinforced to withstand explosions. The AC is designed to filter out all known poisonous gas. While you're here, real time video satellite images of the property will be beamed to NSA. You have monitors in the kitchen, home office, and the master bedroom. There's a loaded nine-millimeter in the glove box of each car. If you'd rather not have firearms, I'll take them with me."

Paul looked at Alicia for a second and said, "We'll keep them. I'll probably relocate the guns from the cars."

Bill nodded and said, "The home is equipped with gun-fire recognition software, giving us real time tracking of an active shooter anywhere in the house or on the property."

David peered through the glass panes in the French doors over-looking the backyard. "Mom, can I take Buddy outside to play?"

"Not right now. We'll do it in a little while."

"But he really wants to go outside."

"Not now, David. In a minute."

"Can I watch TV?"

She spotted a TV screen in a corner of the breakfast nook, stepped to it, found the remote and pressed the power button. "Maybe I can find the Disney Channel." The screen filled with news video from an upscale neighborhood, police cruisers with flashing blue and white lights, TV trucks, investigators and uniformed officers.

A reporter with shoulder-length, dark hair stood by a closed and gated entrance. She glanced down at her notebook, looked into the camera and said, "Authorities are not letting news media near the area where Senator Harvey Fairchild's body was found. Investigators say that Fairchild appeared to have sustained severe wounds to the face and head. The medical examiner indicated the senator died from blunt force trauma. Let's go to the aerial shot we got from Drone Seven earlier today. You can see the area marked off with yellow crime scene tape. That's on a jogging path very near the Potomac River.

"Police say they found an inflatable rubber dinghy on the opposite bank of the river. They theorize the killer or killers used the small watercraft to reach the area where Fairchild was jogging and assaulted him. There have been no arrests. The FBI, of course, has joined the investigation. The president is calling the senator's murder a tragic loss of life. He said Senator Fairchild will be remembered for his tireless, nonpartisan work ethic, and that the nation has lost one of its most fearless public servants. Reporting live from the Windsor Oaks neighborhood in Bethesda, Jennifer Garcia, Channel Seven News."

A middle-aged anchorman appeared on screen, gray at the temples. He leaned forward behind the news desk. "We have breaking news. There has been an apparent attack—a bombing at Mount Rushmore in South Dakota. We don't have any details beyond the fact that an attack happened minutes ago. Witnesses are saying someone used a drone to fly a bomb into the American landmark, destroying the carved face of one of the nations' most revered presidents, the principal author of our Declaration of Independence, Thomas Jefferson. We expect to have video and live pictures momentarily."

Alicia muted the sound on the TV. She looked over at Bill and Paul. "This is horrific."

Bill said, "If you'll excuse me a minute, I need to make a call." He stepped into the adjacent room and closed the door.

TWENTY-SEVEN

Alicia was hesitant to open the door and let David and Buddy play in the backyard. She stood at the French doors for a moment, stared out one of the windows, her son and his dog by her side. There was a high wooden fence, most of it covered in a green blanket of ivy.

She looked back over her shoulder at Paul and then at the images on the news—new video showing the destruction of Mount Rushmore. She opened the door and stepped outside, her eyes taking in every corner, every place where someone might aim a rifle. There were no rooftops, no buildings in any lines of sight. But there were trees. "David, you and Buddy stay right in the backyard. Don't open the fence gate, and don't go in the front yard. Understand?"

"Yes."

She turned, left the door open, and stepped back inside the kitchen. Bill Gray was standing there with Paul, Bill's face pinched, fatigued. He said, "Alicia, I was just telling Paul as much as we know about the explosion on Mount Rushmore. A drone was used. Part of Jefferson's face was destroyed. There was minor damage to the other sculptures. The bomb caused a rockslide and some of the rocks hit the observation area. A little girl, not much younger than David, was struck in the head by a rock. She died at the scene."

Alicia gripped the back of a kitchen table chair, her knuckles white. She looked up at the images on the TV, the sound still muted. "A senator murdered and then a national monument partially destroyed. At the moment, our little island seems so much safer than my own country. I assume the senator's death and the bombing are connected."

Paul nodded. "Most likely. We don't know yet. No one saw anything except the drone coming out of the clouds. The perp or perps got away very fast. No witnesses have come forth to say they saw anyone with or operating a drone. These terrorists want to strike a severe blow to American icons."

Paul stared at the TV for a few seconds. He looked at his son playing with Buddy in the backyard and then at Bill. "It seems their target or targets are linked to Thomas Jefferson and America's first war with the Barbary States. First Eli Dexter is killed. A note on his body read … *remember the battle of Derna*. The militant, Fajar, with his alleged bloodline back to the Pasha of Tripoli, in Jefferson's time, and a current connection to the American deaths in Benghazi. The plane we were getting on … blown out of the sky—Senator Fairchild's murder—and let's not forget to throw in some weird link to Iran. And, somehow, all of this is supposed to be swirling around my family and me?" Paul said sarcastically.

Bill took in a long breath and slowly released it. "That's why the president wants to speak with you. Once again, Paul, your nation needs you to help figure this out."

Alicia touched her neck with two fingers, her face a little flushed. "I'll take David and Buddy inside. After that, I want to use the car to visit my mother. Paul, please remove the gun from it."

"I'll go with you."

Bill glimpsed outside for a moment and said, "If you do that now, the agents need to follow you from a distance."

Alicia folded her arms. "I understand." She opened the door and called David back inside.

Bill said, "The hostiles have most certainly read the letter I wrote to you, killing a CIA agent to get it. And then the bastards hand-delivered it by using one of our former agents. What I didn't tell you is where to find your mother."

"I assume she's at her home."

"Your mother is receiving treatment at Georgetown University Hospital."

"Is my sister there?"

"She has been, for the most part, in the last couple of weeks."

She looked across the room at Paul. "I need to go to her."

"I'll leave with you."

Bill said, "Paul, if you could do it later today, tonight or even tomorrow, perhaps. The president is waiting to see you. It's very urgent."

Paul looked at Alicia. She nodded and said, "It's okay. I'll take David. Do what you have to do." She pursed her lips, exhaled, and reached for her purse.

Bill said, "I'll speak with the agents. They'll take you through a secure entrance to the private basement-level parking garage. You're mother's in room 1114. The car keys are on a hook to the right of the door leading into the garage."

Alicia turned to David. "Let's leave Buddy here. We'll see him a little later. Now it's time for you to meet your grandmother."

Paul walked them to the garage. He hugged Alicia, her body tense, almost rigid. She looked into his eyes and said, "I hate living like this. Armed guards. Satellite monitoring. Our travel restricted. It's like a form of prison. At least on our little island we had the old sailboat. We could go places without the escorts." She inhaled deeply through her nostrils. "I'm sorry … I'm just feeling a little overwhelmed at the moment. I suppose anytime this happens I should look back at how lucky you and I were to survive—to even make it to our island home."

Paul kissed her and then touched her cheek. "We'll be fine, okay?"

"Okay."

He turned to David. "Tell your grandmother I love her. Got that?"

"Why can't you come with us, Daddy?"

"Next time. I have to get Buddy settled in the house and meet with someone."

Alicia and David got in the car. Paul could hear Bill on the phone speaking with the agents in the driveway. He disconnected and made a second call. Paul watched the garage door open, his wife backing out.

She wore dark glasses, driving slowly by the black SUV with federal agents. They followed her down the long drive.

In the kitchen, he heard Bill say, "Tell the president that I have Paul Marcus. We're on the way." Paul stepped into the kitchen as Bill picked up a manila file folder and said, "The president is looking forward to speaking with you."

"I need three of your best miniature GPS trackers, small enough for me to embed in three pairs of shoes."

TWENTY-EIGHT

Paul Marcus and Bill Gray cleared a metal detector at the diplomat's north side entrance to the West Wing of the White House. Two Secret Service agents made the inspection brief and extremely professional. Two uniformed Marine Corp officers watched from their stations near an entrance door to the West Wing. "Wait here, sir," said one agent, his eyes piercing. "You will be escorted the rest of the way."

Bill smiled. "It's been a while since I was here. I can understand the need for more layers of security. A lot's happened in the world in five years."

Seconds later, the men could hear the hard heel footsteps of someone coming down the hallway. Zack Landry, the assistant director of the Secret Service entered the room. Landry was a seasoned pro, having served three presidents. He dressed in a dark suit, military-style haircut, late fifties, ice blue eyes that were unreadable. He extended his hand. "Good to see you, Bill. It was rumored that you actually retired a few years ago."

Bill shook the man's hand, smiled and motioned toward Paul. "This guy's the reason I stepped out of retirement. Zack Landry, meet Paul Marcus."

The men shook hands and Landry said, "It's an honor to meet you. Even after five years, the ripple effect from your exposing the Circle of 13 is still felt around the world, and that's in a very good way.

Up until a few hours ago, I thought you were dead. Damn glad to see that wasn't the case."

Paul smiled. "Me too."

"Between your take down of the Circle of 13 and your crippling the Iranian nuclear program, you deserve the Presidential Medal of Freedom. I hope the president makes the overture."

"Thank you. However, from what I gather, that's not the reason we're here to see the president."

"Well, you still have my vote. If you were military, you'd have the Congressional Medal of Honor." Landry nodded. "A lot has happened in the last forty-eight hours. Senator Fairchild went to Harvard with the President. A strike at Mount Rushmore is paramount to hitting the Statue of Liberty. Let's head to the Oval Office."

They walked with Landry down the long corridor, oil paintings of past presidents lined the walls. Black and white framed photographs of presidential history almost everywhere. Assistants in suits, phones held to their ears—all in alert mode, moved quickly down the long hallway, like phantoms late for Halloween.

No one spoke, as they got closer to the Oval Office. After a few more seconds, Paul looked at the file folder Bill carried and said, "You've been carrying that folder since I met you at the airport. Care to tell me what's in it?"

Bill glanced at Landry in the lead, looked at Paul, started to say something but stopped when they approached a woman in a business suit standing behind a podium with the presidential seal on it. She wore a wireless headset, smiled at Landry and said, "He's expecting you. Please go on in."

Landry nodded to her and two more Marines stationed in the area. He passed them and stood at the door to the Oval Office. "This is where I head back to my area. Bill, good to see you again. Play some golf, okay? You're retired. Paul, welcome home."

"Thank you."

Landry started to say something else, stopped, nodded and walked away. As Bill put his hand on the polished brass door handle to the Oval Office, he glanced up at Paul and said, "The president will mention what's inside this folder and what we hope you can do. I'll go over it in more detail. At least as much detail as we can gleam from something Thomas Jefferson left behind 217 years ago."

Bill opened the door, and they stepped inside the room as the President of the United States looked up from his desk.

TWENTY-NINE

Alicia placed her hand on the hospital room door handle and paused for a moment. She looked at the numbers on the door, 1114, and then glanced down at David, his brown eyes wide, inquisitive. "Are you going in, Mommy?"

She managed a smile, the sound of medical equipment coming from adjacent rooms, the *beep ... beep ...* pulse of a heart monitor, the restrained sound of a woman crying, the TV show *Jeopardy* coming from one room, the smell of human decay and bleach in the recycled hospital air.

Alicia opened the door and stepped inside the room. She had tried to prepare herself for what she might find. But she wasn't prepared to see how cancer had devastated her mother. She barely recognized the woman in the bed. Her mother was sleeping, or maybe comatose. Alicia wasn't sure. Helen Quincy, late sixties, face boney, her long, silver hair splayed over the pillow.

Alicia looked at the monitors to see if there was a digital pulse. There was one. Very slow. Even the beep from the machine sounded muted. Intravenous tubes fed her mother's arms. Oxygen flowed into her nostrils. Her eyes were closed, face drained of life, grayish white, emaciated, much older than what Alicia remembered.

She felt David squeeze her hand tighter. "Grandma looks real sick."

"She is, Davey. But maybe we can make her feel a little bit better." She walked with her son to the edge of the bed. Her mother's hands were clenched, birdlike. Her gold wedding band now too large for her thin fingers. Alicia bit her lip and touched her mother's shoulder. She could feel bone beneath the hospital gown. "Mom … can you hear me? It's Alicia."

Nothing. No flutter of her eyes, her shrunken chest barely moving.

"Mom … I'm home. I brought someone to meet you. His name is David, and he's your grandson." Alicia touched her mother's arm.

"Hi, Grandma," David said, his voice soft. Helen Quincy moaned. She made a dry swallow.

Alicia watched her for a few seconds. "Mom, it's Alicia. I'm back home. I brought my son … your grandson, to see you."

Helen's eyes fluttered open. She stared at the ceiling tile for a moment. Alicia leaned closer. "Mom, I'm right here." She held her mother's hand and fought back tears.

Helen slowly turned her head to her daughter. "Alicia … you're finally home."

"Yes, Mom, I am. This is David. David say hello to your grandmother."

"Hi, Grandma. We came a very long way to see you. Buddy, my dog, is back at the house."

Helen looked at her grandson. She lifted her right hand and said, "Hi David … you favor your grandfather. I wish he were here to see you."

Alicia said, "I think Dad sees us all right now."

Helen smiled, her face muscles weak. She cut her eyes up at Alicia. "I knew you were not dead. When that man brought me the cross you'd given him … I knew. I remember you telling me if I ever saw that cross it was a sign from you that you were alive. I prayed hard and now here you are … my sweet Alicia."

"Mom, I married Paul Marcus. He's David's father. I want you to meet him. He's a good man. I think you'll love him, too."

Her mother nodded, closed her eyes for a moment. "I'm sure I will. Is there some water here?"

Alicia looked on the tray next to the bed and found a cup with a straw and lid. She peered inside. "Yes, here's some water. I'll give you a drink. Let me help you up on the pillows a bit." She leaned in and lifted her mother, felt rib bones through her back, her skin very warm to the touch. Alicia adjusted the pillows under her mother's head, lifted the cup of water and helped her drink from the straw.

David stood at the foot of the bed, watching, not sure what to say.

When Helen finished sipping the water, she looked at David and said, "I am so very glad you came to see me. Come closer, I want to hold your hand."

David stepped closer and reached for his grandmother's hand. She gently held the boy's hand. "I want to hear all about you, David. What do you like to do?"

"I like playing with my dog Buddy. I like to go on the boat with Mom and Dad. And I like pizza."

"So do I. When I get out of here, we'll get us a pizza. I know the perfect place."

"You do?"

"Yes, I do." She coughed and tried to smile, looked at Alicia. "Where is Paul?"

"He wanted to be here today but was called to a meeting with the president."

Helen said nothing for a few seconds. She looked at the TV monitor mounted to the wall. The sound was off but the picture was on, the images of the bombing of Mount Rushmore. Helen tilted her head, her eyes narrowing. "Alicia, what's on the TV? It looks like something is going on at Mount Rushmore."

Alicia looked back at the screen. "They think terrorists flew a bomb into Mount Rushmore."

"Oh dear God." Helen made a dry clicking sound in her mouth, her brow furrowed, eyes squinting. "Do you remember when your father and I took you and Dianne to Mount Rushmore?"

"I do. We had a good time. Dad, the historian as he was, was like a tour guide. He knew the history of the father and son sculpting team. I remember him saying that the son was named after President Lincoln. And he said the original plans were to have the busts of the presidents carved to their waists, but the project ran out of money and was never finish as it was intended."

"Your father was a walking history book, especially about American history. I so wish he could have met David. He's our only grandson." She looked at David and smiled before coughing, a whizzing sound coming from her lungs. "Alicia, was anyone hurt in the bombing?"

"A little girl was killed by a falling rock."

"That's so tragic. Did they catch the person responsible?"

"Not yet."

Helen closed her eyes for a moment and then looked at her daughter. "Is that why Paul is meeting with the president? Is it about this horrible attack on our beloved Mount Rushmore?

"I think that's part of it."

"What's the other part … you seem so troubled? A mother can always tell."

A nervous smile moved across Alicia's mouth. She cut her eyes to David for a second. "It's nothing, Mom. Nothing to worry about." She leaned in and kissed her mother on the forehead.

Helen managed a tired smile. "Take me home, Alicia. I know I don't have much longer. I don't want to die here. Not in this place. You father died in our home. So should I." She paused for a few seconds. "I want to see my garden again. I want you and Dianne to take me home, okay?"

Alicia squeezed her mother's hand and blinked back tears. "Okay, Mom. We'll take you home."

THIRTY

The President of the United States stood behind his desk and gestured toward a bloodstained piece of paper. It was in the center of the desk, sealed in a plastic bag. The president, ending the first year of his second term, folded his arms across his chest. He was in his late sixties, steel gray eyes. His narrow face had the creased, angular look of a veteran cowboy, not a politician. His silver hair was beginning to thin.

Paul Marcus and Bill Gray stood at the opposite side of the president's desk. The directors of the CIA and the FBI stood from two chairs to the right of the president's desk. The Deputy Director of the FBI, Ward Rosenberg, was positioned next to three wide-screen television monitors. The Secretary of State, Patricia Willow, sat to the left next to Sami Botros who served as a senior advisor to the president.

Greetings and small talk lasted less than thirty seconds. The president was angry, and it showed. His intelligent, no-nonsense style of conducting business got him elected twice, the second time by the largest majority in modern U.S. history. He motioned for Paul Marcus and Bill Gray to sit.

The president looked at the note sealed in plastic and then cut his eyes to Paul. "The barbarians aren't at the gate anymore, Paul. They're living right next door, and they're spreading like a plague. Whoever blew part of Thomas Jefferson's likeness off Mount Rushmore, killing a child in the process, will meet a federal death penalty when caught. And they will be caught. What's the latest, Haden?"

The Director of the FBI, Haden McNally, fifties, his ruddy face strained, slipped his glasses on and read from his tablet for a few seconds. "A park ranger, Michael Welch, was found murdered in the brush off Highway 244. We believe this is where the perps launched their drone, about three-quarters of a mile from Mount Rushmore."

The president clasped his fingers together on his desk. "How was he killed?"

"They slit his throat. He bled out. He must have heard the noise and walked up on them. A Jeep Wrangler was found abandoned in the Badlands about fifty miles northeast of Mount Rushmore. The Jeep had been rented at the Sioux Falls Airport. We know the driver's license was forged—a Florida license, and the guy's name on the ID was listed as Ivan Rodriguez. The photo on the license is that of a dark skin man with a full beard. The clerk on duty at the rental agency said he remembers the customer. Said he was soft spoken with a slight accent, but nothing else."

The Director of the CIA, Stephen Parker, glossy head, the flat eyes of a poker player, cleared his throat. "We did find additional tire tracks near the Jeep. There were shoe prints as well. Looks like men's shoes. Two sets. The bombers ditched their Jeep and caught a ride. They could be anywhere."

The president splayed both hands on his desk, fingers spread, with his fingertips less than a foot from the bloodstained note in plastic. "From what you all are telling me, there's a connection between the bastards who murdered Eli Dexter, Harvey Fairchild, and the child and park ranger killed at Mount Rushmore. Assuming from the boot prints near Rushmore, there's at least two. Are these persons the same ones who killed Fairchild, working together with another pair or group, or a case of separate soldiers following the same leader and being assigned to different points of destruction?"

CIA Director Parker held his black frame glasses and gestured with them. "Separate or a different pair, most likely. The travel logistics from Senator Fairchild's murder scene to the detonation of the bomb on Mount Rushmore would have been too tight unless they had access to a private jet and secluded areas to take off and land. That doesn't appear to be the case."

FBI Director McNally added, "We know Fajar Hamad has soldiers here in the homeland. We've been tracking the ones we're aware of, but that's six known people. None are or have been in Bethesda or South Dakota in the last three days. But that could be the tip of the iceberg. We believe all of this is Hamad's doings, and with that, we have a unique new breed of terrorist."

"How do you mean?" asked the president.

The FBI Director gestured to his Deputy Director, Ward Rosenberg, who nodded and said, "If the profilers are right, and we have every indication that they are, we're dealing with a guy who believes he's predestined or chosen by a higher power to reap havoc on the West. When we factor in his supposed family connections to the rulers of Tripoli two centuries ago, we get a Frankenstein hybrid of a monster Muslim who wants to move the line in the sand all the way back to their very first war with America. Look, Mr. President, at the blood of Senator Fairchild on that list of demands. These killers can't stalk a senior member of the U.S. Senate, and spill his blood like they did with our sailors to start the Barbary War."

Sami Botros, the president's senior advisor, shifted in his chair. Dark skin and coal black hair with a trimmed moustache, impeccably dressed. He cleared his throat and said, "With all due respect, Deputy Director Rosenberg, the comment about a monster Muslim is unfair. It's not about this man's ethnicity … it's about what's in his insane head. Muslims don't hold a monopoly on evil any more than do the Spanish, French, or Germans."

Rosenberg looked just above the rims of his glasses, his pale eyes testy. "No, but there are plenty of radical ones, the jihadists, who do."

Botros smiled. "Your surname is Rosenberg. One of Hitler's henchmen, Alfred Rosenberg, a man found guilty of war crimes during the Nuremberg trials, was most definitely a Nazi. However, it would be appalling and presumptuous of me to think all Germans, or someone with the shared surname, such as Rosenberg, would be remotely connected to Nazis. It would be a false stereotype and blatantly accusatory. Fajar Hamad is a soulless killer. The fact that he's Muslim has no more bearing on him than your ancestry to Germany."

Rosenberg's pink face reddened. He leaned forward in his chair, his suit coat stretched by his waistline. "I apologize if I offended you, Sami. We've just had a U.S. Senator, a little girl, and a national park ranger slaughtered by a man and his followers who justify their killings because they believe their Koran gives them the right and the duty to do so. It's not about Muslims, it's about the mind of any person, radical Muslim or some other group, that blindly follows that doctrine of aggression."

"Let's move on," said the president, eyeing the bloodstained paper. "That's one of the reasons you're here today, Paul. Something happened back in Jefferson's day that you might help us with. The other reason, sadly, is that your life and that of your family is probably riding on it."

THIRTY-ONE

Alicia stepped next to the window in her mother's hospital room and tried Paul's burner phone. There was no answer. She looked at David siting in a chair and playing a video game on his tablet, her mother asleep again. Alicia turned up the sound on the TV mounted against the wall. She watched continuing coverage of the assassination of Senator Harvey Fairchild and the bombing of Mount Rushmore.

A nurse entered the room, smiled and took Helen's vital signs, wrote in a chart and left. Alicia could hear voices somewhere out in the hallway. She thought she recognized one of the voices. It was that of a woman.

Alicia walked to the door and partially opened it. One of the agents was speaking with two women twenty feet down the hall. Both women had their backs turned toward Alicia, but still she recognized one of them. It was the near perfect posture, the way she held herself as she listened to the agent. And her unique voice—the controlled energy in her speech.

Alicia approach them and said, "Dianne ... is that you?"

The woman turned, Alicia's younger sister, Dianne Hirsch, broke into a wide smile. She rushed to Alicia and hugged her. "Oh my God!" Dianne said, embracing Alicia. "We thought you were dead! How did you get here? Where have you been?" Her eyes welled with water, tears forming. She sniffled and said, "I was telling this gentleman that my mother is in that room, and I was here to see her."

Alicia smiled at the agent. "She is my sister, Dianne. I know you are just doing your job, but we'll be fine, thanks." The agent nodded and walked toward his colleague twenty feet way. Alicia looked at the other, younger woman, mid-twenties, attractive, eyes gleaming. "Brandi, is it really you?"

"Hi, Aunt Alicia." She opened her arms for Alicia and hugged her, Brandi rocking slightly on her toes.

"Let me look at you," Alicia said, stepping back. "You are so … grown. The last time I saw you, I really didn't see you. It was on television when Iranian guards walked you across a tarmac to a plane bound back home."

Brandi's eyes filled with tears. "From what I was told, I have you to thank for that … and Paul Marcus. Is he … is he dead?"

"No. He's alive and well. And he's my husband." She looked at her sister and niece. "We have a child, a boy. His name's David, and he's in the room with Mom."

Dianne blew out an extended breath. "I'm trying to process all this. My sister comes back from the dead. She's married, and she's the mother of a boy." Dianne glanced down the hall as the two federal agents monitored the flow of hospital staff and visitors. "Alicia, what's going on? Why the bodyguards?"

"They're not bodyguards in the traditional private sector sense. They're FBI agents, and right now they're assigned to us."

"Us? You mean you and your son?"

"And my husband."

"Where's he?"

Alicia started to answer, paused and said, "He's in a meeting with some government officials. You'll meet him."

Brandi shifted her purse strap on her shoulder and said, "All I know, Aunt Alicia, is what your former boss at NSA told us. I think his name was Bill something. He said you and Paul both helped bring down that group called the Circle of 13. It was all over the news and social media, too. And he said Paul had negotiated the deal to have my boyfriend Adam and I released from the Iranian prison. He called the two of you great American heroes in what he said was the most true and ultimate sense of patriotism."

Alicia smiled. "Bill is one of the best of the best."

"He told us after the helicopter you were in crashed off the coast of Sicily, there were no traces of your bodies. I cried for a week."

"I'm sorry. We had to go off the grid completely. I was pregnant. Because of the great possibility of retaliation, especially against Paul, we went into a witness protection program of sorts. We essentially became new people, and I mean new from our identities to the language we spoke and the way we lived. Our home for the last five years was on a beautiful little island in the Mediterranean."

Dianne lowered her voice. "What in God's name happened, Alicia? What got you off the island, or made you leave?"

"Someone recognized us—or Paul. One thing quickly led to the other. Bill let me know that Mom was gravely ill. So we decided to leave. We started in Sicily and left from Rome."

Brandi's eyebrows arched. She spoke in a voice just above a whisper. "That plane … the one someone just blew up off the coast of Sicily … was that … was—"

"We were booked on it. Paul saw something that made him suspicious. He reported it, but after a delay, the airline decided to allow the plane to take off."

Brandi held her hand to her mouth for a moment, licked her dry lips and said, "Maybe we should go inside grandma's room."

They nodded and entered the room. Alicia looked at her sleeping mom and glanced across the room to the empty chair near the window. The tablet was on the floor.

David was gone.

"Mom!" shouted Alicia. Her mother's eyes flickered. "David!" Alicia stepped quickly to the chair, fear on her face.

A nurse entered the room. Alicia turned to her and asked, "Did you see a little boy leave this room?"

The woman, middle-aged, carrying an IV bag, said, "No ma'am."

Alicia bolted across the room and opened the bathroom door. David had his back to the door, peeing in the toilet. "Mom, I'm gonna wash my hands."

Alicia tried to smile. "That's good." She closed the bathroom door and turned to face her sister and niece. "I'm sorry … It's just …"

Dianne smiled. "It's okay. Considering what you've gone through, what you're still going through, I'd be a basket case."

David came out of the bathroom, slightly embarrassed, avoiding direct eye contact with the two women standing by his mother. She said, "David, this is your Aunt Dianne. She's my sister, and this lady is Brandi. She's your cousin."

Dianne stepped over to David, knelt down beside him and said, "It is so good to meet you, David. Do you like animals?"

"Yes. I have a dog. His name's Buddy."

Dianne smiled. "Here in Washington, we have a really cool zoo. Lots of animals live there. Have you ever been to a zoo?"

David shook his head, no.

"The zoo has lions, tigers, elephants and many other animals."

Brandi said, "The first time I went to the National Zoo I was about your age. And I've gone there just about every year since. I have an idea … let's all go. Does that sound like fun?"

David grinned. "Mom can we go?"

Alicia nodded. "Once we're all settled in our new house, we'll make lots of plans."

Dianne stood and asked, "Where is your house."

Alicia took a deep breath. She glanced down at her mother and then looked at her sister and niece. "I can't tell you, at least not now. It's called a safe house. Government owned."

Although in pain, Helen lifted one hand and said, "All in good time. I'm just thrilled to have my two daughters, my granddaughter and my grandson here together."

Brandi stepped closer to her grandmother and kissed her on the cheek. "We're just as thrilled to have you here with us, too, Grandma." She beamed.

Helen leaned a little forward in her bed. "Brandi, help me unclasp this necklace." Helen touched the thin chain of a gold necklace around her neck. Brandi unhooked the clasp and gently lifted the necklace from her grandmother's neck, out the top of the hospital gown. It was a gold cross, a crucifix, a small diamond in the center. Brandi handed the necklace to her grandmother. Helen looked at it, smiled, and held it out to Alicia.

"No Mom," Alicia said. "It's yours."

Helen closed her eyes for a second and then looked at Alicia. "No, it never was, but it gave me two things these last five years. It gave me hope and some comfort because I knew you were alive."

Dianne's eyes widened. "You did? You knew Alicia was alive all this time? Mom, why didn't you tell us?"

"Because she couldn't," Alicia said. "The same man who told you and Brandi about Paul and I ... some of what we went though, Bill Gray—my former boss at NSA, delivered this necklace to Mom. I told her, before I went overseas, that if she ever received the necklace and didn't hear from me, it was a sign that I was alive and would return when I could."

Brandi folded her arms, glanced out the hospital window. Dianne said, "You're here, but you have FBI agents guarding you and you can't even tell us where you live. Can you tell us what the hell happened to you?"

Alicia glanced across the room at David, who'd returned to his video game. "I will soon, Dianne. But I can't right now. To do so could possibly put you in danger."

Dianne cut her eyes to the TV screen; the sound was low, but perceptible. She watched the coverage of the slain U.S. senator, then the screen cut to images of the child killed at Mount Rushmore, and then there was video of the investigation into the plane wreckage off the coast of Sicily. She slowly turned back to her sister. "Alicia, all of this stuff ... these tragedies that have happened the last few days ... are any of them somehow connect to you and Paul?"

Alicia looked down at her mother on the bed, the golden cross swaying from the elderly woman's hand trembling like a pendulum, the sound from the TV news seemed suddenly louder. Alicia said, "I don't know. I can't reach my husband."

THIRTY-TWO

The president stood in the Oval Office, looking out a window to the White House Rose Garden, a lone sparrow hopped between branches on a maple tree. He turned and said, "Harvey Fairchild was one of my closest friends. From our time at Harvard, through the Naval Academy, up until his death … no, his torture and murder." He paused and glanced back at the people in his office.

Secretary of State Patricia Willow, fifties, brown hair worn up, dressed in a dark blue suit, put her glasses on and said, "I'll attend Harvey's funeral with you, Mr. President. Although I didn't know Harvey as long as you had, the time I worked with him was some of my most rewarding experiences. I'll miss him. The nation will miss him, too."

The directors of the CIA and FBI nodded. Bill Gray stood and said, "We'll find them, Mr. President."

Paul Marcus said nothing. He glanced at the bloodstained paper.

The president cleared his throat. "Harvey went from a successful business career into politics because he wanted to make a positive difference. Before I ran for office the first time, I knew the typical American family was fed up with the paralyzed politics and the way most members of congress behaved and conducted the nation's business. Citizens felt that they had no real voice in anything Washington did. Harvey Fairchild fought damn hard to change that by always reaching across the aisle and across the nation. He was one of the best."

The president returned to his chair behind the desk and motioned toward the sealed bag. "That note was what the bastards stuck in Harvey's mouth after beating him to death. Haden, your team tells us there are no prints on it. All the blood is from Harvey. The demands are from psychopaths."

Bill Gray said, "I briefly mentioned to Paul the thrust of their demands."

Secretary Willow said, "Iran's official statement is that their government had nothing to do with the murder or the subsequent demands. Someone working with their Quds Force wants us to transfer a billion dollars into the Central Bank of Iran as reparations from the U.S., through your considerable skill, for shutting down their nuclear reactors. We, of course, deny having knowledge of what you did or did not do."

The president nodded. "So when you and Alicia went off the grid with your apparent deaths, all was fairly copacetic until your cover was compromised. Needless to say, we'll be redefining the nuclear agreement with Iran, orchestrated by my predecessor." The president handed the sealed note to the FBI Director and said, "I don't want to see this again." He looked over to Paul. "This group, loosely associated with Hamas and ISIS, and ostensibly led by a psychopath named Fajar Hamad, wants you, and possibly your family, Paul—they believe you would give them great leverage. They also want us to return Ulan Hamad … Fajar's baby brother, who's in our custody because he's one of those responsible for the deaths of four Americans in Benghazi."

"It's good to know someone wants me."

CIA Director McNally said, "Not only is Fajar Hamad cunning and ruthless, but he's smart and strategic. Combine that with his personal vendetta going back to Jefferson's day, and the fact we picked up his brother for trial here in the U.S. … it makes one pissed off radical jihadist. They pledge to keep killing—"

The president interjected. "We never will negotiate with terrorists. And they—or this nut job—Hamad want me to apologize for Jefferson having waged war on pirates from Tripoli, Algiers, Morocco and

Tunis. Jefferson had enough and had the balls to send our small Navy into the Strait of Gibraltar, along with a five hundred mile march on land from Alexandria, Egypt to Derna, Libya. Two great Americans, Presley O'Bannon and William Eaton led a small squadron of U.S. Marines and a band of mercenaries into Derna. I would love to have been part of that."

Bill nodded and leaned forward. "In addition to the insane demands, this group left their signature calling card on Senator Fairchild ... and they included a deadline. They're saying if their demands aren't met by the end of the next crescent moon, which is in twelve days, they'll unleash a jihad war on America and Israel that will dwarf the 9/11 attacks."

Director McNally said, "For some Muslims, the crescent moon is like the cross for Christians or the Star of David for Jews."

Bill folded his arms and said, "The last thing written on the paper left on Senator Fairchild's body was the same phrase they attached to Eli Dexter's body: '*Remember the Battle of Derna*.'"

"Here's what I remember, and what I will never forget," the president said, lifting a TV remote control and pointed toward a large screen to the right of his desk. The face of Eli Dexter appeared. In the picture, he was smiling. He wore a full dress uniform, Army. The next image was of his body lying in the morgue. Face black and beaten beyond recognition.

Paul looked away. His heart hammered. Fists clenched on the chair armrests.

The president said, "Remember Derna ... I remember Eli Dexter. I think about all of the American sailors the Barbary States captured, tortured and killed. Why? Greed." The president pressed the button again. The image of a little girl, blonde, blue eyed, sitting on a park swing, pink cheery blossoms in the background, "This is Leslie Leman. The picture was taken a week before she was killed when these people blew part of Jefferson's face off the mountain."

He pressed the button again. This time the screen filled with video. The images were of two stoic members from the medical examiner's staff loading a gurney into a dark blue coroner's van. The full-sized gurney wasn't designed for a little child. The girl's body was covered with a sheet and looked small and diminutive in the center of the gurney. In the head area, blood had soaked through the sheet. The stain was small. No larger than a quarter. But it was just as poignant as dead and dying soldiers on a battlefield.

Paul stared at the screen. He thought of his son David. Thought of Eli Dexter when he was a boy, his first little league game, the baseball cap a little too large for Eli's head.

The president pressed the button again. The picture of a park ranger appeared, dressed in his uniform, Mouth Rushmore behind him. "And this is Mike Welch, a national park service ranger who had his throat cut." He turned off the TV screen. He looked at Paul a moment and said, "Bill and NSA, along with the CIA and FBI, have been running psychological profiles on this guy, Fajar Hamad. He's someone with the power of influence and charisma to lead and manipulate people into doing his bloody deeds. He' s a warrior with an agenda that is even deeper than the average vengeful Islamic Jihadists."

"What do you mean?" Paul asked.

"He believes he's a prophet of sorts. Not along the lines of Mohammed, but he definitely knows how to stoke fires that go back sixteen hundred years. He's twisting words in the Koran to invade our homeland to do what he calls death by a million small cuts. He wants to go down as a martyr in a David and Goliath fight with us. But he's clever. He moves constantly like a Bedouin wired with caffeine. In his case, the fuel is hate. We'll find him, but it might not be before he kills others. He appears to select specific prey, like culling them from a herd. But that could change with another bomb into a crowded place. What's the latest on this guy, Stephen?"

CIA Director Parker glanced at notes in his hand. "We believe he's still in Libya. We have three covert Seal and Delta Force teams looking for him. He manages to shuttle all over the Middle East with frequency. Iran, of course, but Syria, Iraq, Saudi Arabia and Lebanon. We believe Russian agents orchestrate some, if not all, of his logistics through the area, but we don't know why."

FBI director McNally nodded and said, "Since the direct attack to Mount Rushmore, the notes left on Senator Fairchild's body, and that of Captain Eli Dexter with the reference to the battle of Derna, we have extra tight security at the Jefferson Memorial. We've notified Virginia authorities to be highly vigilant at Jefferson's home in Monticello. Also, the Jefferson statue at the University of Virginia and the Rotunda there are potential targets."

Secretary of State Willow shifted in her chair and said, "Problem is that there are dozens of Jefferson statues, schools and institutions named after him across the nation."

"And they're all potential targets," said FBI Deputy Director Rosenberg. "With the Jefferson Memorial here in Washington as ground zero. Fajar Hamad, if he's the only mastermind behind this carnage, we need to answer these two questions—what's his Achilles heel and how do we find it?"

"Maybe here," Bill said, setting the file he'd been holding down on the desk.

Paul looked at it, eyed the label, *T Jefferson*, and asked, "What's in there?"

"Something we're hoping you can help us with because Carter's team gave it a hard whack and couldn't break it. Carter was hoping you would take a look. It's something that Thomas Jefferson started during the first war with these people—an encryption, Paul. If you can break it, we might have a better idea where and how to stop this slaughter before it becomes catastrophic."

THIRTY-THREE

Bill opened the file folder on the president's desk and said, "I supposed that somewhere right here in the White House, President Thomas Jefferson wrote this."

Paul eyed the papers. "What exactly are we talking about?"

"Three sheets of paper," Bill said. "Jefferson wrote all of them. One is very legible. The other two, not so much. It's an extremely challenging code, using English, French and mixing numbers in for good measure. Carter Hawkins and his wife found it in the attic of an old home they just bought and are remodeling. It was one of the homes Jefferson spent time in on his trips from Monticello to his summer house at Popular Forest not far from Lynchburg." Bill handed the papers to Paul and said, "He wrote these to Robert Livingston, who was the Minister to France at the time. And he had copies sent to some members of his team, Stephen Decatur and others, facing the pasha of Tripoli and the other Barbary States."

Paul said nothing, examining the encrypted words and then reading the letter. Bill waited a bit and added, "As you know, Jefferson invented the cipher wheel. He encoded at least ten percent of his written correspondence, something no other president did personally before or since Jefferson's time in office. As long as the recipient had the exact cipher wheel, he or she had the advantage to decrypt the message. However, this encryption appears to be much more sophisticated."

The president said, "Probably because a lot more was at stake, as in the future of America, a nation that was only twenty-five years old when Tripoli declared war on the United States. My gut tells me Jefferson knew something on a deeper level about these people and, in particular, the ones with the power. He had to come up with a plan to take down the dictator of Tripoli."

Paul studied the encryption and said, "This will be extremely difficult. It'll take some time."

"We don't have a lot of time," the president said. "What they have in mind at the end of the next crescent moon is anyone's guess." He motioned to the directors of the CIA and FBI. "Based on the profiles your agencies have been doing, I'm starting to think that Hamad has a deeper connection to Jefferson than the fact his family did battle with Jefferson's troops. Maybe there's a love-hate sort of admiration, and idealization that's gone bad and really pissed off this guy. He wants to obliterate Jefferson from our monuments—to tie Jefferson to everything the radical Muslim mindset can't tolerate within the words of our Declaration of Independence. Jefferson dug deep into Islamic history and the Muslim creed. Maybe you can find the connection, Paul, some insight buried on the single page of encryption. It could be a long shot, but it seems to me that the perfect storm of events is coming together, and somehow Thomas Jefferson is the lightning rod. If it exists … some secret from the grave, find it, Paul. And find it before the next crescent moon."

• • •

The wedding was to be held outdoors. Under the oaks and on the grounds of Monticello's west lawn in Virginia. The event was close to the vineyards, rows of grapevines blossoming, the sweet fragrance of budding grapes in early summer, bells ringing from a church across the street. A large white tent was erected, the shade it cast covering a long table and dozens of chairs. Bouquets of lavender flowers were the centerpieces. It was a balmy day with the temperature in the mid-seventies.

Tourists parked in the main lot as did the wedding guests, the only difference was the mix of formal and casual clothing. The wedding party was finishing a private tour of the great house, people spilling out on the grounds, the wedding to be outdoors at the Kenwood Garden with its gazebo and courtyard. The reception was to be held right after the wedding.

The driver of a white catering van followed the small signs to the *Daniels-Campbell wedding*. Karim Mohammed, mid-twenties, clean-shaven was thick in the chest under his white catering jacket. He had black hair, dark skin and facial features of someone with heritage from India, Pakistan or almost any county in the Middle East. Karim could have passed as a graduate student, maybe someone destined for a career in medicine, computer science, education or engineering. He did have some of those technical skills, and he used them in his day job.

At night he built bombs.

All of the bombs had been used by his brothers in the war with the West. This was to be his test of faith, of the ultimate sacrifice. It was the opportunity to become a martyr. To inflict damage or death to non-believers—the infidels, the *kuffars*. The reward would be Allah's good favor, paradise in the never-ending garden, virgins to welcome and honor him for his dedication.

Karim parked and approached the service entrance to the Monticello. There were three cars and two more vans parked, delivery people coming and going. Three uniformed security officers walked the perimeter of Monticello. Two undercover officers from the state police walked through the interior, mixing and blending in with the tourists as the tours proceeded through the great house. There was one state police car in the main parking lot, two troopers stationed there. One security guard watched eight monitors from a back room in the mansion, the gardens, and out buildings—all on camera. One camera caught the activity at the service entrance, the florist, event planners, the decorator and her assistants.

No one paid much attention to the lone caterer. He wore a white jacket over a white shirt with a clip-on black bowtie. He carried a tray of pastries to the back entrance. The security officer at the door, a bear of a man, whose shoes and gun belt squeaked when he walked, looked at the tray of baklava, and asked, "Where are you going with that?"

"To the kitchen. It's for the Daniels-Campbell wedding."

"Not in here. There's another private event scheduled for the library. The wedding just finished. The reception is in the vineyard. You can't miss the giant tent. Reminds me of the traveling circus and the big top they used to advertise. That's way before the activists took pity on the elephants. And now America has no traveling circus. Go figure."

"Yeah, it's a shame. Part of the heritage—the circus." Karim smiled and asked. "Would you like a baklava?"

"They sure look good. But I'd better not. Appreciate the offer, though."

"I will deliver these to the wedding reception. One day I'd like to come back and visit Monticello. I read that Thomas Jefferson was a brilliant man, someone ahead of his time."

"Maybe the nation's finest. Damn shame what happed out in South Dakota. They'll catch and execute whoever did it. It bothered me back when they put a tarp over Jefferson's statue at the University of Virginia—all of those protesters callin' Jefferson horrible names. If it weren't for Founding Fathers like Jefferson, these crazy, ungrateful people wouldn't have a country that gives them free speech and the right to protest. Go figure."

"Excellent point. It was too bad they called Jefferson a rapist and white supremacist. Well, I should get these delivered. I have two more trays. Good talking with you." He turned to leave.

"Hey, whenever you want to tour Monticello, ask for me, John Barker. I usually work weekends. I'll see what I can do to get you a discount."

"Thanks!"

Karim loaded the pastries back in the van, got inside and drove toward the vineyard.

THIRTY-FOUR

Bill Gray lifted a cipher wheel out of his briefcase and sat it on the president's desk. Gray said, "With all the technology and computers we have today, it's not a question of algorithms and linear sequences only. Here's the key Jefferson used to lock his confidential words. Maybe it'll be the key to unlock them. Letters from the English and French alphabets are on the wheel, the most complex one Jefferson ever designed."

Paul picked the cipher wheel up and examined it, turning the cylinders, looking at the letters and numbers. "In the letter that Jefferson wrote, the one that we can read," he smiled and glanced at the paper, "he wrote about studying Islam, the history of the religion and the Muslim people. Why didn't he simply mention his theory in the letter? If it's a theory after all, it is mostly pure supposition or guesswork."

The president said, "Possibly. However, we don't have a helluva lot to go on otherwise. This guy, or this group, definitely has an old junkyard bone to pick with a founding father, and us as a nation. Maybe it was a combination of things—Jefferson, the principle author of the Declaration of Independence, his influence into the drafting of the Constitution—our republic, and ostensibly, our way of life. Which is quite contrary to traditional Muslim—Sharia culture, and even their way of thinking. Combine that with the fact that Jefferson and his Marines kicked some serious butt, and I can see how this militant,

Fajar Hamad, harbors some misconceived grudge. And now that Hamad has funds, Russia and Iran, ostensibly behind him, he's doing his Robin Hood act. He's trying to extort a billion dollars from America and killing members of our military, a U.S. Senator, park rangers and little children who happen to get in his way. I want this guy."

FBI Director McNally said, "Our intel indicates Hamad will even take his extortion demands higher."

"What do you mean?" Paul asked.

"Iran has missiles that can easily hit Tel Aviv. Up until now, they haven't had the nuclear capability to arm the missiles with that caliber of warhead. But they're getting close. We know that the only country Hamad hates more than America is Israel. He must be removed."

Paul nodded. "But we don't know what Jefferson wrote. And whatever it was may have no relevance to what's going on today. It's theory."

"Maybe," said Bill. "But it's not just theory. Not with Thomas Jefferson. He dealt with more concrete facts, or he used science to prove or disprove a concept. When it came to government, to human beings or to being human, it's hard to beat the words he wrote in the Declaration of Independence. Paul, what if whatever it was that Jefferson encrypted is beyond theory. Considering Jefferson's philosophy and his ability to help shape the Constitution that's withstood the tests of time, we think what he encrypted will be more of a time capsule into human events from his era through today and maybe even beyond. We have more of Jefferson's encrypted letters that were decrypted by their recipients. The letters weren't as complicated as the one you have, but you're welcome to them. Maybe for reference."

The president reached for the sealed, bloodstained note in the center of his desk. He lifted it, holding it in one hand, his fingers slightly trembling. "There are causalities of war, but no one comes to the homeland, beats a U.S. Senator to death and shoves a list of demands down his throat. No one comes here and blows one of our presidents off Mount Rushmore, killing a child and park ranger in the process. No one kills a Delta Force soldier, strings his body up like a

Mexican piñata and leaves a calling card around his neck. And no one blows 193 people out of the sky, with you, Paul, and your family, in their sights. Hamad and his crazies have to be stopped."

"But it's not just Hamad. We apparently have two groups to deal with—Hamad and his band of killers in their dual attachment to the Barbary States and Iran, and the Russians," Bill said. "Both, we believe, want Paul, but for different reasons or different end games. The question is this … how close are they working together? How do we keep you and your family safe while we figure this out and take down those calling the shots? And how do we keep the general public safe?" He glanced at the Jefferson letters. "Maybe the answer is in there. Because of all this seemingly connecting back to Thomas Jefferson, maybe you can find a link from the past that will help us beat them now and in the future."

• • •

At the wedding, the best man stood to give a toast to the bride and groom. More than eighty people were seated under the long, white tent, the sides open, allowing the warm Virginia breeze to enter. A wood thrush sang from an oak tree. A DJ stood on a small stage and watched the toasts being made to the newly married couple. The bride, late twenties, dark hair worn in an elegant bun at the nape of her neck, delicate facial features, sat next to her new husband. He was a little older, short haircut, broad shoulders, face slightly red from the good-natured teasing and his second glass of champagne. He was a captain in the Army. At least a dozen members of the wedding party were active military.

One was Special Forces Corporal, Jack Mabry.

As the guests watched the best man stand behind the podium speak into a microphone, Mabry watched the guests. Not the ones he knew, but rather the people he'd never seen. Most were from the bride's side—family and college friends. Some though, were the groom's family. Mabry half-smiled as he observed the flower girls, two under the age of ten, fidget in their wooden chairs as the best man wound down his soliloquy. The family was extended and had deep

Virginian roots. *More uncles, aunts, cousins, nieces and nephews than a typical small neighborhood back in Idaho,* thought Mabry.

One man caught Mabry's eye. He wasn't family. Dressed in a white jacket, black slacks, and black bowtie. *Could be some guy working with the photographers and videographers. Maybe someone on the Monticello event staff.* But the man wasn't doing a job. He was canvasing the area, looking at the people, looking at the open areas between tables.

And he was perspiring.

Odd, thought Mabry. *Why the sweat?* The breeze was cool. A pleasant temperature in the mid-seventies, and the reception was under the shade from large oaks and the tent itself. Mabry sipped his Coke and shifted his weight from one foot to the other, uneasy.

"Let's raise our glasses to the new couple!" shouted the best man, holding up a glass filled with champagne. "To Laura and Chuck Campbell! To your long and happy marriage. To the both of you from all of us!"

The guests raised their glasses, some sipped champagne. Some gulped what was left in their glasses.

Mabry watched the man in the white jacket move through the tent, stepping around the guests who were standing and finishing their toasts. When the man got to the center of the crowd, he paused. Mabry saw him look to the top of the tent and whisper something, his lips barely moving

A prayer.

The loud chortling of a mockingbird came from a low branch in one of the dogwood trees.

The man unbuttoned the first of three brass buttons on the jacket, beginning with the bottom button. Mabry set his Coke on a table and ran toward the man.

The second button undone.

"Bomb!" Mabry screamed. "Get down!"

The top button undone.

Karim Mohammed opened his jacket, turned to face the charging man and yelled, "Jefferson was an infidel! Remember Derna! Praise be to—"

Jack Mabry dove over the last table and body slammed the man who held his finger on a detonation trigger. It was a split second too late. The blast sent shrapnel in all directions for more than two hundred feet. Nuts. Bolts. Screws. Nails. BB's. All shot out in a powerful force of energy and a shock wave that knocked people from their chairs.

Within five seconds, through the smoke and flames, the pain could be heard. "Oh God, Dear God," a woman cried as she hugged her bleeding son. One victim, a teenage boy, dressed in a tuxedo, was lying on his back looking up at what remained of the tent, the sound of moaning and crying all around, the smell of fire and charred skin. People bleeding. Some limping. Many not moving. The teenager looked up at the oyster white tent ceiling, massive bloodstains splattered all over as if painters had slung red paint out of their brushes. One drop of blood fell from the stretched canvas and splashed against the boy's forehead.

He couldn't feel his legs. "Mom …" he stammered, warm tears trickling down the sides of his bleeding face. "Mom … my legs."

THIRTY-FIVE

Paul looked at the bloodstained note in the president's hand and stood in the Oval Office. "Mr. President, if you don't mind, can you put Eli Dexter's picture back on the screen? Not the one after his death, but the one when he first wore his Delta Force dress blue uniform. That's the way I remember him. That's the way I last saw him at his parents house."

The president nodded and FBI Director McNally used the remote control to bring the picture of Eli Dexter back on the monitor, the young man wearing his Special Forces formal uniform, maroon beret on his head, looking directly at the camera, his eyes bright and filled with hope, a wide smile.

Paul looked at the picture a moment and said, "You're right. There are casualties in combat, but no one deserves to have his body put on display in public, to be used as a whipping post, to be desecrated. I don't know if I can decrypt Jefferson's letter, and if I do, we don't know if what he wrote will have a bearing and an insight on all of this chaos today. Granted, there could be a remote connection, and to this guy Hamad's family history, but that's a long shot."

The president pushed back in his chair. "You could be right. However, considering all the circumstances, parallels, and the fact that this sick shit has an old bone to pick with one of Founding Fathers, what do we have to lose? And, right now, without knowing where to find Hamad, it's an option for us."

Paul said nothing.

Bill nodded. "Five years ago, Paul, you cracked an unbelievably difficult code left behind by Sir Isaac Newton. Maybe you can do it again with what Jefferson left."

"To work on this, to give it the time and concentration I need, I have to make sure my wife and son are safe."

FBI Deputy Director, Ward Rosenberg, looked at a tablet in his hand and said, "They are still visiting your wife's mother in the hospital. Less than an hour ago, your wife's sister and her niece met and entered the room. The women want to transfer your mother-in-law back to her home to have hospice care for her. We'll move our security details to cover whatever it takes."

"I need to be there." Paul looked at the image of Eli on the screen. "And after we get Alicia's mother settled, I need to visit Eli's parents. His dad, Liam, was there for me through the years, especially when my first wife and daughter were murdered. I know what Liam and Jenny are going through, what they're trying to process. I have to reach out to them."

FBI Director McNally said, "We'll have agents stay close to you. It's you the radicals want, Paul. You beat them five years ago. They can't shake that fact and how you did it right under their noses."

The president said, "Maybe, with a little help, you can do it again, Paul. Will you try?"

"My reservation has to do with my family. My first wife and daughter were murdered. I traveled to the ends of the earth to find the killer. To find him, I had to find out why he was hired. And it boiled down to my cryptography skills. To work on a code written by Jefferson, like the one written by Isaac Newton, might put my new family deeper into the crosshairs of these fanatics. I don't want to do anything that will do—"

Director McNally lifted his hand. "Hold on! We have a situation. I have an incoming call."

"So do I," said CIA Director Stephen Parker. The men took their calls, both standing and listening in opposite sides of the office. Director McNally shook his head and pinched the bridge of his nose. "Hold on," he said to the person on the other end of the phone. "Mr.

President, we have a situation at Monticello. Can we transfer the call to you and put it on speaker?"

"Do it," said the president, standing.

McNally made the transfer, the president's phone making a soft buzz. McNally leaned over part of the desk, pressed the speaker button and said "Robert, I have the president here along with the Secretary of State Willow, CIA Director Parker and others. What do you have there?"

"An explosion. A suicide bombing. It wasn't inside Monticello. It was at a wedding reception outdoors. Dozens of guests. There are seven known causalities. Many more severely wounded. One witness said the bomber shouted, "Jefferson was an infidel. Remember Derna! The bomber apparently acted alone. He's disguised himself as a wedding caterer."

Paul stared at the image of Eli Dexter on the screen. He picked up the Jefferson file, looked at the president and said, "I'll do what I can. But right now I need to get back to my family."

THIRTY-SIX

P eople watched in bars across the nation. They watched in homes. The big screen at Times Square. Televisions tuned to news channels. Viewers glued to newsfeeds on their phones, tablets and computer screens. The images of Mount Rushmore—a little girl's face, her parents sobbing. The photo of park ranger Mike Welch before his murder. The funeral held for Eli Dexter at Arlington National Cemetery, flag-draped coffin, the military tribute and farewell. The murder site of Senator Harvey Fairchild, marked with yellow crime scene tape. The dead and wounded at a wedding on the grounds of Monticello. Not since the tragedy of 9/11 did the American people feel as invaded. Violated. Assaulted.

A dozen patrons watched inside a posh bar in Washington, D.C., dark wood and leather booths, subdued light. The long bar was made of polished mahogany, smoky mirrors behind premium liquors bathed in soft light. Two patrons, middle-aged men—lobbyists, nursed glasses of expensive scotch and watched the news on the wide-screen TV behind the bar. The bartender, a pale man with a triple chin, used a white towel to polish a wine glass, looking at the screen, too.

A member of Congress was on camera in front of the U.S. Capitol Building, wind blowing his thinning hair, a dark-haired anchorwoman back at the New York City studio, the two on a split screen. She asked, "Congressman Hawthorn, as a member of the House Intelligence

Committee, what are you hearing about these attacks on the homeland in terms of who may or may not be responsible?"

"Well, a lot of militant groups may not be responsible, although some, no doubt, would like to claim responsibility. To our knowledge, no one group, al-Qaeda, ISIS, Hamas or any other organized terrorist group has specifically claimed responsibility. However, the common red thread here is the reference to the battle of Derna. As some of your viewers may know, this goes back more than two and a quarter centuries to the time Thomas Jefferson was in the White House. With the carnage and deaths at Monticello, we believe there's a direct link to a faction with deep-seated hatred toward one, if not more, of our Founding Fathers. The FBI, along with the CIA, are profiling and narrowing this down to a few known terrorists. And make no mistake, the president has every available member of our intelligence and stealth combat forces working on finding these people."

The news anchor leaned forward. "Who appears to be on the short list? You mentioned known terrorists? Who are they and how do they have so many apparent followers here in America?"

"It's no secret that there are sleeper cells here—some could be your neighbor next door, their kids attending schools, all the while the parents—in particular, the father in the environment of Sharia law, is in contact with radical jihadists or terrorists who plan these abhorrent attacks. They enjoy setting off bombs and killing innocent people, because in their minds, anyone who doesn't follow their strict religious doctrine is the enemy."

"Who, Congressman, do you think is behind this? Do we know?"

"We can't always show the cards we're holding, for obvious reasons. Let me just add that we've narrowed it down, and we're coming for these rogue killers."

"We heard that the killers left a list of demands on the body of Senator Fairchild. We heard that if the demands aren't met before the end of the next crescent moon, a tragedy larger than 9/11 may unfold. Do you know what those demands are and can you share them with us? "

"That information would have to come from the FBI. I know that Director McNally has chosen not to release any details at this time.

I believe we need to respect that decision in order not to compromise the investigation."

"Thank you, Congressman Hawthorn. In other news …"

One of the lobbyists turned to the other and said, "This may wind up being as bad, if not worst than 9/11because it continues every other day. We begin looking over our shoulders. Never sure what's around the damn corner."

The other man nodded, sipped his drink and looked at the TV screen, bluish light reflecting off of his glasses. "That's what they want. They want us to be afraid of our shadows. And they're getting it."

• • •

The president paced his office for a moment as his chief of staff tuned in television news feeds on five monitors in the Oval Office. The Chief of Staff, Charles Sanders, was a tall man, neatly parted graying hair, black-framed glasses, his suit jacket off, shirtsleeves rolled to his elbows. They glanced at the news feeds on all five monitors. The president pointed to the screen on the far left and said, "Turn it up, Charlie. Looks like CBS has some numbers."

"And they don't appear to be better." He turned up the sound. The video was of more that a dozen ambulances arriving at a hospital trauma center in Charlottesville, Virginia.

A reporter, her dark hair touching her shoulders, stood near an *Emergency Entrance* sign and said, "A triage team of doctors is doing what they can to save lives. However, the sheer number of the injuries, many critical, is said to be more than fifty-five people. At least twelve are reported dead. Witnesses say the injured and death toll would probably have been higher had it not been for a man who gave his life trying prevent the explosion. He is identified as Jack Mabry, an Army Special Forces soldier who ran toward the suicide bomber and body slammed him just as the man was setting off the bomb. Much of the deadly shrapnel entered Mabry's body, perhaps saving others. Officials are combing through the catering van left behind by the bomber. His identity and his affiliation with terrorists groups are not known. One thing that we do know, according to witnesses, just before he detonated the bomb he screamed this statement: 'Thomas Jefferson was an infidel, and remember Derna.' We know that the words, remember Derna, were written on a sign and left on the body of another American soldier, Eli Dexter whose funeral was held yesterday at Arlington National Cemetery. And although not officially confirmed or denied, we're told that the same message was left on the body of Senator Fairchild. Live from the University Medical Center in Charlottesville, this is Judy Simon. Now back to you in the studio."

The president turned to his chief of staff and said. "Sometimes reporters, in their zeal to be the first, do more damage than good. How the hell did they get that information about what was left on Harvey's body? Let's call an emergency meeting in one hour."

"Here in the Oval Office or the Situation Room."

"Here's fine." The president sat back down and looked at a bust of Winston Churchill on a table next to his desk. "I always admired Churchill. We know him for his statesmanship, his unwavering tenacity in going toe-to-toe with Hitler, never to surrender England. However, he had some experiences in dealing with Muslim extremists back when Churchill was in his mid-twenties. He was a British Army officer at the time and stationed in Sudan. He used his experiences with them to write a book called *The River War*. He wrote that, and I'm quoting here … 'Most individual Muslims show splendid qualities, just like most people. But the influence of the religion paralyzes the social development of those who strictly follow it. No stronger retrograde force exists in the world."

The president stared at the sculpture of Churchill as if he were waiting for him to speak. And then he said, "He wasn't making those remarks toward the Muslim people, many of whom he considered kind and very warm human beings. He was commenting on a faith that he felt championed destruction to those who were not part of the faith. Today Churchill might be considered an Islamophobic. You know what I'd call him, Charlie?"

"What's that, Mr. President?"

"Correct. Damn, correct. I'd have the same opinion if a Methodist or Baptist became radicalized and used passages from the Bible to kill people because they didn't follow the faith the way the radicals believed it should be followed." He glanced at the bust of Churchill and said, "Winston also believed a fanatic is a guy who can't change his mind and won't change the subject. Let's get the meeting started, we have very little time to waste."

THIRTY-SEVEN

Helen Quincy loved the birds. For more than fifty years, she'd kept two birdfeeders in her backyard filled with seed. She was elevated in her hospice bed; the view from her sunroom overlooked her one-acre yard. Through the sliding glass doors, she watched cardinals, doves, finches, wrens, and mockingbirds flock to the feeders, some waiting their turn on the wooden deck railing. Other birds, such as the blue jays, were squawking and jockeying for the best feeding positions.

Helen's adult children, Alicia and Dianne were in the kitchen with granddaughter Brandi. David was in the family room watching a Spiderman movie. Alicia and Dianne would take turns to periodically check on their mother—to hold her hand, help her with medication, a sip of water, or to adjust her pillows.

I never wanted to be a burden on my children," she thought. Her portable bed was in the same area of the home where her husband passed away five years ago. She looked at the family pictures on the wall—Alicia and Dianne from the time they were little girls through their teen years, to young women graduating from college and beginning their lives. Helen stared a framed photo of Ralph and her. It was their trip to Colonial Williamsburg during Christmas, a decade ago, the holiday lights of a historic village in the background, she and Ralph smiling, his arm around her waist, holding mugs of hot chocolate in front of an outdoor Christmas tree. "I miss you, honey," she whispered, her eyes wet with tears. She touched her rosary beads, closed her eyes and prayed.

The doorbell chimed throughout the house. Helen wanted to answer it, to get up from the hospice bed and sprint across the house to greet the guest or the neighbor. She thought about her new limitations. It was the simple things in life, as they were taken away, that reinforced the fate of mortality and how quickly it slips upon you, like a shadow you never really saw. Sometimes you were aware, a slight glimpse here and there when very ill. But the shield of youth repelled disease like faith dissuades evil. But then age compromises everything, except faith and hope.

Helen looked at her blue pajama sleeve. *Hope*, she thought, is like the little black dress in the recesses of your closet that no longer fits, but somehow it is still part of you—part of your past, maybe your future. It's the same courage that guides you into the department store when you first get sick and your body swells from the drugs and treatments.

You buy clothes and take them home to hang in your closet, hoping your health will be restored and you'll slip into new clothes again. But, as your hair sheds and you lose weight from the cancer fight, you no longer open your closet door. The extra pairs of pajamas are kept in your dresser drawer. And so the clothes you bought hang there in the dark, like the wardrobe to a movie that never gets made, price tags to be removed by your children.

Helen looked outside and watched a male and female cardinal in the birdfeeder. The male seemed to keep an eye out for predators as the female ate. And, after a minute, he hopped down the railing and gobbled a few seeds. They flew, both dipping and climbing in flight as they disappeared into the infinity of blue sky.

• • •

It would be an unscheduled stop. Paul drove from the White House south toward the Washington monument and further in the direction of the Jefferson Memorial when he spotted a street vendor selling bouquets of flowers. He pulled over to the shoulder of the road, near a park, stopped and bought a dozen roses and two long-stemmed roses. The vendor was a middle-aged woman wearing a Cubs baseball cap, Redskins jersey and faded jeans. She had playful eyes that looked like she'd just shared a risqué joke. "You're gonna make some woman happy," she said, wrapping the roses in green floral paper. "A bouquet for the wife and two singles, probably for the daughters, right?"

"For one daughter." Paul paid and glanced at the agents who drove by and pulled off 14th onto a side road. He decided not to tell the agents where he was going. An explanation risked someone volunteering to make a decision, maybe suggesting that he didn't go. He placed the flowers on the front seat and eased back on to 14th, heading southwest.

Paul wasn't in the mood for opinions. After hearing about the massacre at the wedding, he thought of a funeral. Not the many funerals in the coming days that would follow the deaths of the wedding party, but rather the funerals for his first wife, Jennifer and his twelve-year-old daughter, Tiffany.

Paul drove west out of the District, through the Virginia country-side, thick woods on both sides of the road, the agents following him as he headed toward Warrenton. It was fifteen miles north of Warrenton where Jennifer and Tiffany were murdered.

It was a warm summer's night in June and his family had gone to town for ice cream cones. They'd enjoy the ice cream sitting together on a city park bench at sunset overlooking a duck pond with lily pads, mallards and a family of white swans. Tiffany loved to feed the ducks. She carried pieces of bread in a Ziploc bag, a dusting of freckles across her nose, eyes the shade of Kentucky bluegrass. Jennifer wore her brown hair below her shoulders, the golden sunset dancing in her chestnut brown eyes, and a smile that stopped arguments with the power of its honesty.

On the way home, back to their turn-of-the-century farmhouse and stables, the skies darkened and a heavy rain poured. Paul drove slowly through the twisting mountain roads. The thunderstorm made driving treacherous, but there was nowhere to safely pull off the road bordered on one side by the sheer edges of mountains and on the other side by guardrails and a thousand-foot drop.

146

When the rain ended, the fog rolled in, almost as if it climbed the steep cliffs and snaked across the road in a choppy sea of foaming white water. Paul and Jennifer spotted a car off to one side near a scenic overlook area. Tiffany sat buckled in the backseat. The car's emergency flashers were pulsating in shades of red through the fog. Someone, a man in a hooded raincoat, squatted by the left rear wheel, trying to change a flat tire. "Maybe he's elderly," Jennifer said. "Are you going to help him?"

"Yes."

Paul remembered getting out of the car and approaching the man in the dark. He never really saw the man's face. But he did see that the tire wasn't flat, the scene had been a ruse, designed to get Paul to stop because they had his file and knew his altruistic personality. And they knew that he was one of the few people in the world who could engineer a cyber bomb from halfway around the world.

Paul remembered the thin cigar the man smoked, the reddish glow reflecting off one side of a scarred and pockmarked face under the hoodie. He remembered the muzzle flash, the sledgehammer force of a 9mm round hitting him in the center of his chest.

And he could never stop remembering the terrified pleas from his wife and daughter. They begged for their lives as Paul lay on his back in a puddle, cold water seeping through his clothes, blood oozing from the gaping wound near his heart. He heard Tiffany's cries in the night. "Daddy! Daddy!" And then the gunshots. Four. Quick bursts. *Pop-pop-pop-pop.* The eerie silence that followed for a few seconds. The sound of boots on the gravel, the feel of water and road grit falling on his face from the killer's boots as he stepped over Paul and fled. As he laid there, life draining from him, the last thing he saw was a fiery meteor shooting across the universe and becoming engulfed in black.

Paul blew out a breath and looked in the rearview mirror at the agents more than one hundred yards behind him. He slowed and turned off the highway onto a narrow road leading through an old cemetery overlooking the Blue Ridge Mountains. He stopped and got out of the car, holding the two long-stemmed roses.

Paul looked back toward the cemetery entrance. The agents had stopped at a respectable distance away. They stayed in their SUV. He walked around headstones, most very old, worn from time and the seasons. He stepped past a wrought iron enclosure to a grave with the statue of an angel next to it. The angel's wings, spotted dark green by lichen, were extended wide, her right hand reaching down, her granite face weathered, dark stains beneath her eyes as if tears had left tracks in time.

Paul continued walking; the motionless air had the scent of cut grass, pinesap and old stone. He stopped at the graves of his wife and daughter. They were side by side—Jennifer and Tiffany Marcus. Paul set one rose next to Jennifer's headstone and the other rose on Tiffany's grave. He stood there for a long moment in silence, two squirrels played tag on a wide oak.

"Jen … Tiff … I'm so sorry I haven't been to visit you in more than five years. Not a day goes by that I don't think of you and how I shouldn't have pulled off the road that night. I now know it was a trap. After your funerals, I went on to uncover some bad things about some very greedy people. In the end, most of it worked out for the good, but I couldn't come back home. I had to start a new life half-way around the world on a small island north of Sicily."

Paul knelt and used his hands and fingers to rake leaves and twigs off their graves. His eyes watered. He slowly stood, a soft breeze moving through the oak branches, casting shadows across the headstones, the solitary moan of a train's horn in the distance coming up from the valley. "Jen … I have a feeling you know I've remarried. In many ways, Alicia, reminds me of you. You both showed me what love is supposed to mean. Tiffany, you have a little brother. His name is David. You'd like him a lot. Buddy is getting some gray fur around his face, but he's doing well."

Paul's phone buzzed in his pocket. He looked at the ID and answered. Bill Gray asked, "Where are you?"

"If you must know, I'm visiting Jen and Tiffany's graves. Why?"

"I just left a debriefing with the president. A suspicious package was left near the statue of Jefferson at the University of Virginia. The bomb squad is en route and the university is in lockdown. Paul, we don't know how many converts Hamad has here following him. But they're good, like shadow people slipping in and out of memorials at will. You can't begin the decryption of the Jefferson paper fast enough."

THIRTY-EIGHT

P aul drove straight to his mother-in-law's home, the dozen roses on
the seat beside him. The agents following him disappeared as he
entered the neighborhood, apparently having spoken with the other
agents shadowing Alicia and David, their car parked under a massive
Chinese Elm tree across the shady street. Paul pulled in the drive
behind Alicia's car, picked up the roses and knocked on the front door.

Inside the home, Brandi Hirsch approached the door and looked
through the peephole. The man was tall and bared a resemblance to
little David. From the pictures Aunt Alicia had shared, Brandi knew
the man standing on the porch, not only was the uncle she never met,
he was the man who'd saved her life when she was thrown into an
Iranian prison. She opened the door and said, "So, what took you so
long to get here? Are those roses for me?" She grinned. "Welcome
home, Uncle Paul!"

She stepped onto the porch and reached up to embrace him.
"Let's hug inside, off the porch." Paul gently ushered her back inside
the house. He looked at the dark SUV parked across the street, two
armed federal agents watching the neighborhood. As he closed the
door, he turned to her, and she asked, "What the hell's going on?"
Brandi looked up at her uncle, confusion in her eyes.

• • •

The robot crawled at the speed of a toddler learning to walk. It slowly approached the statue of Thomas Jefferson in front of the University of Virginia's Rotunda. There were no students or faculty on the sprawling green lawn or near the shady old magnolia trees around the Rotunda. There was no birdsong, only the wail of sirens in the distance. The robot consisted of six full-traction wheels; a base with motors and gears, a dozen distance sensors, two mechanical arms, three cameras, and it was controlled using wireless Bluetooth technology.

Police Sergeant Luke Griggs sat in a van fifty yards away and used a remote control device with two joysticks to operate the robot. Griggs, weathered face, an Army Pathfinder badge tattooed on his forearm, looked at three screens—thirty-inch monitors in the van and watched the statue of Jefferson grow closer. He specifically had one camera focused on the lone backpack at the base of the monument.

Half a dozen members of the bomb squad, all wearing heavy black vests, stood at safe distances and watched the robot roll steadily across the inlaid brick surrounding the monument. The robot's motors made an eerie whirring sound in the quiet of the day, like a chain saw deep in the woods. A sole mockingbird alighted at the top of a balboa tree and eyed the robot. The bird shrieked a series of calls with the cadence and sound of a car alarm going off. The university was on lockdown, everyone told to stay away from the area of the Rotunda.

The robot was one of the most technologically sophisticated in the world. Griggs, an Army combat veteran who used more primitive robots to find and disarm roadside bombs in Iraq, stared at the screen. The robot was now less than ten feet away. Griggs sat straighter in his chair, licked his dry lips and studied the live images.

The police chief, a burly man with a flushed face, sleeves turned up, stood at the back of the van with members of the squad, three detectives and four FBI agents, the agents wearing the letters FBI on blue T-shirts, their Glocks positioned in waistband holsters. The chief looked at Griggs and said, "You're there. Let's see if you can get it out safely."

Griggs nodded. "If it's not a bomb, no sweat. We'll soon find out." Griggs worked robotic handles with squeezable grips to send the same maneuvers to the robot. He used his left grip to lower one of the robot's arms, opened the mechanical fingers and touched the strap on the backpack. He used the other handle to cause the robot's left arm to reach down and gently tug at the straps. The backpack opened. "It's not strapped," he said.

The chief, agents, and detectives watched the TV monitors in the van. The chief said, "Luke, see if you can turn the flap back … maybe take a look inside with one of the cameras."

The dexterity of the robot, coming from Griggs controlling hands, was remarkable. He used the robot's hands to grasp the edge of the backpack and lift the canvas covering. He operated the other arm to tilt the backpack forward exposing the insides. Then he inched the robot a foot closer and used the camera on its front to peer into the pack. The sun was just right, shining down onto what looked like nickels.

"Would you look at that," said the chief, almost holding his breath. "Must be a couple thousand nickels in there. Luke, maybe you can lift it. Move the damn thing out of there."

"All right." He worked the grip handles, lifting the backpack. A stiff breeze came across the lawn, limbs swaying, the breeze causing the pack to sway in the robot's grip. Griggs used the second robotic arm to secure the left side. The backpack fell to the layer of bricks beneath it, spilling to one side, hundreds of shiny nickels with Jefferson's face on one side, his home—Monticello, on the other side, under the statue like silver confetti at the feet of a returning war hero.

THIRTY-NINE

P aul could see and feel the confusion on the face of his niece. Inside the house, he said, "I'm sorry I escorted you off the front porch so fast. There are federal agents in that black SUV across the street. You are probably safe. But after what happened to you in Iran, I don't want to take any chances."

She feigned a smile. "I'm hoping all of that is way in the past."

"Now I get a real hug." He embraced her again. "Your Aunt Alicia and I still have to keep a low profile."

"I understand. Maybe, after all these years, things have quieted down and the bad guys have blown themselves up or something." She used her right hand to pull a loose strand of dark hair behind her ear. "Why are you looking at me like that?"

"You haven't heard?"

"Heard what? What happened?"

"I'll update you and the family."

Brandi managed a real smile, closed her eyes for a second and said, "Okay. That will do for now. I know that you and Aunt Alicia didn't have a chance to return before your lives drastically changed. So, come meet my mom and grandma. Mom's in the kitchen with Aunt Alicia. David is in the family room watching a superhero movie. Grandma ... I think she's asleep. She's doing better since we got her back in her house. She's around family now. Aunt Alicia has been showing us pictures of your house on the island. Oh my God! What a beautiful place! One day we have to go there. I almost forgot, my boyfriend, Adam, and I got engaged after college. The wedding is set for July—on the Fourth, actually. How cool is that? You have to come, because if it weren't for you, there'd be no wedding."

Paul thought about the wedding at Monticello and the horrific deaths and injuries. "I wouldn't miss it," he said, nodding and following his niece through the home.

• • •

Helen felt fatigue behind her eyes. She was back in Colonial Williamsburg, a fresh snowfall, window shopping with Ralph as they walked down Prince George Street, the smell of burning candles and hot apple cider in the crisp air, the sounds of a hammer striking hot iron coming from the open door of the blacksmith shop, burnt orange sparks flying across the anvil.

"Mom, there's someone I want you to meet," Alicia said, stepping into the sunroom with Paul.

Helen blinked a few times, saw a yellow finch alight in the feeder. She slowly turned her head and looked at the tall, handsome man standing by Alicia. Brandi and Dianne were right behind them. "Mom, this is Paul … my husband."

He approached the bedside and Helen smiled. "I have been so looking forward to meeting you, Paul." She lifted her right hand. "I see your face in David."

He held up the bouquet of roses. "These are for you."

Her eyes opened wide. "They're so lovely. Thank you. I need to put them in a vase with water."

"I'll do that, Mom," Alicia said, taking the roses.

Paul leaned over and kissed Helen on her cheek and said, "And I have been waiting to meet you, too, Mrs. Quincy. I'm sorry it's taken us so long to get here."

She nodded and inhaled as deeply as she could, a shudder in her lungs. "In this family, call me Mom. The important thing is that you're here now. I know you and Alicia went through a tremendous risk to do what you did. It was a deep sacrifice, but in the end, you did the right thing."

Paul stood straighter, still holding her hand. "Thank you. That's good to hear."

Helen looked over at Brandi and said, "If you hadn't done what you did ... I'm not so sure that Brandi would be standing here with us today."

Dianne said, "We weren't told much. The man from the NSA that you and Alicia once worked for, Mr. Gray, told us. When he let us know about the helicopter crash that you were in, never finding your bodies ... he told us how you and Paul had negotiated a deal with the Iranians to release Brandi, and all the while you'd devised some kind of sabotage to their nuclear plant. If he knew you two were still alive, I just wish he'd revealed it to us. We didn't have to know where, but thinking she was dead all these years ... it was heartbreaking."

Brandi smiled. "Mom, it's okay. They had to go into seclusion. It wasn't only the Iranians; it was how Uncle Paul solved the old code left behind by Isaac Newton that helped bring down the Circle of 13 billionaires. Even after I returned to the states, it was all over the news for weeks. We don't know the details behind all of that, but I do know I wouldn't be here if it weren't for Aunt Alicia and Uncle Paul. My cousin is in the family room watching a superhero movie; but for the rest of my life, my aunt and uncle will always be my superheroes." She blinked quickly, eyes wet.

"You're sweet," said Alicia. "Mom, how are you feeling?"

"Better. Being back home is where I belong. There's no stronger medicine than the love of family." She nodded and looked at the picture of her late husband on the wall.

Dianne asked, "Paul, are you hungry? I can make you a roast beef sandwich, and we have some sliced turkey, too. Or would you like a salad?"

"I appreciate that, but I can't stay too much longer."

Alicia looked at the file folder in her husband's hands and asked, "How'd the meeting go with the president? Is that where you got the file folder?"

"Yes. There's been another bombing. This one was on the grounds of Jefferson's Monticello estate at a private event, a wedding.

A suicide bomber, disguised as a caterer, blew up a bomb strapped to his chest. He killed and injured a lot of innocent people."

"Dear God," said Helen, touching her rosary beads.

Dianne pressed her hand to her lips and shook her head. Brandi reached for her phone in her jeans pocket and keyed in a newsfeed. She watched the screen, her eyes narrowing, and said, "This is horrible. It says fourteen people are dead and at least fifty-five wounded, many in critical condition." She looked up at Paul, her face almost pleading. "Aunt Alicia shared a little of what made you leave your island home. It goes back to Iran, doesn't it? Is this … is all of this related in someway to what happened to me in Iran?"

"I'll explain as much as I can when …"

The doorbell chimed. Alicia looked at her sister Dianne.

FORTY

For the first time in Dianne Hirsch's life, she was hesitant to open the front door to the home where she and Alicia grew up. She peeked through the drapes in the living room. She could see Nancy Peters standing on the front porch, holding a covered dish wrapped in aluminum foil. Nancy and her husband, Herb, lived next door. He was retired from a thirty-year career with the IRS. Nancy, early sixties, gray hair cut in a bob just below the ears, glanced over her left shoulder, her narrow face tense. She was the perfect example of neighborhood watch, bordering on the fringes of a busybody.

Dianne opened the door and smiled. "Hi, Mrs. Peters. It's good to see you."

"Hi, Dianne, how's your mom?"

"About the same. She's getting some much-needed rest that she couldn't get at the hospital with all the interruptions. You know, nurses waking Mom up to check her vitals, that sort of thing."

Nancy shook her head in agreement. "It's good to have her back home. I baked an apple pie. One of Helen's favorites."

Dianne reached out for the dish. "Thank you so much. When Mom wakes up, I'll let her know you baked this and brought it over to her."

Nancy made a quick smile. "I see with the cars in the driveway that you have company so I don't want to intrude. But I didn't know if you noticed," she paused motioned to the right with her head. "But

156

there is a black car, looks like a Ford Explorer, and it's been parked across the street for two hours. Herb took Buster on a walk with the leash. He said there are two men in the car. But you can barely see them because the windows are tinted darker than usual."

Dianne looked in the direction where the SUV was parked, maybe fifty yards away. "Thank you for bringing this to our attention. We'll keep an eye on it."

She nodded. "How's Brandi?"

"She's good, thanks. I need to get back inside. Thank you so much for the pie. I remember you always made the very best."

Dianne returned to the sunroom and said, "It was Mrs. Peters. She baked a pie for you, Mom."

"That is so thoughtful. I need to visit with Nancy. Is she in the kitchen?"

"No, Mom, she's back home." Dianne eyed Paul and said, "There's a black SUV across the street. Mrs. Peters says two men are in it, apparently watching this house—"

"They're federal agents," Paul said. "They're just trying to keep us safe."

Dianne cut her eyes to her daughter Brandi. "Paul, is someone chasing you or my sister? Is Brandi in danger again?"

"Their anger isn't focused on Brandi. It's the fact that I put a crimp in their nuclear progress. But that's only part of it. We're not sure of all the factions. But it appears one man is driving much of it. His name is Fajar Hamad."

"Where and who is he?" Brandi asked.

"We don't know where yet for certain. He's Libyan by birth, but he's lived and trained in Iran for years. He, no doubt, was in the mix when I planted the cyber worm in the Iranian nuclear system. But, beyond that, this guy appears to have an intense vendetta against Thomas Jefferson and the form of American government Jefferson helped build. Hamad's ancestor was the leader of Tripoli, the first Islamic extremist to wage war on America. So for Hamad, he's making it personal. And he calls himself the Mahdi, a self-proclaimed redeemer of the Islamic faith. What we have is someone who's escalating his holy jihadist war to levels not seen since 9/11. The difference is that he's doing it with a thousand cuts."

Alicia said, "It's apparent that this madman has followers in this country to help him."

"Paul," said Brandi, crossing her arms. "Are we safe?"

"You, most likely, are way off their radar. If they haven't tried to find you in five years, you're probably of no value to them. But it certainly doesn't hurt for you both to be cautious and aware of your surroundings. I'm hoping the safe house Alicia, David and I are in will give our agents time to find and stop this madman."

David walked into the room, glanced at the adults gathered close to his grandmother's bed. He was quiet, peeking up at his grandmother. She smiled at him and he grinned, dimples popping.

"David, are you hungry?" Alicia asked.

"Do we have peanut butter and grape jelly?"

"I bet your grandmother has that. Aunt Dianne and I ate a lot of P-B and J sandwiches when we were growing up, and it was yummy!" she said, reaching out and tickling him.

Dianne said, "I did see some peanut butter in the cupboard and there's jelly in the fridge. Let's go in the kitchen, and I'll make you a sandwich."

"Yippee!" He followed his aunt out of the room.

"I'll help, too," said Brandi, leaving.

Alicia looked at her mother who had dozed off again. She turned to her husband and motioned for him to join her in a corner of the sunroom. "Is Hamad's picture in the folder?" she asked quietly, her face worried.

"No, it's actually a code, maybe a prediction, left behind by Thomas Jefferson. He dealt with the first group of radical jihadists during his term. We're hoping there's something in Jefferson's notes we can use today—maybe an insight he found in war and negotiations with them."

Alicia folded her arms. "So, is the president asking you to try to decipher the code Jefferson wrote?"

"Yes."

Alicia tried to mask the fear in her eyes. "The first time you broke Isaac Newton's code. Although much good came of it, we were targets, and we were chased across Europe. If you break Jefferson's code … what will that mean? Will more of these radical assassins crawl out of their holes and forever threaten our family?"

"We have no idea what Jefferson left behind. But if there's a chance it could help us put an end to Hamad's terror, and if it can let our family have some kind of normal life, it's worth me taking a look at it."

"Do you think you can break the code?" she asked.

"I don't know. It will take some time. It's written in two languages and includes numbers in the mix. Jefferson didn't want it falling into the hands of the wrong people."

"Paul, the first time it was different. You figured out a complex code from Newton that helped expose the Circle of 13 and severely interfere with the Iranian nuclear program. We got Brandi out of that hellhole. But we nearly lost our lives to a Russian hit man, and by the grace of God we survived the helicopter crash into the sea. Now, we have a child."

"That's why I have to try to do something."

She glanced back at her mother. "We're here to be with Mom and family for as long as we can. But soon, we'll have to relocate somewhere else. I know that. Someplace where we're relatively safe again. I have no illusions. We can never go back to Panarea, and we can't live here. But the world is large, and we can find a new home somewhere. I'm just afraid for us, Paul, especially David—working on this code could put you on the radar longer, awaking more people to the fact we're alive and angering others. This could increase the targets, and not just for you—for the three of us."

Paul looked at the folder in his hand. "What if they never stop? Do you want to spend the rest of your life looking over your shoulder, afraid to live? There may be something in here that can put an end to this. Some way to defeat them."

"If it's not this crazy man, Hamad, will it be someone else? Are you waking sleeping giants?" She hugged her arms. "We never were field agents. We analyzed intelligence. In your case, it was code breaking. Only by a twist of fate did we get thrust into this and became hunted by people who are well organized, wealthy, and international serial killers."

"It wasn't just fate. We'd made the decision to get Brandi out of that prison. We knew there were extreme risks and danger involved."

"Yes, but we didn't know it would never end. It has to end!"

"It will." He lifted the file folder.

"May I see it? Can I see what Thomas Jefferson left behind that has now been handed off to my husband centuries later?"

Paul opened the folder to the one page of coding written by Jefferson. Alicia stared at it, her eyes sweeping from side to side, top to bottom. After a few seconds, she said, "Thomas Jefferson, and the other Founding Fathers, helped us give birth to a nation like none other in the history of the world. The Declaration of Independence, cutting ties with tyranny and oppression. I wonder what Jefferson wrote here? And more than anything, I wonder if, from Jefferson's grave, he can make a difference in today's world like he did in a world two centuries ago?"

"Maybe I can find out. I need to get back to the safe house. But before I do that, I want to see Eli Dexter's parents, Liam and Penny. Can you go with me? They live about a half-hour away from here."

Alicia looked across the room at her mother who was waking up again. "I need to spend a little more time with Mom, Dianne and Brandi. Mom's been in and out of sleep a lot ... I want to be here as much as I can when she's awake. Please give Liam and Penny my deepest condolences. Maybe, when things get better, I can actually meet them. I've heard you talk about Liam so often."

"Call me. Let me know when you and David leave and when you arrive at the safe house. The agents will be there to follow you. Don't stop anywhere on the way. There is staff to do our grocery shopping and get anything else we need." He turned to exit.

"Paul ..."

"Yes?"

"Kiss me before you leave. From now on, let's always kiss before we leave and when we arrive, okay?"

"Okay." He leaned down and softly kissed his wife on her lips.

"Be careful going to the Dexter's house. I have a feeling that this time might prove to be as frightening as the first time." Alicia made an effort to smile. "That horrible tragedy that just happened at Monticello … I remember touring there as a teenage girl. On one wall, Jefferson had paintings of the three men he called the Trinity of the Greatest Thinkers the world had ever produced. They were John Locke, Francis Bacon and Isaac Newton. You broke Newton's last known code. I have a feeling you'll do the same with whatever it is that Thomas Jefferson left behind."

FORTY-ONE

P aul wanted to call, but he thought it safer not to do so. He drove
from memory, down twisting roads through the Washington DC
suburbs of Wesley Heights and Palisades. Soon he was in the Spring
Valley area, an upscale neighborhood on the far western edge of the
District filled with old growth oaks and history. He glanced in his
rearview mirror, the SUV with federal agents following at a respectable
distance. Far enough away to look innocuous, but close enough to turn
on an arsenal of firepower if need be.

His phone buzzed. Bill Gray on the line. Paul answered, and Bill
said, "Have you seen the news?"

"No. And I'm almost afraid to ask … what's the latest?"

"The backpack left at the foot of the Jefferson statue at the University
of Virginia wasn't a bomb."

"What was it?"

"A cruel hoax. And it's one with ties back to Senator Fairchild's
murder. As you know, Fairchild's body was found with two nickels
placed over the eyes. The nickel on the left was heads or Jefferson's
likeness on the coin. The nickel over the right eye was tails, if you
will … the rendering of Monticello."

"What does that have to do with the backpack?"

"The bomb squad found more than two-thousand nickels in the
backpack. A message on a typed note read … *Jefferson stands on top
of a bell that doesn't ring for liberty and justice for all. In America, the*

162

bell tolls for the wicked, arrogant and wealthy. For the rest, it is silent.'
I'm too old now, but in my younger day, I would have paid to go bare
knuckles with this guy, Hamad."

"What do you think the message means?"

"Probably exactly what it said. I think the best way to deal with
these militants is to take everything they say and do at face value.
There is no reading into their minds because their brains are seething
with fanatical hate. It is what it is. Nothing more, nothing less."

Paul slowed to a stop in front of a large home that was set more
than two hundred feet off the road. "Bill, I have to go."

"I need to meet with you. I have something that might help you
with the decryption."

"I'll call you back." Paul disconnected and turned into the driveway. The house was two stories, Tudor style, beige, black shutters and
a slate tile roof. Two fireplaces. The driveway was circular, chestnut
oaks, holy and crape myrtle in the yard and around the house. The
garage was a side-entry.

He parked in the drive, got out, carried the Jefferson file in one
hand, nodded at the agents in the distance, walked across the old brick
drive to the front door and knocked. Dark green ivy grew on one side
of a fieldstone wall, the fragrance of crape myrtle and redbud trees in
the air.

He looked over his shoulder. The agents parked in the circle, but
not close to the home. He saw one speaking on his phone. Their
windows rolled up, heavy tree shadows falling across the SUV. A
sprinkler kicked on and made a ratcheting sound to the left of the
house. Paul heard someone unlocking the door. He took a deep breath
and released it. *How do you tell your best friend how damned sorry
you are for his loss? You don't. You just show up as soon as you can
and be there for him.*

• • •

Alicia, Dianne and Brandi stood in the kitchen and watched a live
newscast on a small TV on the counter. Alicia stepped to the door with
a view of the sunroom and her mom sleeping. David had fallen asleep

on the couch watching a movie. Brandi used the remote to turn up the sound.

A female reporter, a breeze tossing her blonde hair, stood in front of the University of Virginia's Rotunda hall and said, "The entire area behind me was completely cleared of students and faculty as members of the Albemarle County bomb squad and the FBI used a remote-controlled robot to investigate a suspicious backpack left next to the statue of Thomas Jefferson in front of the Rotunda." She glanced down at a TV monitor near her and said, "This video was recorded by the bomb squad cameras. As you can see, it shows the backpack falling over and spilling hundreds of nickels on the bricks around the statue. The FBI said there was a note in the backpack that read the following: *'Jefferson stands on top of a bell that doesn't ring for liberty and justice for all. In America, the bell tolls for the wicked, arrogant and wealthy. For the rest, it is silent.'* FBI Deputy Director Ward Rosenberg said there is no definitive evidence that this latest incident involving the nation's third president is directly connected to the death of Senator Harvey Fairchild, the explosion on Mount Rushmore and the suicide bombing at the wedding on the grounds of Jefferson's home, Monticello. However, Rosenberg and others within the Department of Justice say they're assuming that it is … primarily because police say that Senator Fairchild's body was found with two Jefferson nickels covering his eyes. Jane Blackmore reporting live from Charlottesville, Virginia … now back to you in the studio."

Dianne lowered the sound from the TV and said, "This is insane. What do these people want? Why can't we stop them?"

Alicia said, "Because they're everywhere, and the most radical of the extremists … even though they may be a small percent of one-point-seven billion Muslims, can cover a large swath of the planet with people and their ideology."

Brandi folded her arms and said, "After what I experienced in their prison, after what I saw in Iran … their top people spewing hate to the West, you can't collaborate with that mindset. It made me so appreciative of the freedoms we have here. Individual human value means nothing to them … it becomes a single question to the people in charge: What can you do for the state?

• • •

The door opened and Liam Dexter stood there in jeans and a black T-shirt, unshaven, face hollow. He was in his late-forties, powerful biceps and forearms. His eyes slightly red, puffy. He looked at Paul and started a slow grin. "I'll be damned. A ghost at my front door. For the last five years, I thought you were dead."

"Probably should have been, but I got lucky."

Liam stepped out onto the porch in his bare feet. He and Paul hugged. Paul said, "There are no words except to tell you how sorry I am for you and Penny."

Liam straightened, looked at the black SUV in his driveway. "I'm damn glad you're here, but I can tell you have a federal escort. That's gotta mean you're in a helluva mess. What's going on?"

FORTY-TWO

Liam led Paul through the interior of the home, across polished granite floors, and past wide fireplaces. Pictures of Eli and his sister Lisa seemed to cover the hallways, the kids growing up, and many images of Eli in his military uniforms. Liam escorted Paul into a recreation room with a wide screen TV on one wall, a pool table across the room, lots of overstuffed chairs and a sectional sofa. A bar was to the far left. There was a picture of Liam when he played football for the University of Alabama.

Liam said, "It's been the toughest two weeks of our lives. Penny is beyond distraught. I've never seen her like this. Eli's death has shaken her soul to its core. We'll never be the same. I'm afraid for Penny." He paused and exhaled deeply. "Lisa's nineteen now. She's home from Arizona State. She may have to write off this semester. We're all a damn mess. You showing up like this, outta the blue, it'll bring some much needed warmth to the coldest, darkest part of our lives."

"I wish I could have made the funeral. I was in transit and ran into a few obstacles. Caused some delays."

"I'm just glad you're here now. At the funeral, I was numb. Penny had to be slightly sedated to sit through it. Who's your escort in the driveway? I assume it's federal. Just not sure what branch."

"FBI. They're trying to make sure that, when I drive from point A to point B, I get there safely. Not so much the driving, it's just the obstacles I mentioned."

"All that stuff you did five years ago. Bringing down the world's most powerful group of criminals, and I'm including covert world. I never heard of the Circle of 13. Later, I heard it was you who encrypted a cyber bomb into Iran's nuke operation. Man, they had news video of the chopper wreckage off the coast of Sicily. They found the pilot's body on the beach. He'd been shot, like he was dumped from the chopper. And then the bird was three miles offshore in sixty feet of water. I thought you and the woman … what was her name?"

"Alicia."

"Yeah, I thought you two were shark bait, assuming you survived the crash and somehow climbed out before it sank."

"We got lucky. And we got married. I have a child … a son. His name is David."

Liam's eyes watered. "That's the best ending I could have imagined to what I thought was one of the most tragic stories I'd ever heard. We have some catching up to do."

Paul looked at the family pictures against a dark cherry wood wall, the military service medals, ribbons, insignias and patches Eli and Liam had both earned. They were displayed in two different shadow boxes. It was a photographic timeline of Eli following his father's footsteps—the training at Fort Benning and Fort Bragg. Deployment in Afghanistan and Iraq for Liam. Iraq and Libya for Eli.

Paul was amazed at the resemblance between father and son. He thought about David, wondered what he was doing at the moment. Paul looked at one of the medals Liam had won for marksmanship, the Expert Medal, along with a silver star and two bronze stars. He pointed and said, "What these medals don't say is just how accurate you were as a sniper. To eliminate a hostile at a mile takes enormous skill."

Liam shook his head. "Sometimes you get lucky. No wind and the earth stops turning for the two seconds from trigger to impact."

"You were one of the best of the best, Liam. You're too modest."

"How about you, huh? You've broken more codes—complex codes, than anyone in U.S. history. But you never mention it. You brought down one of the most ruthless billionaire's clubs ever known. And I'm bettin' you won't talk about that either."

Paul smiled. "That's because it's classified." He looked at photos, staring at one with Eli dressed in an Army combat uniform with the camouflage pattern, standing next to a tank. "Eli had a lot of your skills. How was he caught off guard and killed?"

"Oh my God … Paul Marcus. Tell me it's you." The woman's voice sounded strained.

Paul turned and Penny Dexter stood at the entrance to the room. Her dark hair pulled back, oval face puffy from tears and fatigue. She wore a long sleeve denim shirt and pressed jeans. She bit her lip, eyes tearing, and said, "I had no hope … thought we'd never see you alive again. And then you come out of nowhere. If you're not a ghost … please give me a hug and tell me where you've been for the last five years."

FORTY-THREE

Alicia didn't want to say goodbye to her mother. She wanted to make up for years of absence in one day. She wanted to create warm memories for David with his grandmother—to experience nature in the state parks, to visit the National Zoo, to play board games and to laugh as only a family can laugh. But she knew that time was the ultimate thief. *And Mom's time was so precious*, she thought, kissing her mother on her forehead as she slept.

Alicia wanted to go grocery shopping and make a homemade dinner, her mom's meatloaf, mashed potatoes and green beans. Maybe pick up a nice bottle of wine to enjoy with her sister and niece. But she and David couldn't stay there, not with the threat of danger lurking over their shoulder. It wouldn't be safe for her mother, Dianne or Brandi.

Alicia said goodbye to Brandi, got David and his toys and walked to the front door with her sister, Dianne. Alicia fished for the car keys in her purse. She glanced at the black SUV across the street, the agents faces obscured in deep purple shade from the laurel trees.

Dianne said, "I so wish this wasn't happening to you, my little sister. You have federal agents as bodyguards everywhere you and Paul go. They'll find these sick people. You have some of the best protection tax money can buy." She grinned. "And I have faith in your husband. Paul did the impossible for my daughter and her fiancé, Adam. He'll do it for you. I feel it in my heart."

"I pray that you're right. But this time it feels much different. Even more frightening, if that's possible. Maybe it's because I'm a mom. And this time our mother is dying and needs us … both of us."

"Why didn't you tell me you were alive? You didn't have to tell me where or any of the circumstances, but you could have told me. I would have held on to hope for as long as it took."

"I couldn't tell you, Dianne. I didn't want to put you in danger."

"But Mom knew."

"In her heart she knew, but that was all. Before I left for overseas for what turned out to be a great and horrific journey, I told Mom if she every received the gold cross she gave me when I was fifteen, if it ever arrived, she would know that I was alive and would return, if I could. I don't regret doing that … especially as I look at her dying."

Dianna said nothing, looked at the SUV a moment, the scent of charcoal and steaks cooking in a neighbor's yard.

Alicia touched the cross on her neck, which her mother had returned, insisting she put it on again for protection. Lifting it toward her sister, Alicia said, "Dianne, if I have to disappear again, I will do my best to send this cross to you so you will know we're okay. I'd better be leaving. I'll get over here as often as I can."

Dianne nodded and gave her younger sister a hug. Alicia's eyes watered. She inhaled deeply and opened the car door for David. He turned and said, "Bye, Aunt Dianne."

"Bye, David. You take care of your mother."

"Okay."

Alicia buckled her son in the car, started the engine, and drove slowly out of the driveway. She looked in her rearview mirror, the black SUV pulled away from the curb. Alicia quickly wiped tears from her cheeks, trying not to let David see her crying.

• • •

Penny Dexter felt small in Paul's arms. They hugged and she started to speak but paused, words seemed trapped in her throat. She stepped back and said, "I hope I didn't get your shoulder wet. I just can't seem to stop crying. A mother isn't supposed to bury her only son ... or daughter, for that matter." She blew out a breath. "How are you, Paul?"

"I'm okay. Better now that I could finally get over here to see you both. I'm so sorry for what happened. There are no suitable words to convey how sorry I feel for you and what they did to Eli. I wish I could have been at the funeral."

Penny used a tissue to wipe the base of both eyes. "Even if you'd been there, I may not have been fully aware. It was so ... so surreal in a nightmarish kind of way. The funeral was a tribute to our son with friends and family, but the scenes, the funeral home, church, and cemetery ... it was as if we were cast in a horror movie with no way out. You have to stay through it, in each painful scene, because it's deeply a part of you. And the hardest of all was watching them lower my son into a grave. I'm sorry, Paul. Can I get you something to eat or drink? We have enough food to feed the troops." She managed a smile.

"No thanks. I'm fine."

"I want to hear what happened to you. But the first thing I noticed is that gold band on your finger. Who's the lucky lady?"

"Her name's Alicia. We married five years ago."

Liam said, "And they have a son."

Penny smiled wide, her eyes suddenly joyful for a moment. "How old is he? What's his name?"

"He's four, and his name is David."

"Where is he? I'd love to see him."

"He's with his mother. We're staying in a safe house."

Penny stared at Paul for a moment, not sure how to process what she just heard.

FORTY-FOUR

Paul, Liam and Penny took seats around a black walnut table in the large kitchen. Behind them in the middle area sat a cooking island with four barstools, copper pots and pans hanging from an old wagon wheel that had been stained and polished. The wheel was suspended above the island by three wrought iron chains secured to the high ceiling. Penny poured herself a glass of red wine, Liam sipped scotch, and Paul chose a bottle of water. He told them of the events leading up to his arrival.

When he finished, Penny said, "I feel so bad for you and your family. The government told the world you'd died. But somehow you wound up or washed up on the shore of an island and stayed there in an odd sort of self-imposed witness protection program for all these years. And now, these recent killings, the murder of Senator Fairchild, the tragedy at Mount Rushmore, the suicide bomber at the wedding … and the death of Eli. You're convinced it's all related, right?"

"If it's not, then someone is going to a deadly and elaborate scheme to make it appear that way. If that's the case, then somebody is trying to point a finger at a phantom when the real perpetrator is penetrating us further each day."

Liam said, "You mean the possibility of someone or some group creating a smokescreen, pointing to this guy Hamad, all the while the real culprits are digging tunnels and coming our way."

"The hard evidence is that Hamad does exist. Our Intel has certified his background with the Russians, Syrians, and most importantly Iran. Iran wants to create chaos in the West, especially in the US. We know Hamad was in Benghazi, and we know he was involved with the American deaths that happened there. He was part of the Red Sector, a guise used by him and his death squad to gain closer access to the CIA's annex and the ambassador's compound. And, on one charred wall, there were the words, *Remember Derna*. The same message was left on Eli's body and Senator Fairchild's, and it was the last thing the suicide bomber yelled before blowing himself up at Monticello. When you combine that with them aiming a bomb-laden drone at Jefferson's face on Mount Rushmore … it's an evidence trail of the same sad and sick agenda."

Penny sipped her wine, looked at a picture of Eli in dress blues on the kitchen counter, her thoughts cloistered, maternal, sorrow dripping from her pores. She cut her eyes over to Paul and asked, "But why Eli? Why did they target him? Liam and I always hoped Eli's tours of duty would be safe. Hoped and prayed he'd always return to us safely. In the back of our minds, we knew that something could happen over there. Just like when Liam was in the service. But what we never anticipated, in our worst nightmares, was what those bastards did to our son's body. No one deserves to be strung up and stoned, to be spit on, to have rocks thrown at our son's dead body." She choked, tears trickling from her swollen eyes. "I'm sorry." She pulled a tissue out of a box and tried to wipe the tears away.

Liam sipped his scotch, his eyes red and tired. "Penny has a good point. We see the common denominator in what you've told us, the reference to the battle of Derna. But out of dozens and dozens of special ops forces in Libya hunting for the Benghazi criminals, why'd they choose our son? Was it simply a fluke, Eli in the wrong place at the wrong time, or something else?"

"Maybe it was me," Paul said in a quieter tone, placing his palms on the wooden table.

"You?" Penny's eyes were wide, skeptical. "What do you mean, Paul?"

"Maybe somehow, Hamad and his followers found out that Eli knew me—that I was his godfather. If so, and if they can make an example out of him, and I hear about it, his death could cause me to come out of hiding. That would expose me and my family to them, and give them a moving target to catch and kill."

Liam said, "That explains the federal agents tagging along."

Paul nodded. "Also, it explains blowing a plane out of the sky, a plane that my family and I were supposed to have boarded."

Penny touched one hand over her heart. "Oh, dear God. Was that disaster meant for your family?"

"Yes. Eli's death came right at the time our identities had been exposed on the Island of Panarea. We decided to leave, to stay off the radar as much as possible, but what we didn't know was that someone had seen us and probably recognized me. That information was funneled to people who want me killed. And this was close to the time that Eli was shot, kidnapped, and killed."

Liam leaned back. "Do you think it was coincidental?"

"I would like to believe it wasn't related. But, no, I think it was deliberate." Paul set the file folder down on the table.

"What's that?" Penny asked.

He opened the folder and pointed to a copy of the encrypted letter. "It's something that Thomas Jefferson wrote. The recipients included were Robert Livingston, America's Minister to France at the time, and three men directly conducting the battle with the Barbary States, specifically Derna and Tripoli. With the Louisiana Purchase, Napoleon rattling Europe, and America trying to get its footing, the last thing Jefferson wanted was for sensitive information to fall into the wrong hands. Some of his encryption had to do with scrambling letters and reassembling them if you had a code—often with a small cipher wheel he invented. Or they had prearranged codes, sort of like email passwords today."

Penny and Liam stared at the scrambled words for a few seconds. Then both looked up at Paul who said, "This encryption, what you see in front of you, is much more difficult. And, according to an accompanying letter written in plain text, the encryption had to do with battling Islamic jihad terror, something Jefferson and the nation experienced from the North African states of Morocco, Tunis, Algiers and what is today … Libya."

Penny reached for her husband's hand on the top of the table. She held his hand, her knuckles white. "Paul, Eli's death in Libya … in Derna … is all of this pointing to something Thomas Jefferson dealt with when he was president?"

"I don't know. But yes, in terms of dealing with the Muslim leaders of the Barbary nations. Whether it will help us today remains to be seen."

Liam looked at the Jefferson papers and crossed his arms. "It's been said that those who fail to learn from history are doomed to repeat it. Why are you showing this to us now?"

"Because I want to break the encryption … or to at least try. Maybe it'll help, maybe bring some sort of closure."

Penny closed her eyes for a few seconds, inhaled deeply. "Paul, do whatever you can to bring these killers to justice. What they did to our son was far beyond some holy war. It was innately evil … evil deeds ordered and done by wicked men who attacked us when Jefferson was president and they continue to do it today." She stood and lifted the framed picture of Eli off the kitchen counter, handing it to Paul. "Please, take this. You were his godfather; and more than that, you helped set an example of excellence for our son. Maybe you can find a way to stop them. For Eli and the thousands who have died as innocent victims through the tirade of evil people who despise anyone who doesn't embrace their religion or culture. Find them, Paul, please."

"I'll do the best I can."

FORTY-FIVE

Paul drove back in the direction of the safe house, the SUV with two federal agents following him in a distance. He replayed his conversation with Penny and Liam, thought about the conversations in the Oval Office—recalled what each member of the president's team had said as the information about the horrific events unfolded—the news from Monticello through intel updates and across the television screens. He remembered the sound of stress in the voices of those in the Oval Office, the look of surprise and horror in their faces.

All but two faces—presidential advisor Sami Botros and Ward Rosenberg, Deputy Director of the FBI.

Paul thought about some of the conversations between Rosenberg and Botros. The flat look in Botros' eyes after Rosenberg used the term Muslim monsters and said, *'These killers can't stalk a senior member of the US Senate, and spill his blood like they did with our sailors to start the Barbary War.'*

Paul glanced in his review mirror and called Alicia. When she answered, he asked, "Where are you and David?"

"Home ... or rather Fort Knox. But I don't think we'll find gold bullion or any part of the nation's treasury in the basement. Maybe a few skeletons down there, considering the history of this place." Alicia smiled, standing in the kitchen and opening bottled water, she watched David play with Buddy in the family room. "Paul, in case you didn't recognize that, I'm trying for some semblance of humor among the horror. Maybe that sounds irreverent, but at the moment—with my dying mother, armed agents in our driveway, a panic button ten feet away, an eye in the sky called a satellite camera watching the grounds, I'm in a coping mode. Where are you?"

"I'll be back there in an hour."

She glanced down at her fingernails, looked at the chipped polish and remembered the times, as a child, Mom would take her and Dianne to get their nails done together. They'd always had fun. Girl talk. Happy talk and happier times. "I guess you don't want to tell me where you're going," Alicia said a bit sarcastically. She sat at one of the barstools in the kitchen. "I'm sorry, Paul. None of this is your fault." She looked out into the backyard. "We can't blame Thomas Jefferson. He didn't start it … I love you."

"I love you, too. We'll talk when I get home." He heard his wife disconnect the phone. He glanced in the rearview mirror, the agents so far back Paul could barely spot their SUV. He dialed Bill Gray's number. After a half-dozen rings, Bill answered and Paul said, "You mentioned that you had many of the known encrypted letters that Jefferson and his recipients—guys like Robert Livingston and John Adams and even Lewis and Clark, shared with Jefferson."

"Yes. I have them in a separate file folder. Looks to be about fifty letters … many still in their encrypted forms and many with the encryption worked out in plain text. All the encryption looks like it was decrypted with the cipher wheel. Fairly basic stuff, using letter sequencing."

"I'd like to examine those, more so for the rhythm of the language, the words they used at the time … the commonalities in wordage, syntax, and inflections those men shared. How quickly can you get the letters to me?"

"I can drop them off at the house."

"I'm not there. I'm near the Arlington Bridge, coming down the Washington Parkway."

"I'm on New York Avenue. Why don't you take the exit for the bridge? The Jefferson Memorial is about the halfway point between us. We can meet there."

"After what happened at Mount Rushmore and Monticello, isn't it potentially dangerous to meet there?"

"That goes for almost any public place in the District. We're both five minutes away. Right now, with the high alert we're under, the very visible and invisible presence of police around the Memorial, it's one of the safest places in the District to meet. Besides, there's something at that location I want to show you. It's something that might help you with your research."

"What is it?"

"Rather than tell you, I'll show you. See you in five minutes."

Paul put on his turn signal and merged onto the Arlington Bridge. He looked in his mirror, a splinter of sunlight penetrating the windshield of the SUV. He could see the agent on the passenger side speaking into his phone. He had a good idea of the thrust of the conversation. *Paul Marcus … the only American listed on the terrorist's demands, driving toward the Jefferson Memorial. Send in reinforcements.*

Paul looked to his right as he drove down Ohio Street, the Potomac River smooth and glimmering in the sunlight. He glanced to his left and could see the waters of the Tidal Basin, the blue sky reflecting off the still, dark water. There was another reflection from the surface. This one was moving. Paul looked up in the sky and watched a Blackhawk helicopter flying a half circle over the Potomac and the 14th Street Bridge.

He drove closer to the Jefferson Memorial across the basin, the monument imposing and in some way autonomous across the tranquil waters.

FORTY-SIX

Paul parked and walked from West Basin Street to the Jefferson Memorial, the whirr of the Blackhawk helicopter in the distance, school children on field trips running toward the rotunda with the columns. Half a dozen street vendors under large red, yellow, and green umbrellas sold food, the smell of pizza, hotdogs and cherry blossoms clinging to the warm air. Tourists snapped pictures and took selfies with the Jefferson Memorial in the background. One man fished in the Tidal Basin. Paul looked over his shoulder, the two federal agents not far behind him.

He noticed more District police officers than he'd ever seen at a national monument in Washington. He spotted men and women in plainclothes who roamed the area not looking at the Jefferson Memorial, but rather scrutinizing the crowds. There was a larger presence of National Park Police as well. The faces cordial but masked in a somber manner that bordered on edginess.

"Is Thomas Jefferson buried here?" a freckle-faced, seventh grade girl asked one of her teachers as they stood in front of the Memorial.

"No," said the woman in a ponytail. "His gravesite is back in his home state of Virginia. The Jefferson Memorial, like those for Presidents Lincoln and Washington, is here to remind us of the roles the Founding Fathers played when they helped create a government for our country, which was just starting out more than two hundred years ago."

Paul walked around a small group of students and climbed the steps leading up to the monument, the nineteen-foot tall bronze of Jefferson standing in silhouette. Paul glanced up at the five members of the Declaration of Independence drafting committee sculpted at the apex of the Memorial. He entered the rotunda, surveying the throng of tourists and middle school students. He looked beyond the six uniformed police officers, to Bill Gray. Bill stood next to the bronze statue of Jefferson, reading the inscribed words on the walls. He held a large manila envelope in one hand under his arm.

Paul approached and said, "You got here before me. So I'm guessing you were a lot closer."

"Maybe a tad. Also, I know the best parking spots. After things settle down, you and Alicia should bring David here. He's not too young to be exposed to greatness."

"I'd like that."

Bill gestured toward the statue. "When Kennedy was in the White House, he had a state dinner with a dozen of some of the world's best scientists, and he told them that the last time there was that much intellect in the room was when Jefferson dined alone."

"I believe Jefferson, the inventor, architect, cryptographer and philosopher was more of a strategist than a politician."

"No doubt. Of all our presidents, living and dead, more people quote Jefferson and the Jeffersonian ideals. This includes the gamut from conservatives, liberals, libertarians, even a few so-called communists who selectively try to cherry pick segments of Jefferson's ideology. But they soon find communism and human rights don't blend well." Bill grinned.

"That is probably one of the best examples of an oxymoron."

Bill nodded, studied one wall and read part of the engraving. "Jefferson wrote, '*I have sworn upon the altar of God my eternal hostility against every form of tyranny over the minds of men.*' I believe, Paul, at least I want to believe, that when we take this career path, the often-invisible path of covert intelligence gathering, we follow what Jefferson wrote. I've come out of retirement, and I know I pulled you into this, again, because of your cryptography skills—you're the best the agency has ever had. But, the real question is this: With having a family now, can you pursue down that path ... capable of seeing it through? Because I know you'll walk into the face of tyranny and horror, and I don't have to crack a code to see the inevitable?"

"I have no choice."

"Yes, you do. But considering the kind of man that you are ... I suppose you don't. No more than men like Jefferson, declaring this nation's independence from those who sought domination of mind, spirit and property. Today, those who challenge us, whether they are an autocratic dictatorship, such as Russia, China, or from those who believe their religious doctrines give them a holy right to harm people who choose not to follow them, it's all part of the compost that grew this nation. Our independence, Constitution, our way of life, took root in the soil of harsh opposition so we could germinate from the decay of tyranny and grow a nation of free thinkers and free enterprise cast in the mold of everything you see inscribed on these walls. Our rights and freedoms, the pillars of our Constitution, are unequalled in the world and unique to the foundation of this nation—America, and its citizens."

Bill stepped away from the bronze statue to the east wall. He watched school children reading the words, listened to their teachers help explain the meaning of what the kids read aloud. Then he turned to Paul. "After thirty-five years of intelligence work, the human and personal sacrifices that go with it, when I see the promise of our Constitution in the faces of young Americans, I feel a certain restorative tonic in my old bones."

Paul nodded. "You once told me you can doubt some of the people you work with, question their motives, but never to take for granted the value of the republic and why that alone is worth fighting for."

Bill smiled. "Sometimes I wondered if you listened to me. Now I know you did, at least occasionally."

Paul laughed. "At least a little bit more than I'm willing to admit. However, I never doubted your dedication. But, Bill, I'm also stepping back in with you because I believe I might be able to make it a safer place for all these kids," Paul said, sweeping his arm toward those exploring the memorial grounds, "and for my family, too."

• • •

The man caught the attention of an FBI agent fishing in the waters of the Tidal Basin. The agent, late thirties, stocky, receding hairline, made a short cast into the water, reeling the plastic worm in slowly. He wore dark glasses and looked up from the Tidal Basin to visitors strolling about the Jefferson Memorial. He watched tourists with maps and ice cream cones explore the area, some on bikes, most walking. Dozens of people sat on the marble steps in front of the monument.

One man appeared alone.

He didn't walk on any of the concrete paths interlacing around the Memorial and about the Tidal Basin. He came into view from a strand of cherry trees and tall elms on the east edge of the property. He walked with an uneasy gait, like a thoroughbred horse, anxious, before the crack of the starter's pistol.

But it was the unusual paring of clothing that first caught the agent's eye—a hoodie sweatshirt, shorts and sneakers with no socks. The man wearing the clothes was in his early twenties, curly black hair, and unkempt short beard. Sunglasses with white plastic frames. There was something under the man's hoodie that caused the agent to be suspect.

There was a bulge—in the stomach area. Odd for a young man with a slender build. And it was even more odd that the bulge didn't have the natural bow of a beer gut. It had the physical traits of something manmade. Square. Maybe circular. The man carried a large Styrofoam cup in one hand, a green backpack in the other hand.

The agent set his fishing rod down and used the radio mic on the inside of his wrist to make the call. "Be advised that there is a male, gray hoodie, shorts, dark hair and beard, approaching the Memorial from the wooded area near the large light pole on the right looking across the basin. He's carrying a backpack in one hand. Something appears to be under his sweatshirt."

A voice in the agent's earpiece said, "Don't let him out of your sight. Jones, Hampton and Anderson—follow him. If he makes a sudden move, use your discretion. Try to keep him from the crowds or getting near the Memorial."

The agent by the Tidal Basin, reached inside his open, untucked shirt and touched the grip of his Glock. He left the rod and reel on the bank and followed the man who appeared from out of the woods.

FORTY-SEVEN

Bill Gray held the manila envelope in his left hand and placed his right hand on the east wall of the Jefferson Memorial. He silently read the inscription on the west wall. After a moment of thought, he said, "Autocratic opposition is the grist that sharpened the sword of our democracy. Like a kite that ol' Ben Franklin flew in an approaching storm, our nation rose in the winds of tyranny blowing against our beliefs of freedom. The Founding Fathers dared to be great, not because they were great men, but because they shared greater ideals for the masses. See that inscription?" He pointed to the wall.

"Yes. What about it?"

Jefferson said … *'I tremble for my country when I reflect that God is just, and that his justice cannot sleep forever.'* He uses that phrase, God is just and his justice cannot sleep forever in here, Paul." Bill held up the manila envelope. "He wrote it in plain text in at least three of the deciphered letters he sent to Stephen Decatur, William Eaton and Presley O'Bannon."

"The Barbary War."

"Indeed. They were some of the men who led the charge against the Barbary pirates, the men who defeated them. In one letter, Jefferson dictates a plan for William Eaton to secretly meet with the pasha of Tripoli's estranged brother, Hamet Karamanli. Jefferson knew the brother wasn't happy with the balance of power in the family, and, under the right circumstances, might be susceptible to a clandestine raid on Tripoli to overthrow his brother. Jefferson had great insight into human psychology and how to leverage that to our nation's advantage. Had he not been president, he may have made one of America's best spies."

Bill looked at the inscription on a wall to his right and motioned. "Up there, Jefferson writes that *'laws and institutions must go hand in hand with the progress of the human mind. And as the people of a nation become more enlightened, as more discoveries are made, new truths disclosed, institutions must advance to keep pace with the times.'* This, along with his firm belief that government has no business dictating or making rules infringing on religious freedom, is, in one passage or another, brought up in these letters." He handed the large envelope to Paul. "Maybe there's something in here or on these walls that you can use."

"Maybe, but this whole thing could yield us nothing."

"That's a possibility. Just remember this, when Jefferson refused to pay ransom or passage fees to travel into the Mediterranean, the Muslim nations in North Africa captured our merchant ships and put many of our sailors into slavery. And then they declared war on us. Jefferson was the first and only president to respond, and much to their surprise, soundly defeated them in their own backyard. You mentioned a few minutes ago that you thought Jefferson was more of a strategist than a politician. We could use some stealthy strategy today. What if it's in there?"

Before Paul could answer, one of the agents assigned to him appeared from behind a column. He wore an open sports coat, tall, a flesh-colored earpiece, the tense eyes of a sniper. Face shiny. A trace of perspiration appeared above his top lip. He said, "Gentlemen, there's been a situation. Let's exit the rear of the Memorial."

FORTY-EIGHT

Bill started to follow the agent when Paul said, "Wait! What situation? I didn't hear shots fired or anyone screaming. I'm not running out the back of this monument until I know what's in front of it with hundreds of tourists and school kids. Are they in danger?"

The agent paused, held one finger against the earpiece, listening. He nodded and said into a tiny microphone on the inside of his wrist, "Copy that ... he's with Bill Gray. Do you still want me to take them toward West Basin Street?" He listened for ten seconds, nodded and looked at Bill and Paul. "We're questioning a man who is either not all there or he could be a decoy."

"What do you mean?" Bill asked.

"The guy fit the physical profile of comparable known terrorists. And in this weather he was wearing a hoodie sweatshirt, carrying a backpack in one hand. When he set it on a park bench near a large group of school kids, walked away and reached under his hoodie, two agents tackled him. Under his hoodie was a Frisbee. In his backpack were canned soft drinks and sandwiches. He was meeting a couple of friends for some Frisbee tossing. He just about got tossed in jail."

Paul said, "You mentioned decoy. How so?"

"A guy looking that suspicious gets the attention of the PD and multiple agencies out here. In the meantime, someone inside the rotunda walks up to you, Mr. Marcus, and shoots you. Sorry to be so blunt. But it happens." The agent looked around at the tourists. A second agent stood near the Jefferson statue.

Bill said, "Better safe then sorry."

"We're still questioning him and his friends. It appears to be okay. I'll be near the perimeter columns."

Paul nodded. "Thanks."

Bill glanced up at the statue and pointed north. "Jefferson is looking in the direction of the White House, always on watch, twenty-four-seven. I've stood on the south porch of the White House and looked in this direction. You can see this Memorial from there. It's in a direct line of sight, and you can almost feel Jefferson's unblinking stare. Too bad we can't read his mind." He turned to Paul. "Good luck with the decryption. Maybe there's something in the letters or here on these walls that will help connect the dots."

"I wouldn't bet the Washington Monument on it." Paul moved the envelope from his left hand to his right, glanced out the main entrance, the silhouette of two police officers in the porte cochère. "Bill, let's take a look at the river." He walked out the left side of the Memorial, the breeze off the Potomac had the brackish scent of an estuary during the spring mating season of migratory birds. Bill followed and stood next to Paul as he looked toward the river.

Bill said, "The water quality is much better than it was when I first moved here. Fishing is quite good, but nothing like it was when people like Jefferson and Madison occupied the White House. John Quincy Adams used to swim naked in the Potomac almost every day in the summer."

"How far upstream from here is Senator Fairchild's neighborhood?"

Bill looked north, his eyes squinting almost as if he had an aerial view of the river. "Probably about twenty-five miles, give or take. The Potomac is more than three hundred miles long."

"And yet the people who killed Fairchild new exactly what spot, what neighborhood, to find Fairchild and precisely what time he'd be jogging on a path adjacent to the river. You told me they used an inflatable dingy to motor across in the dark and wait for him to jog by at the crack of dawn. After they killed him, they fired up their boat and crossed the Potomac like Washington crossed the Delaware. I've been thinking about these recent deaths—murders. I'm curious as to how the killers knew Senator Fairchild's routine so well ... well enough to use a dingy to gain access to him."

"That's a good question."

"And the answer won't be found in any paper written by Jefferson. But it might be found using more modern communications."

"Such as?"

"Such as his phone. Was it on him when his body was found?"

"Yes."

"Can you get the stored numbers on his phone for me ... especially the last numbers he called or received before his murder?"

"Sure, I can have those sent to you."

"Don't do it in any traceable format. You can give them to me on a drive, or write them down the old fashioned way—on paper. If you can give me his phone, that would be best. If not, I'd like to know what, if any, apps Senator Fairchild may have downloaded."

"All right. I've seen this look in your eye before, Paul. Not often, but I've seen it. What are you thinking?"

"I'm thinking that the killers had some assistance. Maybe I can find out who that might have been."

Bill glanced at his watch. "I have a conference call with the White House in a half hour. I need to get to someplace quiet. If I can't get clearance to hand over the phone, I'll scour it and deliver the data to you. Good luck with what's in that envelope. Maybe it'll help you with the really tough one—the single page nobody at NSA can decrypt." Bill turned and walked down the granite steps, soon he melted into the throng of tourists, walking fast, glancing across the Tidal Basin to the White House in the distance.

Paul looked over his shoulder at the bronze face of Jefferson. It was a poker face. Unreadable. The encrypted cards from the nation's third president now dealt to him. He walked quickly down the steps, holding the envelope in his right hand, the sound of hard sole shoes off the cement pathway as the federal agents followed behind him.

FORTY-NINE

The following day, Paul began his work at six a.m. He'd risen before Alicia and David, walked Buddy in the backyard, put on a pot of coffee, entered his home office and read and reread the correspondence between Jefferson and Robert Livingston, jotting down notes. He could hear Alicia and David in the kitchen, the muffled sound of a morning TV talk show.

After more than four hours of research, Paul stood from the desk and wondered just how safe the safe house really was for his family. He thought about what Bill Gray had said, *'All the glass is bulletproof. Door and frames are reinforced to withstand small explosions, and the air filtration unit is designed to protect against gas attacks. Gun-fire recognition software, giving us real-time tracking of an active shooter anywhere in the house or on the property.'*

Paul stepped from his chair and closed the drapes on the only window in the room. It looked out to the backyard. He returned to the desk and stared at the two open file folders near his laptop, the framed picture of Eli Dexter sat on the right side of the desk. The folder on the left was the file he carried since Bill Gray had given it to him during their first meeting in the president's office, and it contained just two pieces of paper, the encrypted letter Jefferson had written and the one in plain text.

The newer folder on the right had copies of every known encrypted letter Jefferson wrote, most with the corresponding paper decryption clipped with it. Paul read many of the decrypted letters, looking for patterns—sequences of letters and the commonalities that Jefferson used. He looked for how the English language was spoken and written at that time. Some of the letters were easily decrypted using an exact cipher wheel with the same prearrangement code. Others had been deciphered using sequential number patterns. All of the letters and matching decoded papers were written with a quill pen, dark brown ink, and the precise cursive penmanship.

Paul wrote block letters, longhand, on a legal pad. He could break the codes quickly, like he was unscrambling a Jumbo word puzzle. The final paper that Jefferson encoded, the one found in the attic, was much more of a challenge. It was written and encoded without the use of a cipher wheel. Paul keyed in his computer, running advanced encryption tests. Rather than encoding letters of the alphabet, the system encoding focused on binary numbers, breaking down mathematical algorithms, beginning with prime numbers. He incorporated dynamic programming, which solves large problems by breaking down puzzles into smaller pieces and linking together solutions.

• • •

Alicia was in the kitchen making breakfast for David when the doorbell rang. The chimes, soft and melodious, sent a chill into her heart. Buddy barked once and sat next to David at the kitchen table. Alicia looked toward the closed office door where Paul was sequestered, working. She used a knife to slice through a stack of buttered toast, put some fruit on a plate next to a piece of toast, and set in on the table in front of her son. "Here you go, David. I'll pour some juice for you in a second. I need to see who's at the door."

"Okay, Mom." David took a bite and handed a blueberry to Buddy who sat under the table near his feet.

Alicia walked by one of the panic buttons in the kitchen, through the house, to the front door. She carried the knife in her right hand. She looked into the peephole and recognized one of the federal agents assigned to her family. He was fairly new to the FBI, early thirties, boyish face, and a college ring on his right hand. He wore a sports coat over a golf shirt. He had an envelope in one hand.

Alicia set the knife on a shelf in the foyer and opened the door. The agent smiled and said, "Good morning, Mrs. Marcus."

She pulled a strand of hair behind her left ear, smiled, and looked at the black SUV in her driveway, the silhouette of a second man in the front seat. "Good morning." She glanced at the package in his hand.

"This is for Mr. Marcus." He handed the envelope to her.

"What is it?"

"I'm not sure of the specifics, but it's some data that Mr. Marcus requested from the bureau. I do know it has top security clearance and came directly from the bureau."

She didn't try to smile. "So it's safe to open this in my home, right?"

"Yes, ma'am."

Alicia held the envelope. There was no name or address on either side. She lifted her eyes back to the agent. He smiled and said, "I can understand your hesitancy. But I promise you there is nothing in there to harm you. No poisons. Nothing toxic or dangerous."

She managed a smile. "Define danger for me, Special Agent Simon. It can be disguised and come in sheep's clothing." She exhaled. "I'm sorry. I'm sure this is harmless, and something my husband needs for his research. Thank you for delivering it."

"No problem. Do you know if you are going to visit your mother today?"

"I haven't gotten that far in my day, why?"

"I was just wondering. We'll have a shift change in a little while. If you were traveling, I wanted to give the next team the heads up."

She nodded, squinting as the morning sun broke through the boughs of a tall loblolly pine tree and rested on her face. "I'll let you know." She turned and went back inside, picking the knife off the shelf in the hallway and returning to the kitchen. She poured a glass of cranberry juice and set it in front of David.

"Where's Daddy?"

"He's in the home office working, doing research"

"What does that mean?"

She smiled. "You know when you and I put together picture puzzles, and we hunt for all the pieces, trying to match the sky and whatever corners and patterns in the picture?"

"Uh-huh."

"That's kind of what Daddy's doing. He's trying to put the pieces of a big puzzle together."

"Can we help him?"

"I wish we could, but this one is very difficult, and it's going to take Daddy a while to work it out."

"Are we gonna go see grandma today?"

"Would you like that?"

"Yes, if we can take Buddy."

"We'll see. Finish your breakfast."

Alicia walked toward the office and paused at the closed door. She knocked softly. "It's open," Paul said.

She stepped inside and held up the sealed envelope. "This came for you via an FBI courier, at least that's what the agent said at our front door."

Paul stood. "Good. It's from Bill Gray."

"What's inside? I only ask because I keep remembering—keep seeing pieces of that plane falling into the sea. I remember the images of some of the passengers that were boarding … a little girl no older than David, flying with her mother. A couple that looked to be on a honeymoon, their faces radiated love for each other … an older couple, probably married for fifty years. Them, and all the others, destroyed in a horrible explosion over the sea."

She held out the knife. "You can use this to open it."

"Mom," David said, running with Buddy toward the office. "Buddy wants to go outside."

"Okay, we'll take him. I'll go with you." She walked to the office door, turned back to face Paul and said, "When I come back, I hope you can tell me what Bill Gray sent to our home."

FIFTY

P aul used the knife to carefully open the envelope. He peered inside, used two fingers to slide out the folded sheet of paper. The paragraph read: *The enclosed drive has all of the information you requested. You'll see the IDs to the numbers he had stored and the apps on his phone. We included numbers from the call log for the week leading up to the murder. Many are numbers from people stored on his phone. They include a dozen senators and as many members of congress. Others are lobbyists, the VP of the NRA, and more. He was speaking with a few people in the president's inner circle, i.e., Sami Botros, Secretary of State Willow, Chief of Staff Charles Sanders and more. The FBI and the agency are following up on everything; however, it seems to be standard phone communications for a senior senator like Fairchild. Nothing appears out of the usual. Good luck, - BG*

Paul inserted the thumb drive in his computer and watched the data load. He scanned through the names Senator Fairchild had stored in his personal contact list. Many of the names he recognized—mostly senators and members of congress, plus one member of the U.S. Supreme Court. But he also recognized names of corporate CEOs for Fortune 500 companies. There were names of family members, and initials only—and even listings he referred to as Popeye, Spiderman, Batman, and finally Superman. Paul assumed the superhero names were people the senator had to disguise, but the numbers were there.

And if there were numbers, there were ways to track people around the planet.

Paul studied the apps that Fairchild had on his phone. There weren't many, a few ride share companies, a weather app, Amazon, and even an app to order flowers and food. Paul could tell that the latest one downloaded was one for a fitness tracker. He keyed in phone numbers with no IDs attached to them, looking for names. He examined the frequency and length of recent calls.

Paul noticed that Fairchild had called Sami Botros, one of the president's closest advisors, three times in the week leading up to Fairchild's murder. Twice Fairchild had spoken with Ward Rosenberg, Deputy Director of the FBI. Both calls less than a minute each. Paul leaned back in his chair, thinking about the heated conversation between Rosenberg and Botros in the Oval Office when Rosenberg said, '*We get a Frankenstein hybrid of a monster Muslim who wants to move the line in the sand all the way back to their very first war with America.*'

Botros had fired back, '*Muslims don't hold a monopoly on evil. Your surname is Rosenberg. Alfred Rosenberg was found guilty of war crimes during the Nuremberg trials. However, it would be appalling of me to think all Germans, or someone with a shared surname, such as Rosenberg, would be remotely connected to Nazis.*'

Paul looked at his watch. When he had time, he'd run more systematic cyber searches using the phone numbers of both men to see if they had a circuitous link back to Fairchild. He returned to the app, the last thing that Senator Fairchild would ever download. The download had occurred at 6:05 a.m. the same morning Fairchild was murdered. '*Coroner puts the senator's death at about somewhere before seven in the morning,*' Bill Gray had said. Paul keyed in the app and the data trail leading from Fairchild's phone to the fitness tracker company.

The trail didn't lead there.

It led to an unknown server in an unknown location. But what Paul could determine was that the app had been a decoy, designed to give the recipient information about Fairchild. The hacker could monitor everywhere Fairchild went and how long he was there. It was as if Fairchild had worn a GPS homing device on his right wrist that could track him anywhere in the world.

Paul called Bill Gray and gave him an update. "There are at least two ways the killers could have electronically monitored Senator Fairchild's movements."

"I know of one … not sure about the other." Bill's voice sounded fatigued.

"His phone, of course, is one. As you know—get the number and a good hacker can get the GPS coordinates and follow the phone as long as the phone owner has the GPS turned on. Some talented hackers can even turn it on remotely, but not many. The second way Fairchild was followed was through his fitness tracker."

"Was? You've already determined that?"

"Yes. It's not difficult. The bad guy emailed a dummy app to Fairchild, one that looked identical to the company that manufactured the fitness tracker. As soon as Fairchild downloaded it, they had him."

"Can you pinpoint where the wolf is hiding?"

"Maybe. The trail has led to multiple servers and bogus IP addresses. I just have to penetrate those. It takes time, and it's taking time away from trying to decipher the Jefferson code."

"Do you want to turn some of it over to the team at NSA?"

"Not yet. Only because of the parallels twisting from Fairchild's death—a senator hand-picked by assassins who left a note referencing Jefferson. From the slaughter of Eli Dexter to all of this recent horror … to where and how it began in Tripoli, there's a meandering, tortuous link to all of it. I just have to break through to figure it out."

"I know under the circumstances, it's damn hard. The pressure to find these guys, before the next explosion or slaughter, is intense. The agencies and NSA are tracking suspects and unsubs all over the world. Fajar Hamad still seems to be the glue, but he's not alone. We just don't know who's in the dark shadows with him."

"Maybe, if I get real lucky, I can shine a spotlight into those shadows."

FIFTY-ONE

Paul stared at a picture of the bloodstained note the killers had left in Fairchild's mouth. He reread the list of demands, looking for key words that he might be able to use in this decryption of the Jefferson code. He read the note left behind in the backpack filled with Jefferson nickels. *'Remember the battle of Derna ... for whom the bell tolls has a silent ring, and always will ...*

There was a soft knock at the door as it opened. Alicia stood at the threshold with a steaming cup. Paul removed the bloodstained note from his computer screen. She said, "I made some tea for you. I bet Jefferson drank tea, and I bet he took a break after spending hours encrypting or decoding messages. How are you coming?" She walked to the desk and set the cup down on a gold-rimmed coaster.

"Thanks. Slowly. It's a challenge."

"Can I ask you what Bill sent?"

"The phone number and app log from Senator Fairchild's phone."

"Why? What does that have to do with something Thomas Jefferson left behind?"

"Maybe nothing. But the list of demands was found on his body from terrorists with apparent ties back to Tripoli and Jefferson. They want the president to issue an apology for what they call aggression from our side when they were the ones holding the ships and our crews hostage, enslaving our people, and then declared war on us. The president has nothing to apologize for."

"You said demands, what else do they want?"

"A billion dollars in reparations for the damage I caused in their nuclear operation. And they want the president to release Fajar Hamad's brother and another man picked up in Libya as suspects in the Benghazi attacks and killings."

David stood at the door and asked, "Mom, can I go in the backyard with Buddy?"

"You have to stay on the patio where we can see you from the window. I'll be there in a couple of minutes. Stay on the patio, okay?"

"Okay. David left, Buddy at his heels.

Alicia looked at Paul and asked, "Why don't you take a break? You've been at it for hours. I'm going to visit Mom. David wants to take Buddy. Can you come with us?"

Paul eyed the photo of Eli Dexter. "I made a promise to Eli's parents to do what I could to help find his killers. And I don't have a lot of time to do it. Hamad and his followers say that, at the end of the next cycle of the crescent moon, which is in about eight days, they'll unleash a major attack on America. I don't know if there is something Jefferson encoded in his letter that may help us today to deal with these people, but considering the parallels, it's worth the effort."

"Paul, is there something you're not telling me? You seem distant. I know you have a lot on your plate, but we've always talked. I feel like you're being evasive, and I don't know why. What is it? You're under no obligation to decrypt espionage letters from two centuries ago. Is there something else?"

Paul cut his eyes from the photo to his wife. "Most importantly, Alicia, I'm doing this for us. Maybe there's a bargaining chip we can use to push them back—to somehow create boundaries and a barrier between them and our family. I have to try."

"You seem to be holding cards close to your chest. Whatever it is, I don't want to be dealt out." She glanced down at the encrypted papers on the desk. "So, tell me, what are you finding among the buried and final encrypted words of the man who carried most of the weight writing the Declaration of Independence?"

Paul sipped his tea. "Jefferson moved from an encryption technique he used for much of his correspondence to one I haven't seen before.

It's not a substitution cipher, one that can be cracked replacing a letter of the alphabet with another, analyzing the number of times particular letters appear. Those are easily cracked using a frequency analysis."

"Maybe for you, but not the rest of the seven billon people on the planet."

Paul smiled and folded his arms, glancing down at the single sheet of paper—coding that looked different from the others. "It's as if he saved his toughest encryption for the very last thing he wrote." Paul moved his index finger along the rows of letters.

Alicia said, "It is different. How would the recipient know where to start?"

"As you can see here, Jefferson wrote this code in vertical columns from left to right, using no spaces or capital letters. The writing forms a grid … in this case … there are forty lines with approximately sixty letters each. One approach I'm trying is to break the grid into sections of up to ten lines each, numbering each line in the section from one to ten. Then I want to see if I can transcribe each numbered section to form a new grid, scrambling the order of the numbered lines within each sector. For the receiver, the key to decoding, I think, was to know the number of lines in each section, the order in which those lines were transcribed, and the number of random letters added to each line."

"Now that I'm thoroughly lost, is it doable?"

"I think so. In Jefferson's day, if you didn't know the key, absolutely no way. But with the computer, we might find something by rearranging all of this in algorithmic math. Still the odds are in the low seven figures."

"Sounds like this is going to take you some time."

"It's not a cakewalk. And there's a chance that I can't crack it. I'm more than a little distracted with what's going on around us."

"I know. It was a risk coming here … but after we discovered that our identities and security were penetrated, coming here was our best option. It's not easy to live with armed guards in the driveway, bulletproof windows, and panic buttons, software to locate an active shooter in the house, and being connected directly to the FBI. It's like a weird form of incarceration with the façade of amenities found in a real home and the reinforcement of Fort Knox." Alicia managed a smile. "As long as we're safe, we'll make do with all of this and the federal agents, too. The flip side is I know a lot about their kids, wives, and even their sports teams."

Paul nodded, stood and stepped to the window. He looked around the fenced and secluded yard toward the patio. Nothing. "I don't see David or Buddy on the patio." Paul bolted out of the room, his wife right behind him.

FIFTY-TWO

"David!" Paul shouted, running out the back door. Alicia followed him, her face fearful. Paul looked to the left, to the concrete extension of the patio. David sat with Buddy at his side against the exterior of the house, the boy playing with a toy plastic bulldozer and a truck. Paul stopped, sucked in a deep breath and said, "Hey, David. Looks like you and Buddy are having some fun."

"We're playing monster trucks." David looked up, flashing a toothy grin, a shaft of sunlight breaking through the trees onto his freckled face. He pushed the toy truck and made the sound of a diesel engine.

Alicia pressed her palms against her jeans as if her hands were perspiring. She said, "You and Buddy come inside. We're going to visit Grandma."

David stood and picked up his toys. "Can Buddy come?"

"Yes, but not every time. Grandma gets tired."

• • •

Rafa Gamal took a seat outdoors at a sidewalk café in the north side of Tripoli. He sat in the corner at a small table under an umbrella, the view of the Mediterranean Sea at night less than one hundred meters, lights from ships in port twinkling off the dark water. There were two-dozen tables at the cafe, all covered with red-checkered plastic tablecloths. Most of the customers had eaten and gone. A twenty-something man and woman sat at a far table, laughing, their faces bathed in warm candlelight, the scent of grilled lamb and lemon in the night air.

Gamal looked at the menu. Although born to a Muslim family, he was non-practicing in the religion of Islam. After working all day, he wanted a glass of wine. None of the cafes or restaurants that he frequented sold alcohol anymore. Some did when Gadhafi was in power. Not anymore. *Maybe Egypt or Morocco would be a better place to live*, he thought. *Libya has gone backwards in its thinking and politics.*

He ordered Turkish coffee, hummus and grape leaves stuffed with ground lamb and rice. He watched a long ocean freighter silently enter the port, the big ship's running lights longer than two football fields, the wheelhouse glowing yellow light as the captain piloted the vessel closer to the docks, the loading cranes in silhouette under the harbor lights.

When a stoic waiter, with a Ping-Pong ball-sized Adam's apple, set the coffee on the table, Gamal's phone buzzed. It was followed by a blast from the freighter's horn as the tie-down ropes were shot out to harbor workers who hustled to secure them to the sturdy bollard posts on the dock.

Gamal looked at the phone. He knew there would be no caller ID. But he rarely made or received calls. He knew the incoming call was business, and he answered in Persian. The man on the phone had the same deep, raspy voice. In Persian, he said, "You excelled in the last job. Your information gave us a profile into the senator's life, one he repeated too often."

"Many of us are creatures of habit. It's often simply a matter of convenience."

"We want you to find out if another man is a creature of habit, too. This person, I know, will be more difficult, more of a challenge."

Gamal sipped his coffee. "I enjoy a challenge. Who is he?"

"His name is Paul Marcus … an American who recently returned home. He is the sworn enemy of the Supreme Leader."

A wicked smiled moved across Gamal's thin lips. "Why would this person be more of a challenge than the last?"

"Because he is one of the world's very best at encryption. You will not be able to surprise him unless, for some reason, he is highly distracted and makes a mistake."

"Everyone makes mistakes. People get careless. Most can't even remember their passwords."

"Paul Marcus is not like most people. He is a genius. He broke an ancient code left behind by Isaac Newton. That revelation opened the door to world events that compromised our relationship with Russia. Marcus, alone, caused a shutdown to Iran's nuclear program, and he did it from a computer many thousands of miles away."

"So … he was the one. The man, among hackers, is legendary. I thought he was dead."

"So did we, and then we discovered he is alive and has a new family."

"I enjoy a good challenge. However, for such a prized quarry, one with the degree of difficulty you described, my price is double."

There was a pause on the other end of the phone. "It will be done."

"When can you begin?"

"In a few hours," he said. Gamal leaned back in his chair and thought, when it comes to the back doors or the underground of the computer world, I will prove Marcus is not better at this Chess game than me.

FIFTY-THREE

P aul worked in his home office for a fifth straight day, looking for the obscure key to unlock the entrance into the mind of Thomas Jefferson. He glanced at his watch: 1:07 a.m. *The crescent moon cycle ends in four days. Time's not on my side*, he thought. He read letters written between Jefferson and the man he had appointed Minister to France, Robert Livingston. Most of the exchange dealt with world events, keeping the United States out of any conflicts arising in Europe, and there were many.

The men discussed their need for increased security within the body of their correspondence. Jefferson sent Livingston a copy of an encrypted letter written by Jefferson's longtime friend, Robert Patterson, a professor of mathematics at the University of Pennsylvania. Patterson had shared with Jefferson a method of encryption he'd devised that, according to Patterson, would be so difficult to decode that it would *defy the united expertise of the entire human race.*

Jefferson used Patterson's model as a guide in his last encrypted letter to Robert Livingston. And now, 218 years later, Paul studied the encryption that was a fusion from the minds of both men, Patterson and Jefferson. "What did you write in here, Mr. President?" Paul whispered, the light from the gooseneck lamp on his desk falling on the encrypted letter. His eyes burned and there was a dull pain above his left eye and into his brain. He eyed the photo of Eli Dexter, replayed the sorrow in Penny Dexter's voice, *What they did to our son was far beyond some holy war. It was innately evil ... evil deeds ordered and done by wicked men who attacked us when Jefferson was president, and they continue to do it today.'*

Paul set the paper down, looked at it for a few seconds, and then quickly hit letters and numbers of his computer keyboard again. His eyes moved from the encryption to his computer screen. His first goal was to analyze the probability of pairs of numbers—the dynamic programing algorithms, taking larger problems and breaking them down into puzzle pieces. He mumbled, "All I have to do is tear it down into grids and then find common links to put the pieces back together in smaller clusters. Hopefully, it'll result in readable cipher ... I just need a digital key to unlock this."

Alicia stood at the open door and said, "It looks like this one has you talking to yourself."

He glanced up at his wife, a robe wrapped around her, pajama bottoms visible beneath the robe. "This one is exceedingly tough. After all these hours, I'm sort of talking to ghosts—those of the third president and some of the men with whom he shared communications, encryptions and plain text."

She stepped in the room. "I wish you could share some plain talk with me. The other day, when you couldn't see David in the backyard from that window, the fear in your eyes was more intense than I've ever seen it." She stood by his desk, glanced at the picture of Eli and looked at the encrypted paper next to the computer screen. "What's going on, Paul? We've always had open and frank conversations. But I still feel you're holding something back from me. What is it?"

"I don't want to frighten you any more than need be. You have enough to worry about with your mom and your family."

"We're family! You, me, David ... my mom, sister, and our niece."

"I know how something as precious as that can be gone in an instant. I lost my first family to a killer. I will do everything in my power to keep that from happening again." He stood and stepped closer to his wife.

Alicia folded her arms and said, "I understand. But I also understand that knowledge is power or can be leveraged to stop danger if you can recognize it. Just by you telling me that you don't want to frighten me anymore than need be does just that—it scares me. Tell me, what do you know that I don't? Was it something the president or Bill Gray told you? Paul, I want to know. I *need* to know."

"The people who killed Eli ... the terrorists who blew up Mount Rushmore, killing the girl and park ranger, the ones responsible for the deaths at the wedding and the murder of Senator Fairchild ... issued a list of demands as you know. One of the demands is for the president to surrender me to this group. It's about retribution, Alicia. It's about making a global statement in the name of their goal of domination."

Alicia said nothing. She held her left hand to her lips, her gold wedding band the color of butter in the soft light from the lamp. She looked up at Paul and embraced him. After a moment, she said, "Before our son was born, you and I accomplished more than anyone would have ever believed possible. I traveled around the world with you to prove the crimes of the Circle of 13. We raced through the other half of the planet trying to stay alive. We defeated them, and you managed to shut down the nuclear advancement of a rogue state. We've been through literal hell on Earth, raced through it, and we came out the other side. I'm here to stay. Together, we are survivors. The president will not bargain with terrorists, and I'm not about to let anyone take you away. Just don't keep anything from me. Okay? Promise?" She pulled her hair behind one ear.

"Okay. I promise."

"It's after one in the morning. Let's go to bed. This puzzle will still be a puzzle when you wake up, but you'll come back to it after a few hours of sleep."

"All right. Let me shutdown." Paul turned to shut off his computer, pausing for a moment to study the screen.

"What is it?" Alicia asked.

Paul said nothing. He sat down, his eyes scanning the entire screen, vertical and horizontal. "Someone tripped an alarm I set up. My mouse pointer moved slightly."

"Maybe you touched it."

"No, I was standing next to you. I saw it. It was almost subliminal, but I know it moved. I set up three nearly impenetrable firewalls— intrusion detection buffers designed to alert me to any outside threat to my work on this computer."

"I wonder how far the hacker got?"

"I'm going to find out."

FIFTY-FOUR

Paul didn't say a word. His fingers moved across the keyboard, pausing as he read the white text against a black background. Alicia stood next to her husband and watched him navigate through the deep recesses of the operating system, stopping to read and return to the keyboard. Buddy trotted in, sat, and looked at Paul and Alicia before jumping up on a small sofa in the room.

Alicia said, "If someone got in, he or she has to be very good. In addition to the firewalls you built, Bill said this system is protected by a similar firewall used in the Senate, House, and many of the computers used in the Department of Justice. Are you looking for malware?"

"No, this hacker appears too sophisticated for that. Or if there's some sort of malware, so far it's undetectable."

"But without a Trojan Horse, it's going to be difficult for a hacker. Someone, somewhere, has to remotely control malware to get it to do what he or she wants and to excerpt the information the hacker wants. Maybe you inadvertently left some digital door cracked."

"I've checked that. Everything's closed. I'm scanning files. I see nothing that the hacker has touched."

"A highly sophisticated hacker, as you know, can cover his tracks. The real good ones can write self-erasing code, create bogus IP and web addresses. Some can even route their attacks through the computers or phones of third-party innocent victims and create the illusion that they are in more than one country at the same time."

Paul continued hammering the keyboard, pausing to search for tracks. "I'm going to create a virtual server, route incoming traffic there, and see if I can build an invisible spider's web to catch this person. Or to at least give me the trails I need to trace a real IP address."

Alicia stood straighter, looked at the closed drapes on the window. "In the medieval era, a family raised the drawbridge, made sure the moat was filled and the castle turrets were armed. Fast-forward some centuries to our lifetime. Just a few years ago, we felt safer with burglar alarms on our doors and windows. Today, intruders can get inside our home without ever picking the lock on the front door or entering through an unlocked window. And with cameras and microphones on our TV's and electronic devices, they can see and hear a lot of our most private world. Maybe the notion of privacy is now an illusion. Even coming from my former life—seven years at NSA, I still find this stuff creepy in a deviant sort of way."

"It's a double-edged sword. Without it, I never would have been able to negotiate Brandi's freedom." He read silently, looking at possible ports of entry, files, and the traps he'd set. Paul leaned back in his chair. "This will take a while. Why don't you go back to bed? I'll be there as soon as I can."

Alicia half-smiled. "I was hoping that when the plane went down, just by chance … by some sad irony, that the bomb wasn't meant for us. That it was a horrible fluke that we were to board a doomed plane. Now that I know these killers have included you on their list of psychotic demands, I'm angry and fearful at the same time. But I'm hopeful, too." She lifted the encrypted letter, the light from the computer screen caught in her pupils. "Maybe the key to removing this cloak of terror lies somewhere in here. I hope you can find it, Paul. Even far beyond our family, this bloodthirsty threat has to come to an end."

"We don't know what, if anything tangible, Jefferson left behind on that paper. My best hope for cracking it is to discover a code or a key that the recipient of this paper had at his disposal. In the meantime, I need to set traps for an exceptional hacker and do it so well he doesn't know that I'm following him."

"How could this person find you here? We haven't been in this so-called safe house very long. That computer is supposed to be shielded by one of the most fortified firewalls our IT people have ever built, and yet someone has found a crack. How?"

"Probably because the hacker had help."

"A breach?"

"I could be wrong, but we have no idea who in the government knows that we're here. Most of the president's inner circle now knows we're in the District. Some of the people in the FBI, obviously, are aware of our location as well."

Alicia said nothing. She set the paper down and walked out of the room, Buddy following close behind her. Paul watched them for a moment, feeling an unusual sense of isolation in the room, unseen but palpable, just like the scent from the cup of tea his wife had left on the desk. He returned to the keyboard, his fingers moving quickly, setting traps and hoping he wouldn't have to wait long to catch what he knew was a unique thief—maybe unsurpassed and the best in the world at deception.

Paul looked up, startled to see Alicia standing back at the office door. After a moment, he said, "Do me a favor … bring me the pair of David's sneakers that he wears the most. And bring me the pair of shoes you wear the most when visiting your mother."

"Can I ask why?"

"Of course." Paul slid a drawer out and picked up a white envelope. He opened it and reached inside to retrieve three small objects, each about twice the size of a grain of rice.

Alicia studied the objects a moment. "Are those what I think they are … trackers?"

"The latest and most powerful for their size. But right now let's call them insurance smaller than a green pea. I'm going to implant one in David's shoes, one in yours and in mine."

"This is in the event one or all of us is kidnapped, right?"

"I hope and pray it'll never come to that, but I want to do everything I can to protect my family, and to find my family anywhere in the world. Promise me that when you leave the house, you will wear the shoes with the tracker, or at least carry them in a bag, okay?"

"Okay, cross my heart."

FIFTY-FIVE

Rafa Gamal sat at his desk in his Tripoli apartment, stared at his computer screen, his wet lips forming an arrogant smile. He leaned back in his chair and lit a Turkish cigarette, taking a deep drag and slowly exhaling. He picked up his phone, stepped closer to his window overlooking Martyr's Square and the large fountain, the water around the perimeter of the circular fountain jetting high in cascading arches, splashing in the pool. An older man, in a red turban, craggy face, sat on the fountain's edge, tossing breadcrumbs to pigeons, the birds shuffling like a trained flock near the sandals on his brown feet.

Gamal made the call, cleared his throat. When the line was answered, Gamal said, "I am in."

The man on the other end spoke Persian and asked, "Where is he?"

"I managed to infiltrate a device used by Paul Marcus. I don't know the exact physical location, however, I can tell it is coming from somewhere in Washington, DC. I will continue monitoring. My goal is to shadow him through his phone, fitness tracker or any electronic device he carries on his person or built into his vehicle."

There was a silence on the line. And then the man spoke. "When you can determine his exact location, contact us immediately. I want to know precisely where he is in Washington DC, where he goes, and how often he goes there. Is that clear?"

"Of course."

The call disconnected. Gamal stepped to his desk, opened the right side drawer and picked up a marijuana cigarette. He lit it, held the smoke in his lungs, sat back down and exhaled, the smoke drifting toward the computer screen. When it cleared, Gamal took a second hit, he closed his eyes, exhaled and stared at the screen.

Something was different.

Gamal spit a charred sliver of pot from his lip, leaned a little closer to the screen and whispered, "Maybe Paul Marcus is asleep at the wheel. Or maybe it is something else. I will find your king and put you in checkmate." Gamal, eyes now dull, tapped at his keyboard. He corrected a few spelling errors, continued, and used his cybercriminal skills to penetrate further into the domain of Paul Marcus.

• • •

Paul opened one of the dummy files he created on the virtual server, marked it the *Jefferson File*, and wrote code that spelled out: *Let's set up a meeting with the WH to discuss the list of demands. The nation is hurting from these barbaric killings. When the Homeland is at stake from mercenaries in the midst, it's time to rethink our negotiation with terrorist's policies.* Paul typed in a phone number with a Washington area code and concluded the message by writing, *THIS IS UTMOST URGENT. The nation can't afford another slaughter or the destruction of an iconic monument—what's next, the obliteration of the Statue of Liberty?*

He watched the movements of the hacker. Studied his quickness— the areas on the phony server that he visited. It was like watching a rat enter your kitchen and sniff the nooks and crannies in search of hidden cheese. As the intruder snooped around the interior of the fictitious world, Paul added fabricated data to files. Salting the mine. Leading the prowler deeper into the dark of the mineshaft.

Every moment the hacker stayed in the simulated environment, was time for Paul to see patterns of behavior, to create more parallel facades that led the hacker to more obscure locations and gave Paul the opportunity to cross-reference global IP addresses, narrowing down possible geographic locations of where the hacker was at that moment. At the center of the honeypot was a fake message and phone number.

Paul watched the intruder sniff around the bogus information, like a shark circles a seal on the surface of the ocean.

And then the predator came in for a taste. It was all Paul needed to set the hook.

FIFTY-SIX

Three blocks from the United Nations Building in New York City lived a den of thieves. It was in the second floor of a remodeled brick condominium complex on 2nd Avenue. A limited liability company owned the two-bedroom unit. No personal names on deeds or property records. Sometimes the unit would be vacant for weeks. Other times, mysterious men came and went. All made no effort to be social. They were reclusive—shadows moving down the hallways. Usually the men arrived late at night and left in the early hours of the morning.

Dabir Nagi was one of those elusive men. Creosote colored skin. Large eyes. Dense, black eyelashes. Hawk nose. The phone call came in as Nagi finished his early morning prayers and stood to glance though a crack in the curtain. A garbage truck lumbered down the street, brakes squeaking, diesel throbbing. The truck stopped every fifty feet to pick up trash on the curb, clanging the metal cans against the sidewalk. One worker carried a dented can back to the curb and spit at a large rat as the animal stood on its hind legs near a ripped black garbage bag. The defiant rat held a small piece of pizza in his claws, nibbling.

From the second floor window, Nagi watched gray dawn evaporate in the heart of the city. He answered the phone in Persian, saying, "Yes."

"He's in Washington DC," came the quipped, deep voice of a man on the other end of the line. "We know he has no family alive.

However, his wife does. Depart immediately. Take three men, more if you need them. We want Marcus alive, if possible. We can assume he and his family are heavily guarded. That will make his capture all the sweeter."

"We will be there before nightfall. Do we stay at the usual place, the embassy?"

"Of course. That's why the Russians have it."

"But we can never trust them either." Nagi peered out the window. Two yellow taxis seemed to crawl down 2nd Avenue. He watched an emaciated man look in one of the emptied and bent garbage cans, scavenging for scraps of food. The man found a half smoked cigarette, wedged the butt in the corner of his mouth, and used a match to light the cigarette. The man stopped and looked at the rat still gorging on pizza. He moved toward the rodent, speaking like he was talking to a pet dog, smoke trailing him as he extended both hands, grinning. The rat dropped back down to four legs, its hairless tail swishing. Then it bolted, running toward a sewer grate, vanishing, and escaping with the pizza.

• • •

Paul hoped he'd see something in a dream that might have an influence on reality. He moved from his desk to the sofa right behind it, sitting down, staring at the large computer screen. His eyes burned and the screen looked indistinct. He watched for movement the way a secluded hunter watches for approaching prey. Finally, he leaned back against the couch and closed his eyes. He thought about the events of late, his conversation with Bill at the Jefferson Memorial, *'Maybe there's something in the letters or here on these walls that will help connect the dots.'*

He pictured the federal agent's shiny face as he ran up the Jefferson Memorial steps and said, *'A guy looking that suspicious gets the attention of the PD and multiple agencies out here. In the meantime, someone inside the rotunda walks up to you, Mr. Marcus, and shoots you. Sorry to be so blunt. But it happens.'*

Paul could hear his wife's voice, but he couldn't see her face. It was dark and she said, *'I'm not about to let anyone take you away. Just don't keep anything from me. Okay?'*

Paul wanted to open his eyes, but they felt welded shut. He heard thunder in the distance, the drum of rain against the window. *Maybe,* he thought, *something will rise from my subconscious that could be scattered pieces to the puzzle—something that will lead to a point of entry.* He replayed some of the day's discussions back in his mind: '*I tremble for my country when I reflect that God is just, and that his justice cannot sleep forever. He uses that phrase, God is just and his justice cannot sleep forever in here.*'

Paul opened his eyes and looked at his watch, 4:27 a.m. He pushed up from the couch and walked out of the room, the soft whir of air conditioning coming from the vents was the only sound. He heard Bill Gray's voice in his fatigued thoughts, '*The AC is designed to filter out gas and other poisons.*' Paul walked through the quiet house, the glow of moonlight coming through the glass panes in the French doors that led from the kitchen to the backyard patio.

He walked quietly into the living room, stopped at the drapes covering a window that opened to the front yard. Paul parted the curtains and looked at the dark SUV in his driveway, creamy moonlight seemed to stream off the black vehicle, like raindrops rolling off the waxed and polished surface of a car hood. He wondered what the FBI agents might be talking about at 4:30 a.m. on a cool Washington DC morning. *Maybe they were asleep at the wheel,* he thought. *Probably not.*

Paul opened the door to David's room and stepped over to his son's bed. David slept in the center, Buddy at the base of bed. Buddy's tail wagged. Paul whispered, "Shhh, just coming in to check on you guys." He petted Buddy on the head and leaned down to kiss David on his forehead, the boy clutching a plush Spiderman toy to his small chest.

Paul stepped out and entered the bedroom he shared with his wife. He stood there in the dark for a moment, listening. He could hear Alicia's steady breathing that deep sleep produces. He undressed down to his shorts, trying to be silent, easing the blanket back on his side of the bed and lying down. He lay there for a minute, light from the moon pouring through a small separation in the drapes over the window.

"I'm glad you came to bed," Alicia said, her voice sleepy. She reached out and touched his upper arm.

After a few seconds, Paul said, "Since we arrived back in the states, I've been having flashbacks about the night Jennifer and Tiffany were murdered. When I'm trying to concentrate on the decryption, I think of that horrible night. Trying to be a Good Samaritan resulted in the murders of Jen and Tiff. I can't shake that mistake."

"You didn't make a mistake. You tried to help someone and you pulled off the road on a rainy and foggy night. You told me that Jennifer even suggested that you help. You both had no idea that the man kneeling beside that tire in the dark was an internationally known assassin, one of the best in the business. He tried to kill us, too, Paul. But in the end he lost. What happened to Jennifer and Tiffany was horrible beyond words, but you are not to blame. Never was and never will be."

"I drove out to the cemetery and put flowers on their graves. After all these years, it seemed different, almost as if I didn't recognize the cemetery. I brushed leaves and broken tree limbs from their graves and just stood there. I wanted to explain some of what happened in the last five years, but found it hard to do. I told them about you and David ... and how Buddy's doing." He reached out and held Alicia's hand. "You're not supposed to bury your family. It happened once ... I can't ever have it happen again. You and David are my rocks and reasons for going on. I'll defeat this second round of evil. I have no choice."

FIFTY-SEVEN

Paul opened his eyes, a shred of morning light breaking through a small gap in the curtain. He rubbed one hand along his unshaven face, his eyes puffy. He stood, Alicia still asleep under the blankets. Paul slipped on his jeans and T-shirt, brushed his teeth and walked quietly back to his office, examining the data on his screen. He could tell the hacker had read the message he left behind and had copied the phone number to one of Paul's burner phones.

After fifteen minutes, Alicia entered with two cups of hot coffee. She said, "Thought you could use this." She handed him one of the coffee cups.

"Thanks. I did fall asleep for an hour or so." He sipped, steam rising.

"Did you break Jefferson's code?"

"No, not yet. But I did set a trap for the hacker. He or she took the bait. Among all of the dummy files I created, one I'd labeled the *Jefferson File*. In it, I wrote a note, ostensibly from NSA or the FBI asking for a meeting at the White House to discuss rethinking the president's terrorist negotiation policy in view of the mass killings and destruction of American landmarks. And I left a bogus phone number. The hacker sniffed around all of it for a while, but finally copied the fake Intel and now I have a port of entry to this person. I'm going to run the diagnostics through the firewalls and see if I can get the IP address and gain access to his world."

"Sounds like you're just a few steps from his or her front door."

"Yes, but it's been a distraction from trying to decrypt the Jefferson paper. The only reason I'm on the offense with the hacker is because this guy got so far in—got through nearly impermeable firewalls to crawl around my servers and hard drives. It's as if he drew first blood in a cyber war. If these people, the ones responsible for the deaths here in America, if they've recruited a hacker of this talent and caliber, they really want to know my moves. They probably want to know what, if anything, I might be doing to their nuclear program again. As I try to turn the tables, I'm hoping to shine some light into where they're hiding. And then the CIA and FBI can send in the troops."

Alicia held her coffee cup in both hands, the steam drifting. Her brown eyes filled with courage and fear. "I hope and pray that it doesn't somehow backfire and they find us before you can find them."

• • •

From the street, the parking lot of the Russian consulate was only visible through the iron gates. A huge wall, the bone white of sun-bleached coral, blocked most of the view. The iron gates to the consulate on Tunlaw Road in northwest Washington DC swung open and the black Cadillac XT5 SUV pulled into the private parking lot. The driver, hidden behind dark tinted windows all around the vehicle, drove through the lot shaded by tall elm trees.

He steered the vehicle toward a second gate, this one leading to secure parking in the basement of the four-story building. Dabir Nagi knew the Americans constantly watched the consulate. Hidden cameras captured vehicle license plates as they came and went from the lot. The second gate opened, and he drove into the subdued light of the basement, the Cadillac's headlamps automatically coming on as the SUV entered the underground.

Nagi parked in the far northeast side of the building. He got out with three other men. None had beards. But all had dark hair and olive skin, average height and build, all wearing sports coats and expensive jeans. Each man carried a briefcase that transported disassembled assault rifles. And each man had a sidearm under his jacket. They spoke in low tones, saying only what was absolutely necessary. Nagi motioned toward the elevator and said, "Let's go meet our hosts."

They walked toward the elevator and veered left, choosing to take the stairway instead. When the door to the stairs closed, Nagi looked up, spotting one of many cameras. He turned to the tallest man in the group, a man with flat, leaden eyes and a small half circle scar on his right cheek that resembled a crescent moon. Nagi said, "We have a long memory and a history of defending our religion that has withstood the tests of time. I can almost smell the fear of the infidel because I know he is close. He mistakenly thinks he is well hidden in this capital of marble monuments to their past leaders and their filthy, unholy lifestyle."

The man with horizontal eyes nodded. "Fajar has been chosen as our martyr. He has special plans for this one. This hunt will be brilliant and blessed."

FIFTY-EIGHT

Paul showered and changed into fresh clothes, then sat back at his computer to see if the hacker had returned. There wasn't an indication that he had. But it didn't matter whether the thief returned because Paul had drilled through firewalls and dummy servers to track the hacker to the other side of the world. After weaving through false web addresses, devices of innocent people, and deeper into the dark web through multiple countries, Paul was removing the last few veils to see if he could find a face or to at least find a location, a place where the hacker operated.

"Let's see what's behind door number one," Paul mumbled as he leaned forward in his chair, fingers moving quickly over the keyboard, white coding against the black background—letters and numbers materializing and vanishing from his screen as if he was flipping through pages of a book. He paused and read the data. He let out a low whistle and whispered, "Why am I not surprised? Of course you are in Libya ... specifically, Tripoli. I found your city, and I will find you."

He sat back in his chair and closed his eyes for a moment, a small smile playing at the corner on his mouth. He pulled up an image of the fitness tracker on his screen, quickly peeling back the covers of coding he'd already done, now moving faster, like a man running into a fiery house in search of people trapped inside. After a few minutes, Paul paused and hit a button to turn the images on his screen into a split screen. His eyes moved from left to right and back again. "Son-of-a-bitch," he whispered. "You do get around from your secluded world in Tripoli."

His phone buzzed on top of the desk. He looked at the ID and answered. Bill Gray said, "You're making the job really easy for the bureau. They tell me you haven't left the safe house in a week. In the meantime, Alicia is driving to her mother's place on a daily basis. That can be risky. Any luck with the decryption?"

"Which one? I'm definitely in a multi-task mode. I bored through a lot of fake real estate, phony web address, and even devices of innocent people to track the hacker to the other side of the world."

"Which side?"

"North Africa. The nation of Libya, and specifically the city of Tripoli."

Bill was silent for a second. He stood in his kitchen and looked out into his backyard. "So, our road leads us to where this whole thing started during Jefferson's time, Tripoli. Do you have the guy's IP, ID, or his specific address?"

"No, not yet. But, unless he becomes aware of my hovering presence, I should soon. Bill, here's the other equivalent. The fitness tracker worn by Senator Fairchild was hacked and the bread crumbs led to the same place—Tripoli."

"So this systemic poison is coming from the same well."

"Yes."

"I'll alert the FBI and CIA, or course, as well as the president."

Paul removed his glasses and rubbed the bridge of his nose. When he looked back at this screen, it was black. "Hold on." His fingers moved rapidly across the keyboard. He squinted, reloading coding and setting algorithms into motion.

"What's going on, Paul?"

"He's on to me. Damn! He's essentially thrown up a cyber shield with some thick walls. The guy's fast."

"At least you managed to track him there. How long he stays is anybody's guess. Maybe you can recoup, find his address, and Special Forces will go in and kick his door down."

"That would be great, but Tripoli is a city of well over a million people. This hacker is good. One of the best I've ever seen. We know the killers took the time to push the note into Fairchild's mouth. The note was, no doubt, written before the murder. What we don't know is if the killers took the time to download the numbers and stored data from Fairchild's phone. I doubt it at a murder scene. But if they did, all of the phone numbers are compromised. In the meantime, for someone with this hacker's skills, he could track Fairchild's contacts through phone GPS, or he might be good enough to use the microphones on the phones as bugs—listening devices to hear conversations as plain as you're hearing me."

"If Fairchild was hacked though the fitness tracker app, maybe that's as far as they got."

"The hacker is in Tripoli. The killers were in Fairchild's neighborhood, and they crossed the damn river to get there. There is no way to tell if they compromised the data on his phone after they killed him. To download that would take a few minutes. They'd be very arrogant to attempt it at a murder scene when they could have simply stolen his phone. But then we'd know all the numbers and data would be robbed. Did they take the time to search for it on his phone? We won't know until …"

"Until what, Paul?"

"Until I can find a link, find a cross-reference, uncover a connection between the numbers and hacker or the killers … or someone else."

FIFTY-NINE

Dabir Nagi and the three killers with him followed the pale-skinned man through the halls of the Russian Embassy in Washington DC. After their initial greeting, in a mix of Persian, Arabic and Russian, they agreed to speak English. Their escort could have been an accountant working for any Fortune 500 or international company in the world. He wore a tailored, powder blue suit, white shirt and dark maroon tie. His fingers were long and seemed delicate. He wasn't an accountant, and he didn't work for any company. Never had. His job always had been and always would be working for the state. Specifically Russia.

He was an assassin. But he rarely used a gun. His expertise was to make murder look like an accidental death. That was with the cases in which the Russian president didn't want to raise suspicion. Although, there was almost always suspicion when a Russian diplomat died of an apparent heart attack or was accidently hit by car.

The pale-skinned man, Victor Orlov, was anonymous, and yet his work was legendary from the old days of the KGB to its modern incarnation under the president, the Foreign Intelligence Service or SVR. When the president did want to make an international statement, usually to Russian double agents, Orlov would find a way to poison them in the slowest, most excruciating way possible. The longer the slow death played out in the news media, the greater the obituary, and the more flagrant the message radiated from the Kremlin.

"We will talk in here," said Orlov, pausing at a locked door leading to a room secluded in the bowels of the building. Orlov leaned closer to a biometric reader. It scanned his light blue right eye, the door buzzed. He walked in with the four men following him. The room had no windows. It had the feel of standing inside a massive bank vault. No pictures on the walls. There was a world map on an eighty-inch television screen attached to one wall. There were a dozen chairs, straight back, leather seat cushions.

A second door opened to the far left of the screen and a tall man entered. He was close to fifty, thinning salt and pepper hair parted on the left, thin red lips, hawk nose, and restless eyes that seemed to scan the faces of all four visitors in the time it takes to sneeze. "Please, sit down," he said, his English perfect. No accent. His name was Dimitri Abaza. He was a high level operative within the SVR. "Welcome to the Russian embassy, gentlemen. Our president extends his greetings to you."

Dabir Nagi nodded and said, "Please convey our greetings and appreciation to your president."

"Indeed. As you know, Russia's interests in the Middle East are to support those leaders who appear to align their goals closest to what we, in Russia, believe in the long run, will be most mutually beneficial. Our pasts are similar. Russia has had a history of defending the Motherland from many invaders. At one time, it severely weakened Russia. However, those days are far behind us. You, as well, have had to defend Iran and certainly Libya from a multitude of invaders. Our greatest mutual threat today is the West, specifically the Americans. And, like you, we have a long memory when it comes to those who have struck out against us. One such man, perhaps an equal of some of the world's greatest minds—men, such as Newton, Einstein, and Popov, is the American Paul Marcus. Not only, as you know, are his cryptography skills the best in the world, he has the unusual talents found in our finest covert intelligence—the ability to think far ahead, almost as if he was moving at blinding speed in a champion chess match. And this makes him a deadly adversary. He singly-handedly dismantled thirteen of the world's best political and economic strategists when he managed to find and publically identify them as the most guarded Circle of 13. We know that Fajar Hamad wants retaliation for the American aggression in Tripoli two centuries ago and that he has … special interests, we shall call it, with Iran. Perhaps we can work with Fajar. Where is he?"

"We never know. Because of his 'special interests,' as you call it, he must constantly move to keep alive. He is a martyr, a holy man and a warrior. Muhammad was a holy man and a warrior as well. "

"But you do know how to get a message to him."

"Of course. Although he is the one who most often initiates communications."

"Communicate this to him. Paul Marcus is less than thirty miles from where you are sitting now. We aren't sure exactly where he is … but it's just a matter of time. When we find him, and we will, would you like to be the first to know? As warriors, I would assume so."

SIXTY

Bill Gray looked at his watch and thought about the crescent moon deadline the terrorists had listed in their note, two days remaining. He held one of the burner phones to his ear, pausing his conversation as his wife, Claire, an attractive women in her mid-sixties, stepped into the kitchen and got a bottle of water from the refrigerator.

When she walked back by him she said, "You don't have to whisper. After thirty-seven years, I know you're talking covert strategy, but remember you retired five years ago, Bill." She half-smiled and walked into the family room and turned on the television.

Bill spoke into the phone. "Paul, can you be more specific? What is the connection? Do you have even so much as an educated guess … hell, at this point, under the deadline of the crescent moon, I'll take a good ol' hunch."

"No, not yet. Maybe soon." Paul glanced out the window at the yard, watched the tree branches swaying in the breeze, the clouds moving in a rambling conga line against the blue sky. "How far away is the satellite monitoring this house?"

"I'm not sure, why?"

"Just wondering whether to shower naked in the backyard." Paul smiled. "You know, Bill, there is something very abnormal about being under constant surveillance. When it's a stakeout, when agents are trying to monitor where a suspect goes or who comes to see him or her, that's one thing. But the safe house and all its imagery, and the heavily-armed escorts, twenty-four-seven, it's a constant reminder of a target on our backs."

"I understand, however, look at the alternative. Until we can remove you and your family as their mark, you all need protection. I'm sorry the idyllic life that you and Alicia had on the island was penetrated. But the hard and deadly facts are that it was, and now we have to figure out how to deal with it to keep you alive."

"I know, I'm just pushing myself hard at this. Not a lot of sleep. And if there's one thing a cryptographer needs, it's some sleep to knock down the cobwebs. But I don't have that luxury, because we don't where Fajar Hamad is going to strike next."

Bill stepped outside on his patio. "Every high school, college, government building, or landmark with Jefferson's name attached to it is as close to being on lockdown as we can get."

"I don't think their next target will be something with Jefferson's name on it. But it will be something that underscores what Jefferson stood for as a founding Father, freedom from tyranny … less interference from government in the lives of the people … and all bridges to liberty. Bill, in the note found in the backpack filled with nickels … "

"What about it?"

"You said the perps wrote, *'Jefferson stands on top of a bell that doesn't ring for liberty and justice for all. In America, for whom does the bell toll? It rings loud for the wicked, arrogant and wealthy. For the rest, it is silent.'* In one of Jefferson's decoded letters to Stephen Decatur, Jefferson writes about the theme of a poem written more than a century earlier by the English poet John Donne. I'm paraphrasing here, but Donne wrote that mankind is not an island in the stream of indifference. He wrote that we, as humans, are collectively part of the continents of humanity. Hold a second, I have the passage here." Paul leafed through some of Jefferson's letters, stopped and read. "Jefferson quotes Donne in a letter by writing this: *'Any man's death diminishes me because I am involved in mankind, and therefore never ask for whom does the bell toll, because it tolls for thee.'* Jefferson was trying to make a point in his dealing with the four Barbary countries.

That verse comes from Donne's poem called Meditation XVII or number seventeen."

"It's interesting that, after two and a quarter centuries, these thugs—one who claims ancestry to the pasha of Tripoli, are twisting that quote around to fit their doctrine when Jefferson apparently tried to leverage it to do just the opposite. What irony."

Maybe there's nothing ironic or coincidental about it."

"What do you mean?"

"I'm not sure, it just seems odd that part of a phrase used by Jefferson in trying to deal with them more than two hundred years ago is being used by these people today. What the hell's the connection?"

"Maybe none."

"Something tells me there is one."

"Why?"

"I don't know … not yet. But somehow and in someway, it feels like this living relative of the pasha of Tripoli is still pulling at threads that have held up Jefferson's premise and the republic form of democracy he helped found. Somehow, they're still trying to unravel the simple philosophy behind the principle of treating others like you'd like for them to treat you simply because we're all in this world together."

"That reasoning didn't work in Jefferson's time, and it sure as hell won't work with them today, not when a group says that if you don't embrace our religious doctrine you are our enemy."

Paul leaned back in his chair, his eyes reddened, almost bloodshot. He whispered, *"Any man's death diminishes me because I am involved in mankind, and therefore never ask for whom does the bell toll, because it tolls for thee.* I may be wrong, Bill, but I do think there's a connection that's resurfacing two centuries later."

"Hemingway used that for the title and that theme in of one of his best novels, *For Whom the Bell Tolls.*"

"And Jefferson used the theme and the power of reasoning in his negotiations with the pasha of Tripoli. His position was that mankind is not an island and basically we're connected through the earth and the lineage of our forefathers. But, it apparently fell on deaf ears or ears that refused to listen. In Hemingway's novel, the main character blows up a bridge."

Bill stepped to a wooden railing on his back deck overlooking the pond. He watched purple martins fly in and out of six gourds he'd hung for the birds on an aluminum pole fifty feet from his house. "Paul, what are you suggesting?"

"Maybe the note in the bag of Jefferson nickels was a veiled threat, hinting at their next target."

"Such as blowing up the Brooklyn Bridge?"

"Or a monument you can see directly from the bridge—the Statue of Liberty."

"Let's hope you're wrong. I'll make some calls." Bill disconnected.

Paul picked up the single sheet of paper with Jefferson's encryption and began analyzing bite-sized pieces of the letters, paring them down into groupings and feeding the sets into the computer, washing them through cycles of algorithms, seeing what, if anything, was in the dark water.

SIXTY-ONE

Alicia stood at her mother's bedside and looked in her fatigued eyes. She remembered her mom's eyes as being filled with light, almost as if they could catch sunlight like fine diamonds and reshuffle the colors of the rainbow, creating a unique sparkle. Her mother's eyes were always like that—the blues, greens and yellows of her iridescent hazel eyes, somehow mysterious, wise and more than anything … playful and loving.

Now Alicia looked in eyes that were dim, the light all but gone, replaced with the ashen look of a rainy dawn, eyes that had dimmed from hazel to a blue-steel gray, resigned to the inevitable arrival of death. But yet her mother, enduring and always the optimist, tried hard to disguise the pain of a weakening body and the agony of leaving her family.

Alicia held her mother's hand, her pulse weaker by the day, her smile fading into a reluctant frown only because she was getting too weak to smile anymore. "Mom, would you like a sip of water?"

Helen looked up, not turning her head. She nodded and said, "Yes, please."

Alicia picked up a plastic glass with a top on it, a straw protruding from the top. "It's empty. I'll refill it." Alicia walked through the family room, checked on David who was sitting on the floor playing with superhero toys one of the federal agents had given him, the agent telling Alicia that his own son had outgrown them. She went into the kitchen where Dianne and Brandi were unloading the dishwasher. "How's Mom?" Dianne asked.

"She drifts in and out of sleep. The sleep part is becoming longer. I guess it's the effects of morphine. I'm getting her some more water." Alicia stepped to the refrigerator. The small TV on the counter was muted. She looked at a female reporter standing in front of the FBI building.

Alicia turned up the sound, the anchorman introducing the reporter's story. "We've learned more about what the terrorists want, and we must say their list of demands, in wake of their deadly aggression, sounds bizarre. Here's Jeannie Lawton."

The image cut to a woman holding a microphone and standing in front of FBI headquarters in Washington, DC. She looked directly into the camera and said, "That's right, Doug. Up until now, the FBI hasn't made the terrorist's list of demands public. However, through social media, the still unidentified terrorists did make the demands public … if they can be believed. The Director of the FBI, Haden McNally, has no comment in wake of all this. The terrorists want the U.S. to pay Iran a billion dollars for damages made to its nuclear program in an incident that happened five years ago. And this is coming after the signing of the nuclear accord we struck with them awhile back. They are demanding the release of two men rounded up in Libya for their alleged involvement in the deaths and destruction of the U.S. compound in Benghazi. They also want the president to release former NSA cryptographer Paul Marcus to them, which is interesting because he has been presumed dead, and we have not been able to receive confirmation that he is not. Marcus, as you may recall, allegedly planted a cyber worm into the Iranian nuclear operation right after he helped negotiate the release of two American hostages held in an Iranian prison for purportedly crossing the border between Turkey and Iran."

Dianne said, "Oh dear God … Alicia." She stepped closer to her sister and embraced her.

Brandi folded her arms, eyes defiant. She said, "There is nothing alleged about it. There were no signs marking the border. It was in a very remote spot. Adam and I were taking pictures of wildflowers.

Out of nowhere came these guys in uniforms with guns." She looked back at the TV screen.

The reporter, glanced at her notes, addressed the camera and said, "Now, the third demand, odd as it may sound to much of the world, is they want a public apology from the president. They want him to issue an apology for what they call former president Thomas Jefferson's aggression in 1804 when Jefferson and the U.S. Marines defeated Muslim forces in what was called the Barbary Wars. An historical footnote, Jefferson sent American troops to Tripoli, which was Libya at the time, after they declared war on the U.S. Back to you, Doug."

The anchorman shook his head. "White House Press Secretary, Hannah Cohen, calls the demands ludicrous and said the president and this nation will not negotiate with terrorists. She added that the FBI and other authorities are circling this group, and it is just a matter of time before they are caught and brought to justice."

Alicia pressed back against the kitchen counter, hugged her arms and said, "I'd be lying to my sister and my niece if I said I wasn't scared."

Dianne, eyes wet, said, "You and Paul got Brandi and Adam home. We thought you were dead. Now that you're here, we're not going to let anyone take you away. They'll find these guys, Alicia. I know it."

SIXTY-TWO

Alex Butler decided to skip lunch. He'd run a little late making the last three deliveries through the outskirts of Philadelphia and wanted to make up time. Butler, mid twenties, thin brown hair like duckling down, was newly married. And with a baby on the way, he couldn't afford to lose a job that he'd applied for twice before getting hired. *'Perseverance,'* he remembered his father always said. *"Nothing beats perseverance 'cause most folks quit too soon.'* Butler thought about that as he drove the brown delivery truck down Wayne Avenue, the warm air heating the inside of the truck.

Butler was cautious by nature, especially in some of the Philly neighborhoods where he made his deliveries. He was raised in Stanton, one of the toughest neighborhoods in Philadelphia. But he didn't stay there. His old high school was now closed. Violence inside and drug deals in the parking lot created a haven for perpetual crime. Traditional education in class evaporated when there were no boundaries to crime on the streets.

Driving the delivery truck through these neighborhoods, he always locked the door and took the keys when he made an infrequent stop. Customers didn't leave packages on their doorstep—at least they didn't for more than a few minutes. And now Butler and the hundreds of other drivers nationwide in the company were taking time-stamped pictures of packages they left next to front doors.

He tried not to think about that as he pulled up to a corner on Germantown. He had one delivery here today. An auto repair shop. As soon as he stopped, parked next to the curb, and hit the button to turn his flashers on, his phone rang. He normally wouldn't even take the time for a call. But his wife, Shelly, was less than two weeks from delivering their first child. He glanced at the caller ID and answered, "Hey, Baby … you okay?" He looked at her framed picture on the truck's console near a small oscillating fan.

"I don't know." There was a slight sob.

"What do you mean?"

Shelly, blonde and petite, stood in her bathroom, spots of blood on the white tile floor next to her bare feet. "I'm bleeding, Alex. I went to the bathroom and there was blood in my pee. When I stood up, more ran down my leg. I'm scared."

Alex licked his dry and cracked lips, his heart hammering. "Look, baby, everything is gonna be okay. Did you call your sister, Abby?"

"Yes. She's in a meeting with one of Bobby's teachers. Can you come get me? I think I need to go to the hospital?"

Alex looked at his watch. He had almost twenty more deliveries. "Yes. I'll be there. I'm not gonna drive all the way back to the office. I'm closer to you from where I am right now. I'll park the truck in front of our house and take you in your car."

"Okay," she moaned. "Please hurry."

"Love you." Alex disconnected, took the package from the truck, ran to the auto repair shop and walked inside. He stepped up to the counter. A fleshy man in a grease-stained, short-sleeve shirt nodded and took the package. "You all right?" he asked. "Look out of breath."

"Yeah, I'm okay. Can you sign?" He set the digital tablet on the counter and the man signed his name. "Thanks. See you."

"You guys are always in a hurry. Always rushing."

"Kinda goes with the job." Alex turned, opened the door and jogged back to his truck. He glanced at his watch, used the key, but realized he didn't lock the truck. Left it unlocked. He climbed inside and sat in the driver's seat. Before he could put the truck in gear, something seemed to drop over his head. It was like a feather touching the tip of his nose, or walking through the woods and a spider's web grazes your ear.

As he tried to look behind him, the wire tightened. Alex fought, trying to reach back to grab the person. But the attacker's strength was too much. Within seconds, the thin wire of the garrote had sliced deep into Alex's throat, cutting his carotid artery in half, destroying his larynx. He kicked at the dash console. Arms flaying. Blood poured down his neck like a coat of red paint. He dug his fingernails into the wound, pulling at the tightening wire. His mouth made a gurgling sound. The capillaries in his eyes burst.

He looked at the photo of his wife wedged next to a small fan on the console. Shelly's smiling face blurred and then darkness.

The killer, a man with olive skin, powerful forearms, dark kinky hair, pulled Alex's body into the back of the truck. The killer wore an identical delivery uniform—brown shirt, shorts and work shoes. He used two white towels to wipe blood from the seat, tossing the towels on the floorboard, getting behind the wheel and driving away.

He set his GPS and drove out of Germantown. He looked in the side-view mirror and spotted the rented car following him. He reached out the window, closed his large fist and lifted his thumb up. He drove six blocks and turned right on North Broad Street, heading in the direction of downtown Philadelphia.

He set his course straight toward the birthplace of American democracy, Independence Hall.

SIXTY-THREE

Paul sat in front of his computer and pored over the Jefferson letters, rereading the transcript from the letter Jefferson had written his Secretary of State, James Madison. Jefferson wrote, *'The American people will not stand for the financial demands of the corsairs of the Barbary nations. Their tributes, as they refer to them, constitute ransom and are the action of pirates. I believed in 1786 the same way I do at the present in regards to this state of affairs. After the Barbary pirates seized the USS Philadelphia, taken Commodore Bainbridge and his crew hostage, it is beyond time for war. The ship, namesake for the city that the nation's independence and liberty rang from, must be returned to us. If not, America will go to war against them.'*

Paul pushed back in his chair and thought about his last conversation with Bill Gray. *'Such as blowing up the Brooklyn Bridge?'* He lifted his phone and made the call. Bill said, "Tell me you've come up with something."

"I believe it'll be soon. In the meantime, I was thinking about that note in the bag of nickels."

"What about it? We have the Brooklyn Bridge and the Statue of Liberty as guarded as humanly possible."

"How about the Liberty Bell in Philadelphia?"

"What about it? Why would they—"

"Bill, they wrote: *'Jefferson stands on top of a bell that doesn't ring for liberty and justice for all. In America, for whom does the bell toll? It rings loud for the wicked, arrogant and wealthy. For the rest, it is silent.'* Based on their movements, I think their next target is the Liberty Bell."

• • •

Dabir Nagi sat in his rental car and watched the delivery driver park on 6ᵗʰ Street close to the rear entrance to the Liberty Bell Center near Independence Hall. It was a balmy day in Philadelphia and hundreds of tourists, many with maps and brochures in hand, ambled around the old streets. They strolled in and out of the historic buildings and museums, down the brick and cobblestone streets to Old City Hall, the Ben Franklin Museum, Carpenter's Historic Hall, and the Signer's Garden—the birthplaces of American democracy.

No one noticed the deliveryman in the brown uniform. He walked through the entrance to the Liberty Bell Center carrying a cardboard box as easily as a vacationer with a camera. He made his way beneath the battery of security cameras, his head low, walking fast, maneuvering down the long enclosed walkway and around tourists.

Dozens of people stopped and looked at the enlarged historical photographs of the Liberty Bell, and the period inscriptions—the chronological events associated with the bell throughout America's past. They viewed short videos and illustrated timelines from the construction of the bell through important American milestones associated with the Liberty Bell and its role in the nation's past—the American Revolution, women's rights, civil rights—images of people from George Washington, Thomas Jefferson, Ben Franklin to Harriet Beecher Stowe to Susan B. Anthony, Rosa Parks, Martin Luther King, John Kennedy and more. The Liberty Bell, and what it stands for, seemed to resonate with all causes of human freedom and rights.

The deliveryman made no eye contact. He headed directly for the legendary bell housed in an area where the public had close access. As he approached the final section, the place where the Liberty Bell was on display, he paused and looked at the dozens of visitors standing near the ropes that cordoned off the bell from human hands.

The people could get within ten feet of the bell; plenty close enough for pictures and selfies in front of one of the most iconic symbols of American freedom.

The Liberty Bell, with the scar in its armor, is a beacon that draws more than one and a half million visitors a year to stand in awe of what the old bell still stands for—hard-fought freedom. Of the top five American historical icons, it takes its place in line behind the Declaration of Independence, U.S. Constitution and its Bill of Rights, and the Statue of Liberty.

A National Park ranger in uniform hosted a tour of more than two-dozen people flocking around the bell. He was an older black man who'd been a park ranger for twenty-five years. He pointed to the crack and said, "If you look closely, you'll see a hairline fracture that leads from the wider crack all the way through the inscription on the bell. Why did the Liberty Bell crack? Anyone know?"

A twenty-something woman, hair in a ponytail, Philadelphia Eagles T-shirt, raised her hand. "I heard it was because the bell was actually used a lot. It was used to convene the state and federal meetings of elected representatives. The metal just got weakened over the years."

The ranger, with salt and pepper hair, a broad smile, said, "Great! That's exactly right. The bell's upholstery, so to speak, became a little too thin. It was recast from time to time and the crack repaired … but once the damage was done, sometimes the old wound comes back. Kind of like a broken bone that never quite heals. Such was the case for the Liberty Bell. Although it shows its age, the inscription on it … the calling card, if you will, is just as fresh today, and perhaps equally important today than anytime in our nation's history. As you can read, it says, *Proclaim liberty throughout all the land and unto the inhabitants thereof…*" The ranger smiled and surveyed the small crowd. "Anybody know where that sentence originated?"

An older man, silver hair, a rosewood cane in one hand, hunched over, looked up and said, "It's from the Bible … Leviticus, passage twenty-five, verse ten, to be exact."

The ranger grinned, sunlight pouring in from the large, floor-to-ceiling glass windows behind the Liberty Bell. "Yes sir, that's exactly right. I do this tour six times a day, five days a week, and I'm lucky if one person knows that verse once a month."

The old man cocked one of his cotton white eyebrows and smiled.

The deliveryman with the cardboard box walked past the crowd. He set the box in a corner, less than fifteen feet from the bell. The man looked out the windows to Dabir Nagi waiting in the rental car. He nodded at Nagi, turned and walked back down the long corridor, pausing for a moment to tape a piece of paper next to the picture of the Liberty Bell during its first and only cross-country tour in 1918. In the picture, Thomas Edison is seen standing next to the bell. The deliveryman taped the top and bottom of the paper to the glass enclosure protecting the old photographs. The paper read: *Jefferson stands on top of a bell that doesn't ring for liberty and justice for all. In America, for whom does the bell toll? It rings loud for the wicked, arrogant and wealthy. For the rest, it is silent.'*

The deliveryman, who just delivered terror in a box to one of America's first bastions of freedom, rounded the building, walked past the parked delivery truck, got into the passenger side of Nagi's car and said, "They all had their eyes on the broken bell. Now is the time."

Nagi nodded, picked up his phone and hit seven numbers on the keyboard. Within five seconds, a massive explosion ripped through the Liberty Bell Center, blowing out all the glass in the large window. Body parts flew from the window like bloody confetti, thick white smoke billowing, hiding the carnage of death and destruction. The Liberty Bell was blown off its housing.

SIXTY-FOUR

Alicia held her mom's hand and said a silent prayer. Her mother stared out the sunroom windows, her thoughts buried. She looked at her daughter and said, "I'm so thirsty."

"I have some cool water for you, Mom." She lifted the plastic glass with the bent straw protruding from the top. "Here you go." She gently placed the straw between her mother's dry lips.

Helen took a small sip and then turned her head to look into her backyard. She watched a goldfinch alight next to the birdfeeder and begin pecking at the seed. The bird's feathers were the color of lemon in the sunlight. Helen managed a small smile and said, "Oh, I so love the little goldfinches. A goldfinch followed Christ on the road to Calvary. The bird picked out thorns from the crown. Alicia, I'm not sure if Dianne put food in the feeder. Would you check?"

"Sure, Mom." Alicia set the water on a bedside table and went out the door.

David walked into the room with Buddy, saw his mom in the backyard and followed her. Buddy stayed close to David. He stopped behind his mother and asked, "Why are you standing out here, Mom?"

She turned and whispered, "Because I don't want to scare the bird in the feeder."

David watched the goldfinch eat, the small bird cocking its head, inspecting the humans less than twenty feet away. After another few seconds, the goldfinch picked up a large seed in its beak and flew to a nearby elm tree.

"Want to help me feed the birds?" Alicia asked.

"Yippee!" David jogged to the birdfeeder, Buddy alongside him.

Alicia opened the bag of birdseed, handed David a plastic scoop and said, "Reach in here and fill it with seed. I'll pick you up and you can pour it in the birdfeeder, okay?"

"Okay." David scooped the seed, his mother lifting him. As he ladled the seed in the feeder, Alicia looked around the perimeter of the backyard where she played as a child. She remembered playing on the swing-set Dad had built for her and Dianne. She recalled holding hands with Dianne and jumping on the trampoline until Mom called them in for dinner. She thought about catching fireflies in a canning jar with the cute neighbor boy, Gerald Ramsey, who lived three houses down the block. They'd sit next to each other on the top of the backyard picnic table, the glow of the fireflies in their eyes, the light of the moon rising over the pines at the end of the yard, the song of crickets in the summer night air.

And now, as she held her son, Alicia looked around her childhood property as if landmines were buried under the soil, the same soil where she learned to turn cartwheels and play hide-and-seek. She heard the sliding glass doors open wider and turned to see her sister, Dianne, stepping out onto the deck.

"Mom really likes watching you and David feed her birds," Dianne said.

"Remember when we were kids, Mom had Dad build half a dozen birdfeeders. I know he'd grumble about the cost of birdfeed, but he never did it in front of Mom. He knew how important it was to her."

Brandi stood at the door, looked at her mother, aunt and David. She said, "The news is going live from Philadelphia. Something bad has happened, and it involves the Liberty Bell."

• • •

Paul put his glasses back on and read the numbers and algorithms on his computer screen. He stared at the screen, not blinking. He returned to his keyboard and punched in numbers and geographic logistics. He followed the trail of the dummy phone number he'd used as bait. It led him through the hidden rooms and chasms in the dark web, which was really a spider's web of victims. Stolen bank accounts. Stolen identities. Bank router numbers. Stolen charge card numbers. Mortgages pilfered. Nude pictures used for blackmail.

All the victims trapped in the web like mummies, encased by the silk wrapping and trappings of criminal spiders and sucked dry. Some victims were nothing but exoskeletons—husks of their former selves. Others were fresh-caught. Identities quickly auctioned and sold for the high-market bid. Paul weaved through the sewer of the dark web. Searching for a door leading to the hacker.

He was close.

He punched less than a dozen more keys and paused, almost as if he was opening a locked and hidden door with a master key. And there it was—the stolen phone number. Paul looked at how the number was being used. The hacker had remotely turned on the microphone and the GPS.

Paul entered the digital heart of the phone and found a link to dozens of other phone numbers—many with international codes. He scrolled through the numbers. Looked at the physical location of cell towers and communications satellites. He leaned in a little closer, whispered, "A number located in Rome. Where will that lead me?" He keyed in more data, following a circuitous digital trail. Within seconds, he was looking at what appeared to be a spreadsheet of other numbers and locations.

Two of the numbers were linked to Senator Fairchild's phone at the time of his murder. One number had a Rome, Italy, country code. The second appeared to have originated from the Washington DC area.

Paul's phone buzzed. He looked at the ID and answered. Bill Gray said, "Have you seen the news?"

"I never like conversations that begin like that."

"And you won't like what I'm going to tell you. All hell broke lose in Philadelphia. You were right about the Liberty Bell. We just couldn't get there fast enough." Gray held his tablet in one hand and his phone in the other, pacing his kitchen. He stepped outside.

"Somehow, one of Hamad's operatives got inside the Liberty Bell Center and blew up half the place. The body count is at seventeen. Many others critically wounded. The Liberty Bell was damaged. The bomber left a calling card, a note with the same written words—the same garbage that was found in the backpack filled with nickels."

"Was it a suicide bomb?"

"We don't know. Hold on Paul. I'm getting a message from headquarters." Bill read from his tablet. "It's an update. Police found what they thought was an abandoned parcel delivery truck about a block from Independence Mall. The driver had been murdered and tossed in the back of the truck with dozens of boxes and packages. The killer used a garrote, almost cut the guy's head off."

"We've got to stop these bastards. I need to call Alicia."

"We're assuming the purpose of the murder was for the killer to impersonate the driver and take a package into the museum. Our guys and the FBI are remotely checking the security camera footage. These terrorists are like a cancer spreading. It's hard for us to cut it out or kill it without knowing the location."

"It might be closer to home than you think."

"What do you mean?"

"I've been tracking the hacker. He's got a lot of people caught in his dark web. Before Carl Busch breached, can you find what number the CIA used, if and when they used a phone to contact him."

"I have a gut feeling that you are doing everything in your power for find Carl Busch since he found you on Panarea. But you've never been one to let revenge obscure your sights."

"It's not about personal retaliation. Not about revenge." Paul looked at the picture of Eli Dexter. "It is, though, to avenge the deaths of others. People like Eli Dexter, the child killed at Mount Rushmore, all those people in the wedding, and those people who died while standing next to the one thing that really personifies our nation's liberty … the Liberty Bell."

"I'll see what I can find out about our tracking of Carl Busch. Give me a few hours."

SIXTY-FIVE

Alicia stood at the back door of her mother's house and saw a lone raven appear. It flew in from the surrounding woods and alighted near the top of the highest pine tree at the edge of the property, exactly where the back yard ended and the woodlands began. They were the same woods she'd played in with Dianne when they were girls. The raven was large, coal black, and seemed to have no interest in the bird feeder. It simply perched on the limb and surveyed the area.

"Come on inside," Alicia said to David. They followed Brandi back inside, Alicia holding the doors for David and Buddy. She said, "David, you and Buddy go play in the rec room, okay? I'll be there in a minute."

"Okay." He walked by his grandmother's bed. "We fed the birds, Grandma."

She smiled weakly. "I saw that. Thank you so much."

"You're welcome. Come on, Buddy."

Alicia stopped by her mother's bed and asked, "Can I bring you anything, Mom?"

"I'm fine, sweetheart. Thanks. Alicia, you don't have to hover over me. You, Dianne and Brandi need to laugh some. Go in the kitchen and tell stories. Have some wine. Tell Brandi about the time her mother tried to bake a cake and set off every smoke alarm in the house." Helen coughed, a raspy sound deep in her lungs.

242

"Okay, Mom." Alicia touched her mother's hand, glanced out the sunroom windows, the raven now closer.

When Alicia entered the kitchen, Dianne and Brandi were standing next to the television screen. They watched news images of firefighters mopping up water around the perimeter of a building in downtown Philadelphia, smoke drifting from what was left of a massive window. Dozens of police and emergency vehicles were in the streets. Blue and red lights flashing.

Yellow crime scene tape crisscrossed everywhere on the outside of the building. There were black body bags lined on a cordoned-off sidewalk, team members for the coroner's office processing the dead. Some bodies were covered in white sheets and lying on gurneys, as paramedics attended to the injured and dying.

"Oh, dear God," Alicia said, holding one hand to her mouth. She heard her phone ring on the kitchen counter, ignoring it, transfixed by the horror on the television screen.

A television news reporter's voice accompanied the live images. The female reporter said, "We are live on the scene of this horrific disaster in the heart of Philadelphia's historic district. From early police reports, we know that a bomb exploded near the Liberty Bell. The viewing area around the iconic bell was nearly filled with visitors, many of them middle-school children. As you can see from the confusion behind us, we don't have a full count of the number injured or dead. Firefighters had to extinguish a fire caused by the explosion. No one is sure how the bomb got into the area of the Liberty Bell, but what is known is that it did substantial damage to the museum resulting in loss of life, perhaps in the dozens." The live shot panned over to the reporter standing in a park-like setting, the smoke and chaos more than fifty yards from her. She wore her dark hair up.

The image cut to a spilt-screen. A news anchorman looked into the camera and said, "Arianna, we understand that police found a typed note apparently left behind by the bomber. Do you know exactly where the note was found and what was written on it?"

The reporter touched one finger to her earpiece, nodded her head. "Yes, investigators found it taped to the glass enclosure of framed pictures of the Liberty Bell as depicted in U.S. history." She looked at her notes. Someone wrote this: '*Jefferson stands on top of a bell that doesn't ring for liberty and justice for all. In America, for whom does the bell toll? It rings loud for the wicked, arrogant and wealthy. For the rest, it is silent.*' She paused and looked back in the camera. "Dan, we're told that was the same message found in a backpack full of nickels left at the foot of the Thomas Jefferson statue at the University of Virginia. If the bomber did, in fact, post the note inside the museum, it appears that this latest tragedy is tied directly to the homegrown terrorists who listed their demands … demands the president said would never be considered or negotiated. From the Independence Hall area of downtown Philadelphia, this is Arianna Price. Now back to you in the studio."

Brandi folded her arms, looked away from the carnage as the anchorman continued with more information. She said, "There are no words."

Dianne turned to Alicia and asked, "Is Paul still trying to figure out the riddles these crazies are leaving?"

"Yes. He's working … he's trying to help the FBI, CIA and NSA find and stop these monsters."

"I hope he quickly reaches light at the end of the tunnel. I'm not sure that we, as a nation, can stand much more of this."

David walked into the kitchen. Alicia said, "David, I'll be in there in a few minutes."

"Mom … it's grandma. Her chest isn't moving up and down like it was before."

SIXTY-SIX

Alicia, Dianne, and Brandi ran to the bedside, all three women knowing in their hearts that the shadow of death had descended on the house. They approached the bed with trepidation, apprehension, not sure what to say or do. Alicia looked at her mother. Her hands were folded across her waist, eyes closed, a look of peace on her pale face. Alicia touched her mother's hand, instinctively feeling for a pulse. There was none. She turned towards Dianne and nodded.

Brandi bit her bottom lip, tears spilling from her eyes. "Grandma," she whispered stepping to the edge of the hospice bed where she touched her grandmother's shoulder and looked over at her mother. Dianne blinked back tears, her lower lip trembling. The sun slowly emerged from behind a cloud, allowing a diffusion of sunlight to creep through the windows into the room, drenching Helen's ferns and half a dozen peace lilies in a buttery radiance. The light fell softly across Helen's face.

Alicia looked at her mother—her beautiful mother, no longer in pain. Her gentle composure restored. Closing her eyes, Alicia could hear mom's voice on those long ago summer's nights. She'd stand at the sliding glass doors, turn on the floodlights and say, *'It's time to come inside, Alicia. Gerald, you can come in, too. But you two should set the fireflies free. It'd be a shame to keep all their pretty light locked up in one jar when we have the dark woods outside. The night critters could use some light now and then.'*

Alicia blinked her eyes, somehow unable to cry. Her mother was no longer suffering and in a better place. Alicia turned her head and looked through the windows at the deck and the birdfeeder. Two goldfinches were on the bars of the feeder. The birds sat next to each other, almost shoulder-to-shoulder, enjoying the thistle. The smaller of the two turned to bask in the grandeur of the sunlight, light bouncing off her yellow feathers, her stomach heavy with eggs that she'd soon lay in their nest.

Alicia thought about what her mother had said earlier, '*A goldfinch followed Christ on the road to Calvary. The bird picked out thorns from the crown.*'

Alicia bent down and lifted David up, holding him tight. "Grandma's not hurting anymore, David. Her body was so sick. She's left it and has gone on to a loving place, to Heaven, where there is no pain. I'm so glad you got to spend some time with her."

"Me, too, Mom. Where is Heaven?"

• • •

Paul heard two cars arriving in the driveway. The garage door went up and one car entered, the other parking midway up the drive. From there the agents could watch the house and part of the road. Buddy trotted into the office first, tail wagging, eyes upbeat. Paul petted him. "How was your day, Buddy? Everything okay at Grandma's house? You know that place even better than this house."

Alicia came to the office door and stopped. She looked at her husband and said nothing, her face told the story. Paul rose from his chair and walked over to her. She lifted her arms, and they embraced. Nothing was said. And then she gave herself permission to cry. The tears flowed as Paul held her tight.

After a minute, she inhaled deeply and said, "I wanted to call you when it happened, but I couldn't. I was numb. Although Mom is suffering no more, the fact that she's gone causes a deep ache in my heart. On Panarea I thought of her every day. I knew that she knew I was alive and that she had hope I'd come home someday. I'm just sad it took me so long." Alicia reached for a tissue, lifting it from a holder near the desk. She dabbed her eyes.

Paul looked at his wife for a moment, his heart heavy for her. "I'm so sorry."

Alicia said nothing, stepping toward the window looking at the fenced backyard, the thick foliage of evergreen shrub hedges almost hiding the tall fence. She turned back to Paul. "We're on earth for such a short time. Dad passed almost six years ago, and now Mom. Dianne's husband, Charlie, is still in Texas on business. He's flying back tonight. Brandi's fiancée, Adam, left work and drove straight over to Mom's house. He helped make arrangements with the funeral home. They came and took Mom away. I learned we had to report her passing to the police, just so they have a record, even in a natural death."

"I'm sorry I wasn't there at the time of her passing."

Alicia's eyes welled. "When Dad died as quickly as he did, much sooner than we expected, Mom told me she didn't lose all of him that day—that moment, but rather her real loss of my father was over time. She grieved at the time of his death, of course. But she truly began to miss him in small pieces ... over the next months. She said it was as if the picture puzzle pieces of their life were slowly removed, one by one. When mail addressed to him ... even the bills, finally stopped coming. When she reluctantly began donating his clothes to charity, the smell of his aftershave lotion on his suits as she took his clothes out of the closet and neatly packed them. Mom said she cried for hours after doing that. Today, when they took her body away, I went in her room and just stood there for a few minutes. I looked at the old pictures of Mom and Dad on the wall and dresser. I smoothed out a wrinkle on the bed and could just smell her favorite perfume on a pillow. And then I went into the sunroom and watered her plants. I watched the birdfeeder through the glass. Although it was filled with seed, I didn't see a bird in it after they took her body away. It was as if the birds and squirrels didn't eat out of respect ... maybe in their own way, saddened. I know it sounds odd. Dianne and I didn't just lose all of Mom today ... we lost her physical body. But the essence of her, who she was—the goodness of her heart, those pieces we will slowly lose over time." Alicia looked across the room at Paul, her eyes heavy with the sorrow.

Paul went over to her. He placed his hands on her shoulders, leaned in and kissed her on her forehead and then on one of Alicia's closed eyes. "Just hold me for a little while," she whispered. "Just hold me, Paul."

SIXTY-SEVEN

B ill Gray sat on his living room couch in partial darkness. There was a low-wattage bulb burning under a lampshade on a table beside the couch. Except for the ticking of a grandfather clock in the corner, the house was quiet. Bill's wife slept upstairs, retiring early because of a migraine headache. He looked at the picture of his daughter, Rachel, on the table. He thought about how Paul had reached out to him from Panarea, *'Dad, meet Bojangles. Three months old. Lisa is begging us to let him sleep with her. Not until he's solidly housetrained ... Bojangles is missing his left dewclaw. Have you ever seen something like that?'* Bill mumbled, "Brilliant. Damn Brilliant."

One of his mobile phones rang. Bill didn't bother to look at the ID. Only one person in the world had the number, and he was the director of the NSA. Bill answered and asked, "Did you get a possible connection on the number?"

NSA Director Lewis Bledsoe, silver hair neatly combed, blue tie loosened, stood in a corner of a massive room filled with people at computer screens, an illuminated world map on a screen that took up an entire wall. He said, "We had to narrow it down to less than an hour of use and only one time. From a tower ping to satellite surveillance, we may have a hit. And I don't think you will be surprised when I tell you who it is."

"I'm sitting down. Tell me."

248

• • •

Alicia stood straighter, glanced at the computer screen and at Paul's reams of notes on the desk. She released a long breath and said, "Mom will be buried next to Dad at Rock Creek Cemetery. They bought plots there long ago. Dad always planned for that kind of thing—way back in his late thirties. I don't know how many people do that today."

"Probably not many."

"Mom died in almost the same spot where Dad passed. Although you never met Dad, I'd like to think that his knowledge of General Patton and World War Two history helped us—helped you, break Isaac Newton's code. Dad was probably one of the few people in the world who knew every line to the poem that Patton wrote called *Through a Glass, Darkly.*"

"I wish he were here now to help me with the Jefferson mystery. I don't think Jefferson wrote much poetry in his time."

"Dad, I believe, liked the contrast found in the sublime power of a poem and the fierceness of a soldier or warrior, especially when that warrior had written the poem, as in the case of Patton. Dad also liked Tennyson's poem about Ulysses coming home as an old man after the war and his world travels, still resolute in the final chapter of his life. Toward the end of Dad's life, I heard him recite some of it, especially the last part."

Paul looked at his wife, mindful of the melancholy and sorrow in her eyes, and asked, "Do you remember any of it?"

"Some, yes. Mostly because I did a paper on it."

"May I hear?"

A partial smile moved across her lips. "Okay … this is the part where Ulysses is thinking about his men. Tennyson wrote, '*Death closes all—but something near the end, some work of noble note, may yet be done. Come my friends, it is not too late to seek a newer world. Push off, and sit well in order to strike the surrounding farrows … for my purpose holds to sail beyond the sunset and the baths of all the western stars until I die. We are the strength in which old days moved heaven and earth. And that which we were we still are. One equal mood of heroic hearts, made weak by time and fate, but strong in our will to strive, to seek and find.'"* Alicia's eyes filled with tears.

Paul handed her a tissue. She said, "Maybe it was because that was one of Dad's favorite poems that I chose to write an essay about it back in college. It's an easy one to remember." She wiped away her tears.

"And it's a powerful one, too." Paul hugged Alicia and asked, "How did David handle your Mom's passing? Where is he?"

"In the kitchen, eating one of Aunt Dianne's chocolate chip cookies. I sat David down and explained to him what happened. He was sad, of course, but understood his grandmother had gone to a new home in Heaven and that her body, with the cancer all through it, wasn't here anymore—that Grandma left it behind and moved on to a better place."

"I'm glad he got to spend a little time with her. She was the only grandmother he had left."

"Paul, I know you've been in front of the computer all day, but did you hear about the horror in Philadelphia?"

"Yes. Bill called and brought me up to speed."

"It's the same sick people, isn't it? The same group, under Fajar Hamad, who killed Senator Fairchild, the little girl at Mount Rushmore and all those people in the wedding at Monticello … isn't it?

"It appears to be."

"With the arsenal of intelligence that this nation has, I don't understand why we can't hunt them down and eliminate them."

"Because this is one of the most sophisticated terror cartels we've ever seen. Bill believes they're partially financed by Russia. Why is that? Because their president has been, and is, positioning Russia as the main player in the Middle East. From Syria to Saudi Arabia to Iran—none of these countries will do anything without thinking of what the Russian president's reaction might be."

"A lot changed in the five years we were on our little island … and most not for the good. I remember visiting the Liberty Bell when I was in Catholic middle school. I was one of those curious kids who always asked the questions at museums and places like that. I'd asked my teacher why it was called the Liberty Bell. She told me it rang out for

250

our freedom soon after the Declaration of Independence was signed. That was certainly part of the reason, but when our group gathered next to the bell, the tour guide said one reason it was called the Liberty Bell was because of what was inscribed at the top of the bell. Do you know what that is?"

"Sounds like a question for Jeopardy. I don't know. What is or what was the inscription across the bell?"

"*To proclaim liberty throughout all the land and unto all the inhabitants thereto.* The guide told us it was taken from the Old Testament in the Bible, Leviticus twenty five-ten. Don't ask me how I remember those things from way back. It just stuck."

"I'm impressed. Maybe you should go on Jeopardy."

"Right now, all I want to do is go to bed. Can you make sure David's showered and fed? I'd love to take in a walk, clear my head, but that's not possible. We were raising our son in a happy and healthy environment on Panarea. We can never go back there. I'm not sure where we can go anymore." She looked at the stacks of paper, legal pads filled with Paul's handwritten notes. "You have to find a way to stop them. Dad used to say that the body of the snake truly dies when you cut off its head. Cut off its head, Paul."

Alicia left the room and closed the door. Paul stared at the computer screen. He'd soon feed David and Buddy and put them both to bed. He wanted to spend a few minutes before bed to talk with his son, to listen to whatever David was thinking about the death of his grandmother and to answer any questions that he could.

He turned back to his computer screen for a moment, looked at the encrypted page Jefferson had written, thought about the bombing of the Liberty Bell and the deaths. He thought about the note left on Eli Dexter's body and the note left on Senator Fairchild's body ... *'Remember the battle of Derna ... for whom the bell tolls has a silent ring, and always will.'* He remembered the phrase from John Donne's poem that Jefferson had used in dealing with the Muslim leaders of the Barbary nations. He thought about what that might mean in relation to the Liberty Bell and perhaps the inscription about liberty engraved on the bell, Alicia's words echoing through his thoughts. "*To proclaim liberty throughout all the land and unto all the inhabitants thereto.*

The guide told us it was taken from the Old Testament in the Bible, Leviticus twenty five-ten.

Paul read from one of Jefferson's letters in a whisper, *"Any man's death diminishes me, because I am involved in mankind, and therefore never ask for whom the bell tolls … it tolls for thee."* He sat straighter, stared at Jefferson's papers and said, "Mr. President, you may not have been a soldier or a poet, but you were a great military strategist, and the poem you picked as part of your strategy was brilliant. And now I think I know why."

SIXTY-EIGHT

The brownstone apartment was located in an upscale area off DuPont Circle in Washington DC. Dabir Nagi and three of his Iranian and Libyan associates pressed a remote control and waited in their black BMW for the gate to swing open. After it did, they drove beyond the building, the driveway secluded, and they entered the property though a locked rear entrance.

Within a minute, they were in the luxurious apartment. It had the best furnishings Russian money could buy—Koket Old World chairs and couches blended with Boco de Lobo handcrafted bookcases, cocktail tables, and chandeliers. Dabir Nagi walked over to one of the windows. The expensive drapes were drawn. He moved them slightly, looking out onto the traffic near DuPont Circle. His men removed their side arms and took seats around the spacious apartment. One man opened the stainless steel refrigerator and removed a bottle of water.

Nagi's phone buzzed. He looked at the ID and answered in Persian. The man on the other end had the deep voice that carried a command, an assurance of authority. He said, "Very good work in Philadelphia."

"It is our honor, sir."

"Where are you now?"

"In the apartment Dimitri Abaza provided."

The voice was silent for a moment. "We appreciate the Russian hospitality, however assume that everything you say and do is monitored."

"Of course."

"Do they know where Marcus is located?"

"Not yet, but we're getting closer. They know the Americans have him in a safe house somewhere. But the Russians tell us there are more than twenty-five so-called safe housed in the District and more scattered in parts of Virginia and Maryland."

"Gamal's Internet nose is better than a camel searching for water under the sand. He says Marcus is somewhere in the District. We have given them a deadline. The destruction of the Liberty Bell is small in comparison to our next target as the crescent moon sets."

• • •

Paul wrapped David in a large, fluffy towel as his son climbed out of the bathtub. He dried David off and helped him get into his pajamas. Buddy sat on his haunches near the bathroom door, watching. Paul said, "Boys, it's time to go to bed."

"Can Buddy sleep on my bed again?"

"Sure. I have to help him up. Buddy's not as young as you anymore."

David wrinkled his nose. "He's ten, right?"

"Yes, that's right. But most animals get older much faster than people do."

"Why, Dad?"

"It's just the way their genes ... it's how they are designed. For example, if Buddy is ten years old, his body is really older only because dogs age faster than humans."

"Then how old is Buddy."

"Maybe as old as me, at least in dog years."

David looked over at Buddy and then at his father, a coy smile forming. "That's pretty old."

"But Buddy can still run faster than me. Let's run to bed. On your mark ..."

"Get set, go!"

In David's bedroom, Paul tucked his son under the covers and then lifted Buddy from the floor to the foot of the bed. Paul kissed David on his forehead. "Goodnight."

He stood and David said, "Mom told me Grandma is in a better place. She said Grandma is in Heaven. Will she come back from Heaven?"

"No ... but up there, she's not hurting from the disease that was in her body. When people die from old age, or when their body is sick or hurt and can't work right anymore, they're able to leave it behind. But your soul, that wonderful force inside your body, doesn't die. Grandma's soul ... her spirit will live with God now."

Where does God live?"

"Heaven ... the whole wide universe ... and even inside you. In your heart."

"Inside me? Does he ever come out?"

"Lots of times. Remember when we picked oranges in our back-yard?"

"Yes."

"The orange comes from the tree. It blossoms as a flower and grows into an orange. You come from God and blossom into the boy you are and the man you will one day become."

David thought about that for a moment, and then looked at Buddy at the foot of his bed. "Mom's sad. That makes me sad." David's eyes welled. He looked away, embarrassed.

"Hey, David. It's okay to feel sad. That's what your heart, your soul, feels. Your mother is sad because her mother got very sick and died. But your mother also is glad that Grandma isn't hurting or suffering. Her soul is just fine. And soon you mother will be fine, too. It doesn't mean she won't miss or won't think of Grandma, because she always will. But in time, she will remember more of the fun times she spent with her mother through the years. And she'll enjoy those memories of the good life they had together as a mother and daughter. Just like she's doing with you as a mother and son ... and like I'm doing too, okay?"

"Okay, Dad."

Paul leaned down and kissed David, turned and left the room. He walked past the master bedroom, the light on, and the muffled sound of weeping coming from behind the door. He placed his hand on the doorknob, but stopped, his heart heavy for his wife. Alicia needed some time alone, time to think—to grieve. He closed his eyes for a moment, his wife's soft sobbing painful. He knew he couldn't take away the pain. But somehow, maybe he could find a way to make them safe again. And, maybe, part of the answer was hidden in encrypted words on old pieces of paper at his desk.

SIXTY-NINE

Paul walked though the semi-dark house, stopped at a window overlooking the front yard. He lifted one piece of the blinds and saw the silhouette of the SUV in the driveway. One part of him wanted to open the door, walk to the vehicle, have them roll down the window and ask them to leave. To pack up and go, never to return. But he knew that would be foolish, considering what he was up against.

He entered the office and sat at his desk. He thought about his last conversation with Bill Gray. '*I have a gut feeling that you are doing everything in your power to find Busch since he found you. You've never been one to let revenge obscure your sights.*'

Paul looked at the hard drive of the hacker, hunted for more victims in the dark web he'd spun, and whispered, "It's not about revenge. It's about human liberty. To some it might be about another section of Leviticus that says, 'an eye for an eye ... tooth for a tooth. But for me, it's about dignity and safety ... and justice."

He spent the next hour tracking the movements of the hacker, thinking about the seismic catastrophes caused around the world from a hacker holed up in a room somewhere in Tripoli, connected to the world through the web, and connected to killers though a shared ideology of hate and greed.

He reread the Jefferson letter, and when he came to the quote from John Donne, he read aloud, the sound of the words somehow more definitive when spoken, '*Any man's death diminishes me, because I am involved in mankind, and therefore never ask for whom the bell tolls ... it tolls for thee.*' "

• • •

FBI Deputy Director Ward Rosenberg's wife was already asleep when he went to bed. He set his two phones down on the nightstand next to his bed, and leaned back into the stack of pillows. He'd swallowed three aspirins chased by three ounces of straight vodka. Sleep, real sleep, was more illusory, his nights punctuated by a film-reel of frenzied dreams with no beginning or ending. Finally he drifted off to sleep, the exhaustion of the day's work yielding to the subconscious mind and all of its pictorial echoes.

He stood, as a boy, at the end of a dock that jutted almost seventy-five feet over the surface of a lake in the Adirondacks Mountains. The lake was dark and deep at the end of the dock. Perched on a slight hill, through the pines, was his family's summer cottage.

An older man, who was a neighbor three cottages down from them, told a story last summer to Ward's family. They all sat around a fire pit near the shore, and the old man said, when he was a child, it was rumored that the lake was haunted. "On account of all the Indian skulls and bones at the bottom of the lake," he said, the dancing orange flames trapped in his dark eyes.

Ward never forgot that.

As he approached the lake, he could hear the sound of a jet ski in the distance, his beagle, Rocky, barking as his two sisters and one brother played in the woods.

Ward stared at a floating dive platform about fifty feet farther out into the vast lake. His uncle had built and anchored it beyond the dock. It was a place to swim out to, to dive from, and to sunbath. But, at age nine, Ward had never swum the distance. Today would be different, he told himself. The floating dock wasn't too far. He stepped to the edge, toes at the end of the warm boards, his reflection off the dark, still water.

He held his breath and dove into the lake, the water colder than he remembered from last summer. He popped to the surface and swam toward the platform. He could see the diving board in silhouette, could see portions of the fifty-five gallon drums that kept the dock afloat. He swam harder. Kicking. Pulling at the water. He didn't seem to be getting anywhere. The floating dock was just as far away. Maybe further. Why? He sucked water though his nose and went under. He clawed his way back to the surface.

He couldn't see the floating dock. Water in his eyes. His heart racing. He'd turn around and go back. But he went under again. This time he was sinking fast. It was cold and dark. No sunlight. His lungs burned. He heard his brother saying, '*Come on, Ward. Don't be scared all the time. You can make it.*'

But he couldn't. He felt his foot touch the mud. Something scurried. Maybe a catfish. He was somehow at the bottom of the lake. He kicked and clawed at the chilly, dark water. There was a glimmer of light. He was back near the surface, and then a loud sound, like bees. He broke through the surface. Sunlight. A man on a jet ski was doing slow circles around him. The man reached his hand down into the water. Ward grabbed it, his tears mixing with the cold lake water.

SEVENTY

P aul glanced at Eli Dexter's picture and reached for the gun. He opened one of the drawers in the desk and picked up the Glock. He chambered a round, wedged the pistol under his belt and untucked shirt. He walked through the house, found Buddy at the foot of David's bed. David was fast asleep. Paul could hear the water running in the master bath, Alicia taking a long, hot shower, trying to scrub the strain from her pores. "Come on Buddy," Paul whispered. "It's your last walk before turning in for the night. You're getting up there in dog world age. No need to put undue strain on your bladder."

He gently lifted Buddy off the bed and set him quietly on the floor. They walked through the house, out the back door, and strolled around the perimeter of the backyard, Buddy sniffing at the fence line, his black nostrils quivering. The night air carried the sweet scent of wisteria. Buddy cocked his head, nose testing the breeze.

Paul smiled. "If you're trying to find the smell of the ocean, forget it Buddy. That's long gone. Literally, another lifetime from where we are now. I'm betting you miss our island home, and you probably missed our old farm in the Virginia backcountry." He rubbed Buddy's neck. "You've been with me wherever I go. The problem is, Bud, I don't know where we go next. There are some bad people out there who want to hurt us. You were there with Jen and Tiffany, and now with Alicia and David. We have to protect them, Buddy. We can't let our guard down. We have to end it. I don't want to have to carry a gun every time you and I go for a walk."

Paul wandered to the far side of the large house, the fence and thick shrubbery like a wall around the perimeter. He looked up to the sky, a bat flying through the soft moonlight. And then a cloud passed in front of the moon, the property growing darker. He waited a moment for Buddy to finish and then stepped quietly around the edge of the garage.

There was a noise.

Paul stopped, looked down at Buddy. The dog uttered a low growl, angled his head to the left, looking toward the dark border foliage. The noise was similar to that of someone softly scratching at a door. Paul slid his pistol from his belt. The cloud cover drifted and the moonlight came through boughs of a large, red bud tree.

There was a movement, a silhouette in the night. A plump raccoon and two young ones waddled at the base of the heavy plastic trashcan partially concealed behind a wooden fence. The raccoons looked toward Paul. Buddy barked once. The animals scurried off into the dark along the fence. Paul smiled at Buddy and said, "That's not a good sign. If a family of raccoons got this close to the house, is it really a safe house? Maybe the satellite tracked their every move. Maybe it's tracking us this very second."

He walked farther around the garage and looked at the SUV parked down the driveway. Buddy started for the front yard but Paul called him back. "Let's stay here, Bud. No need to give the sentinels any reason for alarm." Paul's phone buzzed. The text was from Bill Gray: *Got a match on the number. Call me.* Paul looked down at Buddy and said, "This ought to be good because it's probably going to be bad, if that makes any sense anymore."

When they'd gone inside the house, Paul locked the doors and set the alarm, gently placing Buddy back at the foot of David's bed. As he started toward the office, he paused at the partially close door to the master bedroom. The light was off. Alicia was silent. He knew she wasn't asleep. It was the first night for the rest of her life without her mother.

Paul returned to the office. He made the call. Bill Gray answered and said, "I heard about Alicia's mother. I'm so sorry."

"She's pretty numb. I'm just glad that you alerted us to what was happening with Helen's health and we had a chance to come back. It made a huge difference."

"I'm delighted as well. I just wish it didn't happen the way it happened—with your IDs compromised, a rogue double agent selling you and your family like he'd sell state secrets. The number in Rome … that you found by digging into the hacker's archives, it's not one that was assigned to a Carl Busch, or anyone with the CIA, as far as we can determine."

"Okay."

"However, we've been physically tracking Busch, at least to some extent. That number is most likely one that he used for less than an hour because its tower pings matched with the geographic location that our agents knew Busch was in at the exact time. They're following, trying to see whom he's meeting with, where he goes, and how often he goes there. When he's exhausted his value, he will be eliminated, unless he manages to truly disappear." Bill sat alone in his living room, almost in the dark, a nightlight near the wall casting a soft light off the left side of his face. "Now, my question for you, Paul, is what number from Senator Fairchild's list linked to the one Busch used for that small sliver of time?"

Paul stared at his computer screen the light reflecting off his glasses. "Are you sitting down, Bill?"

"As a matter of fact, I am. I just sipped a very old scotch."

"After I tell you this, you might want to make another pour. The second number linked to the one that Carl Busch used for that brief moment is the number to the Deputy Director of the FBI, Ward Rosenberg."

SEVENTY-ONE

Paul heard nothing except the soft hush of air through the duct in his office. "Are you there, Bill?"

"I'm here." Bill stood from his couch, knocked back the remains of scotch in his heavy crystal glass and set it on the end table near the photograph of his daughter. "Are you certain?"

"Yes."

Bill slowly exhaled, looked at the buttery moonlight falling on the pond at the rear of his property. "Ward was one of the reasons my son-in-law, Justin Silverstein, got his job as an attorney in the Department of Justice. Ward went to bat for Justin. When Rachel and Justin were married, Ward attended their wedding. This one hits too close to home."

"If you are a double agent, or for some reason on the adversary's payroll, it helps if you can be close to the director of NSA, which you were when Rosenberg was coming through the ranks of the DOJ and the FBI."

"I need to make some calls."

"I understand."

"I hope it's confined to Ward and no one else within the bureau, especially at that level. Now things are beginning to make a little more sense."

"In what way?"

"Russian influence peddling far beyond attempting to manipulate U.S. elections. Special Counsel Charles Kurger's investigation is uncovering rocks where American lobbyists have deep connections with authoritarian regimes that do everything from hiring Western public relations firms to shaping the regime's image to retaining Western lawyers who file libel suits against the critics of these governments. And, when people like former congressman-turned-lobbyist, Robert Benson, sit on the board of Russia's oil giant, Rosneft, it looks bad. The Kremlin is saying that our politicians-to-lobbyists are no more virtuous than anyone in the Kremlin or in Ukraine, for that matter."

Paul nodded, pushing back from his chair. "Combine that with the way Russian trolls used social media to target and *friend,* if you will, unsuspecting Americans, and many U.S. organizations, all in a covert effort to mine personal data. The brave new world is as close as a computer mouse or mousetrap."

"Sami Botros, when he was a member of congress, and now inside the White House, was one of the few who wouldn't take PAC money when he ran and won two successful terms. He's been vehemently outspoken when it comes to influence peddling, foreign and domestic. Ward tossed the shadow of suspicion toward Sami Botros. Botros had mentioned to the president that he had reason to believe there was a mole at the top of the DOJ. Any other surprises you have from the data off Fairchild's phone?"

"Not yet. The dummy phone and number I've used to track down the hacker …"

"What about it?"

"I had removed the battery and placed it in a safe right here in the safe house. How safe is that?" Paul managed a smile. "I think I can use it, either via text or voice, to set a trap for the hacker and ostensibly for the people paying him. And I'm betting that's Hamad or someone very close to him."

"How will you do this?"

"By engaging in a fake, maybe scripted conversation with you or someone you designate. In it we can reveal a bogus place where I'll be with my family at a certain time. We can do it in an area where it will give the bad guys some camouflage, such as the streets of a large city, a wooded park, plenty of those in the District … or wherever you and the agencies suggest, maybe even an isolated house."

"We can't use you and your family as bait."

"I'm not suggesting that we have to be visible. The information can reveal we're ostensibly in a home or building. If it's a home, you can place highly skilled operatives in it and agents hidden along the perimeter. It might draw Hamad's people there. This could be a good opportunity to toss a net around them and force them to talk. Your next arrest could be Hamad himself. That way you can cut the head off the snake."

Bill said nothing for a moment, stepping close to his glass doors and looking at the moonlight off the still surface of the dark water. "What if we take it one step further? I can bait Ward Rosenberg with the knowledge. He'd be the only one privy to it. If he informs Fajar Hamad or whomever Rosenberg is working with in the Kremlin, then we take a bad seed out of the bureau and also capture these people who are intent on blowing up our historical monuments and killing innocent people. I'll let you know in the morning. Goodnight, Paul. Why don't you get some sleep? You sound exhausted."

"I'm going to work a little more tonight, give Alicia some time to process the passing of her mother. Goodnight, Bill." Paul disconnected and turned to face his computer. He thought about what Alicia had said, '*To proclaim liberty throughout all the land and unto all the inhabitants thereto. The guide told us it was taken from the Old Testament in the Bible, Leviticus twenty five-ten. Don't ask me how I remember those things from way back. It just stuck.*'

Buddy walked in the office and lay down next to Paul's desk. "Hey, Buddy, are you a little restless? Me too. Let's see what we can find." Paul's fingers flew across the keyboard. He whispered, "Leviticus twenty-five-ten. Mr. President, I'm betting you used the Old Testament Bible *verse* from the bell that rang the Founding Fathers proclamation and Declaration of Independence to announce liberty throughout all the land and unto the inhabitants there too—the Americans of the young republic. Your encrypted letter has eighty lines with sixty letters each. I can break it down into twenty-five sections." Paul paused, staring intently at the screen, eyes moving across the letters and grids.

He glanced down at Buddy and whispered, "I'm missing one component … and that is how many grid sections to create. And because there are nine letters in the word Leviticus, I can alternate the letters for a grid of up to nine lines each.

"And If I take the number ten, as in *verse* ten, I can number each line in the section from one through ten. So, if this works … if I can find the correct algorithms, it means that I have a key to the code—the number of lines in each section, the order in which those lines were transcribed, and just as important, the number of random letters added to each and every line."

Paul paused and moved his fingers across the keyboard, his eyes darting from the keys to the screen. He licked his dry lips, a slice of moonlight coming though a crack in the curtains across the window.

He mumbled, "I'm looking for a series of two-digit numbers. In cards, it's called two of a kind, but in cryptology it's called a key, not unlike turning the dial on a combination lock, and listening for the tumblers to fall in place." *If the key is the number 68, I will move the six to the first line of the section and then add eight random letters. If the next number is 51, I will move row five to the second line and add one letter. But to do this, I will use what was not available in the days of Jefferson and Robert Patterson—a computer that can crunch numbers and spit out algorithms.*

Paul took a deep breath. Typed in the words … *and therefore never ask for whom the bell tolls … it tolls for thee.*

He looked at his watch: 10:57 p.m.

And he waited.

• • •

Bill Gray placed a call to FBI Director Haden McNally's mobile phone. When McNally answered, Bill said, "I know it's late, Haden … but I need to ask you something."

McNally stood in his kitchen, jeans and T-shirt, setting down a glass of milk. He asked, "What's going on?"

"Before Paul Marcus and his family left Panarea, only three people knew he and Alicia were still alive. Did you share that with anyone on the bureau at any time?"

There was a moment of silence, McNally rubbing his temples, thinking. He said, "Yes, I mentioned it in strict confidence to my Deputy Director, Ward Rosenberg. Why?"

SEVENTY-TWO

T he enigmatic communication slowly began to reveal itself. After 218 years, an encrypted letter written by Thomas Jefferson and sent to Steven Decatur, one of the commanders in the Barbary War, was appearing as if two centuries of fog were lifting off the pages.

Paul used the code, keying in block letters that were represented from the decrypted letters. His fingers moved swiftly, finding the correct sequence of letters that transformed into words, and words into sentences. Authoritative sentences. Paul read what Jefferson had written:

> 'We will go to war. We have no other choice. The declaration of war against the United States and steadfast unwillingness of the pasha of Tripoli, to consider our terms, has led us into war. Let us not tread lightly, but be bold and defeat those who choose to seize our ships and sailors. The capture of USS Philadelphia exemplifies the dire strait in which this conflict has escalated into war.
>
> We seek peace and a treaty that establishes the boundaries of a tangible and lasting armistice. In order to achieve that, let us extract from the story of Cain and Abel. The pasha, in my view, rules with arrogance and a degree of narcissism. Ego blinds a man to live in the present because his suffering from the past causes him to plot for the future, consequently he will expose his Achilles heel often through his own ego. From what we know

about his brother, they do not share the same arrogant temperament. We know that the pasha's deposed brother, Hamet Karamanli, is living in exile in Alexandria, Egypt. We further recognize that Hamet harbors resentment toward his brother, Yusuf, for what Yusuf did to him.

I tender to you the authority, in the time of war, to find Hamet, if possible, and then extend an olive branch offer to restore him as ruler of Tripoli with the following conditions: All American ships, crew and property be released immediately. The practice of extorting monetary levies against any nation entering the Mediterranean Sea shall be forever abolished. Tripoli, Morocco, Algiers and Tunisia shall reimburse the United Sates of America the sum of one million dollars in damages to its ships, stolen cargo, human imprisonment, and restitution of wrongful duties previously collected by the Barbary States for the last two decades.

Paul sipped from a bottle of warm water, mouth dry, his thoughts racing. He continued reading Jefferson's words:

"In my endeavors to negotiate peace with Pasha Yusuf Karamanli, I shared the essence of the poem written by John Donne. Although it is secular in foundation, its principal is founded in the roots of righteousness, shared in part by the Bible and the Koran. Donne wrote: 'Any man's death diminishes me because I am involved in mankind, and therefore never ask for whom the bell tolls, because it tolls for thee.'

My purpose in sharing that one sentence is to extol the virtues of living in peace. By waging war, we kill and destroy many on both sides. And those who survive will not be any happier for the losses. However, I fear my proposition has fallen on deaf ears as it did two decades ago.

Many years ago, John Adams and I met with the Minister of Tripoli in London. He informed us that it was written in their Koran that all nations, which do not acknowledge the Prophet Muhammad, are sinners. He said it is the right and duty of the Muslim faithful to plunder and enslave the sinners. All these years later we have not, and clearly will not, now or anytime in the future, convince militants to reconsider this creed. The preamble to the Constitution seeks to secure the blessings of liberty to support the legislative pillars within the Constitution. That is only achieved in a democratic republic where human rights and individual freedoms are ensured by a government designed specially to protect these immutable rights. The birth of our nation was founded on principles that all men are created equal. Their Creator bestows them with certain absolute rights, including life, liberty and the pursuit of happiness. To safeguard that, our government is designed with constituents of separate but equal powers, and when these powers are united when considering matters, they should make every effort to guarantee the individual rights inherent to the republic from which the Constitution stands. The government shall not hinder or dictate laws prohibiting the right to assemble and the orderly voice of the people. Nor shall the government offer directives that prohibit the freedoms of religion. God, who gave us life, gave us liberty at the same time. The hands of force may destroy, but cannot disjoin them. Governments should make no law prohibiting the free exercise of religion, thus there should be a separation between church and state to guarantee that the boundaries of religious freedoms are not crossed or compromised.

Paul paused. He sipped from a bottle of water, his heart racing. He wanted to run to the bedroom and show Alicia what he was reading. But he needed a moment to process the information, to see what bearing, if any, it might have to the present dilemma. He continued using the code to search for words. Jefferson wrote,

"I have sworn upon the altar of God, eternal hostility against every form of tyranny over the mind of mankind. One can often forecast the future based on careful study of a long, repeated history and past actions of governments or people aligned with unalterable principles. I predict the Barbary States, under Islam, will not separate religion and state because they are inseparable

within that canon, now or in the future unless change is started by the people themselves. When a code of conquest by religious differences establishes a hostile force, there can never be significant negotiation to maintain peace and human freedoms when state and religion, incarnate as one, will justify aggression by scripture or an ensuing jihad war. All people of different beliefs in matters of religious faith, must accept and allow others to practice their religion as they choose, for it is not the right nor duty to harm those who do not believe as they do. In any religion that embodies the state to subjugate its people, change, if it is to transpire, must come from education and within the people if their collective desire can rise higher than those who wish to dominate them. A greater force must meet whoever prescribes to this autocrat tyranny and uses it for conquest and harm against others, in or out of domestic and religious boundaries. If not, all the freedoms essential to people, as individuals, will be forever lost. Any nation that subverts its people through totalitarian rule under the canon of religious doctrine, including the condemning of education, deprives them from self-determination and government for the people and by the people. The democratization of those states in which authoritarian rule reigns, compelling an interchange of clear elections to the legislature, will result in a transformation to democracy for its people. If customs and rituals of the past pave the course of the future, and the future is not altered to reflect the faults and pious inequities of the past, societies will be doomed to repeat injustices to one another. Human division will grow like a sickness in the heart of mankind at a much larger scale as ethnic populations and hallowed dogma expand in proportion and yet opposite each other.

Gentlemen, you and your Marines, will have a long and arduous march from Alexandria to Derna or into the city of Tripoli itself. We will supply you with United States naval fortification. You should attack from the land and the shores. The march and the battle will be worth it because everything this nation and its Constitution stand for is at stake. We now live in *a world with no real physical boundaries, when a minority of belief can become a majority of principle. The only borders are the ones of greed and conquest instituted by depraved men with motivations and agendas sowed in ancestral retribution from the time Cain slayed Abel.*

I wish you Godspeed in this endeavor. War has been declared on the United States and all for which our Constitution stands. To give it, and this nation, a bridge over the rivers of domination, to withstand the tests of time inflicted by those who would destroy the principles for which it stands, may you and your men fly on the wings of eagles. Let freedom ring and proclaim liberty throughout all the land and unto all the inhabitants thereto.

Th Jefferson

Paul leaned back in his chair, a slight headache above his right eye. He looked at a third sheet of paper. This one was no more than two paragraphs. And Stephen Decatur signed it in plain text. Paul used the key code to decipher the boxed letters.

Within two minutes, he wrote:

Dear President Jefferson, by now you have, no doubt, been informed by Commodore Richard Dale and others in the military campaign that Tripoli has fallen. The United States, although suffered loss of men and property, the USS Philadelphia was burned to the waterline, was victorious. Our men, and the mercenaries we recruited, fought honorably and won a victory that will open trade doors to the Mediterranean for America and all of Europe. Lieutenants William Eaton and Presley O'Bannon are true leaders. Other nations of the Barbary Coast have agreed to sign the terms of the peace treaty.

I will stay through to administer that task. I wish to inform you, sir, that Pasha Karamanli, after signing the treaty, departed Tripoli in a state of anger to take refuge in what is known as the Jabal Caves, the caves of the ancient tribes. These are caves in the Nafusa Mountains some one hundred kilometers south of the city of Tripoli. I learned it was the ancient home of his people. He has taken a militia of his best warriors.

Before his departure, he swore retaliation. He said it may not happen in his lifetime or that of his sons, but one day, he predicted, one of his distant grandsons would rise up and wage war, and do it on the anniversary of the fall of Derna, and shout the war cry, remember the battle of Derna.

I do not know, sir, whether anyone will remember what we, as a new nation, accomplished here. However, I do believe that the example we set on these shores will long be remembered and feared in the hearts of those who wish us harm and dominate us by proclaiming their aggression as a holy right and calling.

Under your leadership and motivation, inspired by the tenets in our Constitution, let it be remembered that we are one nation under God.

Respectfully yours,
Stephen Decatur

Paul opened the door on the left side his desk, picked up an unopened bottle of scotch and twisted off the cap. He lifted a clean glass from the same wooden decanter holder and poured a drink. He turned off his computer, barely in silhouette from moonlight against the drapes. He closed his burning eyes, sipped the whiskey and thought about how the past was about to intersect with the present.

SEVENTY-THREE

He could hear his wife breathing in the dark. It was a half hour later when Paul entered the master bedroom, undressed down to his boxers and quietly got in his side of the bed. Alicia's breathing was steady, in a deep sleep. How long she'd been asleep he didn't know. He lay there for a moment, eyes stinging, thinking about the correspondence between Thomas Jefferson and Stephen Decatur.

Paul tried to pull the blanket over his legs when the movement stirred Alicia. She reached for him, her hand touching his shoulder. "Is it really you?" she asked, her voice groggy. "Or am I dreaming? What time is it?"

"A little after four."

"You're not Superman. Sleep deprivation is its own form of kryptonite."

"I broke Jefferson's code."

Alicia sat up. She reached for a light on the bedside table, fumbling to find the switch. She turned the lamp on and said, "You broke the code … oh my God. What is on those pages?"

"A lot. Some of it had to do with Jefferson's military strategy in defeating the Barbary States. And a large part was Jefferson's reasoning to Stephen Decatur, and others in America's first war, why he had no other choice. Jefferson based his decision to go to war on his personal history with Muslim leaders of the Barbary States, and his research of Sharia law. Through covert intelligence, Jefferson knew that the pasha of Tripoli had an ostracized brother who was thrust into a family exile. He knew the brother might be open to working with America to overthrow his own brother and be restored to the pasha position. Jefferson picked some of the best soldiers he had to conduct the operation. And it worked. They recruited the deposed brother, marched 500 miles across the desert, and coordinated an attack on Derna from the land and sea."

Alicia looked across the bed at Paul. She pulled a strand of hair behind one ear. "And now, all these years—centuries later, the notes found on two bodies read remember the battle of Derna. That's an aberrant vendetta."

"Jefferson made a prediction. He wrote that nations, following Sharia law under Islam, would not separate religion and state because they are inseparable within that canon, now or in the future unless the people themselves want change. After his experience in dealing with leaders who believed the Koran gave them the right and responsibility to attack those who didn't follow their religion, he did a lot of research relative to Islam and its interpretations. He said, when a code of conquest by religious differences establishes a hostile force, there can never be real negotiations to maintain peace and human freedoms when state and religion, personified as one, will justify hostility by misrepresenting scripture or an ensuing jihad war."

"Doesn't sound like much has changed since Jefferson's time."

"What has changed is that more than one and a half billion people are Muslim. How may are strict followers of Sharia law? I would believe a small minority. But what Jefferson suggested was this: that unless radical Islamic followers, Christians and any other religions, can accept and allow difference in beliefs, the world will always be a dangerous place to live and will eventually collide with enormous deadly consequences. He proposed that when the world moved from swords, knives and dueling pistols to weapons of large-scale destruction, a minority could harm a majority. Jefferson had no concept, at least I don't think he did, of nuclear bombs, but his deadly comparison is spot on and amazing for his time."

"Will any of this information help the FBI prevent one of Hamad's soldiers from detonating a suicide bomb in front of a national monument, stop them from flying a drone-laden bomb into the Statue of Liberty ... or will it free us, you, David and me from their vengeance?"

"Maybe."

"How?"

"You wanted me to cut the head off the snake. To do that, I have to find out where the snake's hiding. I think I might be getting closer. Soon, I may know exactly where to look."

"I hope it's sooner than later."

"The encrypted correspondence between Jefferson and his men ... especially Stephen Decatur ... gives me a much better insight into what they had to go through to beat the leader of Tripoli more than two centuries ago. A lot has changed, no doubt. But I'd bet some things are still the same."

SEVENTY-FOUR

Ward Rosenberg arrived at his FBI office a half hour late. He hadn't slept well, the same reoccurring dream—drowning in dark water. There was no way to the surface because the surface wasn't perceptible. He'd had the dream twice in the last week. He thought about the news story months ago of a sightseeing helicopter crashing into the dark, cold waters of New York's East River, the chopper flipping over and quickly sinking fifty feet to the muddy bottom of the river.

He entered his office, finishing a large black coffee, tossing the empty paper cup into a trashcan. His chest felt tight. He pushed the images of the dream from his thoughts, loosening his necktie a notch, just enough so he didn't feel his caffeinated pulse against his starched collar.

His secretary made a cursory knock at his glass door and entered the office. She walked with a sense of urgency, early fifties, sunlight through the window highlighting slivers of gray hair amid the dark brown. She had four phone messages on pink paper in her left hand. She looked at her boss and said, "Traffic was a bear on the beltline this morning. I just put on a fresh pot of coffee. Would you like a cup?"

"No thanks, I've had two already."

"Director McNally called first thing. Mr. Gleason said he could join your one o'clock meeting in the small conference room on this floor." She handed him the messages, turned to leave and paused. "Is everything okay?"

"Yes, Maggie. Why?"

"Oh nothing really. But after working with you for the past five years, I can usually tell if something is bothering you."

"It's just more cases than we can handle. But what's new with that?"

"Not a whole lot. Crime and criminals are on the increase, and our budget can't keep up." She smiled, turned and left.

Rosenberg returned Director McNally's call. The director answered on the first ring and said, "Ward … something's come up. We need to meet immediately. My office." He disconnected. Rosenberg slowly replaced the receiver on the phone cradle, thinking about the director's abrupt call. It was no secret that the president and McNally had disagreed over some recent fundamental issues. *Maybe McNally was getting the boot,* Rosenberg thought. *Maybe now was his time to assume the top spot.*

• • •

FBI Director Haden McNally stood in one corner of his large office watching four TV monitors mounted to the wall next to an American flag on a brass stand. He turned when Ward Rosenberg entered the office. "Lock the door, Ward. We don't need any more damn interruptions."

Rosenberg nodded, locked the door and approached the director. McNally said, "The people of our nation are growing weary of constantly being on high alert for the next terrorist's attack. This crescent moon deadline is fast approaching. All we need is air-raid sirens howling in the background to give it the kind of apocalyptic texture that the damn media help cause by hyping bad news to the point of ad nauseum. Everything they say has to have a screaming banner at the bottom of the screen that tells us it's a breaking-news alert. Maybe I should crawl under my desk and lay in the fetal position."

Rosenberg smiled. "Good morning, sir. Perhaps both of us should cut back to decaf."

McNally inhaled deeply, grunted and said, "Sorry, but there is no one in the bureau or the DOJ more frustrated than I am at what's going on in our country. Who, in a million years, would have thought homegrown terrorists would be targeting our national monuments, specifically ones connected to Thomas Jefferson? We've discussed it in our playbook of possible terrorists' scenarios, but never did we think it would happen because a so-called relative to a ghost of the former dictator of Tripoli would be waging guerilla warfare on American soil."

"As you know, Haden, it's just a matter of time—a very short time, before we nail him. We know Fajar Hamad has not left Libya. He moves between Benghazi, Tripoli and Misrata."

"The question we need to answer is how does Hamad direct his followers, his guerilla soldiers here in America, from Libya as if he were hunkered down in a mosque with fanatics hell bent on destroying this country."

"I've sounded the alarm, and I'll do it again. But it seems to fall on deaf ears within the White House. As you know, we've been monitoring Sami Botros since we obtained a FISA warrant. Botros had lunch with Saajid Tahir, the imam who heads up the Islamic Center of East Michigan near Detroit. Tahir is believed to have recruited for Al-Qaeda from his mosque, which, for all practical purposes, is a front for jihadist propaganda and the extreme radical interpretation of Islam. They met for dinner at the Café Enab in Georgetown. Botros didn't have his phone on him at the time, so we couldn't hear their conversation. But the dinner lasted more than two hours. We had eyes on them the whole time, and saw Tahir give a folded slip of paper to Botros."

"But we have no idea what was on that paper."

"No, but I guarantee you it wasn't his grandmother's recipe for hummus."

"Do you think Botros is empathetic to Imam Tahir's radical activism, or are they old friends from the Muslim hood of Detroit who share a common friendship, background, but not an ideology?"

"I think we'd be damn naïve if we thought that."

"Have the wiretaps produced anything we can use?"

"No, Bortros seems to prefer meeting with people in person in busy restaurants."

McNally looked at the images coming in on one of the TV screens. The video was the aftermath of a recent school shooting in Texas. Seven students and one teacher were shot and killed. Nine more were in critical condition at hospitals. The shooter, a disgruntled former student, took his own life. There were images of body bags and crying teenage students. Interviews with shell-shocked survivors. Politicians espousing conjecture, weighing in on whether to ban the sale of assault rifles to teens and how the Second Amendment figures into the scene. There was sad and agonizing video of a mother in a business suit who just arrived at the school and learned that her daughter was murdered in math class. The mother held one hand to her trembling lips, tears streaming, her pain excruciating. She steadied herself against her car, bent over and vomited onto the parking lot.

Director McNally shook his head. "It's bad enough when we have adversaries come into our country and destroy our national monuments and kill innocent bystanders. But when we have our own pissed off high school students who flunk out or were told to leave, and they show up two days later with an assault rife and two hundred rounds … maybe we should pass a law requiring a thorough background check to breed."

Rosenberg said, "We have agents from Dallas and Houston on the scene, but it will boil down to a dysfunctional misfit who made the decision to become a mass murderer."

"My first case with the bureau was working the killing field left behind when Timothy McVeigh blew up the federal building in Oklahoma City. The aftermath, the smoldering and charred remains of the building, the stench of death all around—people crying … lost souls. When I was a cop, trying to get hired into the bureau, some of the most dangerous cases we'd work were called domestic disturbance. You'd arrive at the perp's house to find blood all over the kitchen or bedroom. Usually some guy, often a mean drunk, had beaten his wife to a pulp, and he wanted to do the same to you."

"I don't regret never having gone through those stages of law enforcement."

"It's the best basic training for what we do because you learn on the streets, you become better at reading people. Spotting liars." He paused a moment. "On another note, Paul Marcus seems to be having one hell of a hard time decrypting the Jefferson letter. He's been cooped up in the safe house for two weeks. He made a request to take his family to the old farmhouse his grandfather built. Paul lived there as an adult before going into witness protection overseas. He wants to take his wife out there, ride horses, and just breathe some fresh air. And he wants a little privacy."

"That could be problematic."

"Maybe. But he's willing to risk it. He wants limited bureau protection, maybe two agents posted at his gate to the property. It's more than two hundred acres off State Road 600 north of Sperryville. They want to spend one night in the old farmhouse before he returns to the safe house. Says he can do his work just as well there as anywhere else."

"Do you think that's a good idea?"

"As long as we're careful about it. Have two of our best assigned to the gate, maybe a day and just one night won't hurt. Besides, if it'll help him finish the project that the president asked him to do, let's roll."

"When?"

"Today."

SEVENTY-FIVE

B ill Gray spoke briefly with the two agents assigned to the safe
house. They stood next to their black SUV in the driveway, the
morning sun coming over the tree line, a robin hopping across the
front yard. One agent, tall, wide-shouldered, sports coat tight near the
biceps, removed his sunglasses. The second agent, close-set hazel eyes,
cleft chin, folded his arms, glanced at the safe house and at the
entrance to the driveway.

Bill said, "I gather it was a quiet night. When's the next shift?"

The taller agent responded. "They should be here in a half hour."

Bill nodded. "I hear Paul Marcus and his family will spend some
time at his old farmhouse near Sperryville. Will you guys be assigned
to them out there?"

The second agent said, "Haven't heard. I wonder if that's a good
idea considering the bounty on Marcus's head. From what we hear,
Fajar Hamad won't stop coming until he or Marcus dies."

"Maybe we can arrange the former."

"We're trying. In the meantime, Hamad's got enough nut jobs in
the homeland to launch a few more suicide bomb attacks. When Paul
Marcus took down the Circle of 13, he became, what we call in the
bureau, the ultimate whistleblower. A man willing to take on thirteen
of the world's most powerful people has guts. But he paid a price." The
agent pursed his dry lips and shook his head. "I gotta admit that his

protection program was the best we've ever seen. So good, in fact, we had no idea he was still alive."

Bill looked toward the house. "We have to make sure he stays alive." He turned, got back in his car and drove to the front of the house. Bill walked up to the door and knocked. He waited a half-minute, the sound of someone with a leaf blower somewhere in the neighborhood. He could hear Buddy bark inside the house.

Alicia opened the door, Buddy standing next to her. The dog trotted onto the large front porch. Bill said, "Hey, Buddy. Good morning to you, boy." He petted Buddy and looked up at Alicia, worry visible on her face. "Alicia, I'm so sorry to hear about your mother."

"She not suffering anymore. I'm glad we got to spend some time with her, and we owe that to you. Thank you."

"You're welcome."

"Come in, Bill. Paul is expecting you."

Bill stepped inside the house and said, "I knew he'd break Jefferson's code. It wasn't easy, though. Maybe he can explain to me how he did it, and if I'm lucky, maybe I'll understand it." Bill smiled, following Alicia through the house and into the kitchen, Buddy in the rear, his tail wagging.

Paul stood next to the kitchen counter sipping black coffee from a thick mug. David ate Cheerios at the table, a spoonful of milk splattered next to the bowl. "Good morning guys," Bill said, stepping close to the counter.

David waved and Paul said, "Glad you could make it out here. Coffee?"

"That'd be great, thanks."

Paul poured coffee into a cup, handed it to Bill and said, "Let's go to the office, and I'll show you what I've found."

Alicia said, "Bill, would you like some breakfast? Eggs and toast?"

"I appreciate the offer, but I grabbed a Danish before I left the house." He followed Paul into the office.

Paul sat in front of the desk. He gestured for Bill to sit on the couch, the computer screen on, reflecting light off Bill's glasses.

Paul said, "I'd mentioned to you the name of an English poet, John Donne, who died a hundred years before Jefferson was born."

"Yes, the for 'whom the bell tolls' reference."

"That poem, *Meditation XVII* or number Seventeen, seems to have had a strong influence on Jefferson. A lot of Donne's later work dealt with the fall of mankind, but this one, *Meditation XVII,* embraced the humanity of man, and how no one is really an island. Jefferson used the number seventeen as a key component in his grid. The other elements came from the reference for whom the bell tolls as in the Liberty Bell ringing for freedom. The engraving on the bell, another *verse* Jefferson quoted, originally came from Leviticus twenty-five ten. Those two numbers, gave me the key."

"Amazing … truly amazing."

"In Jefferson's encrypted letter, he wrote all of the message text vertically, columns from left to right. It formed a tight grid with no capital letters. Seemingly, no start or end points … unless you had the key, then it was relatively simply to decode. And to do that, the recipient had to know the number of lines in each section, the order in which those lines were written, and the number of random letters that the sender added to each line."

"You got that from a three-hundred year old poem and the engraving across the Liberty Bell?"

"Yes."

Bill leaned back in the couch, looked at the steam rising from his coffee cup. He lifted his eyes up to Paul. "You have a helluva gift. You've taken the baton from Jefferson and ran with it."

"Stephen Decatur had those key components, too. So he could sit down and decipher them fairly quickly."

"What did Jefferson say in the dispatch to Decatur? Anything we can use, because if there is, I'm calling the president from this room."

"It wasn't just Jefferson's communication to Decatur … it was what Decatur let the president know as well. Jefferson laid out a strategy for a land and sea war against the pasha of Tripoli. To make it successful, Jefferson knew he'd have to offer something more than shock and awe and no extended plan for leadership. He'd have to have a plan, a business model if you will, that would establish some form of government in Libya or Tripoli, if he was to take out the pasha and leave an open hole for all kinds of factions, tribes and insurgents to crawl out."

"What was his strategy?"

"To have Decatur and Patrick O'Bannon hunt down the pasha's brother. Jefferson knew the older brother had been ousted by the younger brother and sent into exile."

"Where was he?"

"Jefferson's intelligence agents, and he had some in those days, heard that the older brother was hiding in Alexandria, Egypt. Jefferson's team worked the system; found the brother and convinced him to join them to overthrow the younger brother. And they walked five hundred miles across the desert—a band of U.S. marines and dozens of Muslim mercenaries that Decatur, William Eaton, and Presley O'Bannon had recruited. At the appointed time, the ground troops hit Derna from one side, and our naval forces did it from the shore. The rest is history."

"Did Jefferson have an insight that might help us battle a great, great grandson of the same guy Jefferson fought?"

"To some extent, yes. Jefferson, in the dispatch to Decatur, seemed to want to justify his reasoning for war. And it came from the fact that the pasha had drawn first blood on us, refused to release our ships and men, and wanted ransom money. Jefferson also drew upon his history in dealing with leaders of the Barbary States and fundamental tenets in a religion, through radical interpretation, that can opt to wage war on those who do not follow it's a doctrine."

Paul gave Bill an analysis of the rest of the letter. He printed a copy of the words he'd deciphered, handed the pages to Bill and said, "This is the complete deciphered text from Jefferson's letter and that written to him from Stephen Decatur, who elected to stay in the Barbary States, trying to help the older brother, Hamet Karamanli, establish himself in a leadership role in Tripoli. Also, Decatur stayed behind to negotiate the same peace treaty with the other three Barbary nations, Algiers, Mocorro and Tunisia. In my opinion, there ought to be a statue or two of guys like Decatur, Eaton and O'Bannon erected somewhere here in Washington."

Bill held up the pages. "Maybe, in light of all this … we can get it done."

Paul leaned forward in his chair, hands on his knees. "You have a copy of Decatur's dispatch back to the president. In addition to him choosing to stay through the transition of power, and have the other Barbary States sign the treaty, Decatur said, that the pasha, Yusuf Karamanli, fled the city, swearing revenge—maybe not in his lifetime, but in that of the sons of his sons. Thus today, Fajar Hamad, is reciting the battle cry, *remember Derna* … the same thing the pasha shouted on his way out of the city to seek refuge in the mountains."

"The number you found for Ward Rosenberg's other phone, the one that's supposed to be one of the secure connections at the FBI that no one can trace—except, of course, you and the hacker that wormed his way through our firewalls—can you pull it up?"

"Okay. What are we looking for?"

"We set a trap. He may not have fallen for it. But since it came from Director McNally, maybe he took the bait. There may be a raid on your old farmhouse. If it is, Rosenberg is the link."

SEVENTY-SIX

P aul turned to his computer, keyed in a series of numbers and letters, and waited a moment. Bill Gray stood, placed his coffee cup on a coaster and watched Paul move through firewalls at the speed of light. "What do you see?" Bill asked.

"The private number Rosenberg uses, and he uses it very infrequently, a call was made from it yesterday afternoon at 5:19."

"Who did he call?"

"I don't know who's attached to that phone, but if you give me about ten seconds, I can tell you where the phone is or was located." Paul worked the keyboard, his eyes squinting. He looked from the screen over to Bill and said, "It appears that the call went to a secure location here in Washington."

"Where in Washington."

"The address is 1239 Tunslaw Drive."

Bill stared at the screen and stood straight. "That's the Russian embassy."

Paul said nothing, his thoughts racing.

Bill said, "When you combine a guy like Fajar Hamad with the Russians, you get one hell of a deadly cocktail mix. What could they possibly have on Ward Rosenberg to get him to turn?"

"I don't know. Maybe a few million dollars in bribe money."

"While you were in Panarea, I made sure your old farmhouse was kept in good shape. I need to run by my house and grab the key."

"Why?"

"I'll need it. That's the trap. Director McNally told Rosenberg that you and your family were taking a day and a night to slip out to the farm, to have security less obvious, maybe a detail near the entrance to that long driveway of yours, to give you and your family some down time in a place that doesn't feel like Fort Knox."

Paul sat back in his chair. "And so if the Russians or some of Hamad's men come calling, you can do two things—surprise them and get the drop on whoever arrives, and you nail Rosenberg."

"That's the plan. Let's hope that it works."

"Let's hope the farmhouse stays in good shape."

• • •

The farmhouse was more than one hundred years old, painted white, black shutters, pitched gables, metal roof, brick chimney, large front porch with four wicker rocking chairs. Trimmed rose bushes bloomed along the front of the home, red and white roses on the bushes. The property and home had the lived in look of a family.

But that was a deception.

The house had been empty for more than five years. The property deed was changed to reflect the new imposter owners. Paul continued to own the home, 160 acres of rolling land and the stables. However, Bill Gray had the name changed on the deed to give the indication of new ownership, all part of the guise to keep Paul and his family safe seven thousand miles away from the Blue Ridge Mountains on the Isle of Panarea. A caretaker, hired by NSA, kept the home and property in good condition.

Today, twelve federal agents—nine men and three women, along with seven members of the U.S. Marshal's office worked the detail. The team, all heavily armed entered the property and staked out areas to watch and wait without the enemy knowing that they were there. The agents walked the lay of the land, the old red barn, the wide creek, and along parts of the fence-line. They surveyed to spot elevations in the surrounding foothills, looking for any place an adversary could enter.

They canvased the house, placing hidden cameras in strategic areas to record whatever happens as irrefutable evidence for when the time came to take the perpetrators to trial. The senior agent, Mark Holland, early fifties, large hands and flecks of gray in his bushy eyebrows said to half a dozen of the agents inside the house, "Let's get the television going, work the drapes all around so they're closed but allow enough light to filter through. We don't know if the perps will come tomorrow during the day or wait until nightfall. They may not come at all, but they do know the Marcus family is supposed to be here, and that security will be at a bare minimum to give the family a little privacy. If I was a bettin' man, I'd wager they'll make a hard and fast go of it."

"I'd agree," said one of the female special agents, her brown hair in a ponytail, the letters FBI on the front and back of her shirt."

Holland nodded. "Let's head out to the porch and make sure everybody there understands exactly what he or she is expected to be doing the next forty-eight hours."

They walked onto the wooden porch, the scent of blooming roses in the breeze. There was the rapid sound of a pileated woodpecker drilling into the limb of a tree near the barn, the bird's large head adorned with a triangular crest of red feathers.

Holland motioned for the team to gather around the porch. Agents and marshals formed a semi-circle, and he said, "The challenge is to contain the property and yet leave room for the hostiles to enter without any of us being spotted. The Marcus property abuts a national forest on the back two thirds. The nearest neighbor is a half-mile away on either side of the frontage road. So basically, the only real way in here is to come up the drive from the road. As you know, that drive from right here to the road is at least two football fields in length.

'We've made arrangements to park in a farmer's field about a half mile away, off the road so they won't spot our vehicles. We'll have a car parked close to the entrance of the driveway. The hostiles will either try to take out that unit or they'll enter from another spot, and that's limited. We're facing assassins. They're highly trained and as ruthless as they come. When your enemy professes to have no fear of death because paradise with its harem is waiting for him … that's a whole different mindset. Let's go over a couple of scenarios. None of them will look too promising so consider the terrain and what we're facing. Remember, the homeland is under attack. Let's defend it."

SEVENTY-SEVEN

Ward Rosenberg was wrapping up for the day in his office. His secretary had left an hour earlier. A few special agents and research techs were in some of the offices. Rosenberg locked his door and walked across the large office area, around cubicles and other glassed-in offices. Special Agent Roger Berlin, put his sports coat on coming out of his office. Rosenberg nodded to him and said, "Thought you'd be out on the task force at the farm property."

"I wanted to go, but I'm still assigned to the safe house. It's not that easy to keep eyes on the place, primarily because you don't want to disturb the family. There's a private entrance to a small bathroom off the back of the garage, but I hate to use it." He grinned. "I don't drink coffee on my shift."

"I guess it's not like you're doing surveillance in an urban area where you can get out of the car and hit the head in a restaurant bathroom while your partner keeps eyes on the stakeout."

"You got that right. And at the safe house, there are so many cameras and satellite cameras if you take a piss behind a tree, you can be seen. I'm heading over there in a few minutes. Gus Verini will be joining me."

"Tell Gus I have some hockey tickets for him. The Capitols are surprising everybody this season." Rosenberg turned to leave.

Berlin said, "I'd like to be on the stake out at the farm property, but I heard the Marcus family won't even be there."

Rosenberg stopped, turned around. "Where'd you hear that?"

"From Mark Holland. But who knows, plans change in a heartbeat around here as we try to stay a few steps ahead of the bad guys. See you Thursday."

Rosenberg nodded, his jawline hard. "Have a good night." He watched the agent leave, and then turned around, unlocked his office door and made a call on one of his secured phone lines.

• • •

The next day, Paul woke before sunrise, walked quietly into the kitchen and put on a pot of coffee. As the coffee brewed, he moved through the house and looked out the blinds, the SUV with the agents just visible at the end of the drive under the soft moonlight. He walked back to the kitchen and poured a cup of coffee. He thought about what Bill had said, *'There may be a raid on your old farmhouse. If it is, Rosenberg is the link.'*

Paul sipped his coffee, stepped back to his office and turned on his computer. He sat and waited for a moment, steam rising from the coffee. Then he keyed in information to access Rosenberg's phone number. He could see a second call was made to the same location off Tunslaw Drive—the Russian embassy. Paul picked up his phone, called Bill Gray and said, "Rosenberg made another call to the same place."

"When?"

"Last night. A little after six."

"The question is why … what could he have to report that would warrant a second call so soon?"

"I wish I knew."

"When is the funeral planned for Alicia's mother?"

"In two days, Friday."

"What if your family didn't attend?"

"Bill, Alicia is torn apart. She feels guilty for having been gone so long, and when she returns home, her mom dies within the first week. I'm not sure I could ask her not to be there with her sister and the rest of her family. Do you have any indication they'd try something at the funeral?"

"No, but we don't know who Rosenberg is talking with at the Russian embassy."

• • •

The only sound came from the cicadas in the woods. The FBI agents and U.S. Marshals were scattered around the perimeter of Paul Marcus's farm property. They spoke occasionally and only in brief whispers over the radio. A sniper in camouflage fatigues stood on a metal deer hunter's stand near the top of a tall pine tree less than one hundred yards from the entrance to the property. He looked through his scope, watched a sparrow alight on the rusty chain across the driveway.

Cars and pickup trucks came by infrequently. The sniper had counted eleven all day. He looked at the Blue Ridge Mountains in the distance; the rippled peaks and valleys appeared to be great sleeping dinosaurs with purple arched backs, serrated against the blue horizon.

After more than ten hours, Special Agent Holland opened his radio microphone and said, "Drew."

"I'm here." Special Agent Drew LeGault dressed in camouflage, held a pair of binoculars and stood behind an oak tree, he had a clear view of the road. He was a half-mile away from the property.

"Anything coming?" Holland asked.

"No. Clear."

"How about you, Susan … anything?"

Special Agent Susan Stone, dark hair pulled back in a ponytail, looked to the west. "Clear in my direction."

"Okay. It'll be night soon. Let's change up some positions, give everyone a chance to stretch their legs, but let's do it in segments. We'll get everyone night goggles and thermal scopes. My gut tells me if the hostiles are going to pay the Marcus family a visit, they're going to attack at night. We have some fresh legs arriving at sunset. Anybody who doesn't want to be relieved let me know now."

Holland stood in the brush off the main road. There was silence on the radio. He swatted at a gnat and smiled. *Damn good*, he thought. The only sound came from a crow cawing in the distance.

• • •

FBI Director Haden McNally sat in his large office and listened to one of his special agents summarize a report. The agent, a woman with dark auburn hair to her shoulders, blue suit, said, "We have confirmed that the calls were made to a phone within the Russian embassy. Each one was less than one minute. Not a lot of time for detailed conversations."

"No, but time enough to tip someone off, if that is indeed the case. I've known Ward for twenty years. It simply doesn't make sense. Maybe he's following confidential leads … working on something at a high level that he hasn't shared."

"Wouldn't he share that with you?"

"I'd think so, but sometimes that's not always the case."

The agent shook her head. "I wish that were the case, sir. However, our techs retrieved images that were sent to one of Rosenberg's phones. He'd most likely thought he'd deleted them."

"What kind of images?"

"They depicted him in bed with a woman. We've identified her as an operative, a woman extremely well trained in the art of seduction. They'd met at the St. Regis one afternoon, according to the time-stamped images we retrieved from one of the cameras in the entrance." She pressed two keys on her tablet, placed it on the desk in front of McNally. "These came from whomever is blackmailing him … and it's not too hard to guess. Most likely it is someone who is reporting directly to Dimitri Abaza."

McNally looked at the picture on the table, Ward Rosenberg nude, kissing a nude woman in bed. McNally said, "It's time to meet with the president and the attorney general. Keep your eyes on Ward. I'll call you soon." He reached for his phone and made a call.

Ward Rosenberg said, "Hey, Haden. You still in the office?"

"Where are you?"

"Just passing the Jefferson Memorial."

"I trust it's still in one piece."

Rosenberg forced a laugh. "Looks to be."

"Turn around, Ward. We need to chat." The director disconnected.

Rosenberg pulled over to the side of the road. He swapped phones and made a call. After three rings, Dimitri Abaza, sitting at a desk in the Russian embassy, answered. "Good evening. What do I owe the pleasure of this call?"

"Stop the bull shit! They're on to me."

"How do you know that?"

"I just do. I've worked there long enough to know. I need asylum. For me and my family, and I need it tonight."

"Where are you now?"

"Across from the Intercontinental Hotel."

"There's a bar next to it. Have a drink and calm down. I'll see that Victor Orlov meets you there in a half hour. He will work out the details to get you and your family smuggled out of the country and onto an Aeroflot plane."

"Dimitri, don't even think about double crossing me. I will spill everything I know if you leave me out to dry. And it'll go all the way back to the Kremlin. Are we clear?"

"Of course. You are an extremely valuable asset. You will live in Russia. You have earned your place. Sit at the bar, Victor will find you in twenty-eight minutes."

SEVENTY-EIGHT

The President of the United States pushed back from the long table in the Situation Room, removed his wire-frame glasses, and looked across the table at Attorney General Samuel Gross. The president said, "I never would have suspected it … Ward Rosenberg. We need to find out immediately who he's working with, what he told them and when."

Gross, late fifties, flushed bulldog face, had carved a reputation in his previous career as one of the most tenacious prosecuting attorneys in the Department of Justice. Three of the Al-Qaeda terrorists were serving life sentences in the Supermax prison near Florence, Colorado, due to their crimes and Gross's calculated prosecutorial strategy. He said, "If it pans out the way it's looking, this would be treason in its most severe form, considering what's happened in our nation within the last month."

The president cut his eyes over to FBI Director Haden McNally. "Haden, have someone go arrest Rosenberg."

"Yes sir." McNally stood, stepped outside the large room and placed a call.

• • •

The bar had a rich look and feel, polished dark wood, secluded booths. It was a watering hole for attorneys, lobbyists, politicians, and their mutual constituents. The establishment could have been transplanted from an exclusive country club, the cigar box smell of Ivy League whiskey and money. Ward Rosenberg sat alone at the end of the long bar. He nursed a drink, Belvedere vodka over ice, twist of lime.

He didn't see the man enter. Somehow Victor Orlov seemed to pop up, as if he came in from a rear entrance. He wore a dark gray suit, white shirt and blood red tie. He was small in stature, but had a big smile. It was the smile of a politician, focusing, for the moment, on you. As if no one else was in the room until someone else was in the room. He said, "You are half a drink ahead of me."

"How quickly can you get my family and me on a plane?"

"Within three hours. If we need to, we can charter a jet should an Aeroflot flight not be available. Just take a deep breath, and let us help you."

"You need to realize what I'm facing?"

"Have you spoken to your wife?"

"No, not yet. I wanted to see what options you had to offer."

"I understand," he nodded, his blue eyes slowly closing and opening, like an animated caricature out of a fairy tale. He caught the bartender's attention and said, "Like my friend here, may I get a vodka, Beluga? But no ice, please, and no lime."

"My pleasure," said the bartender with a neatly trimmed red beard and a Leprechaun's twinkle in his green eyes, red spotted bowtie like a butterfly under his chin.

Orlov took a seat next to Rosenberg and said, "They have nothing on you. How could they, really? A few phone calls don't prove anything, especially when they were so carefully worded … so generic. Nothing definitive to tie you to divulging covert intelligence."

"Is that what Dimitri told you?"

"It is true, is it not?"

The bartender served the drink and said, "Can I get you gentlemen an appetizer or two?"

Rosenberg shook his head. "No, we're fine, thanks."

The bartender nodded and left to serve another customer, a woman, at the end of the bar. Orlov sipped the straight vodka.

He said, "Let me check flights." He opened his phone and hit a few keys, his pale eyes seemed to absorb the glow of the screen like an owl looking into a rising full moon. "We're in luck."

"What do you have?"

"There's what you Americans call the red eye. It is the last flight out from the states tonight to Moscow. It leaves after midnight out of Dulles. You will arrive the following day in Moscow and be met at the plane. Will that serve your needs?"

"Yes."

Orlov raised his glass in a toast. "To your new life. Cheers." He knocked back the vodka. Rosenberg sipped his drink. Orlov said, "Perhaps it is time to speak with your wife. It might be rather challenging for her to leave at such an abrupt notice. In that event, we shall block off four seats on all subsequent flights until you decide."

"Thanks."

"It is the least we can do." Orlov picked up a paper napkin and used a pen to write down a number. "This is my direct number. Call me as soon as you speak with you wife so we can make arrangements, understood? We need to relocate you. I hope she will understand the urgency."

Rosenberg took a long sip from his drink. "Give me a minute. I'll step outside to call her. You'll have your answer in a few minutes." He picked up the bar napkin with the number, folded it and slipped the napkin in the inside pocket of his sports coat, got up and walked outside. He stood at the top of a short flight of marble steps leading to the street level, two taxis lumbering down Pennsylvania Avenue. The hotel's doorman greeted the driver of a black Mercedes S 650, opening the car door. Rosenberg stood away from the main entrance next to a large stone pillar and tapped the number next to his wife's name on his phone screen.

She answered. "Are you still at the office?"

"Glenda ... listen very carefully. Something has come up. I will explain it in depth soon, but right now I need you to pack a bag for you and Gabriel."

"Pack? What? Why? What's going on, Ward?"

Rosenberg started to respond but couldn't remember his wife's name. His head pounded. Vision blurry. He removed the phone from his ear and tried to focus on the screen, on her picture. It was indistinct, as if the screen was somehow shimmering in his hand. He tried to return it to his ear, but couldn't—the phone felt like a dead weight in his hand.

"Ward! Where are you? Ward!"

His wife's pleas sounded shrill, a whisper in the wind, a fading signal. He dropped the phone on the concrete, reached for one of the massive pillars to steady his balance. His arms didn't work. He couldn't make his arm extend to the pillar. His legs felt as if electricity was shooting through his thighs, calves and down to the soles of his feet. Burning. *Taser,* he thought. *Why? Can't stand anymore.* He couldn't form words with his mouth. He tried to walk, but fell, rolling down the steps.

He lay on his back for a moment. The hotel doorman rushed over and said, "Sir! Can you hear me? Sir! Somebody dial nine-one-one!"

Rosenberg didn't respond. He stared at the man in the uniform. The man's mouth moving, but the words garbled, as if a cell phone signal was coming from underwater. His heart slammed in his chest, ribcage exploding. He felt he could hear blood rush under his skin. He coughed up the metallic taste of toxins and blood, white foam spilling from lips that were numb. *Poisoned. I've been poisoned.*

Within seconds, more panicked onlookers gathered around, fear in their eyes. Two people dialed 9-1-1 at the same time. A woman held her hand to her mouth, eyes frightened. Rosenberg's breathing was labored. Wheezing. He tried to fill his lungs, but there was no air. His head spun. And then, in the semi-circle of onlookers, Victor Orlov's face materialized. He had the same expression he'd displayed at the bar, the mock smile, and the sleepy eyelids of a wooden puppet.

And he was gone.

Rosenberg thought he heard the sound of approaching sirens. The crowd of terrified bystanders faded like ghosts as his attention focused solely on trying to swim to the floating dock at his family's summer cottage. He was so tired. Arms like putty. His legs and feet were weighted to the point of near paralysis. He slipped beneath the lake, his body plummeting though the water, from a cool temperature at the surface to cold in the deep. It no longer was a lake where he'd watch sunsets with his mother as his dad prepared a fire pit near the beach.

It was a vast deep and dark pit with no way to escape. He fought, but his body didn't respond, he tried to hold his breath, but his lungs were bursting, as if he'd inhaled acid. His right foot touched the muddy bottom, sinking above his ankle in silt. It was darker than the blackest night he'd ever felt. He rolled onto his side, fingers sinking into the mud, clawing. And then he felt something. *Maybe a rock at the bottom of the lake.* He touched the smooth, round surface—a surface too circular for a natural rock. He felt two holes, his fingers entering as if he'd found a bowling ball. And there was a third opening below the sockets. Not as round. And below that were the jagged points of teeth and a jawbone.

A human skull.

Rosenberg managed to kick from the mud, suddenly caught in a current, swept deeper into the lake and the bones of the ancients who'd perished in its cold grasp.

SEVENTY-NINE

The moonlight gave off enough light for a sniper to kill a man. The marksman, perched on the deer hunter's stand fifty feet up in the tall pine, looked through his night-scope and sighted on an opossum waddling across the driveway entrance to the Marcus farmhouse. The image of the animal through the scope was a shade of chemical green, the opossum's eyes the glow of red coals in the white ash of its face.

The agent set his rifle in the crook of a limb, watched and waited, fireflies rose from the bottomlands and moved in a hide-and-seek courtship game through the leafy pines. From the direction of the farmhouse came the high-pitched wail from a screech owl.

And then there was manmade light.

It was the moving light from a vehicle coming up the twisting rural road in the foothills of the Blue Ridge Mountains. The sharpshooter keyed his radio microphone and said, "In-coming vehicle, eastbound. Appears to be a single unit."

Senior agent Mark Holland opened his mic and said, "Roger … let's put some eyes on whoever's coming. It's getting late, so for somebody to be out in these parts … we can assume they live nearby. I-66 is seventy miles away."

"Got a visual," said a U.S, Marshal sitting in a parked, dark green Jeep fifty feet off the road behind some scrub oak. "Looks to be a Ford Explorer. Dark gray. Can't tell how many subjects are in the vehicle."

"Copy that," said Holland. "Let's see where it goes."

Within half a minute, the SUV came closer to the property, less than eighty yards away. All of the agents hiding in the thickets around the perimeter of the farmhouse could see the headlights. They listened for instructions over the radio should the driver enter the property and exit the vehicle. Some hoped the driver would turn off the road and gain access to the property. The stakeout was arduous and, at times, boring. Waiting for action as opposed to creating it.

The agents watched and waited. The driver of the SUV slowed near the entrance to the farmhouse. In the headlights, some members of the surveillance team could see an opossum shuffle across the road, scampering into the undergrowth. The driver only slowed to avoid hitting the animal. After the opossum was gone, the driver resumed speed and passed the driveway, not a touch of the brake lights, the vehicle gaining speed and disappearing a quarter mile down the road and around the bend.

Special Agent Holland keyed his microphone. "All clear. Let's keep at it. Who knows what might happen at midnight."

• • •

Alicia tucked David into his bed, pulling his Spiderman blanket up to his small chest. Buddy, as usual, was curled at the foot of the bed. She leaned down and kissed David on his cheek and said, "Love you. You guys get some sleep."

"Mom …"

"Yes?"

"Are you still real sad about Grandma?"

"Yes, and I'll always be sad about your grandmother's death. But remembering her life makes me happy."

"You cried bunches."

"Yes, I did. We have her funeral coming up, and I'll cry some more."

"What's a funeral?"

"It's usually in a church or a cemetery … a place where family and friends meet to say goodbye to a loved one who has died. The body of your grandmother will be buried in a cemetery in a special place next to your grandfather."

"Can Buddy go, too?"

Alicia smiled. "No, this time it's people only."

David looked at his dog and said, "I don't think he minds."

"Goodnight, sweetie."

"Goodnight, Mom."

She walked out of the room and turned the shower on in the master bath, looked down the hall, the light still coming from the office.

• • •

Paul glanced at the photograph of Eli Dexter on his desk and placed a call to Eli's father, Liam. He answered and Paul said, "Liam, it's Paul … I know it's late, but I needed to call you. Is Penny with you?

"Yes, she's in the other room, why?"

"I broke Jefferson's code."

"No shit … wow! Of course you broke his code. I never doubted you." Liam stood in the family recreation room and looked at some of the pictures of his son in military uniform.

"It wouldn't have happened if I hadn't had access to a good computer." He glanced at Eli's image. "Jefferson wrote the letter to one of his top field agents, Stephen Decatur and William Eaton, who were directing the raid against the leader of Tripoli at the time. The leader was the guy that Fajar Hamad says he's related to."

"Is there anything we can use from Jefferson's letter to find Hamad? All I want is five minutes in a closed room with him." Liam looked up on the fireplace mantle at a long-distance marksmanship medal he'd won twenty years earlier for smashing a world record for distance and accuracy.

"Maybe we can get you that. I can't promise anything yet, but I didn't want to leave you and Penny in the dark. I don't have anything I can hang my hat on, but I'm working on it. I'm analyzing patterns of behavior—military, philosophical, religion … the politics and people of the North African states, in particular Libya—Benghazi, and much of the Middle East. Jefferson, in his letter, laid out a strategic plan to attack Tripoli by taking out Derna, and his troops did it from the land and sea." Paul summarized the decrypted information and added. "Jefferson's team recruited the older brother, Hamet Karamanli, who actually was the rightful heir, as a replacement when they toppled Yusuf, the younger brother." Paul heard a beep on his phone, looked at an incoming text. "Liam ... I'm getting a text from NSA. I gotta go. Tell Penny we'll get this guy."

"Thanks for the update."

Paul disconnected, looked at his watch and read the text. It was from Bill Gray: *Call me ASAP.* He made the call and Bill said, "Paul ... Rosenberg is dead."

"Dead? How?"

"Poisoned. Looks to be the handiwork of the Kremlin. He had a drink at a bar near the Intercontinental Hotel. We didn't find much on the security cameras. However, the bartender described the man who had a drink with Rosenberg. From what we could gather, his name is Victor Orlov. He's SVU, one of the best assassins they have. He used some kind of deadly nerve agent, probably sarin. It took Rosenberg about ten long, excruciating minutes to die. And he died right before paramedics arrived. They had to wear HAZMAT suits to remove the body from the front of the hotel on Pennsylvania. There were a helluva lot of terrified bystanders. The news media are all over this. The Kremlin is sending a horrific message ... again saying if you work both sides, we'll put polonium in your tea or spike your cocktail with sarin."

"What did they have on Rosenberg to leverage against him to work as a mole? And how are the Russians working in tandem with Hamad's group?"

"The age old use of high stakes blackmail. Rosenberg apparently succumbed to the advances of a beautiful Russian operative, highly trained in the art of seduction. The question remains ... what did Rosenberg know about the Russians or Hamad that justified the kind of public execution he just suffered less than five blocks from the White House?"

"We do know that Rosenberg made a second call to someone in the Embassy of Russia not too long after his first call." Paul paused, looked at the letters he'd decrypted at the edge of his desk. "Hold on a second. You said FBI Director McNally set a trap for Rosenberg, letting him know that he, McNally, just learned my family and I would be heading to my farmhouse for a couple of days. If we assume the first call from Rosenberg to the Russians was to tell them that, or to tell whomever is in their embassy that information … then why make a second call to the same number unless he had new information."

"What are you suggesting?"

"That somehow Rosenberg knew we weren't going to be at my farmhouse. How'd he find out, and what if he told them we'd be here instead? With dozens of agents out at my place in the Virginia countryside, that could leave this house more vulnerable. I assume there hasn't been any movement at my farmhouse yet?"

"I've been in touch with McNally. He's in the FBI's command center. Between the hit on Rosenberg and all the firepower out at your farmhouse, the last twelve hours have been trying."

"Wait a second, Bill. I'm going to walk to the front of the house to see if the agent's car is visible at the end of the drive." Paul lowered his phone and moved through the house, keeping lights off. He approached the front windows, slowly parting the curtains and peering outside. He could see the outline of the SUV under the moonlight. He raised his phone to his ear. "They're at the end of the drive, at least the SUV is there. Sometimes, depending on the moon, streetlights of where they park, I can make out silhouettes in the car. Not tonight."

"These guys shutoff the dome light and get out to stretch their legs from time to time. Also, they have the key to that private bathroom near your garage. They take turns going so someone always has eyes on the front. Let me see if I can get one of their cell numbers from McNally or have McNally call them. They need a heads up anyway in the event Rosenberg told the wrong people where to find you on a night we'd set a trap for them and Rosenberg. I'll call you right back."

EIGHTY

S pecial Agent Roger Berlin had never received a phone call from the director of the FBI until tonight. Berlin sat behind the steering wheel in the SUV parked at the end of the driveway leading to the safe house. His partner, Special Agent Keith Hale, sat on the passenger side watching the house. He looked toward the road and the locked gate across the driveway. A streetlight on a high steel pole lit much of the entrance to the drive. Moths circled the light. A bat darted in from the black, snatching a large moth.

Berlin answered his phone. "Berlin, this is Director McNally. What's the status out there tonight?" McNally stood in the center of the FBI's Command Center at its headquarters in Washington. More than two-dozen analysts and agents sat close to large monitors receiving fiber optic and satellite feeds from potential hot spot areas around the world. One was the safe house.

"The usual, sir. Quiet. We have eyes on the house, the main entrance, and we have a wireless satellite feed to the cameras around the perimeter of the property. All we've seen in more than two weeks was a family of raccoons the other night."

"Let's hope it stays that way. Who's on duty with you tonight?"

"Keith Hale."

Hale cut his eyes over to his partner, not sure who was on the phone or why his name was mentioned. Berlin looked at his wristwatch. "Director McNally, may I ask you something, sir?"

"Of course. What is it?"

"I've been with the bureau for thirteen years, and I've never received a call from you. Not that I was ever expecting one. Is there something going on tonight that my partner and I should know?"

"We have reason to believe that it is going to remain quiet out at the Marcus property near Sperryville."

"May I ask why?"

"Some new intel we received. And if it's correct, there could be a greater chance that the safe house may have been compromised."

Berlin sat straighter, looked toward the deserted street and glanced at his partner. "Well, I'm glad you called. Thanks for the heads-up. I'd seen Deputy Director Rosenberg earlier today, and he thought the focus would be on the farmhouse. I'd mentioned to him that I figured it'd be a quiet night at the safe house, even though the Marcus family would be here, because the bureau had leaked that the family might be visiting the farm. At this point, until we find Fajar Hamad, we have to be protective on all fronts."

"When did you speak with Deputy Director Rosenberg?"

"Before Special Agent Hale and I started our shift."

"The deputy director was killed tonight."

Berlin gripped the steering wheel. "Killed? What happened?"

"He was poisoned. We suspect a Russian assassin. It has the clear trademarks of the Kremlin."

Berlin said nothing for a moment. Special Agent Hale looked at his partner and asked, "What's going on?"

Berlin started to answer when Director McNally said, "We're sending a couple more units your way."

"Sounds good. Sir, why would the Russians hit the deputy director? Doesn't make sense unless …"

"Unless he was working for them. We believe he was. Rosenberg didn't know that the Marcus family was not going to the farm property."

"I think I understand what you're saying. If there's a breach here tonight, Rosenberg was the one that told them."

"Yes."

"Damn … I didn't know. I had no idea—"

"You're right, you didn't know. Water under the bridge. Just be vigilant out there tonight."

"Thank you, sir, for the call." He glanced down at the monitor in the dashboard, looked at the four stationary camera images of the property. I think I'll have a check around the backyard. Keith and I will be on radio if you need us."

• • •

Paul stepped back inside his home office. Alicia was in bed, lights off in the master bedroom. Paul's phone rang. He looked at his watch, midnight, and answered his phone. Bill Gray said, "Director McNally's in the strategic operations area of the bureau with a few dozen techs, analysts and agents. He's been speaking with the president. McNally alerted the agents, and he's sending more troops just in case we need them."

"I have two hand guns, a sleeping wife, my son and his dog. If anyone makes it through the federal agents and the bulletproof glass and doors, I'll stop the first few. I just hope it's a few. Then, maybe we'll have a better chance."

"Paul, assuming Rosenberg tipped them—Russians and Iranians as to your location, chances are he told them you're in a safe house with guards and twenty-four-seven satellite camera surveillance. They may simply lay low and wait for a better time ... or maybe we'll get to them, specifically Hamad, and negotiate with a gun to his temple. We'll see just how close he is willing to get to martyrdom."

• • •

From a secluded conference room in the center of the Russian embassy in Washington, DC, Dabir Nagi opened the cap on a bottle of water. He took a sip and glanced up at a framed photograph of the Russian president. No smile—a penetrating look into the eye of the camera. His three colleagues sat in comfortable chairs around a small table and played cards.

Nagi looked at his watch, picked up a secure phone and made a call to a secluded spot in the Libyan outback more than 5,500 miles away. A man with a deep but soft voice answered in Persian and said, "What do you have?"

"We know where Paul Marcus is hiding."

"Where?"

"A safe house in a neighborhood northwest of here. We know it's heavily guarded, but with enough men we could attack. The mole inside the FBI supplied the information to the Russians. They eliminated him." He looked up at the photo of the Russian president. "They want Marcus, too, but for a different reason."

"Russia's history in dealing with the Americans is much shorter than ours. For them, it is strategic. For us, it is personal. An old wound that can never be healed properly until the infidels admit they were wrong in first attacking Derna, toppling and inserting new leadership. This is their pattern throughout the Middle East. They come in and remove leaders, prop up puppets they can manipulate, and conduct business in their best interest. We showed them in Benghazi that we would not tolerate it. And now, on American soil, we are demonstrating our broad reach. They, like mice, are afraid."

"Yes, Fajar. You knew … you are a prophet."

"Praise be to Allah."

"What do I tell the Russians?"

"Nothing. I will speak with Dimitri Abaza. There are rooms for you and your men at the Rosewood Hotel. We will contact you with our plans. My brother will taste freedom again, and Paul Marcus will die a slow death."

EIGHTY-ONE

P aul awoke on the couch in his office when the dawn crept over the tree line. He sat up, lifted his pillow, picked up the pistol and locked it in one of his desk drawers. He showered and put on fresh clothes as his wife and son had breakfast. When he entered the kitchen, Alicia poured a cup of coffee for him and said, "You look like you've been hit by a car. Still handsome, but in a long-haul trucker kind of way." She smiled.

"I didn't sleep well." He smiled at David and pretended to take a bite out of his toast.

David said, "You can have it, Daddy. There's lots of toasty toast." Buddy sat at his feet anticipating dropped food.

"Thanks, David. But daddy's just going to sip some coffee now and work my way into breakfast in a little while." He smiled.

Alicia said, "If you came to bed, and didn't fall asleep on that couch, you might feel better."

"I didn't want to wake you."

She looked at her husband, his unshaven face and puffy eyes. "Paul, you cracked Jefferson's encryption. You've done all you can. It's up to the FBI, CIA and others to find Fajar Hamad."

"My goal is to make it safe for my family. We don't want federal agents delivering our groceries forever. My work isn't done until you and David can walk through a park without bodyguards." He stepped closer to her and lowered his voice. "The deputy director of the FBI, Ward Rosenberg, was murdered last night."

Alicia folded her arms, glanced at David, slipping Buddy a piece of toast, lowered her voice and asked, "Murdered? Where? What happened?"

"Poisoned. He died in front of the Intercontinental Hotel on Pennsylvania. Bill and FBI Director Haden McNally believe Rosenberg was a mole … supplying the Russians with sensitive information. Alicia, one of the phones Rosenberg had access to, a secure phone that could be traced, was used to contact Carl Busch, the CIA agent who breached and caused our safe haven on Panarea to evaporate."

"Oh my God … does this mean that Rosenberg has leaked our location here to Fajar Hamad or the Russians or anybody else hunting for us?"

"I don't know. Bill and McNally don't know what, if anything, Rosenberg may have told them. No one trespassed on our farm property last night."

"Paul, my mother's funeral is tomorrow. I'm supposed to meet with Dianne today to work out the details. Can I even plan Mom's funeral?"

"Of course you can. The agents will be respectful, like they've been the last couple of weeks. They'll stay in the shadows, but they'll be present in the event someone approaches you or David."

Alicia turned and looked at the backyard. A slight breeze was blowing, slightly moving the bushes that hid the high fence encircling the property. She looked at Paul and asked, "Are you coming to the funeral?"

"Yes. I will be there with you."

"Brandi and Adam are getting married in July. My hope and prayer is that we can attend the wedding, the reception, to go as a family and not have armed federal agents there." Alicia picked up her purse. She looked at her son. "David, you want to stay with Daddy while I run some errands?"

"I want to go, too."

"I'm just going to meet with Aunt Dianne and talk about some things."

"Will Brandi be there?"

"I don't know."

He looked over at Paul and then cut his eyes toward his mother. "I still want to go."

She picked up her purse. "Okay, kiddo. But Buddy stays here today."

• • •

An hour later, Paul put on a fresh pot of coffee and walked back into the office, Buddy following him. He keyed in the GPS numbers to track the signals given off by chips he'd inserted in Alicia and David's shoes. After a few seconds, he found one signal coming from David's shoe, the signal just barely moving, indicating that David was not traveling in the car with his mother. They'd most likely arrived at Helen's house.

Alicia and Dianne were meeting at their mother's home, David probably watching a movie. Paul felt a tug of sorrow move within him. Not only sorrow for Alicia and Dianne due to the death of their mother, but the sorrow that comes from having to cope with the threat of aggression when the family should be given the time and space to grieve.

The other GPS signal was coming from close to where Paul sat, down the hall and in the master bedroom. He got up from his chair and walked to the master bedroom, opened the closet door and looked at his wife's shoes. He lifted a pair off the floor, the same pair that he'd fitted with the GPS chip. '*Promise me that when you leave the house you will wear these, or at least carry them in a bag, okay?*'

'*Okay, cross my heart.*'

EIGHTY-TWO

Paul sat back in front of his computer, upset with Alicia, his body and mind tired. He cut his eyes up to the screen, the pulse of the GPS chip in the heel of his son's shoe like the light from a dim star tucked in the corner of the universe. He thought about the encrypted words Jefferson and Stephen Decatur had shared. He picked up a page of the decrypted letters and read, *"Let us extract from the story of Cain and Abel. The pasha, in my view, rules with arrogance and a degree of narcissism. Ego blinds a man to live in the present because his reprisal from the past causes him to scheme for the future, consequently he will expose his Achilles heel often through his own ego."*

Paul set the page down and whispered, "Jefferson, you figured out the pasha's weak spot ... I have to do the same with Fajar Hamad to defeat him. There are probably a few things that haven't changed in 225 years, he handed down ego and places where Fajar could be hiding."

He picked up Stephen Decatur's decoded letter and read, *"I wish to inform you, sir, that Pasha Karamanli, after signing the treaty, departed Tripoli in a state of anger to take refuge in what is known as the Jabal Caves, the caves of the ancient tribes. These are caves in the Nafusa Mountains some one hundred kilometers south of the city of Tripoli. I learned it was the ancient home of his people. He has taken a militia of his best warriors."*

Paul sat straighter in his chair, leaned forward, and keyed in numbers and letters. The screen filled with a satellite image of earth. He tapped a half dozen keys and the earth turned, North Africa filling the screen. Paul's fingers moved across the keyboard and the satellite image of Libya appeared, he zoomed into the coordinates, the camera image flying toward a large mountainous area. The mountains were high, rocky, some areas covered in what appeared to be scrub trees—maybe olive trees. The mountains were crisscrossed with squiggle dirt roads, some no larger that goat trails.

He used the satellite images to track from above, looking for signs of people. There were dozens of earthen brick, adobe-style builds—farms, wedged in and out of the plateaus. Paul knew that somewhere in the mountains were the caves that became the refuge of the ousted pasha of Tripoli and now they could be the hiding place of his great, great grandson.

Paul called Bill Gray and said, "I think I know where Fajar Hamad may be hiding?"

"If you do, somehow you've been able to accomplish what dozens of our Delta Force, Seal teams, and federal agents haven't found yet. And they've stealthily combed Libya, from Tripoli to Benghazi."

"But have they looked in the Nafusa Mountains?"

"Where?"

Paul saw something on his computer screen that was almost subliminal. He used his mouse to delete images of the Libyan mountains from his screen. He looked at the GPS pulse image coming from David's shoe.

Bill, holding the phone to his ear, walked up to FBI headquarters, and said, "I hope you can get a little more specific. The next deadline is almost here. The cycle of the crescent moon ends in forty-eight hours. We have no idea what this guy's planning, or whether the Russians, hidden behind a cloak of anonymity and denial, will offer him any further assistance."

Paul's mouse pointer barely moved, as if it was an accident—the hacker could have sneezed causing the tiny movement. But it was enough to catch Paul's eye. "Hold a second, Bill." He stared at the screen, the blink of the GPS image from David's shoe still coming from his grandmother's house.

And then it moved.

The dot was traveling down the street and out of the neighborhood. Paul watched it and knew the hacker was watching it, too.

"Paul, are you still on the line?" Bill asked.

"Yes. We have a problem … a big problem." Paul's eyes followed the dot.

"What?"

"The hacker from Tripoli got through my reinforced firewalls. He's in my system. He's following the GPS tracker in David's shoe. They know where Alicia and David are at this very second."

EIGHTY-THREE

A licia could see the two agents in the distance, following her car. She turned to the right at the end of the neighborhood, looked in the rearview mirror and pulled onto the main road. David sat in the seat next to her, strapped in his seatbelt, playing a video game with Marvel animated characters. He looked up at his mother and asked, "Can we stop and get some ice cream?"

"That sounds like a fine idea. Maybe our FBI friends will want ice cream cones, too. I know a great place. It's about five miles from here. They have the best pistachio on the planet, or at least they used to when I went there."

"Did you go there with Daddy?"

"No, that was before I met Dad. But I bet he'd love it, too. You can try it ... they'll give you a sample on a little spoon." She glanced up at the mirror, the agents behind two cars, trying to be as inconspicuous as possible. "Oh, I forgot to tell your Aunt Dianne something. I need to make a quick call." She lifted her phone from its slot in the console cradle and hit one button to call her sister.

• • •

Paul moved closer to the computer screen. He said, "Bill, I'm going to put you on speaker phone. I need to use both hands for a minute. Where are you now?"

"Just entering FBI headquarters."

"Alicia and David are traveling south on Connecticut Avenue approaching Oxford. Can you let the agents following them know that their location is compromised."

"Absolutely. We'll have additional escorts join them."

Paul hit the keys with machine gun bursts from his fingers. He looked at the firewalls and traps he'd set for the hacker, zeroing in on the point where the latest attack originated. "You bastard ..." he mumbled, his eyes following lines of code. "Bill, when the hacker doubled back and basically used a cyber battering ram to knock through the walls, the traps I set opened him up. He wanted to get in so bad he compromised his location."

"Where is the son-of-a-bitch?"

"Tripoli. To be exact it's 1527 Mizran Street. Looks to be about a block from the fountain at Martyrs' Square. We need to get somebody there quickly. This guy might be able to see that I've found his hideout. If so, he could be gone in minutes. I need to call Alicia."

"Call me back when you're done." Bill disconnected.

Paul hit the number to Alicia's phone.

• • •

Alicia listened to her sister Dianne for a minute and said, "With my adjusted schedule, I haven't had a chance to ride out to the cemetery to speak with them about Mom's gravesite."

Dianne, still at their mother's house, sitting at the kitchen table, paperwork all around, said, "I spoke with them this morning. I gave the phone to Charlie, and he took care of the arrangements for us. Everything there is taken care of, as is the funeral home for the showing ... Alicia, I hate the sound of that word. The last thing Mom would want was to be showed."

"I know. But she has lots of friends and family that would like to walk by the casket and say their own personal goodbyes."

• • •

Paul stood in front of his computer, the number to his wife's phone ringing. "Come on, Alicia, pick up." After a few rings, it went to voicemail. He disconnected and immediately tried again, paced the floor, and walked out of the office with Buddy following him. "Alicia, answer the phone. Come on!"

• • •

Alicia listened to Dianne and looked at the incoming call. She could see it was Paul again. She started to interrupt her sister, but Dianne was getting emotional, talking about their father's death, how she'd cried more at that time than when their mother passed, "And I loved Mom just as much as Dad," she said. "Maybe the reason I cried so much after his death was because it came so quick. He was sick but I thought he had more time. Didn't you feel the same way?"

Alicia looked in the rearview mirror. The agents were still two cars behind her and David. She said, "I think you're right. I was on the phone with Dad when he passed. He was describing a sunrise to me … what I remember the most was …"

• • •

Rafa Gamal watched the GPS signal from his computer screen. He sipped an energy drink and smiled, sat back in his chair and made a call. There was light static on the line when the man answered in Persian and said, "Do you have something for me as the crescent moon of our forefathers prepares to display itself in the sky?"

"I have a GPS signal from someone in the Marcus family."

"Who and where?"

"I do not know the answer to the first part of your question. But they are traveling down Connecticut Avenue just passing Oxford in northwest Washington DC. They are moving at approximately twenty kilometers per hour."

"How do you know the signal is from Marcus or someone in his family?"

"Because I am the best at what I do. That's why I can command my fee. I managed to—no I will be blunt, I tricked Paul Marcus and reentered his computer recently and found the screen where he monitors the GPS movements. I will deduce that either his wife or son are wearing the chip because I get one signal from the moving location, a car presumably, and two signals from a stationery position, a house or building, most likely."

Gamal leaned forward in his chair, lit a dark Turkish cigarette, exhaled a smoke ring and watched it slowly drift toward the computer screen where the light from the screen illuminated the ring of expanding white smoke. "The vehicle has come to a stop."

"Where? The address! Now!"

"Tracking the prey this way was not part of our negotiation. Another half million buys you an address for the vehicle and house."

"Done! Where is the vehicle right now?"

• • •

Alicia pulled off the road and into the parking lot to Carl's Ice Cream Shoppe. It was built in the 1950s and had the retro, low-slung feel of a diner at the birth of rock 'n roll. Cinderblocks painted the color of lilacs. A checkered awning wrapped around the front. A rosy neon sign that spelled *Carl's* sat on the top of the one-story building.

EIGHTY-FOUR

P aul paced the floor of his office. He tried to call his wife again. No answer. He called Bill and said, "Alicia could be in trouble. If the hacker is relaying her location to anyone working for Fajar Hamad here in Washington, we have a dangerous situation."

"Where is she now?"

Paul looked at the computer screen. "She's slowed down ... the location is Connecticut Avenue just past Primrose. That's the location of an ice cream shop. Carl's Ice Cream Shoppe. Bill, call the agents assigned to her. They need to be on high alert."

"Done."

• • •

Alicia leaned toward David in the front seat of the car and said, "We'll eat it inside. I don't want any ice cream spills or drips in this new car."

David grinned. "I'll lick the cone."

"And you'll do it over a table with a napkin tucked in your shirt. Stay right here. I'm going to get out of the car and open your door."

"Okay, Mommy."

Alicia looked around the parking lot. Except for the agent's black SUV pulling into the lot, there was only one other car, and older model Buick. She waited a moment for the agents to park. They opened the front doors on the SUV, both men surveying the premises, dark glasses on, pistols under their sports coats.

One of the agents walked over to Alicia's car. He motioned for her to lower the driver's side window. When she did, he leaned down and said, "Mrs. Marcus, would you like for me to go inside and order something for you?"

She smiled. "No thanks, Larry. You've been with us going to the doctor's office and grocery shopping. I've been promising David an ice cream since we left Panarea. This place is certainly off the beaten path, it's not like David and I are walking around the Washington Memorial. Why don't you and Chuck come inside out of the heat and have an ice cream with us. We can sit at the same table together. Bodyguards with ice cream bibs. I love the concept." She smiled wide and laughed. She held her hand to her mouth and said, I think that's the first time I've laughed out loud since before the plane blew up over our heads."

The agent nodded, quick smile. "I understand. You and your family have been going through some stressful times. It will get better, and soon."

"You sound like my husband. But the fact of the matter is that we're scared to bury my deceased mother because of what's going on around us. It's no one's fault. It's complicated, and just the way it is. So, that's why the simplicity of a scoop of pistachio on a sugar cone sounds so appealing." She opened the car door. The agent backed up, the radio earpiece just visible in his left ear.

Alicia walked around the car and opened David's door. She reached in to unlock his seatbelt when a car pulled in directly behind her. A second car pulled in the lot and came to an abrupt stop one parking space away from her car.

She was boxed in—no retreat.

She looked up through the windows to the agent near her door. In the next five seconds, her world stopped.

The agent reached inside his jacket and pulled a gun.

From behind her came shouts in a foreign language—Arabic.

Four men in black pants, T-shirts, and black ski masks. Two in each car.

She stood and looked toward the agent just as his head exploded.

A scream was trapped in her throat. The second agent crouched behind his SUV and fired his gun. He hit one of the attackers in the center of his chest. A flower of red blossomed instantly as the man fell backwards onto the pavement.

"Mommy!" David cried out.

More gunfire. *Pop—pop—pop.* A second man in the car directly behind her car slid down, no longer visible at the wheel. Alicia tried to get in the car to protect her son. She felt a strong hand on her shoulder pulling, the barrel of a gun wedged into her temple. Her attacker screamed at the FBI agent. "Lose your gun or the woman dies!"

"Mommy! Don't hurt my Mommy!" David tried to unbuckle the seatbelt; his instinct to protect his mother.

Alicia watched in horror as the agent crouched behind the SUV, sighted down his gun barrel, the muzzle aimed at the man holding her. He fired two shots at the agent. One hit the front side window, glass blowing out. The second round entered the side of the SUV above the tire. Alicia broke free. She jumped back in the car next to David and tried to unlock the glove box in a futile effort to get the pistol.

"Mommy!" he cried, tears streaming down his cheeks.

The man she'd escaped from grabbed her by the hair, pulling hard, jerking her out of the car and onto the pavement. "Daddy!" David screamed. "DADDY!"

The assailant aimed his Beretta at Alicia, the dark muzzle of the barrel like the eye of a Cyclops. Black. Unblinking. Deadly. But it was the look in the attacker's eyes that was more foreboding. Even through the partial disguise of the ski mask, through openings in the mask, the eyes toyed with her. Amused. Hungry for a kill. The thin, wet lips mocking.

She held one hand up, anticipating the bullet tearing through her body. Before he could fire, a round entered the man's neck, just below the chin. He fell backwards, frenzied breathing, the burble of air mixed with blood—a shattered larynx.

Alicia heard the agent run toward them, trying to save David and her. Another man came from around the side of his car. Alicia could see him stooped near the rear of the car, tracking the agent's moves. He raised his gun.

"Look out!" screamed Alicia.

The man fired. Two quick bursts. She heard the agent fall, moaning slightly, his breathing labored. The assailant slowly stood and walked around Alicia's car. No hurry. His prey mortally wounded. She watched him aim his Beretta. He fired once.

The agent stopped breathing. Alicia got up, tried to run around her car, the keys still in the ignition. *Maybe I can backup into the car and push it away,* she thought. She got as far as her door, turned to open it. The man pointed his gun at her and fired. The round hit her in the stomach with the force of a line-drive baseball.

She fell onto the parking lot, the left side of her face against the pavement, the stench of a half smoked cigarette on the pavement, the stickiness of vanilla ice cream partially dried in the cracks of the asphalt. There was the sound of sirens in the distance, growing closer. With her face against the parking lot, she could see beneath her car to the other side. She watched the man's shoes. Black running shoes. White laces. He stopped at the open door, reached in and unbuckled David's seatbelt.

"Nooou!" David screamed. "Mommy!"

The man lifted her son out of the seat, David kicking and screaming. The attacker ran toward his car with David. Alicia heard the car door slam. David's muted screams and pleas, his sobbing. The sound of the engine starting, the car backing up and leaving, tires squealing.

Alicia laid there in the parking lot, holding her stomach with one hand, blood seeping between her fingers and trickling across the stains of white left from the vanilla ice cream on the ground. She saw Paul's face. They were on the sailboat. Paul at the helm, his face tanned and smiling, seagulls squawking in a turquoise sky that mirrored the still waters of the Mediterranean. Paul motioned for David to join him. David climbed in his dad's lap and reached for the wheel, his small fists barely able to grip the helm. He grinned, dimples popping, the *swoosh* of the water against the hull, David's laughter unbridled and mixing with the chortle of the gulls following in the boat's wake.

And then the sea turned black as coal, whitecaps rolling. Alicia held the rigging and lifeline, looking at the dark horizon. She turned back toward the cockpit. David and Paul were gone, the helm spinning with the uncertainty of a roulette wheel, sails straining in the wind, the boat tipping dramatically, the angry sea coming across the hull and pulling Alicia down in its dark grasp.

EIGHTY-FIVE

David sat in the center backseat of the strange car. The two men in the front seat removed their ski masks and spoke in a language that David didn't understand. *Why did the man driving take me? Is Mommy hurt?* He didn't know. The man drove the car fast, making quick turns. David felt sick. His stomach churned. His head throbbed. He pulled his knees up under his chin and gripped his legs. *Where's Daddy?* His lower lip trembled, tears spilling from his eyes.

The man on the passenger side turned around and faced David. He shouted, "Be quiet! No crying! You are here only because your father is a very bad man."

David stopped crying and stared at the man with the dark beard. He said, "My father is not bad. My father is good!"

"Shut up!"

David glared at the man who said something to the driver in the strange language. They laughed, and he knew they were laughing at him. David felt a sudden anger. The more they talked and laughed, the angrier he became. He kicked the back of their seat once.

The man on the passenger side, Fadi, turned around. He reached back and grabbed David's legs, pulling off his shoes. "Give me my shoes!" David yelled. The man dropped the small sneakers into a cardboard box. He reached inside his jacket and removed a sheet of paper, putting it inside the box, folding the flaps in place.

The driver said something in Arabic. They pulled up and stopped behind a Metrobus that was in a loading zone in front of a bank and grocery store. Fadi got out of the car, holding the box, and jogged up to the bus as the driver was closing the door. He banged on the door and the driver opened it, Fadi entering the bus. He paid his fare, walked past a dozen passengers, and took a seat in the very back. He sat alone.

As the bus pulled away from the curb, Fadi sat, holding the box in his lap. He stared at the driver who looked at him in one of the rearview mirrors for a moment. As soon as the driver kept his eyes on the road for a few seconds, Fadi took the box off his lap and hid it under the rear seat. He looked at the cityscape as the driver entered more of the metro area of greater Washington DC.

At a distance of half a city block, Ibrahim Omar drove the car and followed the bus. After another half mile, when the driver pulled over at a bus stop, Fadi got out, walking casually down the street. He looked back over his shoulder, a flock of pigeons taking flight from foraging next to a park bench. As the bus continued toward downtown, Omar eased the car up to the curb and his partner got back inside.

David glared at the man, tears in his eyes. "I want my shoes."

Fadi looked in the back seat and said, "Your shoes will serve a great purpose. You should feel honored. Your shoes will bring your father to us. Then you can be together again. That, boy, will make you happy, yes?"

David stared at the man in silence. He thought about his mother. *Where was she?* He tightened his lips. He would not let them see him cry again, because he wouldn't cry again. Maybe never.

• • •

Paul stood in the living room of the safe house and peered out the front window, the SUV at the end of the drive, the silhouettes of the agents in the front seat. He called his sister-in-law, Dianne, and asked, "Have you heard from Alicia?"

"No, Paul, not since she and David left a little while ago. Is everything okay?"

"I don't know. I think she stopped at an ice cream shop along the way."

"We'll that sounds harmless, particularly with two bodyguards in tow."

"She's not answering her phone, and that's not like Alicia."

"You want me to try her for you?"

"That'd be great. If you reach Alicia, please have her call me. It's urgent."

"I will." Dianne stood in her mother's kitchen, looking at the paperwork from the funeral home and cemetery. "Paul, I know what you and Alicia are going through … frankly, it's more than most people could cope with … and now with the loss of Mom. I'm worried for Alicia. She's under a lot of stress, and trying to always have a brave face for David. Tell me … are the FBI, CIA and whomever, any closer to finding this guy and his band of killers?"

"They're making progress, getting closer. It's just a matter of time, I think. And through it all, they're charged with trying to make sure no one else gets hurt or killed attending weddings, or visiting our national monuments."

"I'll see if I can reach my sister. Stay safe." She disconnected.

Paul slipped his phone into his back pocket and walked down the driveway toward the agent's car. As he got closer, the agents opened both doors to the Ford Explorer and quickly got out. Paul looked at their anxious faces and could tell something had happened. The driver, a square jawed man with an accountant's neatly parted haircut, said, "Mr. Marcus, sir, you need to get back in the house."

"Why? What's happening?"

"There's been an incident."

"What incident?"

"It's Mrs. Marcus, sir. Four hostiles in two cars blocked her car in when she stopped in the parking lot of an ice cream store—"

Paul felt his knees weaken, his heart slamming in his chest. "Is my wife okay? Is my son okay?"

"From what we understand, Mrs. Marcus was shot. She's alive and being airlifted to the hospital. Two of our agents were killed on the scene. Before they died, they'd killed two of the hostiles."

"What about David?"

"Your son, sir, was kidnapped. I'm so sorry."

Paul reached for the hood of the SUV, bracing himself, his breathing fast and shallow. He looked at both agents and nodded. "What hospital? Where'd they take my wife?"

"Georgetown Hospital."

Paul turned and ran back to the house. He entered and sprinted to the office, Buddy following at his feet. Paul hit a few keys on the keyboard and watched his computer screen. He looked at the GPS dot coming from David's shoe. "Still in the area," he whispered, picking up the phone and calling Bill. When he answered, Paul said, "I'm going to Georgetown Hospital. Alicia's been shot."

"I just heard moments ago. I'm getting an update now and—"

"Bill! Listen … I'm sending you the coordinates to track David. They kidnapped him." Paul glanced at the screen. "The signal is coming from Massachusetts Avenue at Rocky Creek, moving at about twenty-five-miles-per-hour. The FBI and SWAT need to get these coordinates immediately and stop them before they have a chance to hide David or worse."

"David was taken because they want you, Paul, and they know that holding David hostage is the way to find you."

"I don't know if my wife is dead or alive. They've kidnapped my son. I've never felt so helpless. I'm going to the hospital. Please call me the moment David is found. If they want to negotiate, I need to be part of it."

EIGHTY-SIX

As he passed the general waiting area, being escorted to a more private section, he counted eleven people in the room, some reading magazines, others texting on their phones, some staring at a wide-screen TV mounted to one wall, the news on, sound off. An elderly man in shorts and a Tommy Bahamas shirt had his face buried in his hands. Three federal agents stood near the doorways, watching people arriving, occasionally speaking into radio mics clipped to the cuffs of their sports coats. The smell of bleach and anxiety stifled the air.

The wait was interminable, but Paul knew the longer he remained in a secluded and guarded area of the hospital trauma center, the greater the odds were that Alicia was still alive. No doctor had come forth with news—good or bad as Alicia underwent emergency surgery.

Paul looked at his watch. *Why hasn't Bill called? Did they find David?* He wanted to be with the SWAT team hunting down the animals that kidnapped his son, but he dared not leave the trauma ward of the hospital with Alicia in emergency surgery. He stepped across the large room to a window. The outside view was that of a lush garden, purple and white impatiens alongside the thick border grass. There was a small, flowing water fountain just beyond the park benches, the water cascading over smooth stones and emptying into a grotto with koi fish cavorting just below the surface.

In the background, he could hear the TV newscast as someone turned up the sound in a nearby hospital room. A reporter said, "We want to warn our viewers that some of the video footage is quite graphic. The facts, as we know them at this point, are this: four people were shot and killed in the parking lot of Carl's Ice Cream Shoppe in the northwest section of the District."

Paul picked up a remote from the coffee table and turned on the TV in the room where he was. The reporter continued. "Two of the dead are said to be FBI agents. An initial investigation indicates the agents had returned fire after four men in two separate cars entered the lot and blocked a car driven by Alicia Marcus. She is the wife of the former NSA cryptographer, Paul Marcus, who is on the list of terrorist's demands, insisting that Marcus be handed over to an Islamic faction only known by their signature name—*Derna*. Both, formerly, were assumed dead after they disappeared five years ago because of their heroic actions allegedly linked to dismantling a powerful group called the Circle of 13 and crippling Iran's nuclear program—that was until Paul Marcus' name appeared on the demands' list."

Paul glanced at the federal agents who stood near the door. They remained stone-faced, ignoring the news reports of the carnage and information about his former activities.

The reporter, a thirty-something man in a sports coat, white shirt, no tie, stood on the opposite side of the street, Carl's Ice Cream Shoppe in the background. There were dozens of police and investigators on the scene. He said, "We'll cut to the surveillance footage from a nearby camera across the street. The images are somewhat grainy, but you can see the attackers blocked in the car driven by Alicia Marcus. An FBI agent drew his gun. Less than five seconds later, all shots were fired ... including one that struck Mrs. Marcus as she tried to protect her young son, David. She fell to the pavement and one of the two remaining attackers snatched the child from his mother's car and sped away with the other man."

Paul studied the images, queasiness building in his gut fueled by a surge of adrenaline driven by vengeance. He looked at the make of cars, the physical traits of the two men, the way they moved, their hand signals. And the way one man ran with David, throwing him in the back seat like he was a sack of potatoes before driving away. He couldn't see Alicia, the view blocked by her parked car.

But Paul did see the man fire a single shot.

A shot that entered his wife's body.

Paul turned away from the TV and looked out into the garden, an oasis in the midst of suffering. He closed his eyes, clenched his fists, thinking about David and Alicia ... trying to remember the last thing he said to either of them. He said a silent prayer, opened his eyes and watched a sparrow alight at the edge of the grotto and dip its beak into the water, the little bird tilting its head back and swallowing.

He could hear Alicia's voice like a whisper, *'One summer my Dad put up a hummingbird feeder ... mom would sit on the deck as the hummingbirds darted around the feeder, sticking their long beaks into the nectar beyond a fake flower. Mom held the feeder a few times and chatted with the hummingbirds like she was calling a puppy. One hummingbird would come in, fly around her and the feeder for a moment, and then land on her finger between sips of nectar. It was amazing.'*

"Mr. Marcus?" the voice was deep, a sense of sorrow in his tone.

Paul turned around. "Yes."

A doctor, mid-fifties, dressed in scrubs, narrow face, blue eyes that had seen a lot of suffering, folded his arms. There were two tiny specks of blood on the edge of his glasses. "The surgery went as well as can be expected. Your wife will need to stay in the IC ward as we monitor her recovery."

"She's going to make it, right, doctor? Alicia is going to live ... just tell me that, please?"

"She should recover. However, she'd lost a lot of blood before the paramedics got there. Her heart had stopped en route to the hospital. It was touch and go. The bullet did damage to her stomach, intestines, spleen and one kidney. But she appears to be quite a fighter. Her sheer resilience, I believe, played a big factor in her survival thus far."

"Can I see her?"

"In a little while, and only for a brief period." He glanced at the outside garden and back over to Paul. "She's very lucky, maybe even miraculous in her survival. Miracle is not a term, as a doctor, I often use. But sometimes it's the only way to describe what really can't be defined in medical terms." The doctor glanced around at the federal agents on guard, the people in the waiting room, dropping his voice. "I only heard snippets of what happened today. I'll assume the attack on your family stems from this terrorist group that's being led by the fanatic in the news who is trying to avenge the Barbary States war, the nation's first under Thomas Jefferson, correct?"

"Yes."

The doctor removed his glasses and used a wrinkled, off-white handkerchief to clean the lens. "In my line, I deal, literally, in fighting death. When man, and not some sort of accident, causes the injuries, I always take pause at the horror. How could someone do that to another human being? Madness and a mission too often are the same. We'll move your wife to IC recovery in about a half hour. Then you can see her."

"Thank you."

The doctor put his glasses on and turned to leave. He stopped, looked back at Paul and said, "I heard they took your son. There's a reason your wife is still with us. I believe that reason will prevail for your son as well." He nodded, his eyes fatigued. The doctor turned and walked down the corridor, holding a fob up to an electronic sensor, the doors to the IC operating rooms opening and quickly closing as he walked inside.

Paul's phone buzzed. He answered and Bill Gray said, "Tell me Alicia is okay and recovering."

"She's out of surgery, but she's not out of the woods. The bullet did some internal damage to her spleen and one kidney … " The words stuck in Paul's throat.

"It looks like one or more of the attackers abandoned their car and is traveling on a metro bus."

"Is David on the bus?"

"It's hard to see from the road, but the GPS signal is coming from it. So we're assuming David is seated on the bus with this guy. We have some of our very best agents in quiet pursuit. At the next bus stop, one of our top people with a sidearm is going to board the bus. David's safety is our utmost concern. That's why we're using this approach. If it comes to a show of arms, our guy won't miss. That's a promise."

"What if David is sitting right next to him? My wife is fighting for her next breath. I can't chance that with my young son, too."

"Paul, the alternative might make it worse. If we stop the bus, surround it with police and heavy firepower—the guy could shoot everyone on the bus, including David. He might then turn the gun on himself to punch his ticket to paradise. Boarding the bus as a passenger, not looking like police or an agent, will gain us the surprise and advantage over this guy. Stay there and take care of Alicia. We'll bring David back to you."

"Bring him back alive. That's all I ask."

EIGHTY-SEVEN

It was the journey no one wants to take. Maybe the longest walk of Paul's life. He followed a nurse down the extended corridor from the waiting room to the trauma center unit, beyond inaccessible operating rooms, past the central station, doctors and nurses in pea-green scrubs reading patient charts and computer screens. Somewhere in the unit a woman screamed out in pain. At a distance, one federal agent shadowed Paul and the nurse.

They walked by triage areas where patients were treated, some of the trauma bay curtains partially open as doctors fought to stop hemorrhaging and extend lives. The bays clung to the slight odors of disinfectant and the coppery smell of spilled blood. Three teenage boys, victims of gunshot and gang violence, had been brought in on gurneys. A white sheet was pulled up on a body, a tag on one toe.

An older black man, salt and pepper hair, dressed in a custodial uniform, mopped fresh blood off the floor of one bay. He swept up discarded paper wrappers and plastic ripped from needles and syringes used to sustain life. His face was lined from age and saddened from senseless death.

"Your wife is in room 202," the nurse said, pointing toward an extension hallway to the left. Paul nodded and followed her directions, the agent staying back, keeping Paul in his sight. The room was less than fifty feet from the nurses' station. He paused at the door and took a deep breath. *Alicia Marcus* was written on an ID sheet. Paul slowly opened the door and entered, not prepared for what he was about to see.

Alicia was lying on a bed that was raised to keep her head and upper body elevated. Her eyes were closed and she was attached to at least a dozen plastic tubes and wires monitoring her vital signs. Paul could hear his wife's heartbeat and see the EKG digital readouts on one screen. The constant *beep … beep … beep.* Other screens monitored her breathing and blood pressure. From across the room, she looked so small and fragile.

He stepped to her bedside. IVs ran to both of her arms. The sheet across her chest barely moved as she breathed in and out. Her face was slightly swollen, a bruise on one cheek, lips dry and cracked. He reached down and touched her left hand, a fleck of dried blood on her gold wedding ring. He tenderly held her hand, emotions welling inside.

Paul leaned down and kissed Alicia's forehead. He stroked her hair. "I love you … you can't leave me … not after what we've been through together. You have too much to live for. Stay with me. It's not your time, Alicia. I know that's not for me to decide … but I know it's not. David needs his mother. I need you, and you need us. I will fight for you. I'm going to find Fajar Hamad. In the meantime, you get well … you hear me?" Tears rolled down Paul's face, softly falling on Alicia left hand. "We have a wedding to attend. When Brandi and Adam pledge their vows to each other, I want you to be there … just like you were when I promised to love and cherish you … for richer or poorer … in sickness and health … then, now … and forever."

A final tear streamed down his cheek and splashed against Alicia's wedding ring, the fleck of blood washed away.

• • •

Special Agent Thomas Martinez could shoot a handgun equally well with his left or right hand. Being ambidextrous had given him the life and death edge twice in his seventeen-year career with the FBI. His eye-hand coordination was among the FBI's very best, so good, in fact that, as a courtesy he no longer competed professionally in matches.

And twice a year, he was asked to spend three days teaching new recruits firearms use at Quantico.

Today, Martinez looked like he could have been a homeless man, digging deep in his pockets for enough change to ride the Metrobus. He stood alone at the marked bus stop near the intersection of 6th and K streets. He wore a gray hoodie, black T-shirt, jeans with grass and dirt stains on the knees. Martinez had a week's worth of whiskers on a face that could have belonged to a construction worker or oil field roughneck. His skin had the tanned and leathery look of someone who'd spent a lot of time outdoors doing physical work, large hands. Martinez had spent his outdoor time training for full marathons.

But no amount of training can prepare anyone to face a possible murder-suicide scene. When there is no fear of death, there is no fear of consequences. There are no bargaining chips when the perpetrator is ready to cash in all the chips. Police and hostage negotiators can better deal with someone high on drugs holding a hostage, or someone, in a fit of jealously, holding a hostage. There is always a chance they can be talked off the ledge. Not so with a murder-suicide combatant drunk on the Kool-Aid of a ticket to paradise.

Martinez thought of that as the Metrobus pulled up in a gust of diesel fumes, and screeching brakes. The door opened with a loud *swooshing* sound, and the portly driver looked at Martinez through Coke bottle glasses. As Martinez stepped aboard, he said a silent prayer, his Glock under the hoodie, a Colt Mustang XSP wedged in an ankle holster on his right leg.

He pulled change out of a smudged pocket in his jeans, fed the machine, and turned to take a seat on the bus. He quickly scanned the passengers, making it appear that he wasn't looking at faces—wasn't looking at anyone. The first person he wanted to see was a boy—David. There was a little blonde girl sitting next to a woman that Martinez assumed was her mother. And they were in the first five rows.

Martinez walked slowly, head partly down, holding on to the overhead balance rails as he made his way to the back of the bus. He counted sixteen passengers—seven black, six white, two Koreans and one woman from India, a red Bindi dot near the center of her forehead.

No small boy.

No one wore a beard.

No one fit the profile of the two men seen on the video surveillance cameras at Carl's Ice Cream Shoppe.

The bus driver looked up in his wide rear-view mirror, all the passengers visible. "Please take a seat, sir," the driver barked, his voice high-pitched. "We're on a schedule."

Martinez sat in the last row, last seat. The driver pulled away from the bus stop and merged into traffic. Martinez looked out the back window, spotting at least three cars with agents. He glanced up in the sky and saw a helicopter following at a distance. He slipped an earpiece in his ear and pulled a small microphone from his cuff. He whispered, "The boy's not here. None of the two subjects from the ice cream shop are here either."

Senior Special Agent Andrew Perkins watched the bus through one of the surveillance cameras streaming video of the moving bus from the helicopter. Perkins, tall as most pro basketball players, cotton white hair, stood in the FBI command center, watching one of six large monitors above the consoles that resembled the control room of a television network. Twenty agents and a dozen technicians worked phones, live satellite and mobile camera feeds. Two video streams came from the dash-cameras mounted in the agents' cars. Perkins spoke into a microphone at one of the video consoles. "Are you positive the boy is in none of the seats, maybe laying down? The GPS signal is definitely coming from that bus."

"But it's not coming from David Marcus's shoes ... at least he's not wearing them on the bus because he isn't on the bus."

Perkins shook his head. Director McNally walked up to him, watching the monitors. McNally said, "Tell him to look around the seats. The perp must have left the boy's shoes somewhere in the bus."

"Martinez, Director McNally wants you to look around or under the seats. Maybe the shoes are there. Also, ask the driver if he saw a man and boy that fits their descriptions."

"All right. I'm in the back of the bus now. I'll start here."

A passenger, an older black woman wearing lavender-framed glasses attached to a beaded strap, sitting in a seat five rows ahead of

Martinez, turned to look at him. She stared for a moment, watching Martinez speak to no one visible. She raised her thin eyebrows and turned back around, sticking a scratch-off lottery ticket in her straw purse with a fake sunflower blossom on one side.

Martinez squatted down and looked under the seats directly in front of him. Nothing. Then he turned and looked under the back seat.

There was a box. A small one—flaps folded, one over the other, on each side to hold it closed.

Martinez opened his mic and said, "I may have found it. There's a small, cardboard box under a backseat."

Director McNally looked at the bus on of the monitors and said, "There could be a bomb in there. Stop the bus now! Get everybody off!"

EIGHTY-EIGHT

P aul stood next to Alicia's bed when a doctor entered the intensive
care room and nodded at him. The doctor was the same man who
had delivered the news about Alicia to Paul in the private waiting room
earlier. Two nurses followed him. The doctor touched Paul's shoulder
and said, "Mr. Marcus, we need to take a look at the wounds and
check her vitals. If you wouldn't mind stepping outside for about ten
minutes while we did that, we'd appreciate it."

"I really appreciate the care you've given my wife so far. Thank
you for saving her life."

"I wish we could take all the credit, but that's not the case. Your
wife had some help. As I mentioned, I don't toss the word miracle
around much, but there are some rare exceptions. You wife is one of
those."

Paul looked at Alicia, her eyes closed—a slight flutter of her
eyelashes for a moment. One of the machines beeped louder. "If you
would, please update me after you examine her," he said, turning to
leave the room. As Paul was walked back to the secured area allotted to
him, his phone buzzed, Bill Gray calling. Paul answered and Bill asked,
"How is Alicia?"

"She's in recovery. But she's far from out of danger. One of the
surgeons said it's a miracle she's alive."

"She's a fighter. Paul, the GPS from David's shoes led the agents
and SWAT teams to a Metrobus. When one of the agents boarded the

bus, David wasn't on it. There was no indication he'd ever been there. The agent found a cardboard box in the back of the bus. He let all the passengers off and drove the bus into the center of a large empty parking lot adjacent to some new construction off Eisenhower Boulevard."

"What's in the box?"

"We don't k know. The bomb squad is on the scene processing it now. Damn news media are having a fit trying to get close enough for live coverage in the event it blows. The agent questioned the bus driver, showed him a still pic lifted from the video in the lot of the ice cream shop. He told the agent that a man resembling one of the two in the photo boarded the bus, rode for a few blocks and got off."

"Where'd he get off?"

"E Street and 3rd."

"And they still have David."

"We'll find him."

"God willing, Alicia is going to wake up after recovery from surgery. She's fighting for her life because of a fanatic who refers to my wife, on one of his nice days, as an infidel, and tried to kill her. When she wakes up, the first thing she's going to ask me is where's David? What do I tell her, Bill? What do I tell a woman who is clinging to her own life … that her son may have lost his? That can't happen."

"I'm betting it won't. We'll find and rescue David. They're not going to kill him because it's you they want. He's their high card. I bet we'll hear from them very soon. And we need a helluva good plan to protect David and you."

"I need to call Dianne, Alicia's sister."

• • •

A member of the bomb squad stood in the open doors of the bus parked in the center of the empty lot. He wore a heavy-duty blast suit and helmet with a protective bulletproof glass visor. The nearest buildings were a block away. Federal agents and police officers stayed at a safe distance from the bus, standing behind parked squad cars, vans, and SUVs.

The bomb disposal expert set a robot down inside the bus, placing it in a position to be controlled by a radio signal. The robot, the size of a vacuum cleaner, resembled a small Army tank with its continuous caterpillar tread on all six wheels. The man in the bomb suit walked slowly back to an area cordoned off where another member of the squad worked controls to remotely operate the robot.

The men lifted their protective visors in order to better see the screen that was receiving a wireless, live video feed from the robot. The same feed was patched through to the FBI's command center where Director Haden McNally, Bill Gray and six senior members of the bureau watched.

Through the robot's center-mounted camera, the operator navigated it down the middle of the aisle to the back of the bus, the small box just visible under the rear seat. The operator, a man in his mid-thirties with intense blue eyes that didn't seem to blink, said, "The flaps on the box don't appear to be taped down … so I might be able to lift them open."

The other member of the bomb squad stared at the screen, "Let's try to open it. If it does blow, the bus has been in service on and off for five years. The loss won't be as bad as a new model. And there are no innocents around."

The operator grunted and inched the robot closer. He stopped it a foot away from the cardboard box, used a joystick to extend one of the robotic arms, opened the claw hand and clamped down on the edge of the first flap. The operator gently tugged to release it and then lifted the other flaps one by one. He used the controls to tilt the box so the robot's camera eye could peer inside.

"Look's like a child's pair of tennis shoes," he said, into a mic attached to a headset. "There's also a piece of paper in the box." He used the mechanical arm to lift each shoe out, using the second arm and motorized hand to peer inside each one. "Looks like they're empty inside." He used the metallic arms to turn each shoe over, examining every inch of them, from the top to the soles.

In the FBI Command Center, Director McNally stepped a little closer to one of the wide-screen monitors. He opened a microphone near a console and said, "This is McNally. Can you get an angle on that piece of paper? Looks like something was written on it."

"I can give it a try," said the operator, moving one of the three joysticks and staring at the monitor in the parking lot. He used the robot's mechanical hand to grasp the right edge of the paper and lift it from the bottom of the box, holding the note in front of the camera lens. The operator and his partner stared at the paper, not sure whether to read it aloud.

Bill Gray looked at the screen in the Command Center, put his glasses on and read aloud.

> *"Release Ulan Hamad. Transfer the one billion into the Central Bank of Iran. Deliver Paul Marcus before the crescent moon cycles or the next box you open will contain the head of the boy. Remember the battle of Derna - for whom the bell tolls has a silent ring, and always will.*
>
> *-Fajar Hamad*

McNally eyed Bill and said, "He signed his damn name. Could Fajar have managed to slip into this country? Could he be right here in the District calling the shots?"

"He could be anywhere, and that's what he wants us to think. He could be feeding pigeons in front of the Lincoln Memorial while his suicide squad tries to blow up the Jefferson Memorial ... at least that's what he wants us to believe. I have to call Paul and let him know they still have his son. How the hell do I tell him they're threatening to decapitate David? Before Alicia was shot, Paul had mentioned something, a long shot, about a place Fajar Hamad may be hiding. And right now that long shot may be our only shot."

EIGHTY-NINE

Dianne Hirsch wasn't prepared for what she was about to hear and see. She sat at the table in the small kitchen of her mother's home going though paperwork related to her mother's affairs and finances. The TV was on in the background. A news reporter, her hair worn up, stood near the parking lot, the city bus in the distance, dozens of police and emergency vehicles in a sea of flashing blue, white and red lights.

The reporter looked into the camera and said, "Police originally thought they were dealing with a bomb on a bus. After some tense moments, that appears not to be the case. They used a remote controlled robot to open a small cardboard box left at the back of the bus by one of the men identified as the shooter of Alicia Marcus and the kidnapper of her young son, David. Police and FBI said they had reason to believe the terrorist's act would extend to a Metrobus filled with passengers. Alicia Marcus is reported to be in critical condition at Georgetown University Hospital. There is no word on the condition or of the whereabouts of her son, David. And police say the kidnappers have not contacted them or the boy's father, Paul Marcus."

As the reporter continued with details of the horror in the parking lot at Carl's Ice Cream Shoppe and the fact that David's tennis shoes were found in the box with a chilling note, Dianne stood from the table, placing one of her hands over her mouth, nausea swirling in her stomach. She braced herself against a kitchen chair, looked for her phone on the counter, almost stumbling across the floor to pick it up and call. She noticed there was one missed call. If it was from Paul. Her mind raced. *He must have called when I went to the bathroom.*

Dianne returned his call, and after four rings it went to voice-mail. She said, "Paul, it's Dianne. I know you tried to call me. I just saw a news report on TV. Dear God ... what's happened? Are you at the hospital? Where is David? Please call me!"

• • •

Ibrahim Omar would not be taken alive. Neither would his partner, Fadi Zahir, sitting in the passenger side of the black Lincoln Navigator as Omar drove just under the speed limit through the heart of Washington, DC., constantly checking the rearview and side-view mirrors.

David Marcus was in the back seat. He looked at the buildings, recognizing the Washington Monument. He stared down at his shoeless feet, thought about his mother, father, and Buddy. David fought back a deep sadness.

Omar pulled the Lincoln into the private driveway of the brown-stone home in an upscale area of DuPont Circle. He stopped, entered a four-digit code on the lock system and waited for the ornate iron gate to swing open. He drove behind the building and into an underground parking area. Four other luxury cars were parked. Omar turned around to face David and said, "This will be your new home for a little while." He stepped out of the car and opened David's door, reached in, sternly pulling the boy from the back seat.

"This is not my new home," David said, standing on the concrete parking area in his stocking feet. "I want Mom and Dad."

Omar locked the door and walked around the car. "We want your dad, too. Let us see how much he wants you. Walk with us."

"No!"

"What did you say to me?"

"I want to go to my home."

Omar slapped David in his face, the blow almost knocking the boy down. "Your first rule is to obey and keep your little mouth shut."

David fought back the tears, his left cheek stinging, the man's handprint rising on his small face. "Follow us," said Omar, his black eyes cold.

They walked up steps and entered the home from the rear. The men led David through a hallway. On one wall hung a painting of the Potomac River at sunset. On the other wall was a painting of the ancient Iranian city of Persepolis, mostly in ruins. They moved though the kitchen and into a large living room with opulent Old World furnishing.

Dabir Nagi stood near a window. He turned around, unsmiling, and looked at David. "So, you are the son of Paul Marcus."

David said nothing.

"Where are your shoes?"

David pointed to Omar. "He took them from me."

"Well, in that case. He will have to get you another pair. It is only fair, yes?"

"I want *my* shoes."

Nagi shook his head. "I am afraid that is not possible. You see, the only way to get your shoes is for your father to bring them to you. He knows where they are. Let us see if he will deliver them to you."

NINETY

Paul sat in a hardback chair next to Alicia's bed. He held a phone to his ear and listened to Bill Gray give a summary of what happened when the bomb squad opened the box. "Fajar Hamad signed it, or one of his followers signed his name. Regardless, he's now about as brazen as it gets. We haven't seen anything like this, attacks on American soil, since 9/11. The next crescent moon sets in less than twenty-four hours. One of the problems is their communications ... it's basically one-way. They blow something up or kill someone and leave demand notes behind for us to read. We don't know where they are or how to communicate with them unless we do it through the news media, and that's always tricky at best."

Paul looked at his wife's face, the sound of heart and blood pressure monitors constant in the background. He stood from his chair and asked, "Have any of our operatives arrived at that address I gave you in Tripoli?"

"No, they're en route, coming from outside Benghazi to Tripoli."

"Good. Have them stand down, to stay very close to the address but don't rush the place and knock the door down ... not just yet."

"Why, Paul? Why not just take this terrorist geek out?"

"Because he may be the fastest way that we can communicate with them."

"What are you going to do?"

"I'm going to try to contact him. If I can, maybe I can figure a way to bring these killers out of wherever they're hiding."

"How? By using you as bait?"

"I'll do anything I have to do to save David's life."

"Whatever you do, it has to be coordinated through the CIA and FBI, because you will need backup, and you may only get one shot at this before something goes horribly wrong."

"Maybe one shot is all I'll need."

"You mentioned something about a mountain range where you thought Fajar Hamad might be conducting his operations. What do you have?"

"The Nafusa Mountains, about 125 miles southeast of Tripoli. There are some ancient caves there that go back to the time Islam was founded, maybe even earlier. They're called the Jabal Caves, but they're beyond caves in the traditional sense. Hundreds of years ago, they were carved out of the mountains into a series of large, connecting rooms, linked through intersecting cave-like tunnels. From goat herders to farmers, they've used those caves as homes for centuries. The original pasha of Tripoli fled there after his defeat. Maybe that's where Fajar is calling the shots. He could be using generators and satellite uplinks to stay connected with his followers. In Decatur's letter to Jefferson, he said Yusuf Karamanli fled there vowing revenge. What if that's the place where Hamad is conducting his strategic terror, following the vows of his great, great grandfather centuries earlier?"

"I'll get with the president, secretary of state, and the joint chiefs. We'll find those caves and see what, if anything, is in there."

"Jefferson, in his dealings with Karamanli, believed the Achilles heel was an ego that blinded them to the present because their view of the future was fueled by their arrogance and perception of misdeeds in the past. Hamad, if he's somewhere in those mountains, a surprise attack—just like Derna two centuries earlier, may be easy to find because he already thinks he's leading the battle and his guard could be down."

"We'll start satellite recon immediately. There are enough Special Forces ops and agents hidden in Libya to deliver the firepower, especially in a surprise. We just have to find Hamad. We know he has followers here, and at least two of them have your son."

Paul glanced at his watch, calculated the hours before the setting of the next crescent moon. "I need to go, Bill. I have a trap to set. My prey is in Tripoli. What I hope will happen is that he takes the bait and the trap springs somewhere in Washington."

"If you make contact with this guy, keep me posted on every move. You, alone, planted a cyber bomb in the Iranian nuke operations five years ago, but to rescue David … you're going to need help and manpower. We won't have a second chance with David's life."

"I'll call you." Paul disconnected, stepped over to Alicia's bedside. He looked at her sleeping and bruised face, bent down and kissed her forehead. "I'm going to bring our boy home. I promise you."

Paul left the hospital room, called Dianne and filled her in on what happened and Alicia's status. And then he headed back to the safe house to write the most important short message in his life.

NINETY-ONE

David's life hung in the balance of words Paul was about to write. He sat in front of his computer for a minute, thinking about what he was going to compose. He knew that the way he worded the message could have a direct impact on his son's life. He had to get it right to even get a response. And based on the way the hacker responded, if he did answer, Paul would begin to set the trap he had in mind.

His fingers moved across the keyboard in careful, even strokes as the words appeared across his screen: *This is Paul Marcus. Tell Fajar we will comply with his demands. And tell him this: I am the man you want. Now, you can come get me. I will surrender to you and go back to Iran or Libya with you only if you set my son free to live in peace with his mother. We can have an exchange. If you have access to a plane, we can board and leave, but only when my son is set free.*

Paul read his message, removed seven firewalls he'd built, keyed in the IP information and hit send. He stood, his heart pounding. He looked out the window, a robin hopping across the back yard. Buddy lifted his head from sleeping on the couch in the room. Paul said, "I know your life is in disarray, Buddy. Maybe, when this is over, we, as a family, can go to the farm and take a long walk though the Virginia woods. I bet you miss that."

Buddy tilted his head and came as close to a dog can come to smiling, his eyes bright. Paul glanced at the screen. There was a message. Rafa Gamal wrote: *The great Paul Marcus … the world's best in cryptography and cyber espionage. How does it feel to have met your match? Unfortunately, due to the nature of my work, I must remain anonymous … so our secret remains between us. I will dispatch your information to my employers. If they wish to respond, you will know soon.*

Paul read the message, his mind turning over the possibilities. He wrote: *Since my son is believed to be somewhere in Washington, the exchange can happen here and before the setting of the crescent moon. Isn't that what Fajar wanted? If they have transportation, a plane perhaps, it can leave with me on board. It will not be shot down. It's your call. There are plenty of smaller airports that can accommodate your needs.*

Paul hit send and waited.

• • •

Delta Force commando, Mike Nolan, studied the satellite images of the Nafusa Mountains on his computer screen in an adobe house on the outskirts of Misrata, Libya. He wore an earpiece in one ear and a wrap-around microphone so he could use both hands on the keyboard. His face had a ruddy, windswept look from spending months on covert missions in and out of the Libyan deserts. His lips chapped, blue eyes slightly bloodshot.

A dozen members of Delta Force were in the house, some of the men looking at aerial maps and printouts of the mountain range, others polishing weapons and sipping black coffee. Preparing for battle.

There was a palpable edginess in the air. Not fear. Testosterone mixed with adrenaline. None of the soldiers were afraid of combat. But every man gets ready for battle in his own way. There are internal demons of fear to be leashed and external demons of war to be unleashed on the battlefield. Each man knew that failing to prepare for the next few hours would be preparing to fail, and that was not an option.

"Listen up," said Mike Nolan, pushing back in his chair next to a thick wooden table. "NSA is sending us a live satellite feed from one of our birds above Libya. We'll have drone images here soon, too.

You guys gather around the screen." The men came closer to Nolan's computer. He reached down and enlarged the images of the live video feed. The mountains were rocky, almost barren of trees, reddish sandy soil, and boulders scattered everywhere, many larger than diesel locomotives.

"Looks like the surface of Mars," said one of the men with a grin.

Another man nodded and said, "Or maybe the Grand Canyon with a lot of red in the soil and mountains. Does command have any idea where Fajar might be, assuming the desert rat is holed up in those mountains?"

Nolan said, "There is some movement in and out of the terrain. NSA's been looking at the whole Nafusa Mountain range, tracking everything from goats to camels. Some of those mountains have an elevation of more than three thousand feet. The range is close to fifty miles long. Lots of hidden valleys in there. They've spotted some goat herders. A few farmers, too. What they grow in that kind of soil beats the hell outta me. They've seen some old trucks moving along the dusty roads, which look like goat paths."

"What about the caves? What are they called?"

"Jabal Caves. They're actually scattered all over the mountain range. Lots of people lived in them before mud and adobe houses a thousand years ago. Some refer to them as ancient troglodyte caves. The cave dwellers spent generations carving and enlarging them, making interconnecting rooms. They lived like Fred and Wilma Flintstone. There are caves with interlocked passages that are like small neighborhoods, long ago abandoned. We just have to find the right ones."

A tall, rawboned commando smiled and said, "It'd be nice to chopper up there and drop in for beer and a Brontosaurus burger with the Flintstones. Betty was hot, and I'd bet she would get you to yell yabba dabda doo. Talkin' about getting' your rocks—"

Nolan lifted his hand, palm out, listening through the earpiece. He leaned forward in his chair, typed in coordinates from the keyboard and stared at the changing images on the screen. "Got a visual," Nolan said into the mic. He looked up at his men and added, "They're flying a quiet version of an unmanned aircraft, sort of like a Predator drone, through the mountain range right now. We'll take the feed."

The men watched the images on the screen. It resembled a fast-paced video game. The live pictures were of the mountains in front of the camera and on either side, the wide-angle lens capturing the topography as the drone flew between the mountains, diving into the dark valleys, soaring two-hundred feet above winding trails that led to abandoned mud houses that seemed to be cast onto sides of hills and at the edge of barren plateaus. The red soil was a near blur as the drone flew over and into the mountain range.

"Look there," said one of the men, a week's worth of whiskers on his face, the light from the computer screen reflecting from his pupils. "There's movement, and it sure as hell isn't a goat herder."

The image cut to an overhead shot by a satellite camera in sync with the drone. The remote drone operators piloted the aircraft from hidden command centers in the Nevada desert. They used laser controls to fly through the twisting landscape—speed, altitude, longitude and latitude all displayed on the corner of the screen in real time.

"Would you look at that," Nolan said. He released a low whistle and pointed to the screen. There were live feed images of a half-dozen men moving around the entrance to a cave. The men, dressed like Bedouins, were heavily armed. "I see at least one satellite dish near a boulder close to the entrance to a cave. There are three vehicles, all appear to be covered in camouflage cloth."

One of the men leaned a little closer to the screen. "Looks like that cave leads to sort of an open air room. There are four men in there. Appears to be at least one rocket launcher."

Nolan stared at the images, not blinking. "Okay, we have the coordinates. We'll map the best way to gain access by surprise. Looks like we're in for a helluva fight on our hands. This one started with our brother Eli Dexter." He stood and inhaled deeply. "It extended to killings and destruction on America soil. They hit our Mount Rushmore, and now we're about to hit them in their mountains." He glanced at the watch on his wrist. "A soldier philosopher, much smarter than me, once said the two most powerful warriors are patience and time. Gentlemen, ours and that of our country's patience has run its course. And now the hostiles are out time. Let's roll!"

NINETY-TWO

Paul walked into David's bedroom and simply stood there in the late afternoon light. Buddy followed him. It had been six hours and no response yet from the hacker or his "employers," doubtless it was Fajar Hamad directly or indirectly. Paul stepped around electric train tracks in one corner of the room, the tracks made a figure eight on the hardwood floor. The train's engine, five cars, and a caboose were still where David had left them.

Paul walked over to a small desk and dresser. On the desk were toys, some plastic late model cars and a model plane. It was a replica of a Gulfstream G650, long-range jet. Paul picked it up off the desk, held it in both hands, slowly turning it over before replacing it on the stand. He studied a picture on the wall, the image of a better place and time. It was of David, Alicia and him sitting in the cockpit of a sailboat, all smiles, the blue sky and Mediterranean Sea almost identical at the horizon.

He walked back to the office and looked at the computer screen. There was no reply. He called the hospital and got through to the nurses station in the intensive care unit. Paul identified himself and asked, "How is my wife? Has her condition improved some?"

The middle-aged nurse sat behind a console and studied a computer, patient data on the large screen. She said, "Mrs. Marcus is in serious but stable condition, an upgrade from critical."

Paul pinched the bridge of his nose, his eyes burned. "Thank God."

"Oh, Mr. Marcus ..."

"Yes."

"Your wife's sister and some other members of the family are in the waiting room. They've asked about you, sir. I just thought you might want to know."

"Good, yes ... thank you." He disconnected and called Dianne. He said, "Alicia's been upgraded from critical to serious but stable."

"That's what they told us a few minutes ago. But they won't let us back there to see her. All I want to do is whisper in Alicia's ear, to tell her we love her and are here for her. Paul, have you heard anything about David? We've been watching the news, but no one seems to know what's happening ... does Alicia even know they've taken David?" Her voice choked.

"I don't know. We'll find them. That's what I'm trying to do this very minute. We'll find them and get David home safe." Paul glanced down at his computer screen. There was a message. He said, "Dianne, I have to go."

"When are you coming back to the hospital?"

"I don't know. Right now I have to find my son so when Alicia wakes up, David will be the first person she sees."

"Okay, Paul."

He disconnected and sat down to read the message. It was from the hacker, the man's name still unknown to Paul. But he had his address, and that would prove to be enough. The message read: *If you do not want your son's head delivered in a box, here is what you will do. You will meet us at a place of our choosing and you will be there when we say to be. You will bring Ulan Hamad. We will exchange the boy for you and Ulan. Your government will deposit one billion dollars into the Central Bank of Iran, we have included a routing number. And your president will admit that the battle of Derna was American aggression and apologize.*

Paul sat down and wrote: *Agreed to your terms. Where do we meet and when?* He hit the send button and waited. After more than an hour, Paul called Bill Gray and said, "I made contact with the hacker."

"What did you say?"

"Basically that I will swap myself for David. I'll send the message to you for dissemination. I let them pick a place to meet, suggesting that it be a place where they can fly out, assuming they have their own get-away jet. With their oil money, they'll have a fleet of them."

"You think they'll just fly out of Reagan or Dulles, you on board and federal agents holding your son at the exchange point? They'll kill him and you, Paul, if they get a chance."

"Maybe not. Fajar Hamad would rather stick me in a bamboo cage and parade me through the streets of Tripoli or Tehran or both if he gets the chance."

"Speaking of Hamad, we've been flying birds and drones over the Nafusa Mountains. We've spotted at least a dozen heavily armed militia almost dead center in the mountain range. Although we haven't spotted Hamad on camera, we have identified two of his top lieutenants. A Special Ops team is going through reconnaissance and scouting, getting into position to hit them hard."

"Bill, they need to hold off until we can try to execute the plan to swap me for David. If Fajar Hamad is in that cave, and we take him out, there will be no exchange and his people will kill David on the spot."

"I'll speak with the president and the joint chiefs. In the meantime, let's hope you can get a bearing on where to find the people holding David. Call me as soon as the hacker from hell responds to you. We have one of our best ready to approach him. Maybe we simply do that now, break a few bones and make him talk."

"It's too risky. David is in too much danger. Let me try to get these killers in the open somewhere. You can send the troops in then, as soon as David is safe."

"All right." Bill disconnected.

Paul stood from his chair and desk. He turned to Buddy and said, "I bet you could use a walk outside."

Buddy jumped off the couch. Paul reached inside one of the desk drawers and lifted out the pistol. He held it in his right hand as he and Buddy walked though the house and opened the back door. They walked outside, the evening air cool, inky sky filled with glowing stars, the sweet fragrance of night blooming jasmine in the air.

As Buddy made his rounds in the yard, Paul stood near a large sweet gum tree. He thought about Alicia and David. He stared up to the heavens and whispered a silent prayer for them. Paul looked to the southeast and saw a crescent moon tilted in the sky. He glanced at his watch, 11:30 p.m. The moon would set at midnight and tomorrow night it would enter its final phase as a crescent moon.

Buddy walked up to Paul and sat on his haunches beside him. He crouched down and petted Buddy. Something caught Paul's eye. A meteor cut a blazing trail through the night sky, crossing directly in front of the crescent moon. He and Buddy watched the shooting star travel with a rooster tail of fire streaking across the coal black sky—a man and his dog, the nightlights of the universe shining down on them.

"Let's go inside, Buddy."

They went back to the home office, Paul placing the pistol on the desk near Eli's picture. There was a new message on the screen. Paul read it slowly, his pulse picking up the more he read: *We will make the exchange. You exchanged for your son. You bring Ulan Hamad. In lieu of the transfer of funds, your president will agree to remove all of the tariffs and trade sanctions he placed against Iran last year. He can make that announcement to the news media the same time he apologizes for America's first war on Derna. If you agree to this, we will meet at place of our choosing. Time is running out, Paul Marcus.*

Paul inhaled deeply, stared at his keyboard for a moment and then wrote: *We agree to your terms. When and where do you want to meet for the exchange?*

Paul leaned back in this chair and waited. The response came almost immediately: *There is an abandoned airport in the Blue Ridge Mountains of Virginia. Your CIA used to train there. How do we know that? Because you trained some of our Iraqi operatives there when you were helping to stage a coup. It is called Donovan Field, named from the man who started your OSS, William Donovan. We know your history much better than you know ours. The field is fourteen kilometers west of Sedalia off Road 602. We will have a plane ready to leave with you and the man you are holding. One more thing, we know you will have your U.S. Marshals escort Ulan Hamad. However, all we want to see is you standing next to the runway with him. If you have anyone come within five hundred meters of the plane, we will cut the boy's head off and roll it across the airfield. Meet us at 6:00 p.m. sharp on the rise of the crescent moon.*

NINETY-THREE

B efore Paul made the call to Bill Gray, he went online to study the airport, to look at the surrounding topography. It wasn't an airport, only an airstrip almost hidden in a small valley in the heart of the Blue Ridge Mountains. He studied satellite images and some old photos he found online. The airfield was just under 3,500 feet in length and paved. There was only one small building used for an office at one time. There was no flight tower, no surrounding buildings within more than three miles. Paul wondered how Fajar's people even found the airfield.

At 3,500 feet, it was long enough for most private jets to land and take off. He studied the surrounding mountains. Something caught his eye. He enlarged the image. A forest service fire tower came into view. Paul hit the keys, looking for information about the tower and its distance to the airfield. The tower was no longer in service and a padlocked gate at the base kept people from climbing the steps. Paul zoomed out of the satellite map and tried to calibrate the trajectory from the tower to the airfield.

He looked across the desk at Eli's photo, released a low whistle, picked up the phone and called Eli's father Liam. When Liam answered, Paul said, "You may literally have a shot at taking out someone who killed or was responsible for the death of Eli."

"Paul, what the hell are you talking about?"

"Fajar's people are going to do a prisoner exchange, if you will. They're handing over David in exchange for me and Fajar's only brother, Ulan Hamad."

"Where and when?"

"It's an abandoned airfield in the Blue Ridge Mountains. I think the government still owns it. Used during the wars for pilot training. Liam, there is an old fire tower about three quarters of mile away from the airfield. It appears to be built near the top of a mountain. You might be able to get off a clear shot or two from that angle."

"Three-quarters of a mile away. Paul, I haven't shot distances like that in years. I'm sure the Army's got snipers with younger eyes."

"You used to tell me that your eyes focused on the mission, giving you reason and the vision to hit a target at great distances. Eli, or his memory will give you the edge no one else could bring through the scope. And since my son, David, will be there, I'd like to have you behind the trigger more than anyone."

Liam glanced across the room at a shadow box filled with Eli's medals and Army Special Ops pictures. He stared at his rifles behind the glass of his gun case, the McMillian TAS-50. "Okay, Paul. Tell me when and where. And tell me my target or targets."

"I'll get back with you in a few minutes." Paul disconnected and called Bill, giving him the details of everything—the last message from the hacker, information about the airfield, and his conversation with Liam Dexter. "If I want to see my son alive, to put a stop to Fajar Hamad's killings on our soil, this is the best chance we have."

"The president won't negotiate, you know that."

"He doesn't have to. I did. We do it all the time in covert exchanges. The president doesn't have to drop trade sanctions, not from what amounts to holding us ransom. The apology for Thomas Jefferson kicking their butts is only something that Fajar Hamad wants because of the circumstances. So the real issue is a prisoner swap. Hamad gets his brother, and I get my son."

"Why wouldn't we simply shoot the plane down before it can leave Virginia?"

"Because they're gambling that I'll be aboard and assuming our guys wouldn't kill me for a handful of them. Also, they're probably banking on the risk of lost lives on the ground if we shoot it down."

Bill stood next to the pond on his property, two Canadian geese swimming toward the center. He said, "I'm calling the president and the directors of the FBI and CIA. We're going to need some buy in; and Paul, you're going to need more than your friend Liam sitting in a fire tower almost a mile away. Do nothing until you hear from me. Is that clear?"

"Yes. Thanks, Bill."

"Don't thank me yet. Don't thank me until David is safe and Alicia is up and walking. If you go to the bathroom, take your phone. We have very little time to pull this together."

• • •

The pilot of the Gulfstream G650 didn't file a flight plan. He didn't have to. A decoy jet, the exact make and model, was flying from Dulles to Roanoke, Virginia. The pilot of the Gulfstream, a former fighter pilot in the Iranian Air Force, had his orders. He flew the jet from a small executive airport forty-three miles from the heart of Washington DC.

On board the Gulfstream were five heavily armed men. Their mission was to secure and protect Ulan Hamad, get him on the plane with the infidel Paul Marcus and his son. The pilot and his co-pilot, a Russian trained fighter pilot, spoke in Persian as they flew under the radar, taking an obscure circular approach to landing the jet. As they came closer, they flew not far above Jefferson's Monticello home, veering slightly southeast. Three minutes later, they made their approach and landed the new jet on an old runway in the heart of the Blue Ridge Mountains.

NINETY-FOUR

Paul was in the shower, eyes closed, letting the hot water beat off his back and shoulders. He thought about Alicia. His last call, before entering the shower, he was told her condition remained the same—serious but stable. He thought about David. *Were they treating him with compassion? What did David have to endure? And, when it was all over, how would the experience scar David? It's no question that it would scar—the only question was how deep would the wound be and would it ever fully heal?* But first he had to get his son home.

Through the torrent of water, he heard his phone ring. He turned off the shower and answered. Bill Gray said, "The president was reluctant to buy off on this, but he sees it as the best option. In the meantime, Special Ops and the Seal Team are trying to find Hamad in his rattlesnake lair. If he's not there, we have problems."

"We already have problems. My little boy his being held hostage, and my wife is clinging to life in a hospital because of these thugs. They blew part of Jefferson's face off Mount Rushmore, destroyed the Liberty Bell and killed a lot of innocent people between there and Monticello. I think the president is making the right decision to go through with this."

"We've been studying just about every square foot of the old airfield and the surrounding area. There is only one road leading in and out of the place. It's unpaved, a gravel road. There are a few areas we might be able to place snipers, but very few. We're not going to even try to stick somebody on the damn fire tower. It's too far, Paul. You might as well tell Liam Dexter to shoot from a mountaintop. Do you really want him up there with your son right in the thick of things?"

"That's exactly why I want him there—because my son will be on the ground. Liam will not hit him, and I'm counting on him hitting as many hostiles as possible."

Bill took a deep breath and let it out. "All right … if he can take the first shot, if he makes a kill, our team will stand up from their camouflaged areas. All you have to do is grab David and try to get the hell outta there before your head is blown off. Hamad, no doubt, will have armed men on the plane. We assume the men bringing David are coming from ground transportation. And we assume they'll hop on the plane and leave their vehicle there. How you get your son to safety is going to be a challenge."

"I know, but I don't see any other way."

"Okay, the U.S. Marshal's office will bring Ulan Hamad. We'll have you walk with him to the runway. In the meantime, we're assuming they will let David walk to the Marshal's vehicle. It's going to be tense and very dangerous."

• • •

Liam Dexter used bolt cutters to break though the padlock at the base of the fire tower. The tower stood near the top of a mountain. He opened the gate and a black snake slithered through the knee-high weeds near his feet. He began to ascend the old wooden steps. Some we're missing. Others were rotten. He carried the rifle on a sling over one shoulder, a backpack with an extra round of ammunition, and a pair of binoculars. He had been given a radio for communications to other members of the team far down in the valley. He wore an earpiece, the microphone was hooked to the earpiece and curved to align close to his mouth.

As he ascended the steps, he looked around the mountains and valleys. It was late afternoon, shadows growing from the trees, as the sun moved lower in the west. He looked at the airstrip in the distance. He could see a jet at one end and a black SUV near the jet. There was no sign of federal agents and U.S. Marshals. But Liam knew some of them were there, fanned out along the perimeter of the airstrip, most in heavy camouflage, ready for the signal.

He counted twelve flights of rickety steps before he would get to the lookout area at the top of the tower. He paused near the top, a bald eagle soared over a mountain summit, and the wind blew from the north at about three miles per hour. A wasp flew close to Liam's face. He looked up. A wasp's nest the size of a car battery was under the base of one of the large steel girders that supported the tower. He watched the nest, teeming with wasps, some just lifting their wings, agitated.

Liam didn't move. He stood there for a minute and then slowly continued his climb, making every effort not to disturb the wasps. The wooden steps creaked and groaned under his weight. Finally, he climbed the last few stairs and stepped onto a planked observation deck that surrounded the shanty known as a fire tower cab. He could see for miles in any direction, the Blue Ridge Mountains seemed to rise and fall to the edge of the earth. He set his rifle down, removed the backpack, lifted binoculars to his eyes and looked at the airstrip.

He saw no movement in and around the jet or the SUV. He could not see through the vehicle's tinted glass windows. He observed the surrounding trees, watching the way leaves moved. He could see the faded orange windsock next to a cinderblock building not far from the runway. The windsock indicated a breeze was blowing from the northeast. Liam checked an electronic temperature and humidity gauge he wore on his wrist next to his watch.

He had just enough room to lie prone on the deck and setup his rifle on the tripod. Within less than a minute, he was looking through the scope at an airfield almost three-quarters of a mile away. More than 1300 yards.

He surveyed movement through the scope. Two black Ford Explorers pulled up near the old block building. Paul Marcus and two U.S. Marshals got out of one vehicle. When the door to the second opened, two more marshals stepped out with Fajar Hamad's only brother, Ulan Hamad. He was tall and wiry in build. Dark eyes and a shabby beard the color of last year's bird nest. His hands were cuffed in front of him. His body language spoke superiority.

Ulan grinned at one of the marshals and said, "I told you my brother would come, perhaps not in person, but his power is felt everywhere. You will see."

The marshal, gray eyes the color of his gun, said, "Don't bet the farm on it." The marshals walked with him to the edge of the airstrip.

Liam sighted the rifle crosshairs across Ulan's chest. He keyed his microphone and said, "I have a bead on the guy in the cuffs. Waiting for instructions."

• • •

They left under the cover of darkness. If it were a modern day sheriff's posse, it may have been one of the fiercest in U.S. history. There were thirty-two men. They were a mix of Seal Team, Delta Force Special Ops, and federal agents who could have passed for Bedouin gypsies in their beards and clothing.

Some traveled in trucks, vans, and Range Rovers southwest from Misrata toward the Nafusa Mountains. Others members of the group were arriving by air. They would parachute in from a high altitude, 18,000 feet, free-falling a thousand feet every six seconds through the night air, deploying their chutes close to earth.

Captain Mike Nolan led the forces on the ground as they drove the winding back roads through the desert, watching to make sure they weren't being followed. Careful to stay at a steady speed, the group traveled in different increments so it didn't appear as a caravan, yet the men could assemble quickly if need be. Nolan sat in the passenger side of a ten-year-old Land Rover. He looked at the portable screen he carried, real-time travel coordinates displayed with the topography they were entering. He opened his small microphone and said, "Heading southwest and going left about one kilometer past a mosque on the right. Copy?"

Nolan listened as each group of six men said "Roger."

After a few seconds, the Special Ops commando driving the Land Rover glanced over to Nolan and said, "I'm glad Command is sending us in there. I don't know how many of us will be coming out ... but I damn guarantee you Fajar Hamad is going to be carried out."

362

"We could have hit the area with a drone. But Fajar might survive that kind of strike. Regardless, we need every bit of data on their computers … names … places … people."

The driver nodded, watched the road in front of him. He drove past a mosque, three cars in the parking lot. Lights coming from two windows. He said, "We're going to be entering the foothills of these mountains in a few minutes. Sir, this is our fourth mission together. I don't know if I've ever said it before, but I want to say it now. You're the kind of soldier I strive to be. You lead us by example, and you always raise the bar. It's been an honor."

Nolan grinned and said, "Thank you. But we're not done yet, so no speaking in past tense. It's an honor for me to lead the team, each and every time. Right now it's present, and in the moment, means that it doesn't get more defined as we approach combat." He looked ahead, the mountains cast in silhouette under a sky filled with stars and a crescent moon rising over the largest peak. Nolan motioned to the northwest. "That's where we're heading. You can just about follow that sliver of moon, it's got just enough light to shine down on Fajar's Hamad's head.

NINETY-FIVE

P aul stared at the black SUV. The front of the SUV was facing him and the U.S. Marshals. *Was David inside? Was he in the jet, less than one hundred feet away, the engines running, ready to race down the runway and gain altitude, flying over the mountains.* He knew the jet could fly for eleven straight hours and land in many other countries without the need for refueling.

Where's my son? Where's David?

The two marshals escorting Ulan Hamad walked slowly, their eyes on the SUV. One agent walked directly behind Hamad, the agent's right hand on the grip of his holstered pistol. The maneuver sent a message: *If bullets start flying, little brother is getting one in the back of his head.*

The doors on the SUV opened slowly. The door on the front passenger side and then the two rear doors opened. The driver's side remained closed. Three men got out. All wore unkempt beards, hands resting on the grips of pistols holstered to their belts. Paul could tell they were wearing bulletproof vests. *Not good,* he thought. These men were anticipating a fight. But what they weren't expecting was a sharpshooter in a fire tower who was following their every move through his scope.

Where is David?

And then the driver's side door opened. Dabir Nagi carried David in his left arm, his right hand holding a Sig Sauer P225 to the child's head. Nagi walked by his three men, they followed in a rather tight pack, all hands on sidearm grips.

Paul's hands clenched into fists. He fought back rage. David spotted his father and screamed, "Daddy! Daddy!"

Nagi whispered something into the boy's ear and David became silent, tears now rolling down his cheeks.

Paul yelled, "It's okay, David. You're going home to see Mom and Buddy."

David looked at his father, confused, his little face hurt, lower lip trembling. Nagi lowered David to the ground, but held a hand onto the collar of the boy's shirt and the Sig point at the back of his head.

A federal agent, wearing combat camouflage in a thicket near the block building, keyed in his microphone and whispered, "Okay ... we can see the four hostiles. We assume there are more in the jet." He looked up the mountain to the fire tower far in the distance. "Liam, what's your best angle? Do you want to try it from that far out?"

Liam moved the crosshairs from one of the hostiles to the man who stood behind David. He said, "The big guy holding the gun on David. I have him in my sights. Hell, yes, I want to try it."

The agent said, "Good. Chris ... you take the hostile to the far left of the boy. Ed, can you take the guy to the far right wearing the sandals and the smoking jacket.

"On him," came a response.

"Chuck ... can you get a clear one into the guy who looks like a wrestler."

"No sweat," the agent said.

"We can't do anything until the boy is released. Everyone, stand down until we have the right opportunity."

• • •

In a cave on a remote and desolate range of mountains in Libya, far from the Blue Ridge Mountains of Virginia, thirty-two warriors, the best of the best, closed the gap on criminals. Under the cover of night, Navy Seals and Special Ops Delta Force commandos following the leadership of Captain Mike Nolan, encircled a region known by some elder Berber tribesmen as the *Mountain of Ghosts*.

But it was here where men, very much alive, were holding camp and plotting destruction ranging from ethnic clashes in the Middle East to bombings in the West.

It was where Fajar Hamad was calling global shots to his followers. Hamad and more than thirty men occupied a series of rooms, two carved vertically into the limestone side of mountains. The largest, the center family room, had been dug and carved out of the stone 900 years ago. Its sheer walls extended thirty feet from the stone floor to an open sky. During the heat of the day, it was cool in the desert. No roof. Moonlight, stars and candles lighted it at night. In the rare event of rain, a shallow trench was carved in the stone floor that led to an opening on the side of the mountain.

Fajar Hamad, dressed in a bone-white tunic, red-checkered keffiyeh around his head, salt and pepper beard to his chest. He wore a thirteen-inch dagger or janbiya in a jeweled sheath on his hip. The hilt or handle was made from rhinoceros horn, the knife more than two centuries old and once carried by his great grandfather.

Hamad's eyes were unreadable, black as motionless swamp water, something sinister just below the surface. His face had the leathery look of a man who'd walked through Sahara desert winds. Dark circles under his eyes grew darker each day. Hamad sat at a wooden table and read communiqués on his laptop screen. He looked up to the night sky in a room without a rooftop, stars twinkling and a crescent moon almost straight above the mountain.

Out of the corner of his eye, he saw movement. A fast blur falling just in his peripheral vision. *Maybe one of the large Pharaoh eagle owls diving on a rodent,* he thought. He was wrong.

From the large center family room, a place adorned in Persian rugs on the walls and colorful pillows on the floor, there were five tunnels that led to nine separate rooms, most lit by candles and battery-operated lights.

A dozen of Hamad's men moved in and out of the dwellings, some cooking lamb on a spit at the main entrance to the cave on a mountainside plateau, the glow of orange flames falling on deeply tanned faces. Some of the men played card games, Bara and Tannab, sitting four players to each small wooden table. There were four tables.

AK-103 rifles were aligned against two walls close to the men. All carried 9mm pistols on their belts or in their tunic waistbands.

Hamad looked at maps on his computer screen. He spoke softly and low, in Persian, to his key followers in Benghazi, Tehran, and Washington, DC. He'd received two calls from Moscow earlier in the day. He anxiously awaited word of his plan to take Paul Marcus from America. Hamad looked at the difference in time from Libya to Virginia. *I should know something by now*, he thought. *Ulan should be in communications with me.*

Hamad placed a call to the Russian embassy in Washington, was put through to Dimitri Abaza, and he said, "I have heard nothing from my brother. He should have been on the plane by now. Where is my brother?"

• • •

Rafa Gamal carefully prepared his favorite cannabis cocktail. He sat at his wooden desk next to his wide screen computer and measured the compounds: one ounce of ground hashish, one ounce of marijuana, one ounce of Turkish tobacco, and a half ounce of opium, all blended well. He packed his hookah pipe, lit it, took a long drag and held it deep in his lungs for fifteen seconds before exhaling. He repeated it three times within two minutes.

He leaned back in his chair propped his feet up on the table and gazed at the computer screen. He pulled a still frame from a video news report of American, Alicia Marcus, gunned down in a parking lot, the image of two dead FBI agents in the background. Gamal grinned, the drugs in his bloodstream and brain, hallucinations beginning, the screen stretching the size of a billboard, Alicia Marcus lying on her back, her head shaped like a goat with red lipstick, paramedics around her.

Gamal stared at the image, put ear-buds on and played *Karma Police*, a song by Radiohead. Gamal took another long hit from the bong, his eyes listless, lips wet. His back was turned to his apartment door. He looked at the screen, a smile trying to form on his numb lips. With the pounding music in his ears, he never heard the American operative pick the lock and enter.

The agent, six-two, broad shoulders, black T-shirt and faded jeans, carried a Russian made 9mm Makarov pistol. He crept through the smoke in the room, layers like white stratus clouds. The stench of the burning drugs irritated his eyes. He approached Gamal in the chair, eyes closed. The agent jerked out one ear-bud and shoved the gun nozzle into the ear. Gamal opened his eyes, as if he was coming out of a dream, his mind sluggish. The agent whispered, "The only way we could find you was through Paul Marcus. He extends his regards." The agent shot Gamal through the head, blood and brain matter splattering across the computer keyboard.

He wrapped Gamal's dead, warm hand around the pistol grip and then set the gun on the floor next to the chair. He pulled out a small plastic bag and plastic spoon from his pocket with spent gunpowder in the bag. He placed a slight amount on the spoon and blew on it, scattering a hint of gunpowder onto Gamal's hand. He positioned Gamal's right arm to hang from the chair, just above the gun.

He turned and left, locking the door on his way out.

NINETY-SIX

Ulan Hamad had no fear of death. That's because Ulan was sure he would live. He would board the jet with the infidel, Marcus, and fly back to Tehran to a hero's welcome. In the remote chance that he should die tonight, paradise surely awaited him with a hero's welcoming. Either way, he could not lose. He smirked at Paul Marcus.

The two marshals with Ulan stood near Paul and the other two marshals. Ulan pointed at Paul and said, "You get your kid, but lose your life. When he grows up, maybe we'll come back for him. We will remove your seed from the face of earth."

Paul said nothing. He watched the men holding David come closer. Then they stopped, less than fifty feet away. The man gripping the gun to the back of David's head shouted, "Marcus … come forward. You want your son? You can come to him. One, and only one, of your agents can follow you to take the boy back. And then we get on the jet and travel to a land far away."

Paul nodded, took a deep breath and started walking toward the men holding David. He was close enough now to see the pain and horror in his son's face.

• • •

Dimitri Abaza sat at a polished mahogany wood desk in the Russian embassy in Washington, a state-issued photo of the Russian president on one wall, the desk spotless. No paper. Abaza poured straight vodka into a glass on a dark felt coaster and said, "We know your brother was escorted from his holding cell by U.S. Marshals, and they were en route to the old airport. We have not heard anything one way or the other."

"Why did you not send some of your people as insurance?"

"Because that was not part of our agreement, Fajar. Now is not the time to ask for something that should have been addressed days ago."

"A man should not have to ask for what is obvious."

"We helped secure the jet. Even found the pilot. A man should know when to pick fights for gain not to avenge a loss. In Russia we too remember our past so we are not destined to repeat it. However, we choose not to draw blood from the sons of long ago enemies. As you know, one reason we chose to assist you is because of your pledge to ensure that Iran buys more goods and expert service in your nuclear program. All your life you have wanted to draw a nuclear line in the sand with Israel, but this personal vendetta with Jefferson's America keeps raising its age-old head. Assuming you get Paul Marcus and the return of your brother, then what? How can you help direct the future of Iran and Libya when you are recycling old ghosts?"

"Because a Muslim man never forgets his past and those who transgressed against the Koran."

Abaza sipped his vodka, looked out the embassy window to the lights of Washington DC. "Fajar, you remind me of an old Asian Hindu I once knew. He believed in Karma, a hidden system that he thought kept a personal diary, a running total, of a person's deeds and worth—his or her life though many lifetimes, to determine fates and fortunes through each level of reincarnation. That is what you sound like to me … a man living his life through that of his ancestors, never following his own path, never becoming his own man."

"Be careful what you say, Dimitri. You need me more than we need you. We delivered the Deputy Director of the FBI to you. Find out if that plane left Virginia, and if my brother was on it with Paul Marcus." He disconnected, stared at the computer screen, the black swamp-water eyes burned like cottonmouth moccasins slithering just beneath the surface.

Captain Mike Nolan stood on a small plateau three hundred yards away from the opening to the cave. Seven men flanked near him. He used night-scope binoculars to watch Hamad's men. "I see nine outside the cave on the small plateau," he said to a tall commando standing next to him. "Can you spot any sentries?"

The soldier looked through his binoculars, moving from ledge to ledge. "No sir, not from this point of view. Security appears lax."

"Maybe that's what they want us to think. In the meantime, some of 'em could be buried in the sand and breathing through a reed just waiting to spring up." He smiled. "But what might be buried are land mines." He looked at a shorter man to his left, stubble on the man's ruddy face. Nolan said, "Allen, you Williams and Fitzgerald, use your ground-penetrating radar as we move off the beaten path toward the hostiles. You see anything that looks like a mine, stop in your tracks. Every man will do the same behind you three. Got it?"

The men nodded, "Yes sir."

Nolan pulled his microphone mouthpiece closer to his dry lips and said, "Jumpers ... everyone in place?"

"Roger," came the replies. One man removing his parachute on a mesa just beyond the mountain said, "We'll have three men ready to rappel over the side of that largest room in fifteen minutes."

"Roger," said Nolan. He looked out into the shadows with his binoculars, lowered them and said, "South flank ... we're ready to move. Are you getting in position?"

"Ready, Captain. Just say when."

Nolan looked at a mountain ledge two hundred yards opposite the cave. He said, "Snipers ... you ready?"

Two snipers lying in prone positions on the edge of a rocky ledge looked through their scopes directly down into the entrance to the cave. One of then moved the rifle crosshairs to the chest of a man cooking the lamb on a flaming spit. The sniper said, "Ready ... Randy's got the three on the left of the cook. I have the chef and the four dudes passin' the hookah pipe."

Nolan said, "Stand by ... move and maneuver as planned. If something does come up unexpectedly, use your training, experience and your head. We'll all figure it out at that time. Get ready."

NINETY-SEVEN

U.S. Marshal Cody Stevens wasn't proud of his kill rate. He wasn't ashamed of it either. Two years ago, during his lunch hour, he'd been in a bank to deposit his check when three men ran in brandishing guns and screaming at customers and employees. They wore masks and demanded money. A retired cop, overweight, working as a security guard, had just come back from the restroom when he walked into the mayhem.

He'd started for his gun when one of the men shot him in the gut. The distraction was all Stevens needed to reach inside his jacket and pull out his Glock G20. Witnesses later said that Stevens shot and killed three men in less than five seconds. Before the smoke cleared, he walked outside, found the driver in the waiting getaway car, made a cursory effort to arrest him. When the driver reached for his gun, Stevens shot him in the face.

Today, Cody Stevens eyed Dabir Nagi. Stevens, a man with the lean look and casual walk of a rancher, stayed next to Paul, his hand on his sidearm. The two groups of men stared at each other—the law and the lawless. If it were 1881, it could have been the meeting at the O.K. Corral in Tombstone, Arizona. But it wasn't. It was an abandoned airfield in a remote section of Virginia, and a child's life was in the balance. Hands were on guns. But nothing left the holsters. Not yet. A mockingbird called out from the top of a hemlock tree. A slight breeze rustled leaves in a stand of sugar maples. Paul could feel a trickle of sweat roll down the center of his back.

There was a movement in the shadows of the open jet door. Except for Liam, no one noticed it because all eyes were on David. When Paul and the marshal were a few feet away, Paul crouched down and extended his arms to his son. Nagi said, "You can go to your father. He shifted his pearl black eyes to Paul and said, "From the door of the plane is a rifle barrel pointed directly at the boy's back. If anyone tries anything, the boy will die on the spot. Understand?"

Paul said, "Yes." David ran up to him, hugging his father, his little arms holding Paul's back, his hands gripping Dad's shirt. "Everything is going to be okay, David. I promise you. Okay?"

The boy nodded, tears in his large blue eyes.

• • •

Captain Mike Nolan used hand signs the last fifty yards of his approach. They could hear the sound of gas-powered generators outside the cave. All of his men were in place, waiting for the word to execute the plan. Nolan, and twenty-five of his men, fanned out in a large half circle before the small plateau and entrance to the cave and its network of rooms. He whispered in the mic, "Topside … what's your position?"

One of the three men, who'd parachuted into the inhospitable terrain, crouched on the side of the mountain and peered over the edge of the opening into the great room. He said, "We're ready to rappel into the main area, sir. I have a visual. Four hostiles are playing cards, and a guy that matches Fajar Hamad's description is talking on a satellite phone. Three more men are in front of computer screens. Looks like one guy is sleeping on a mat in a corner area."

Nolan said, "Okay. We'll assume more are in other rooms. Snipers. It's time. Fire at will."

The two snipers on the mountain ledge, one hundred yards across from the entrance to the cave, glanced at each other and nodded. They sighted on their targets. Through his scope, one shooter could clearly see the man cooking the lamb, the fire reflecting off his creased face. The cook reached with a knife to slice a piece of charred meat off the lamb. As soon as he placed it in his month, his lower jaw was shot off. He fell into the fire. One man had just taken a long drag off the hookah pipe, exhaling through his nose, when a bullet went between his eyes.

In seven seconds, seven of Hamad's men were dead, and Mike Nolan and twenty-five warriors were entering the cave, three rappelling from the roofless opening. The Americans were met with five men reaching inside tunics and belts for pistols. Only one cleared with his Sig before he was shot through the neck. The other four died trying.

As Nolan and his troops entered the great room, a table of men ran from their card game to the semi-automatic weapons lined up against the walls. Fajar Hamad ran towards a connecting tunnel. Mike Nolan followed. Inside the great room, three of Hamad's men were killed before they could lift their guns. Six additional members of his regiment entered the room, pistols drawn. One shot a Navy Seal in the shoulder. As the man aimed for Nolan's back, one of the Airborne soldiers, clinging to a rappelling rope, put a round through the man's left eye. The commandos dropped from the open-air roof into the smoke and firing of weapons. A dozen of Nolan's men fanned out into the connecting tunnels, the sounds of gunfire all around.

Fajar Hamad ran through a tunnel lit from candles and portable battery lights. He could hear the American following him. Hamad entered what appeared to be a bedroom area, mats on the floor, a desk and two chairs. He exited through a tunnel just wide and high enough for him to run through. In fifty feet, he was outside the mountain, on a ledge that was a small plateau. He hid behind a rock formation to the left of the mouth of the tunnel, under the stars and light of the moon. He held his breath and listened.

The American was coming.

Closer.

Silently, Hamad slid the long dagger from the jeweled sheath. He had used the knife to behead a man three years ago. Tonight he would do the same with the American.

Nolan stopped running. He listened, the gunfire now gone, replaced by the moans of injured men. He hoped very few were his own men. He listened for sounds further in the tunnel. Nothing.

He walked as quietly as possible in his combat boots, his shadow flickering against the wall from the light of candles. He assumed some of his men would follow soon. But he didn't want to risk Hamad disappearing from an obscure tunnel carved through the mountain. *Move on!*

Nolan held his Glock 19 in his right hand. A few more steps and he could see where the tunnel opened into another room. *Was Hamad there, or had he managed to escape through another passageway?* Nolan wouldn't know until he entered the room. A dozen more steps. He heard nothing, but he smelled something. It was human body odor, and it was close.

Nolan wrapped both hands around the pistol grip and stepped into the room. He moved the muzzle back and forth in the shadows. Nothing. And then he saw the entrance to a smaller tunnel. *And escape path.*

He moved through the entrance. Within twenty feet, he could feel the outdoor night air coming through the shaft. He stopped walking at the exit, the silhouette of other mountains visible in the distance under the starlight.

He bolted through the exit, rolled once on the flat rock and came up catlike. There was no sign of Hamad. Nolan could hear the clatter of generators running.

A slight sound came from behind him. Someone in sandals taking fast steps.

Nolan turned around just as Hamad drove the long knife into Nolan's chest, the blade sinking to the hilt, an inch of the knife protruding from the back of Nolan's uniform. Hamad's eyes were wide, seething with hate and pleasure at the same time. He whispered, "Don't die too quick, infidel. That will come when I cut your throat like I butcher a lamb."

He pulled the knife out and made a swipe at Nolan's neck, just missing the carotid artery. Nolan stepped back. He could feel blood pouring from his chest and back at the same time. He didn't have a second to aim the Glock. He simply pointed and fired. The round hit Hamad in his stomach. He fell back against the side of the mountain, his thin, wet lips forming a perverse smile. He charged, wildly swinging the dagger.

Nolan fired another round. This one tore through the left side of Hamad's chest, destroying a lung, bones and arteries. The dagger slipped from his hand, falling next to his right sandal. His knees were weak. Difficult to breath, blood trickling from the left corner of his mouth. He smiled and said, "You may stop me, but you can never kill me because you cannot kill the cause."

Nolan holstered his Glock. Stepped toward Hamad and said, "You hung a young man up to die at the entrance to Derna. You wrote remember Derna. I say this, remember Eli Dexter." Nolan hit Hamad hard in his lower jaw, knocking him flat on his back. He looked up at the sky, stars seemed close. Hamad's open eyes locked on the crescent moon right before a cloud covered it like a veil in the universe.

• • •

The federal agent in camouflage clothing near the cinderblock building keyed his microphone and whispered, "Liam, we were just told there is a hostile in the jet, standing just inside the doorway, and he has a drop on the boy. Can you see the perp from your angle?"

"Yes." Liam moved his riflescope off Nagi and shifted it to the plane's open door. At the top, just inside the jet, he could see the man's shoes and pants. And then the sun came out from behind a cloud, sunlight flooding into the cabin. Liam could see a man aiming a rifle in the boy's direction. Liam whispered into his mic, "I have a clear shot. The bullet will be there three seconds before the sound. By that time, if I get lucky, I will have dropped the guy who held a gun to David's head."

The lead agent said, "Go for it."

Liam factored in the wind, distance, humidity and the trajectory of the fifty-caliber round. He aimed just above the cabin door and whispered into the mic, "This one's for my son, Eli." He squeezed the trigger. Instantly chambering a second round and sighting on Dabir Nagi. Liam squeezed the trigger a second time.

The man in the doorstep to the plane would never know what hit him. The round went into his neck and snapped his spinal cord. He

376

fell out of the plane, tumbling down the boarding steps. A second later, Dabir Nagi's head exploded, a spray of pink mist falling on the three men who stood next to him. Before they could pull their pistols out, the agents opened fire, dropping the remaining three men. Paul pushed David down and covered him with his body.

Ulan Hamad bolted and ran. He stopped at Nagi's body, stooping to pick up the Sig Sauer. U.S. Marshal Cody Stevens fired a single shot, hitting Hamad in his stomach. He fell to his knees, looking at his gut in disbelief, holding both hands against his ripped stomach, blood pouring through his fingers. He fell backwards next to Nagi. Hamad stared at the fire tower in the distance, the sun down behind the mountain, and a crescent moon emerging from the horizon, visible in a twilight sky far behind the silhouette of a tower on a mountain.

Liam's third target was the jet. He fired two rounds into one of the engines, the bullets destroying the turbines, white smoke pouring from the engine. The next seven rounds were shot through the fuselage and cabin. One bullet ripped through the cockpit, killing the pilot in his seat. A second man fell dead as he tried running to the back of the plane, a 50-caliber bullet hitting him just above the ear. The co-pilot screamed, "I give up! Don't shoot!" He held his hands above his head and walked down the steps to the ground, falling to his knees.

In less than thirty seconds, it was over, smoke drifting in the air above the old airstrip. All the federal agents came from their positions around the perimeter of the property, running toward the plane.

Paul rose to his knees and held David close to his chest. "I'm proud of you, David. Mom will be, too. Let's go home."

EPILOGUE

Virginia, near Monticello - Four months later

It was a perfect day for a wedding—a Fourth of July wedding. That's what Brandi and Adam wanted. Somehow, very fitting, a wedding—a celebration on America's birthday. The old church, built in 1870, was painted white with a cherry red roof and a steeple with a large brass bell inside.

Peach colored roses mixed with fist-sized red and white blooms grew from bushes that lined the front of the church. The fragrance of rose petals drifted in the air. Century-old oaks cast purple shade in dark grass as guests arrived to witness Brandi and Adam exchange marriage vows. The church property bordered Monticello and some of the vineyards planted by Thomas Jefferson.

Paul, Alicia and David walked up the wooden steps to enter the church. Alicia had healed well, a scar barely visible on her stomach. Today, Paul held her hand, meeting ushers, the wedding party prepping for pictures and getting in place. A cardinal sang from a cottonwood tree, guests arriving as white seed blossoms floated through the warm summer air like confetti. The ushers helped seat everyone, and soon the church was filled to capacity, more than one hundred people were there to witness the wedding.

Happening at a quick pace after the attacks against the U.S., the work was almost completed in restoring and rebuilding the sculpture of Thomas Jefferson on Mount Rushmore. Dozens of artisans, from twenty-one countries, worked around the clock on the project, carving, patching, sanding and restoring. The news media called it the most "united facelift in history." News outlets from around the world followed the progress.

The Liberty Bell had survived the explosion with damage, but not as much as originally feared. The old bell was knocked from its perch and a chunk blown away. Here, too, after the damage on the building was fixed, a team of sculptors and welders, like all the king's men, patched up the bell and put it back in place.

Record crowds were flocking to see the Liberty Bell. An article in National Geographic said the damaged inflicted on the bell and its restoration was a testament to what America stands for under the Declaration of Independence and the Constitution. Op-ed pieces called it a metaphor to the constant attack on liberty and freedom. The new bruises, in an ironic way, were simply more scars, badges of honor, worn to maintain freedom and all for which it stands.

"And damn worth it," the president of the United States had told the media aboard Air Force One as he traveled from Moscow after a two hour "line in the sand" meeting with the Russian president. Détente was reached on Syria, Iran and Libya. There would be less interference by both nations and more involvement from the United Nations in the Middle East. Before the meeting, the American president, along with his secretary of state, had conducted a live video session with Iran's president. The nuclear agreement would remain in place, with conditions, Paul Marcus and his family were to be left alone and economic sanctions would be lifted. After the agreement and some initial reluctance on Iran's part, the president said, "By the way, your embassy building here in Washington is still vacant. We've been cutting the grass there since 1980. In the spirit of our new accord, you can remind your Supreme Leader that we've left the light on for Iran. It's your move, but don't wait too much longer, the property is valuable … could make a nice hotel."

Paul thought of that when he saw Bill Gray and his wife taking a seat in one of the long wooden pews. They sat beside Liam Dexter and his wife, Penny. Bill had kept in constant contact with Paul as negotiations began after U.S. troops killed Fajar Hamad and thirty of his men. Two were taken prisoners, both more than willing to describe, in detail, the ferocity of the fight. Although nine Americans were wounded, Captain Mike Nolan severely injured, none had died, and Nolan had recuperated and retired.

Paul, Alicia and David took seats in a pew sitting next to Dianne and her family. They chatted briefly and then the pianist, a middle-aged woman wearing rhinestone glasses, began playing the wedding song. People turned in the pews and watched as Brandi entered the church with her father. She was radiant, her white wedding dress drenched in the soft sunlight coming through the stained-glass windows.

Brandi walked with her father down the aisle, the guests smiling, a tear spilling from Alicia's eyes. She squeezed Dianne's hand as she watched her niece take a place beside Adam, the man who was about to become her husband. The same man whom Paul had helped free from an Iranian prison five years ago. For Alicia, at that moment in time, it felt like the remnants of a dream without definition. A place in time long ago.

And it was.

• • •

An hour later, the wedding reception was held on the grounds of Monticello, in and around the Montevallo Pavilion, on top of a hill with a commanding view of the Blue Ridge Mountains, the setting sun casting the mountains in silhouette. Paul and Alicia waited for most of the guests to enter the pavilion. They stood there a moment, watching the sunset. She said, "It feels so good not to have an FBI escort everywhere we go." She watched David try to catch a yellow butterfly flitting about the border flowers. Thank you, Paul." She held his hand.

He smiled, looked over her shoulder to two men blending into the wedding party. He knew they weren't listed on the guest roster, but the agents were there, covert and a subtle reminder to him that he'd be relocating his family soon. But he wanted Alicia to enjoy the moment, so he simply smiled and said, "No reason to thank me. I'd thank Liam for his accuracy and all the men who rooted out Fajar Hamad and helped bring their aggression to a close."

"But without your guidance, the information you somehow managed to decipher from those papers, I don't know if our people could have found them nearly as fast."

Paul looked toward Jefferson's house, Monticello. "I had some help."

Alicia leaned in and kissed her husband. "You two make a pretty good team."

Paul smiled. "Thanks … let's join the party. David, come on."

Inside the pavilion, after dinner, guests watched Brandi and Adam cut the cake and take the first dance, bridesmaids and groomsmen following, a few clutching beers, wine or mixed drinks. A disc jockey cranked the music and teased with the guests, encouraging the new bride to toss her bouquet, followed by one of her garters. Brandi, after her second glass of wine, was happy to oblige.

Alicia chatted with her sister, Dianne, both women beaming. Alicia finally relaxed. David cut into a slice of wedding cake, doing his best to fit it into his mouth and not drop it on his new suit jacket. He was successful. Paul leaned over to Alicia and asked, "Can I get you a drink?

"Not yet. Ask me in a little while, and I'll take you up on it."

"I'll do that." He stood and walked around the celebrating guests toward one of two bars at the far end of the pavilion. Bill Gray and Liam Dexter were nursing glasses of scotch and swapping stories. Paul ordered a glass of cabernet and stepped over to them.

Bill lifted his glass in a toast. "To taking care of business and taking care of America."

"I'll drink to that," said Liam, lifting his glass.

The men toasted and Paul said, "I don't know if you set some kind of long distance shot record firing from that fire tower on top of the mountain, but in my mind it was literally the shot heard around the world."

Liam sipped his drink. "I had a strong incentive … the memory of my son, Eli, your son, and our nation. I was shooting for all three. I just got lucky."

Bill said, "I think it was more than luck." He glanced at Paul. "Alicia tells me you guys are looking to relocate. I imagine the safe house is more than restrictive." He grinned and sipped his drink.

"Thought we'd move out and let the government offer it to a family that will need it more than us." Paul smiled.

Liam said, "I hope it stays that way for you and your family. You've been through enough."

"Are you going to move back to your farmhouse?"

"Alicia and I've talked about it. Right now, even the old farm is too close to Washington. Maybe Washington State might work." He sipped his wine, watched the guests dance and have fun.

Bill nodded, glanced at the party and said, "You did what most everyone at NSA and the CIA for that matter, said couldn't be done. You broke an almost impossible code, decrypted a message that is as relevant today as it was when Jefferson wrote it. It was prophetic ... and pertinent. Jefferson offered the olive branch first but the solution wasn't that."

"Maybe we'll find it one day." Paul looked at the last remnants of golden sunlight through the windows. "If you gents will excuse me, I need a little fresh air."

They lifted their glasses, and Paul walked across a section of the pavilion. Bill observed him for a moment, almost like a father would watch a son leave for a tour of duty in the military, not knowing if he'd ever see him again. He knew, and Paul knew, the government would be relocating his family soon, and that he'd always be looking over his shoulder no matter where they went.

Paul walked outside and crossed to a grassy area with a spectacular view of the rolling hills to the east. He glanced over his shoulder and could see a little white and red church in the valley with the steeple.

Someone inside the old church rang the bell at sunset. The ringing traveled through the valley and onto the hills, the clouds above them mauve and scarlet, the trees in deep purple shade. Paul looked at Monticello down the hill. He could hear the words of Thomas Jefferson with the church bells in the background, *'Any man's death diminishes me because I am involved in mankind, and therefore never ask for whom does the bell toll, because it tolls for thee.'*

The End

CPSIA information can be obtained
at www.ICGtesting.com
Printed in the USA
BVHW041127120120
569282BV00014B/406/P

9 781723 357893